The Body in the Basement

Phyllis G Humphrey
1994

KATHERINE HALL PAGE

The Body in the Basement

St. Martin's Press   New York

I would like to acknowledge Barbara Brackman, quilt detective extraordinaire, and her excellent guide to identifying and dating antique quilts, *The Clues in the Calico*, EPM Publications, Inc. Thanks, as always, to Ruth Cavin, my editor, and Faith Hamlin, my agent, for their insight, advice, and above all, friendship.

Illustrations by Phyllis G. Humphrey

Library of Congress Cataloging-in-Publication Data

Page, Katherine Hall.
     The body in the basement / Katherine Hall Page.
        p.   cm.
     "A Thomas Dunne book"
     ISBN 0-312-11470-2
     1. Fairchild, Faith Sibley (Fictitious character)—Fiction.
2. Caterers and catering—Maine—Fiction.   3. Women detectives—Maine—Fiction.   I. Title.
PS3566.A334B63   1994
813'.54—dc20   94-25764
                                                                       CIP

First edition: October 1994

10   9   8   7   6   5   4   3   2   1

Editor's Note

The Body in the Basement includes, at the end of the story, six full recipes from Faith Fairchild's (fictional) cookbook, *Have Faith in Your Kitchen,* as well as a number of descriptions in the text of the way Faith and Pix make some of the delectable New England dishes featured in the action.

In praise of aunts, and uncles, this book is dedicated to:
Ruth and Charles Samenfeld
and all my dear cousins

Two residents are standing on the post office steps in a small Maine coastal village observing the increased traffic on Memorial Day weekend.

"Well, this time of year always brings two things: the summer people and the black flies," says one.

The other nods. "Yup, but you can kill the black flies."

—Anonymous

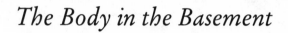

The Body in the Basement

Chapter I

There were days when Pix Miller was forced to agree with her husband, Sam's, observation that "Don't worry, Pix will do it" would be the epitaph carved on her tombstone in the family plot in Maine.

She was at the plot on Sanpere Island now, thinning the potentilla that grew on her father's grave. The sky was slightly overcast and the woods that surrounded the cemetery were dark and dense. She preferred to be there on sunny days, when the white birch trunks shimmered and the stately emerald evergreens looked as if they had been and would be there forever. The dead were not dead on those days, but came alive in memory as she walked past stones with familiar names to their own bit of earth, the ground covered with wildflowers until Freeman Hamilton came with his scythe.

Today as Pix looked down at her father's grave, she had no trouble remembering that first shock, the first grief, although he had been gone for a dozen years. She put down her clippers and stretched out on the green, very green, grass. "Pix will do it." Apt, extremely apt.

She sat up, feeling a bit foolish at the picture she presented—spread-eagled on her forebears. If there was anything Pix Miller was not, it was foolish, however much she tried. She plucked a piece of grass from the ground, slit it with her thumbnail, and put it to her lips. The ensuing high-pitched whistle was gratifying. She still knew how. She'd taught her children the trick, just as she'd taught them all the other things she'd learned on the island when she was young: how to sail, canoe, and swim; where to find the best clams, best blueberries, best shells; to leave nests undisturbed and to walk silently through the forest; to get every last morsel from a boiled lobster and to wake up in anticipation each morning.

That was how she had awakened this morning. It had taken about thirty seconds for her to realize she was not in her bed in Aleford, Massachusetts, but tucked under the eaves in her bed in Maine. Pix didn't waste any time getting to Sanpere for the summer, and this year was no exception. Yesterday at exactly twelve noon, she'd picked up seventeen-year-old Samantha at the high school, then swung by the middle school for twelve-year-old Danny and turned the Land Rover, packed to the gunnels, due north. She had already driven her oldest, nineteen-year-old Mark, to Logan Airport in time for the early shuttle to Washington, D.C., where he was spending the summer as an intern in their local congressman's office. Mark had protested the ungodliness of the hour all the way to Boston, but Pix was too busy running through her mental lists, making sure she hadn't forgotten anything, to pay him much mind.

At the airport, he had given her an affectionate bear hug and said, "It's okay, Mom. I know you can't help yourself. The old Siren call of Sanpere, and probably they'll be a few moments this summer when I'll wish I was there, too. When it's a hundred degrees in the shade in D.C."

Pix had had a sudden hope. This was the first summer the

whole family wouldn't all be together for at least part of the time. "It's not too late to change your mind, sweetie. We could swing by the house and get some of your more rugged clothes." Mark was dressing for success these days.

"Mom, I said, moments, 'a few moments.' Sure, life on Sanpere is gripping: 'Mrs. Walton will be entertaining her daughter and family from Bangor for the weekend' and 'Sonny Prescott has a new lobster boat, which he has named the *Miss Steak*.' Health-care reform and balancing the budget are going to seem pretty tame." Mark had rolled his eyes. "Time to let one of us fly."

"But you'll come up Labor Day weekend?" Pix was trying to hold on to the end of the string.

Mark said something that could have been a yes or a no, the string snapped, and he was gobbled up by the crowd of morning travelers just beyond the terminal's automatic doors.

Still absentmindedly picking at the grass, Pix realized this was going to be a summer of women, not an altogether-bad thing, of course, but different. On the way up last night, she'd dropped Danny off at his beloved Camp Chewonki near Brunswick for a virtually whole-summer stay, and Sam probably wouldn't be able to get away until the Fourth of July, and then only for a few days until his August vacation.

Samantha had picked up on her mother's mood the night before as they drove through the darkness, bent on getting to their cottage no matter what the hour. "We'll have fun—and think how easy the housework is going to be, and the cooking." Pix had brightened considerably at this prospect. She didn't mind the housework, but unlike her friend, next-door neighbor, and now employer, Faith Fairchild, food preparation as a pleasant activity was up there with lighted matches under the fingernails. If Pix had not been endowed with a superabundance of Puritan guilt, it would have been Hamburger Helper every night—instead of merely some nights.

Faith was the Faith of Have Faith, an extremely successful

Manhattan catering company that Faith had recently re-opened in Aleford. She'd moved to the village following her marriage to the Reverend Thomas Fairchild. Pix's responsibilities at the catering company didn't involve cooking. Keeping the books, counting forks, and other organizational feats were the areas where Pix excelled.

Over the years, Pix Miller had developed a reputation for getting things done. And having earned it once, she kept on earning it. She was the townwide coordinator for the Girl Scout cookie drive, although Samantha hadn't been in uniform for years. Then there was the United Way appeal, Town Meeting, the library board of trustees, and so forth. She'd ceased being a room mother now that her children were out of elementary school, but she still held her seat on the PTA Council. And she did all this along with chauffeuring these children to soccer, ballet, French horn lessons, ski team, swim team, as well as making their Halloween and school-play costumes. Some Alefordians called Pix a superwoman, but she didn't feel like one. She'd talked about it once with her friend Faith in a sudden burst of self-examination: "I'm not working, so I feel I can't say no, and everyone always calls me. I don't want to disappoint them—or my kids—but sometimes I wonder how the heck I got in so deep."

Faith had taken a dim view of the whole thing, especially the notion that Pix wasn't working. As a minister's wife, Faith lived in fear that she would end up in charge of the Christmas pageant or fund-raising for a new roof. Fortunately, Pix had taken this job. "You *have* to start saying no. You know the slogan, 'Just Say No'. All this is not so different from doing drugs, Pix. I think you've gotten to the point where your system needs it and you have to go cold turkey. Besides, now you are gainfully employed and you have a perfect excuse."

It was hard for Pix to face the fact that Faith might be right—that Mrs. Miller had a reputation to uphold and had grown dependent on the praise she got from all these unpaid jobs. But then again, often no one knew she did them—except Pix herself—so she supposed it was the same thing. That night, more confused than ever, she'd talked about it with Sam. He'd been slightly exasperated with Faith, not an unusual occurrence. "Pix, you like to help out. You're good at it. There's nothing wrong with any of that. Except, you take on too much and don't have enough time for us—or yourself. Pure and simple. Samantha's driving now and Danny's the only one who really needs you. You can start getting out of some of these other things—like the cookies." Sam was always annoyed at how much room the boxes took up in the garage. He had to park his precious sports car outside for the duration.

Pix had stopped listening after the phrase "Danny's the only one who really needs you." Where had all these years gone? It was like shrubs. You put them in and they looked so tiny and inadequate, then before you knew it they had outgrown the space and you had to get a backhoe to yank them out. Maybe Danny would go to college nearby. With all the colleges and universities in the Boston area, Mark had to pick one in Colorado and Samantha was considering Reed in Oregon.

Her mind drifted back to the present. A summer of women—three generations of women, to be precise. Pix's eighty-year-old mother, Mrs. Arnold Lyman Rowe, Ursula, was already in residence at The Pines, the immense "cottage" Ursula's father had built for his family by the shore in the late 1890s.

In those days, the rusticators' journey was not a five-hour drive from Boston, but one stretching out over two days, starting with the embarkation from the Eastern Steamship pier on Atlantic Avenue—complete with steamer trunks, portmanteaus, wicker lunch hampers, hatboxes, and all the other bulky accoutrements necessary for a back-to-nature summer. Ursula Rowe reflected ruefully on the soft-sided nylon luggage that sufficed for her now and told her daughter there would never be a better way to travel than those long-ago voyages.

Mother. Pix blew another shrill note on a blade of grass. Just as she was bewailing the departure of her fledglings, she was wondering how to clip Ursula's wings a bit, and once they were clipped, what would Pix do with her? Ursula resisted every effort to change her way of life and Pix was plagued with anxiety about all the things that could happen to her mother, still living alone both in Aleford and on Sanpere, rattling around The Pines with only Gert Prescott coming in a few times a week to do for her. Yet, where else would Mother go? Mother and daughter got along very well, but Pix was not sure how it would be if they were ever under the same roof. She had the strong feeling any roof Mother was under would soon become Mother's roof, and while Pix as a dutiful and loving child might be able to cope with this herself, Sam would not like it. At all. As it was, when everyone was on vacation on the island at once, away from work and school, ready for leisure activities specifically with Pix, she felt as if she were slowly being stretched to fit Procrustes's bed—pulled in opposite directions by her loved ones. She could navigate the road between her own cottage and The Pines blindfolded.

But something was going to have to be done about Mother. She even refused to wear one of the Medic Alert medallions supplied by Blue Hill Hospital. "There are so many people going in and out of my house every day that if anything ever happened to me on this island, you'd know before I did," she'd told Pix. There was some truth to this. Sanpere was a close-knit community; some might even call it too close-kit. But still Pix worried. Mother was so stubborn.

Just like Samantha. Pix had unfortunately assumed any adolescent turmoil on her daughter's part would be over at age seventeen. Recently, it seemed Samantha was making up for lost time, a late bloomer—not that she stayed out until daybreak or had pierced her nose. But "Oh, Mother" punctuated their conversations with alarming frequency. Lately, Samantha hadn't seemed very interested in completing her collection of island mosses, last summer's all-consuming passion, *and* she was letting her hair grow, abandoning the style Pix favored for what she feared might be "big hair."

Pix looked around. It was a typical Maine day, which meant the sky was perfectly blue, the air clear, the sun pleasantly warm. If she was at the shore, the water would be a slightly darker blue, with an occasional whitecap. She took a deep breath. For Christmas one year, her brother had given her a can of Maine air, the kind they sold to tourists up at Bar Harbor. She'd laughed along with everyone else, then late that night she'd gotten out a can opener and opened it, closing her eyes and burying her nose inside before it could mix with the Massachusetts molecules. She didn't think it was her imagination. There was a hint of balsam and a crispness, then it was gone. She opened her eyes to look into an empty can that she quickly threw away before anyone could tease her.

Arnold Rowe, her brother, an orthopedic surgeon, was thirty-nine, six years younger than Pix, and there were just the two of them. He and his wife, Claire, lived in New Mexico. Arnie was attentive to Ursula—from a distance—and of course reaped all sorts of glory merely by showing up. He was the fair-haired son, and if Pix hadn't loved him so much, she might have resented all the attention he got, arriving in Sanpere on vacation or for fleeting holiday visits in Aleford when he would not be called on to drive Mother to doctor's appointments, Symphony on Fridays, tea with her friends, the flower show, the . . .

Arnie and Claire would be arriving sometime in July. Mother had had his boat taken out of storage and all was in readiness for his return. Gert would leave Arnie's favorite, a strawberry-rhubarb pie, for the first night's dinner, and then they'd see very little of the two Rowes, what with sailing, golf, tennis, cocktails, and dinners at their innumerable friends' houses on the island and mainland. They wouldn't see them, but the house would still be in a whirlwind as they dashed from place to place. He'd leave with regret: "Where did the time go? We'll take that sail to Vinalhaven next year, I promise." Things would settle down, and Pix would find herself missing the clutter of Arnie's tennis things and golf clubs in the hall.

All this reminded Pix: she had taken Mother's supply of sheets down to Aleford for the winter to wash and repair. "You can't get percale like this anymore," Ursula asserted, and Pix agreed. The linens were like silk. She'd have to unearth them, or her brother and his wife would be sleeping on mattress ticking. She laughed at herself and felt better. Sure Arnie and Claire were a little self-centered, but they were also fun to be with and very generous to their nephews and niece. With no children of their own, they encouraged visits; Mark had once spent a whole vacation with them, exploring cliff dwellings and learning about the Anasazi.

Pix stood up and stretched. The first day with one foot still in Aleford was always a little difficult. It would take some time to get into her island rhythm—maybe another hour or two.

After returning home, she spent the rest of the afternoon unpacking. Samantha had left her a note saying she'd taken her bike over to Arlene Prescott's house but would be back by five o'clock, in plenty of time to go to Granny's. Ursula had invited them for dinner this first night. Arlene was Samantha's best friend on the island. They'd known each other all their lives and each year picked up where the last had ended. They had been faithful pen pals when younger. More recently, the correspondence had degenerated to a few postcards. Presumably, teenage life on Sanpere was just as time-consuming as it was in Aleford—even with the closest mall sixty miles away.

Pix unpacked her clothes. It didn't take long. She smiled to herself at what Faith would say about her choice of raiment.

On Sanpere, Pix lived in jeans, shorts, and turtlenecks or polo shirts, depending on the weather. Tonight, though, she'd change into a skirt. Mother had worn pants all her life, but she didn't like to see them at dinner. Pix donned a white wrap-around skirt and, with a nod to Faith, paired it with a bold black-and-white-striped Liz Claiborne shirt. She slipped on some red espadrilles, washed her face and hands, combed her hair, and was ready. When Samantha came home, she eyed her mother approvingly. "You look nice, except you forgot your lipstick."

"No I didn't," Pix replied. "I'm on vacation."

"Oh, Mother." Samantha went off to get ready, a process that took considerably longer than her mother's titivations.

She emerged in what Pix knew was the latest fashion, but it still looked like something she'd give to the thrift shop: a long flowered-print housedress with a crocheted vest on top. To complete the ensemble, Samantha was wearing a pair of heavy-soled black boots that managed to suggest the military and orthopedics at the same time. Sam's hair was at that in-between stage where everyone either comments, "Are you growing your hair?" or says, "You need a haircut." Pix chose the latter.

"Your hair is so cute when it's short, and think how easy it is for the summer." They'd had this conversation before.

Samantha explained patiently, "I want it to look good when I go back to school. Up here, it doesn't matter what I look like and please, Mom, for the last time, I don't want to look cute. That's not the idea."

"Well, attractive, then." Pix knew she should shut up, but old habits die hard.

Her daughter nobly chose to ignore the remark. "Why don't we go to Granny's? You know how much she hates it if we're late."

"We're never late!" Pix protested.

"There's always a first time." Samantha smiled sweetly. "Why don't I drive?"

Pix sat in the passenger's side, wondering when the reins had slipped from her grip.

Ursula Rowe greeted her daughter and granddaughter. "Don't you both look lovely."

"You're looking pretty spiffy yourself, Granny," Samantha said as she gave her a kiss.

Gathered in the hallway, the three generations bore a general resemblance to one another, most blurred oddly enough in Pix, not Samantha. They were all tall and had good posture. Ursula, in her ninth decade, carried herself as proudly as she had at Miss Porter's in her second. Ursula's high cheekbones were softened in her daughter's face, only to emerge sharply again in Samantha's. All three had the same thick hair. Pix and Samantha's was the dark chestnut color that Ursula's had been before it turned snowy white. Pix's was cropped close to her head. Her mother's was almost as short but curled slightly, whether by nature or art, she did not reveal. Samantha's eyes were a deeper brown than her mother's and grandmother's. Her father's genes had turned almond into chocolate.

"Shall we go in?" Ursula linked one arm through Samantha's, the other through Pix's. Pix felt a sudden rush of well-being. It was going to be a good summer. She'd tend her garden, put up a lot of preserves, spend time with her mother and her daughter, and maybe clean out the attic at The Pines, a herculean task that had been put off for twenty years of summers. And she'd make Arnie take her over to Vinal-haven.

Over the creamed haddock Gert had left, they talked about the summer. Ursula had been on the island since Memorial Day. Unencumbered by school-age children, she spent May to October on Sanpere. Pix was dying to ask her the latest gossip, but their custom of not discussing such things in front of the children, even when said children weren't children anymore, was too strong, so they stuck to safe topics.

"When do you start working, Samantha? Have some more beans, Pix dear. They're the last of last year's."

"Monday. The campers arrive tomorrow, but Mr. Atherton said he won't need me until then. I'll be there in the mornings to teach the younger children sailing, stay to help with lunch, then I'm through for the day. I promised the Fairchilds that I'd be able to take care of Ben and Amy when they come up in August, so that will be in the afternoons."

"Phew, that's quite a schedule."

"Yes." Samantha laughed. "But think how rich I'll be!"

"Are you going to have any time for fun?" Her grandmother looked concerned.

"It's all fun! Besides, Arlene is working at the camp, too—full-time, so I wouldn't be seeing her, anyway. And I don't work weekends."

"It's nice that Jim Atherton keeps the camp going. It must have been the early thirties when his parents started it. He certainly doesn't need the money." Ursula exchanged a sharp glance with Pix hinting good gossip to come.

"A labor of love," Pix remarked. "I can't imagine Jim without the camp, and Valerie seems to enjoy it, too, although it's not really her thing."

"What do you mean, Mom?" Samantha asked.

"Well, Valerie Atherton is some kind of interior decorator. I think she likes having the camp around to keep Jim busy while she goes antiquing."

"It's funny. We're so close to the camp if you go by water, but we don't really know them. I guess it's because none of us ever went there. I haven't even met Mrs. Atherton. My interview was with him."

"I think you'll like her," Ursula said. "She's not as flashy as she looks."

Samantha brightened, "This is going to be interesting."

"You know she has a son about your age from her first marriage."

"Yeah." Samantha made a face. "Arlene says he's a real dork."

"It couldn't have been easy for him, moving to the island, especially after losing his father the way he did," her grandmother commented, correctly translating Samantha's opinion. "Now, why don't you clear the table. We can have our dessert on the porch. Gert left your favorite—lemon meringue pie!"

"What a sweetheart! Please thank her for me." Sam jumped up from her chair and began to clear the old, large, round dining room table with alacrity.

"I'll make some coffee," Pix offered, wondering how she could drop a gentle hint to Gert Prescott that Pix's own personal favorite was black walnut. Gert probably figured Pix made her own pies, but she figured wrong.

After consuming two pieces of pie, Samantha went down to the shore to poke around and watch the sunset. Her mother and grandmother stayed on the porch in the fading light.

"More coffee, Mother?"

"No thank you. I want to sleep tonight."

Ursula was a notoriously sound sleeper, and Pix laughed.

"You could drink the whole pot and not worry."

"So *you* say. Nobody knows how much I toss and turn. Now, when is Samuel coming?"

"Not until the Fourth. Maybe the weekend before, if he can get away. He's preparing a big case and it goes to trial soon. It all depends how long the jury takes. We could get lucky." As Pix spoke, she realized how much she was going to miss her husband. It happened every summer. She didn't want to leave him, but she really wanted to go—and it was wonderful for the kids.

"Now, tell me what's been going on since you've been here," she said to her mother.

"Not much. You know how quiet things are in June. It's

heavenly. And the lupine was the most spectacular I've ever seen."

Ursula said this every year. Pix had come for a long weekend one June especially to see the fields of tall purple, blue, and pink spiked flowers. She had no doubt that every year would be better than the last, because no memory could equal the impact of that palette stretching out—in some parts of the island, as far as the eye could see.

"No scandals? Come on, Mother, you're slipping," Pix chided.

"Let me think. You heard that the manager of the IGA is keeping company with his ex-wife's sister? And the two sisters have, of course, stopped talking to each other and the ex-wife has to drive clear off island now every time she needs a quart of milk.

"And what else? Oh, I know. It will probably be in the paper this week, but Gert told me about it this morning. They had a real scare at the nursing home. When Karen Sanford went to open up the common room, she found glass all over the place, and she'd left it spick-and-span the night before. Obviously vandalism. So she called Earl to come investigate. Turns out the vandals were a Yoo-Hoo bottle that had exploded and knocked over a tray of dishes!"

"It will definitely make 'Police Brief,'" Pix said when she finished laughing. What a change from reading the news at home, she thought to herself. Sgt. Earl Dickinson was the one and only law-enforcement official on the island—and so far, the only one needed. It reminded her.

"Do you think Earl and Jill are going to get married?" Jill Merriwether was the proprietress of a gift shop in Sanpere Village.

"It's certainly about time, but they seem to be content the way they are and so long as they both feel the same, it's fine."

"I know what you mean. If one or the other starts getting itchy for the altar, then there could be a problem. Still, I don't know why they don't. It's nice being married." Pix had no regrets.

"Then, as you might imagine"—her mother continued to catch her up—"there's a lot of talk about the Athertons. I didn't want to say too much in front of Samantha, but their house is finally finished and everyone's calling it 'the Million-Dollar Mansion,' which is quite likely close to the truth. I don't think there's a person on Sanpere who doesn't know they have six bathrooms, three with bidets."

"The bidets may have taken some explaining."

"True, but the gold-plated faucets didn't."

"Where did Jim get all his money? The fees at the sailing camp have always been pretty steep, yet nothing that would produce an income like this."

"His mother's father invented scouring pads or some such thing and money made money. Keeps on making it, if the house and those boats of Jim's are any indication."

"So they really intend to live on the island year-round. I'm not so sure I'd want to be here all winter. It gets pretty quiet." Pix thought of her constant round of activity in Aleford and realized with a start that she'd miss it if she moved.

"Your father and I considered living in The Pines when he retired, but when it came down to it, there were too many things and people we didn't want to leave."

The two women paused in their conversation and looked out across the water at the sunset. They could see Samantha silhouetted against the horizon. The Pines had been built to take advantage of "the view." There was a large front porch and one extending off the second-floor bedrooms. It was an ark of a house, with rooms added to the rear as needed. By modern standards, it was dark. The windows were small and the interior pine paneling old-fashioned. The only remodeling that had been done since it was built was to the indoor plumbing and the addition of a gas stove and other modern appliances in the kitchen. The old woodstove was still used for heat and Gert kept it blackened, its chrome sparkling. Pix had seen a similar one for sale in an antiques shop for five hundred dollars. Her mother had been stunned.

The sun was a ball of fire, descending rapidly into the sea, leaving streaks of purple, pink, and orange as it fell that would have seemed garish in any other context. Flashy. It brought Pix back to the Athertons. It wasn't that Valerie dressed in gaudy colors or was dripping with rhinestones. Her jewels were real, especially the large diamond solitaire Jim had given her as an engagement ring. It was that she *dressed*. She wore *outfits*. Blouses matched shirts and pants. Sweaters matched both. Her shoes matched her scarves, as did the polish on her perfectly manicured nails. Pix's nails, clipped short, tended to suggest activities like weeding and clamming. Valerie's indicated pursuits like sunbathing and page turning.

"Let's see, the Athertons have been married for about three years, right? And they used to spend the winters in Virginia, where Valerie lived?"

"Yes, we all thought Jim was a confirmed bachelor. He met Valerie when he was sailing someplace in the Bahamas. It was just after her husband died so tragically."

Pix had heard the story. Valerie, Duncan, and Bernard Cowley were sailing when a sudden tropical storm hit, almost destroying the boat and sweeping Bernard overboard. Valerie had developed an understandable aversion to boats of any size or shape amounting to a phobia and refused to set foot on one. That her new husband ran a sailing camp was definitely ironic.

Pix looked over at her mother. She'd been widowed a long time. It was a prospect Pix kept firmly shoved way in the back of her mind. She sincerely hoped she and Sam would go at exactly the same moment.

"And what are you going to do with yourself while Samantha's busy making all this money?" Ursula asked.

"The usual—and maybe this year we'll tackle the attic.

Then remember, I'm overseeing the Fairchilds' new cottage."

"I'd almost forgotten about that. Seth Marshall is building it, isn't he?"

"Yes, and tomorrow I want to go over and see how much he's done since Memorial Day."

Faith and Tom were building a modest house on a point of land not far from the Millers. The Fairchilds had hired Seth Marshall as the architect and contractor after seeing his work. It was a very simple plan, yet Faith had still wanted Pix to keep an eye on the progress. Pix had steadfastly refused to accept any money for the job, insisting that having the Fairchilds as neighbors on Sanpere as well as in Aleford was reward enough. Besides, Pix argued, she was the one who had lured them to Sanpere in the first place, with somewhat startling results. But Faith had pressed hard. She knew the amount of time Pix would devote to the project, so finally they'd compromised on an amount. Pix grudgingly agreed, especially when Faith threatened to bar her from the site if she wouldn't take the money.

It was the kind of thing Pix loved doing, and being paid for it seemed wrong. There was nothing more exciting than watching a new house go up. She loved all the smells—from the fresh concrete of the foundation to the fragrant fir of the framing. She'd miss out on the concrete. Seth would have poured the foundation long ago. They'd seen the gaping hole in May.

"It will be nice to have the Fairchilds on the island," her mother remarked. "I'm not surprised they decided to settle here. Sanpere has a way of getting into one's blood."

"Just think. This is your eightieth summer on the island. We should make a banner to carry in the Fourth of July parade."

Her mother sighed. "I've lived a very long time. Maybe even too long."

Pix was used to this sort of remark, but her heart never failed to tighten. "Don't be silly."

"Oh, I'm not silly. I'll tell you what the funny thing is, though. Eighty years old and I still feel twenty inside. It's all gone so fast."

Pix stood up and called Samantha to come in.

Too fast. Much too fast.

The next morning proved to be another typical Maine day and Pix proposed to Samantha that they pack sandwiches and walk out to the Point to check what progress had been made at the Fairchilds' cottage. Her daughter agreed wholeheartedly. She was curious about the house, too.

"Show me the plans before we go, and let's take the dogs."

Pix had assumed any walk they took would automatically include the golden retrievers that she regarded as canine offshoots of the Miller line: Dusty, Artie, and Henry.

"Of course we'll take the dogs." She leaned down to stroke Dusty. "Do you think you can keep up with us, old lady?" Dusty's muzzle was turning white and she no longer raced into the mud at low tide when one of the children threw a stick, her former favorite and extremely messy pastime.

It was close to ten o'clock by the time they set off, feeling vaguely wicked about skipping church.

"We'll start next week," Pix vowed. "Most people don't even know we're here yet."

"Granny does," Samantha reminded her.

"True, but look at this sky. Surely this is a day that the Lord hath made, and I'm sure both the Lord and His representative on earth would be glad we're enjoying it."

"Hey, Mom, I don't even like going to church here. It's so boring compared to Reverend Fairchild's service. You don't have to convince me."

Through a quirk of faith, and through Faith's quirks, the Fairchilds had managed to buy the entire forty-acre parcel of land known locally as the Point, a long finger of land stretching out toward the open sea. It had one of the only white, sandy beaches on Sanpere and was a popular spot for swimming and picnicking. The Fairchilds had given most of the land to the Island Heritage Trust, saving a few acres for themselves at the very end. An old road had been improved and they had been able to get the power and the telephone companies to string lines out to the site—no mean accomplishment, Pix had informed them. Faith had been surprised. "How could we possibly be out there without power or a phone?" She was even more surprised when Pix had told her that the Millers hadn't had a phone at their cottage, by choice, until the kids had started to go to sleep-away camps off-island and Pix's nerves couldn't take it. "It was wonderful. A real vacation when no one can call you." Faith had privately thought this New England eccentricity in the extreme. No phone!

Today, Samantha and Pix were following the road straight down the spine of the Point. They'd take the shore way back, clambering over the rocks when the tide was lower. The road went through the woods, but there were openings that cut down to the sea. Judging from the number of sailboats out, local pews were pretty empty this Sunday morning. The sun sparkled on the surface of the water and the clouds in the sky were as white and billowy as the sails beneath them. Pix thought how much of their lives on Sanpere was governed by the sea. Their days were planned around the tides. When it was high, they swam. When it was low, they dug clams, gathered mussels, or simply combed the beaches for shells, peering into the jewel-like tidal pools at the starfish, sea anemones, tiny crabs, and trailing seaweed. The Millers' cottage was not on deep water, unlike The Pines. First-time visitors were always shocked at the broad expanse of pure mud revealed where a few hours before the ocean deep had beckoned. Pix had grown to prefer the change, charting the summer by the time of the tides.

She remembered suddenly what the tide had revealed to her friend Faith several summers earlier and shuddered. She stepped determinedly along and almost bumped into Samantha, who was crouched down on the shady path leading from the road to the construction site.

"What are you looking at?"

"Someone dropped a key," Samantha answered. "It looks like an old one. Isn't it pretty?" The cut work on the top of the key was done in intricate swirls.

"Hold on to it and I'll ask Seth next time I see him if anyone has lost it. I'd take it, but these pockets have holes in them, I'm ashamed to say."

"If that's all you've got to be ashamed about, Mom, you're in good shape." Samantha shoved the key in her jeans pocket. If no one claimed it, she'd wear it on a ribbon around her neck.

Pix was debating whether to follow up Samantha's comment with a veiled inquiry as to what Samantha might be ashamed of that would lead her to make a comment like this. She stepped into the sunlight; news that Samantha was running a lunch-money extortion ring at school would have been welcome compared with the news that greeted her eyes.

Seth Marshall hadn't done a thing since Memorial Day. No, she quickly took it back. An ancient cement mixer had been brought in and there were empty cans of soda and other potables on the ground, nestled next to Twinkies wrappers and squashed Mother Goose potato chip bags.

"Mom! Didn't you say they would be framing the house by now?"

Pix was speechless. She nodded dismally. The Fairchilds hoped to move in at the end of the summer. They'd be lucky if the roof was on before bad weather struck.

Her anger mounted, and she found her vocal chords worked after all. "Wait until I get hold of Seth! This is totally inexcusable!" Pix's voice, which at times like these assumed the strident tones of a sideshow barker by way of the Winsor School and Pembroke, rang out indignantly in the crisp Maine morning air. She strode to the edge of the hole where the basement was supposed to be, the dogs following at her heels. "I know he's not dead or injured. It would have been in *The Island Crier*." The Millers subscribed to the Sanpere weekly paper year-round. Next to *Organic Gardening*, it was Pix's favorite reading material. "He'd better have a pretty darn good excuse!"

"Look over here," Samantha called. She was behind a stand of birches the Fairchilds had specified be left. "Aren't these the things they use to stiffen the concrete? It must mean they're going to do it soon. They wouldn't leave them here to rust."

Pix went over to get a closer look.

"You're right. These *are* reinforcing rods, and here are some anchor bolts. But even if they pour tomorrow, we're still weeks behind schedule. And in any case, they couldn't pour any concrete without putting in the footing forms, and I don't see any sign of them."

Samantha tried to cheer her mother up. "Come on, let's go down to the shore and eat our sandwiches. It's not like it's your fault. Mrs. Fairchild will understand." Samantha correctly zeroed in on the thing Pix was dreading—telling Faith.

"I know, but I'm so mad at Seth, I could scream. Promises, promises. I should have known better and called him every day."

"Well, scream if you want to. It will make you feel better. Tiffany Morrison says her therapist told her to, and it's awesome."

"Why is Tiffany seeing a therapist?" Pix was suddenly sidetracked. The Morrisons owned a real estate agency in Aleford and had always seemed like the perfect apple-pie family. Maybe that was the trouble.

"Oh, you know, the eating thing. She won't eat anything, then she eats like crazy. I think she first started doing it to get her parents' attention. They're always so busy. Then it kind of got out of hand. She tells us about it in gym, and it's totally gross. But she's doing okay now. I guess the screams worked."

They both laughed, then Pix said, "Really, an eating disorder is no laughing matter."

"That's not what we're laughing at," Samantha pointed out sensibly. Sometimes she thought the term *guilt trip* had been coined for her mother.

Pix felt much better. She'd call Seth as soon as she got home. Then once she pinned him down to a firm date—and she would tell him she would be there watching—she'd phone the Fairchilds and might providentially get Tom.

She called to the dogs. Dusty and Henry came running from the woods, barking happy doggy greetings as if they had been crossing the country for months, desperately trying to find their people. But the third dog did not emerge from the greenery.

"Artie! Artie! Arthur Miller! Come now! Do you see him, Samantha?"

"No, but he can't be far. He never strays from the others."

Pix found him immediately. "Oh, naughty, naughty dog!"

Artie was down in the cellar hole, digging furiously. He glanced up at the sound of his mistress's voice, then went back to his work.

"What is he doing? He must have found an animal bone."

Pix jumped in, landing on the soft earth. She went over to the dog and grabbed his collar. "Stop it this instant!" As she pulled the dog away, she noticed that what he had unearthed was not a bone, but a piece of fabric.

"Samantha, look what Artie's found. I think it's part of an old quilt."

"I'll get something to dig with."

"It's probably in tatters. Remember the beautiful Dresden Plate quilt I saw in the back of Sonny Prescott's pickup? He was using it to pile logs on, to keep the truck clean!"

"Here's a stick. It was all I could find."

Pix took it from her and scraped away the dirt. So far, the quilt seemed to be in good shape.

"It looks like a nice one. I love the red-and-white quilts," Sam said excitedly.

"Me, too." Pix crouched down and tugged at the cloth. "It's Drunkard's Path. I've always meant to do one, but sewing all those curves seems much harder than straight lines."

"Artie, sit!" The dog had come to her side, about to resume his labors. The other two were looking over the edge of the excavation, puzzled expressions on their faces. At least this was how Pix interpreted them, and she prided herself on knowing her dogs' moods.

"Look at Dusty and Henry. They're all confused. People aren't supposed to dig like this." Dirt was flying out behind her as she dug deeper. "You pull while I dig."

Samantha gave a yank and a large chunk of earth flew up, revealing more of the quilt. And as it unfolded, something else was exposed.

That something else was a human hand.

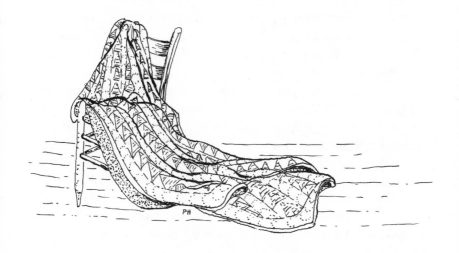

Chapter 2

At first, Pix thought it was one of those plastic joke hands that had been all the rage in Maine the previous summer—sticking out of someone's trunk or trash can. The first time she'd seen one, she'd laughed. After a while, it got boring—and ghoulish.

This hand wasn't plastic.

Pix and Samantha looked at each other, aghast. Samantha was the first to speak.

"It's a dead body, isn't it?" she whispered. Her face looked pale and sickly.

Pix gently lifted the hand with the stick. It was flaccid and curiously heavy. The cuff of a blue denim work shirt was revealed. Pix assumed there was an arm attached, leading to all the other parts wrapped in the quilt in the shallow grave. She nodded and stood up. Her legs were shaking.

"I'll stay here and you go to the Hamiltons' for help. They're the closest. Take the dogs."

"No, Mom. Keep the dogs with you."

"All right," Pix agreed. The dogs could slow Samantha down if they decided to chase a squirrel or even a leaf blowing across the path. She felt immeasurably comforted to have them stay.

The two women climbed out of the hole in the ground at the lower end, opposite the spot where the body had been buried. As they walked across the level dirt, Pix gave a thought to the footprints they were obliterating, but there was nothing they could do about it now. From the moment the dog had jumped in, the murder scene had been messed up.

Murder scene. Murder. There couldn't be any doubt. This was not the way loved ones were laid to rest.

Samantha paused briefly to give her mother a hard hug. "Is this really happening?"

Pix held her close. "I'm afraid so, but I can't believe it, either. You'd better go," she said, holding her tighter.

Samantha broke away and ran off toward the road. She was a fine athlete, and as her mother watched her graceful long-legged stride, the horrible discovery they had just made was forgotten for an instant—but only an instant.

The first thing Pix did was to tie the dogs to one of the trees. She didn't want Artie or the others to continue the exhumation. She sat down on a granite boulder, a massive one disgorged by the inexorable progress of the glacier, and tried to think.

But the horror of their discovery was making rational thought impossible. At least she'd been able to send Samantha for help. What was filling her mind now was the picture of that hand lying there on the ground, disembodied. It was growing larger and larger in her imagination. She hadn't even noticed whether it was the right or left, and what did that matter, anyway? What mattered was that it was a person, someone who had been alive perhaps only a day or two ago. She took a tissue from her shirt pocket, blew her nose, and swallowed hard. She sat up straighter. So far, she'd done what she was supposed to; now she had to force herself to think of something besides that hand.

For instance, whose it might be? She hadn't heard anyone was missing on the island, and her mother would certainly have mentioned it the night before. If it wasn't someone local, the police were going to have a difficult time identifying the remains. The end of the Point was a lonely, sheltered spot. A boat from anywhere along the Maine coast—or the Eastern Seaboard, for that matter—could easily land and dispose of a body without anyone knowing.

But . . . Her thoughts were sliding back into their old, familiar logical patterns. The killer had to be someone who knew about the construction, someone who knew the foundation hadn't been poured yet. It was too unlikely that an individual looking to get rid of a dead body would just happen upon an excavation site. No, the whole thing did not point toward chance. It pointed toward someone well acquainted with what was happening on Sanpere. Roughly 95 percent of the population.

The initial shock and disbelief were beginning to wear off and Pix was drawn to the edge of the basement, above the body. She looked down. The hand was dead white against the dark soil, just as she'd left it. She hadn't imagined the whole thing and naturally nothing had moved. She jumped into the hole again, being careful to land on the same spot and retrace her steps. Somehow, Pix couldn't continue to sit on a rock with a corpse lying a few feet away and not investigate further.

She didn't disturb anything; she simply stared at what had already been revealed and noticed several things she had missed before. There was a noticeable but small X sewn in blue thread near the border of the quilt where people sometimes put a name and date. Roman numerals? The beginning of a date? X was ten. She remembered that much from her years of Latin.

The hand looked like a man's—or that of a hirsute woman who worked with her hands. The nails were short, uneven, and one was blackened—the way a nail gets if you close it in a door or hit it with a hammer. It was the left hand, but there was no ring on the ring finger, although that didn't mean who-ever it was wasn't married. Few of the men around here wore wedding bands, except to please their wives when they dressed up. The kind of work they did was not kind to jew-elry.

The final thing she noticed sent her quickly up above-ground. The quilt was indeed a red-and-white one, but there were two reds, one a slightly rusty one—dried blood. It had been a violent death.

Back on the rock with the dogs stretched out next to her, she realized she could be here a long time. It would take Samantha at least a half hour to get to the Hamiltons' house at the beginning of the Point. Nan would be in church and prob-ably not home yet. It was Sunday, so Freeman Hamilton wouldn't be out pulling his lobster pots, and Pix hoped he was puttering around the house and not off someplace. He wouldn't go too far, though, and risk being late for his Sun-day dinner.

Freeman wasn't a churchgoer. Said he liked to talk to God directly. She remembered what he'd told her once when she was a girl and he and Nan were a young married couple. He'd come by with some lobsters for her grandfather, pointed to the view of their cove, with islands that seemed to stretch beyond the horizon across the wide expanse of deep blue water, and said, "You know, if you want to speak to God, it's a local call from here."

Pix thought a few words with the Almighty were most cer-tainly in order now, but her mind was teeming with so many questions, such as how long the body had been there, that she settled for a few devout entreaties for the peaceful repose of whoever the unfortunate soul might be and a Godspeed for Samantha.

Pix realized that she felt oddly distanced from the event. Was she in shock? Or was it because the hand still seemed like plastic and without a fully identified being, the death wasn't a reality yet? Nothing had been personalized, except their reactions to the idea of murder.

She must be in shock, she thought, to be thinking this way and to be thinking about what she was thinking so consciously. She was going in circles, but she wasn't frightened. Whoever had brought the body here was long gone. She tried to imagine what might have happened. An unknown man (presumably) was stabbed to death by person or persons unknown, wrapped in a quilt (why a quilt?), taken to this out-of-the-way spot either by boat or car, and buried. It would have had to have been at night. It would have been risky to come during the day, when there was a chance the construction workers might be around. She saw the scene vividly: the body wrapped in the quilt to keep the blood from leaving any telltale signs, carried from the car or boat, and placed in the basement; the digging of the grave by the dim light of a flashlight beam—make haste; make haste—finally leaving the corpse and slipping back into the role or roles played everyday, with no hint of the night's work crossing a face. Her breath was almost taken away at the audacity of it all. If Pix hadn't brought the dogs, the concrete basement floor would have covered the grave and no one would have been the wiser. The Fairchilds would be living above a crime and never know it.

But wouldn't the dead person have been missed eventually? What kind of person has no one asking his whereabouts?

Pix stood up and walked farther away from the house. Sketching the scene in her mind had removed some of the distance—or the shock was wearing off. She began to feel queasy and afraid. Where was Samantha?

Think about something else. There's nothing you can do. Why had she stayed behind? They both could have gone for help. But it had seemed wrong to leave that hand so exposed, untended. The sky was filled with the shrill cries of gulls and terns. She shuddered at the notion of their beaks pecking at the hand, unearthing more of the body in the basement.

She threw her head back and gazed up at the circling birds: herring gulls; laughing gulls; two cormorants, portentous black creatures, necks bent like shepherds' crooks as they landed on the rocks; arctic terns, streamlined and elegant, swooping gracefully among their gull cousins. She watched as one lone tern hovered over the water, then suddenly plunged headfirst after a fish. A hundred years ago, this tern would have been prey, not predator. Pix's mother invariably mentioned it at least once a season when watching the birds dart and dive. Thousands at a time were killed in their summer nesting grounds and island women were hired to skin them, preparing them for the New York feather market to grace a hat or trim a dress. The terns were saved from extinction just in the nick of time by the first Audubon Societies and legislation controlling the plumage trade.

The terns were summer people. They were from "away" and had nested on the islands at their own peril. The corpse lying here under the sky, was it someone from away, as well? Someone unknown and unfamiliar to the island who could vanish without a trace? Vanish as the terns nearly had?

Samantha must surely be at the Hamiltons' house by now.

Think of other things.

It was almost July, but the long hard winter buffeting the island with snow and heavy rains until late April had delayed the already-short growing season even further. And now it was dry. There wouldn't be the traditional fresh peas to go with salmon for the Fourth of July. No one had been able to sow much of anything Memorial Day weekend because the weather had been so bad. Pix imagined what her garden would look like in August: green tomatoes that she'd have to bring back to Aleford to ripen between sheets of newspaper; lettuce; too many zucchini; the eggplant was doubtful— Her pessimistic reverie was interrupted by a loud shout.

"What the hell are you doing here!"

She hadn't heard anyone approach, and it was obviously not Freeman Hamilton, Samantha, or Sergeant Dickinson.

She jumped to her feet and ran in the direction of the shore, with some notion of trying to attract attention from a passing sailboat.

The tethered dogs were barking their heads off. As she raced down the slope toward the beach, her heart pounding with fear and from the exertion, she glanced back at the animals and caught sight of the intruder. It was Seth Marshall, glowering. His long dark hair, heavy mustache, and the anger in his eyes made him look like a pirate from a children's book illustration.

Pix stopped abruptly and turned around. Her own anger of an hour ago returned full force, fueled in addition by the fright he had given her.

"What do you mean what am *I* doing here? How about what the hell *you* were supposed to be doing here? I thought you were building a house. The foundation isn't even poured!"

Her voice was booming and she was almost face-to-face with him before she collected herself. Seth Marshall knew when and where the concrete foundation was going to be poured. Seth Marshall had a handy pickup filled with shovels and all sorts of other digging equipment. Seth Marshall's mother was a quilter.

"I didn't know it was you." He was almost apologizing. "Don't want people messing around out here."

"When were you here last?" She wanted some information before she broke the news.

"Look, Pix, I can't afford to turn work down. I told the Fairchilds that when they hired me. I've got to make enough in the spring and summer to last me all year. The Athertons needed some repairs at the camp before they could open and I've been over there the last few weeks. And I've been finishing a cottage for some people on the reach road. But we'll be here every daylight hour from now on. The soil is good and dry. We'll be able to get everything done, even the floor, by the end of the week. The Fairchilds will have their place before Labor Day. That's a promise."

Pix heard him with only half an ear, although that half did cause an internal comment of promises, promises, before zeroing in on the matter at hand—literally. She'd have to watch out. Her mind was running amok. So, Seth claimed not to have been at the site for several weeks. The police could probably tell how long the soda cans and other debris had been around. Without carbon dating, it would be impossible to say when the venerable cement mixer had been set in place.

There was no point in delaying further. She had to tell him. He'd spot it the moment he walked over to the excavation, and he was moving that way.

"There's a dead body buried in the cellar hole. My dog started to dig it up."

"What!"

Seth's bushy eyebrows rose clear out of sight, disappearing somewhere into his mane of hair.

Pix was patient. It was a lot to take in. "The dog was digging at something and when we went to see what it was, it turned out to be somebody's hand. There's a very dead person over there. Wrapped in a quilt."

"A quilt?" Seth seized on the word, the only one suggestive of normalcy.

"Yes, a patchwork quilt."

"I don't believe it!"

Pix knew he wasn't referring to the quilt. "Come and see for yourself." He followed her over to the edge of the pit he and his crew had dug in the spring. There hadn't been anything other than rocks in the ground then.

"Holy shit! It's a hand!"

Pix nodded. It was the third time she'd approached. The hand was beginning to look familiar.

"We've got to get Earl out here!"

"Samantha was with me and she went to the Hamiltons' for help. They should be here soon."

"I've got a shovel and a pickax in the truck. You sit out of the way and I'll dig him up. It could be pretty nasty."

Pix figured Seth would want to take action. Most men usually did, however she'd been close enough to her friend Faith's sleuthing activities to know that they should leave well enough alone. Not that she had exactly, but digging the body up would definitely be regarded by the police as tampering with evidence, and she told Seth so.

Without something to do, he seemed visibly shaken and went to the truck for a beer.

"Want one?"

Pix did, but somehow the picture she might present to her daughter, Sergeant Dickinson, and Freeman Hamilton, who would surely not stay home once he learned there was a body on the Point, was a bit unseemly. Not to mention that it would be all over the island that she had been drinking with Seth Marshall while someone lay stone cold only a few feet away. Not by any stretch of the imagination could this be called a wake. At a wake, it was customary at least to know the name of the deceased.

"Do you have anybody new working for you this summer? Anybody who's been missing for a while?"

Seth came and sat down next to Pix on her boulder. The dogs had long since quieted down and were snoring peacefully in the afternoon sun.

"You're trying to figure out who it is, right? Well, I haven't. It's the same crew as last summer, and some from the summer before. The Atherton kid was helping us on the camp work, but I told his folks I couldn't afford to hire him for other work. They were paying him for what he did there. Or didn't do is more like it."

"Have you heard of anyone missing? Here or on the mainland?"

Seth shook his head. "Of course, we don't know how long the body's been here, but I haven't heard anything at all, and you know the way news gets around."

31

Pix continued to pursue her line of questioning.

"I assume the whole island knew you were working out here and had dug the hole for the foundation."

"Yup, it wasn't a secret."

"But who knew you hadn't poured yet?"

"Probably all the same people, since I've been at the other places instead of here for some time now. But I was planning to pour this week. Not too many people would have known that."

They were getting somewhere.

"Who would have known?"

"Okay now, let me see. I was ordering the lumber for the footings at Barton's and I may have mentioned it then. I told my mother, because she said you would be here soon and if I didn't get going, you'd have my hide, which is true." Seth smiled and the pirate was replaced by a mischievous little boy—little boy, despite his thirty-odd years. He'd been one of the island's footloose and fancy-free young bachelors for so long, it was hard to think of his ever settling down—or getting any older. He lived with his parents in Granville, the larger of the island's two main towns, Sanpere Village being the other. His mother, Serena, was a member of the Ladies' Sewing Circle with Pix's own mother. The Sewing Circle. That tore it. If Serena knew, it might as well have been listed under "Coming Events" in *The Island Crier*.

Small-town life made criminal investigation nearly impossible. There were rarely any skeletons in anyone's closet, because at one time or another, some friend or neighbor had opened it "by mistake," ostensibly looking for something else. "How's your uncle Enoch doing?" asked in the right tone of voice would be enough to elicit the information that he was drying out up to Bangor and how the hell did you know, anyway?

All this was running through Pix's mind, along with the inevitable conclusion that she couldn't figure anything out, island mores or no, until she had found out who the corpse had been for a start. She abandoned her previous line of inquiry.

"So, this is definite? You're going to start work tomorrow?"

"If Earl will let me," Seth replied.

They sat in companionable silence for a while. There was a slight breeze and the leaves in the aspen grove behind them rustled softly. Seth took a pull on his bottle of beer, then asked, "Did it seem like it was attached?"

Pix knew what he meant. "I think so."

"Could be part of him is here, part someplace else."

"I hope not," Pix said, her queasiness returning at the idea of dismembered body parts turning up at construction sites from Kittery to Calais.

They were quiet again, subdued by the grisly suggestion, but Seth couldn't stay still for long.

He smacked his forehead dramatically. "I must be losing my mind. I've got a CB in the truck. I can call Earl myself and find out what's keeping him." He walked rapidly toward the pickup and soon Pix heard the crackle of static and Seth's muffled words. He was back within minutes.

"He's already on his way. But I bet Freeman beats him."

Scarcely were the words out of his mouth when Freeman's truck pulled in and screeched to a halt, sending gravel flying in all directions and starting the dogs barking again. Samantha flew out her door and was at her mother's side before Freeman had even opened his. When he stepped out, Pix could see he had his Sunday clothes on, which meant several less layers than usual. His fisherman's tan—forearms, face, and neck—was a deep mahogany color, contrasting with his thick mat of light gray-white hair.

Samantha spoke, her voice full of concern: "Mom, the police will be here right away. Are you okay?"

Considering the only danger had been from her own overactive mind, Pix was able to answer, "I'm fine. How about you?"

Freeman answered for her, "She was a little wobbly when she first got to me, but she's calmed down some. Nan came home and that helped." He did not seem surprised to see Seth and nodded to him. "Hello, Seth. Where's this body of yours now? Lucky I decided to fix Nan's washer today instead of going fishing with Charlie Porter."

"It's over here, in the foundation. And it's *not* mine," Seth added snappishly.

The two men went over to the edge of the excavation. Pix decided she'd seen enough of the hand to last her a lifetime and returned to her perch on the rock, making room for Samantha and holding her near. Her daughter still looked very pale and seemed to be shivering in her jeans and T-shirt despite the warmth of the sun.

"Gorry," they heard Freeman exclaim. "Think someone cut him up in pieces?"

Seth's speculation and Freeman's further reaction were cut short by Sgt. Earl Dickinson's arrival. Uniformed, tall, and ramrod-straight, he looked very official. And with his closely cropped light brown hair and deep blue eyes, he looked very handsome. He addressed Pix and Samantha first. "Show me where you found it and how you got down and up."

Earl Dickinson was a man who always went straight to the point. When it became apparent that the earth had been disturbed by both of them, as well as Artie, the sergeant jumped in the hole himself, inspected the evidence, and climbed back out. "No one else been in there?"

Pix answered for them: "No."

"All right, then, stay out of it. I've got to call in to report, then we can talk. The state police are sending a unit."

He was back in a few minutes with his notebook out and pen clicked. They sat on and around Pix's boulder, at his feet like so many schoolchildren. First he wanted to know exactly when the Millers had arrived and how the body had been partially unearthed, then he asked all the questions Pix had. Did Seth have anyone new working for him? When had Seth been at the site last?

After he was finished, he closed his notebook with a sharp snap and buttoned it into his pocket, along with the pen. "Not a whole lot you folks can do here, so I suggest you go home and keep your mouths shut as much as is humanly possible when everyone on this island will be asking you what's going on. Until we dig him out, we don't have anything to go on, except that somebody appears to have used a perfectly good quilt as a shroud."

The sergeant's vocabulary was taking on a new richness, Pix noted. Maybe it was Jill's influence. But he had hit upon the thing bothering her, too. Yankee thrift being what it was, why not wrap the body in an old tarp or burlap? She wanted to tell him about the mark she'd found on the quilt, yet heeding his caution, she decided to wait until they were alone. Not that she didn't trust Freeman and Seth, especially Freeman.

"Then Samantha and I will be going. I'd like to get her home." And into her nice secure little bed with a cup of chamomile tea, she thought.

"I'll take you," Freeman offered. Seth looked a bit lost and said he'd stick around to keep Earl company until the staties showed up.

"No, you go along, too. We know how to get a hold of you if we need you," Earl said. Effectively dismissed, Seth mumbled what could have been a good-bye and roared off in the pickup.

"Needs a new muffler," Freeman commented.

Earl nodded and Pix half-expected him to take out his notebook and make an entry, but most of the pickups on the island needed new mufflers. It wasn't considered a citable offense, unless you were caught drag racing on the old cemetery road in Granville, a road so blackened by burned rubber that locally it was called "the speedway."

So they went their separate paths to spend the afternoon

trying not to think about what was uppermost in their thoughts: Who was the body in the Fairchilds' basement—and who had put it there?

The dead man turned out to be Mitchell Pierce. While not exactly an island resident, he was not unknown on Sanpere, having spent time living there off and on while he was working at his purported craft: the restoration of old houses. But Mitchell also lived all along the coast from Camden past Bar Harbor, depending on where he was working. And to complicate matters still further, he was known to disappear for months at a time, purportedly (again) to the Pacific Northwest. *Purport*, in various forms, was a word that turned up often in conversations about Mitch. In addition to his restoration work, he dabbled in antiques, buying and selling. In fact, he bought and sold almost anything from Mercedes coupes to odd lots of canned goods. He was a man who lived by his wits and it was a well-known fact that these wits often took him close to the law. *Provenance* was something that Mitch defined broadly, as it suited his own needs. An exquisite piece of folk art could have been made in 1890 or 1990. What mattered, Mitch was quick to point out to his detractors, was that it was exquisite.

In another era, Mitch might have sold snake oil, and the pitch he made to new purchasers of old houses was not unlike the slippery patter of his antecedents. His charm was hard to resist and levelheaded Boston businessmen found themselves uncharacteristically turning their houses and charge accounts at Barton's Lumber over to Mitch so he might bring the dwelling back to its pristine glory. Mitch got free rent and free rein. Sometimes the customers were satisfied. Mitch *did* know what he was doing. And sometimes they returned in the spring to find hide nor hair of him, their pipes burst, and an astronomical bill waiting at Barton's. Still, he kept getting jobs.

It wasn't that he was particularly good-looking. Short, with a wide widow's peak, the adjacent bald patches threatening to spread back across the dome of his head, he'd developed a paunch at thirty; now at forty, it could be described less kindly. He had an impish grin, an infectious laugh, took no one, including himself, seriously, and was wonderful company.

He'd done some work on The Pines a few years ago and Ursula stood over him the whole time. He'd expected nothing less and they parted friends, but Pix hadn't fallen under his sway. She didn't trust him—not on her tintype, and especially not on his.

It was Mother who called to reveal who the dead man was, of course.

Ursula was miffed that Pix hadn't informed her immediately about her grisly find, but Pix had always been a good little girl. So when Earl told her to keep her mouth shut, she took it as a sacred trust.

"But certainly you could have said something to your own mother!"

"I didn't even tell Sam. Now, of course, I can, since everyone seems to know even more than I do and I found him." Pix often found being good didn't shower one with the rewards implicitly promised.

"Why don't you come over here for tea and we'll talk about it. How is Samantha?"

"She slept when we came back and seems fine now. Arlene and her boyfriend asked her to go to the movies in Ellsworth and that should take her mind off it. And it will help when she knows who it was. I doubt she ever met him. If it had been someone she knew, that would have been worse."

"All right, then. When she leaves, you come on over."

Pix agreed and hung up. She really ought to call Sam now and most certainly should call the Fairchilds. Tom was probably out on parish business. Maybe it would be better if they were both together and she could tell Sam at the same time, because the first thing he'd do after hanging up would be to run next door. Besides, her mother might have picked up some more things and Pix would have further information for them. She'd wait until she came back.

Feeling like the abject coward she knew herself to be, she waved good-bye to Samantha, whose color was back, and set off for tea and maybe sympathy.

The tea tray was on the front porch and her mother was waiting. The family took as many meals outside as the weather and time of day permitted. None of the Rowes liked to be indoors when they could be enjoying the view and the air up close.

"It must have been terribly upsetting for you, darling," Ursula said, taking Pix's hand in both of her own.

"It was." Pix sat down in one of the wicker chairs that they had never thought to cushion. The latticework that appeared on the back of one's legs when one was wearing shorts was a kind of badge of authenticity. "I was mostly worried about Samantha. But she seems to be all right, even a little excited. None of her friends have ever found a body," Pix added with a slight grimace.

"A dubious distinction at best, but I'm glad she is not upset. The whole thing is puzzling, though. Who on earth would want to kill Mitchell? He was always a complete gentleman when he was here, although I know others have not been so fortunate in their dealings with him. He did a beautiful job removing all that dry rot in the back addition. I'd hoped he would be able to repair the latticework on the porches this summer. I suppose it's too late now."

"Much too late, Mother. The man is dead."

"I know, dear. I told *you*, remember."

Pix did.

"I hope the Fairchilds weren't too disturbed by all this. It's not the way one likes to start a new house."

"I haven't reached them yet." Pix skirted the truth. "But I don't think they'll be too upset. It just happened to be their basement. It could have been anybody's—and they didn't know him."

"This business of wrapping him in a quilt . . . such an odd thing to do. What was the pattern?"

Pix was amazed there was something her mother didn't know.

"It was a red-and-white Drunkard's Path—very nicely done, tiny hand stitching. It looked old. Although, I couldn't see much of it." And there were those bloodstains obscuring the work. Pix gagged on her tea and her mother had to pound her vigorously on the back before she stopped coughing.

"Well, whoever did kill him must be an exceptionally nasty person."

"I think we can assume that," Pix said.

"No, besides being evil. Drunkard's Path—it's just plain nasty to call attention to Mitchell's drinking problem. He's been fighting it for years."

Ursula must have grown very close to Mitchell over the dry rot, Pix speculated. There didn't appear to be much she didn't know about the man. No reason not to take advantage of Mother's winning ways.

"Did he have a family? I never heard that he was married."

"No, he never married. I don't think he was really very interested in women—or men. Just things. He definitely liked things, especially beautiful and valuable things. Of course he must have had a mother and father, but he never spoke of them—or any brothers or sisters. He did mention that he grew up in Rhode Island, though."

"We should tell Earl that. It might be a lead."

"I will, or you can tell him. Mitchell knew a great many people on the island, but not many people knew him. He minded his own business."

And probably for very good reasons as far as Mitchell was concerned, Pix thought.

"Seth knew him best, I'd say."

"Seth!"

"Yes, when he was a teenager, he worked for Mitchell. I've often heard Seth say he learned everything he knows about building and restoring houses from Mitch. They were very close for a time. You know the way boys that age look up to someone a little older who seems to know everything. I think Mitchell even lived with the Marshalls one winter. Maybe Seth can repair the latticework. I hadn't thought of him."

"Not until he finishes the Fairchilds' house," Pix said firmly. "The latticework has needed repair for several years and it can hold out a little longer."

She took another cup of tea, turned down her mother's offer of sherry as sunset drew nigh, and set off for home to make her phone calls.

The Pines was across a causeway connecting Sanpere and Little Sanpere. It was a short road, but it twisted and turned precariously above the rocky shoreline. It was another favorite place for the local kids to drag and had witnessed several tragedies over the years. There were no guardrails. Large rocks had been set on either side and this year they were painted with bright white luminous paint to help keep drivers on track. It wasn't a road she liked to think of Samantha negotiating at night.

She passed through Sanpere Village with its lovely old ship captains' houses, some with widow's walks, facing the sea. Her friends Elliot and Louise Frazier lived in one, and Louise was planting geraniums in a huge old blue-and-white stoneware crock in the fading daylight. Pix waved and continued on. The Fraziers belonged to the same group that Pix fancied her family did—people not orginally from Sanpere who either now lived here year-round or had been coming in the summer for so long that the line between native-born and "summer person" had blurred. They weren't islanders, but they were close to it. Elliot Frazier had been the postmaster for years and both he and Louise had served on many of the town's boards. They were even further across the line than the Millers and Rowes, although if there had been an honorary islander award, Pix's mother would have won it years ago. Being admitted to the Sewing Circle amounted to the same thing.

As Pix drove across the island on one of the three roads that connected the loop Route 17 made around the circumference, she thought about all these distinctions and wondered why people always found it so necessary to put other people in neat little categories, and why indeed she prided herself so much on her own label.

Many of the summer people actively fought the moniker—buying their clothes at the fishermen's supply, driving beat-up old trucks, and studiously avoiding the vacation community on the island. These same people tended to count how often they received the traditional island road greeting—a few fingers casually raised from the top of the steering wheel and maybe a slight nod as vehicles passed.

The rusticators, families who had been coming for generations, had always hired local people to work for them as caretakers, and cooks and they didn't pretend—or in some cases want—to blend in. Their ways had been set by a grandmother or grandfather in '02 and successive generations found no reason for change. They sailed. They took vigorous walks. They picnicked—with the same immense wicker hampers outfitted with thermos bottles, china, utensils, a rug to spread on the ground, and a folding camp stool if required by an elderly member. They wore squashed salt-encrusted, white canvas sun hats that did not prevent their faces from turning a ruddy bronze, complete with peeling nose, by August.

Where did Mitchell Pierce fit into the social scheme? Pix wondered. He wasn't a summer person, but he was from away. He was more intimate with the native population of Sanpere, since he'd boarded in various island homes at times. These people generally spoke approvingly of him, even after some major disaster when a foundation he had finished crumbled because there was too much sand in the concrete. He loved to listen to the old-timers' stories and could recount the history of the island better than most who had grown up here. He played the mandolin passably and was a popular addition for musical evenings, where he was sure to be asked for "Rainbow" and "The Girl I Left Behind Me." Yet his last series of misadventures had left an unpleasant taste even in the mouths of these supporters.

He'd been working on a large Victorian mansion originally constructed by a shipyard owner in Sanpere Village. The current owners, wealthy summer people, lived in Chicago during the winter. Mitch had charged not only building supplies at Barton's but also food at the IGA and bread and other baked goods at Louella Prescott's. Louella ran a small bakery from her kitchen and had learned the same delectable recipes from her mother that her sister, Gert, had. Both women were noted especially for their pies, and in Louella's case, the best anadama bread in Maine, or perhaps anywhere.

Mitch had disappeared midwinter and was sighted up in Northeast Harbor with a booth at an antiques show. He told someone there that he planned to return to Sanpere to finish the job and settle his accounts, but he never again crossed the bridge to anyone's knowledge—and there were plenty of people looking for him. Barton's was a big outfit, and in any case, the owners of the house he was working on would be forced to cover the bill, since they'd given Mitch carte blanche. But Louella, and Vincent at the IGA, had trouble absorbing the loss. Mitch had run up quite a tab. His habit of turning up on your doorstep with a pie in one hand and a few pints of the expensive ice cream Vince stocked as a luxury item didn't seem the generous and kindhearted gesture it once had. Local opinion was that Mitch should come back and face the music.

Pix could almost hear what people were no doubt saying now. Well, old Mitchell is back, but the only music he's facing is harp music, and that might be doubtful.

She added another category for people like Mitch.

The Fairchilds were clearly going to be summer people, arriving for a vacation, pure and simple, leaving only their footsteps behind.

Samantha's employers were a blend, since Jim's family had been coming for such a long time, plus they were now living here year-round. But Valerie's southern accent alone would keep them at arm's length as outsiders for years.

Jill Merriwether drove past Pix on the opposite side of the road. They'd reached the two steep up and down hills that were so much fun to drive, like a roller coaster. Jill gave more than the laconic salute—a big smile and a wave. Had she heard about Mitch?

Pix suddenly remembered that Jill had added antiques to her shop. She'd talked about it during the Memorial Day weekend and mentioned that Mitch was one of her suppliers, so she must have known how to get in touch with him. Pix made a note to herself to talk to Jill and try to find out where Mitch had been living.

Jill's shop was close to the Sanpere Inn, lovingly restored six years ago by its new owners and saved from certain ruin. Mitch had worked on that, too, she recalled. The inn sat next to the millpond, facing the harbor across another small causeway. In a short time, it had become well known for its picturesque location and fine cuisine. Jill had quickly noted that its clientele was more interested in nineteenth-century marine paintings and pine chests than in mugs decorated with lobsters or jars of blueberry jam. She'd been excited about getting into the antiques business and had told Pix she was reading everything she could get her hands on. Pix reminded her not to overlook finds at the dump. A previous enterprise in Sanpere had obtained most of its stock that way when various local people traded up for a matching living room set from Sears, complete with his and her recliners, leaving the old rickety stuff off to one side by the household trash.

Pix turned down the long dirt road to their house. No matter how often she did this, she always felt an immediate sense of well-being. The first cove she passed had been posted for red tide this summer and no clamming or worming was allowed. But the cove at the foot of the meadow by their house had always tested out fine. It was illegal to cross private property to get to the shore, though anyone could come by boat and did. She'd see them bent over the mud with their short-handled rakes. Clamming and worming were backbreaking work. Digging in the mud for sea worms and bloodworms, freshwater bait, wasn't any better. Eking out a living on Sanpere had never been easy, but it was especially hard during the current recession. Men and women had to be Jacks and Jills of all trades. And that brought her back to Mitch again.

Which of his enterprises had led to the grave in the basement? Who had wanted him dead? Someone left with a half-finished or botched job? But they'd be more likely to sue or at least try to get him to complete the work, wouldn't they? She also couldn't see Louella working herself up to a murderous frenzy over unpaid bills for baked goods. But then there were people on the island who might get pretty steamed on her behalf, particularly after a night filled with too many beers.

Someone had had a reason. When they could figure that out, they'd have the murderer. This was the way she understood it usually worked in books. Look for a motive. Who inherits? Who had been scorned? Some event in his past? Something to do with his family? Maybe the whole thing was totally divorced from his shady occupations.

The newspapers played up random craziness, serial killers selecting victims at whim. But altogether too much thought had gone into the planning of Mitchell Pierce's death—the location, the timing, maybe even the quilt, Drunkard's Path. Had he been killed because he drank too much? Maybe it was insanity, some crazed temperance fanatic?

She pulled the car to the side of her house. The simple Cape wasn't an old one, but the seasons had worn the cedar shingles so that it looked as if it had been in place for centuries. Pix's garden added to the image. It was filled with old-fashioned flowers: delphinium, cosmos, phlox, oxeye daisies, and coreopsis. A combination of fragrances from the old varieties of peonies and the rosa rugosa bushes welcomed her home.

Inside, the cottage had been furnished with castoffs from The Pines, yard-sale finds, and a gem or two from local auctions. These embellished the myth that it was an old house, as did the Boston rocker needing some new paint and the gently faded chintz slipcovers on the down-cushioned sofa. The braided rugs scattered across the pine floorboards had been made by Pix's grandmother in shades of muted rose, blue, and green. Field guides, knitting projects, sailing charts, and Samantha's tennis shoes were strewn around the living room.

Other than the shoes, there was no sign of Samantha. She was still at the movies. Pix decided it was now or never. She *had* to call Faith. Having refused Ursula's sherry, she felt justified in pouring herself a scotch, dropped an ice cube in it, and dialed Sam.

He answered on the fourth ring.

"Hi, honey, I was going to call you two tonight. I was just out in the backyard in the hammock. You wouldn't believe how hot it is here!"

"That's nice," Pix said, then realized the inappropriateness of her remark. "I mean, that must be terrible."

"All right, what's wrong?"

"Samantha and I walked out to the end of the Point today to check on how the house was coming along. . . ."

"Is Seth doing a good job?"

"He hasn't done much of any job so far, but that's—"

Sam was as indignant as Pix had been earlier and she decided to let him have his say before finally interrupting. "Darling, we found a dead body on the site. In the excavation, actually."

"What!"

Pix told him the whole story. It was turning out to be a much-needed dress rehearsal for her star turn with the Fairchilds. Sam agreed to give her fifteen minutes before he went over.

"I know they're both home. I just saw Tom pull in and Faith has been in the yard with the kids all afternoon. They went inside about an hour ago.

Baths, supper, stories, Faith would be pretty busy.

But not too busy to answer the phone.

"Pix! This is great. I didn't think we'd get a report so soon."

Pix took a deep breath and a large mouthful of scotch.

"Is Tom around?"

"Yes, he's reading to the kids in the living room. Why do you ask? Don't tell me. They've screwed something up. Put something in upside down or left us with no doors!" Faith was attempting to speak lightly.

"Samantha and I went over this morning to see how things were progressing and one of the dogs dug up a dead body in your basement—or rather, the hand. The police uncovered the rest."

"I can't believe it!" Faith turned away from the phone, "Tom, get on the extension. Quick!"

"We had trouble believing it ourselves, but . . ."

"This is going to put us terribly behind schedule," Faith wailed.

From the extension, Tom asked, "What is?"

"Pix found a body buried in our future basement, and I know how the police work. It will be weeks before they'll let us continue. We may have to get all sorts of new permits and getting the ones we have was like something out of Dickens."

Pix graciously decided Faith must be in shock. She also decided she needed to get back into the conversation.

"The man who was killed was Mitchell Pierce. I don't think your paths ever crossed. He never had a permanent place on the island." Until now, she added silently. "He restored old houses, sold antiques, and tended to move around a lot."

"Isn't he the one who left Louella Prescott holding the bag?" Faith had become friendly with the baker.

"Yes, that was Mitch."

"I can't see Louella committing murder over a few crullers, though."

This time, Tom interrupted.

"How are you and Samantha? It must have been terrifying for you."

Pix felt a warm glow, a combination of Tom and Johnnie Walker.

"It was at first, but we're all right now. Fortunately, the dog only unearthed a hand."

"Oh, Pix"—now it was Faith's turn—"I've been such a jerk, thinking of my own petty concerns when you and Samantha have been through a horrendous day. What can we do? Should I come up?"

"No," Pix and Tom said in unison, Pix adding, "There really isn't anything you could do, and I know how busy you are getting ready for all those Fourth of July parties."

The Fairchilds' doorbell rang audibly in the background.

"That's probably Sam," Pix told them.

"Why don't you get it, sweetheart," Faith said.

Tom said good-bye and hung up the phone.

"Now, Pix," Faith said sternly, "I know you've seen me get involved in a number of murder cases, but it's not something I recommend, and I think you should stay out of all this as much as possible."

Pix found herself feeling somewhat annoyed. Who had located Penny Bartlett missing in Boston last year? It hadn't been Faith, but none other than her faithful friend and neighbor. Surely this same friend and neighbor should be able to ferret out a few salient details about Mitchell Pierce's death here on Sanpere, where she knew not only the names and characteristics of all the flora and fauna but the two-legged inhabitants and their habits and habitats, as well.

"Please, Pix, listen to me. It could be dangerous. I'm sure it's a total coincidence that someone picked our particular cellar hole, but you can't be too careful."

It was all Pix could do to refrain from comment, something referring to Faith's possible reactions upon hearing these same words. But Faith had become her dearest friend, and if she was a bit insensitive, a bit self-absorbed, a bit like a steam roller, other sterling qualities more than made up for it.

So she said, "Yes, Faith" as meekly as she could muster and hung up with promises to stay in touch with everyone on the hour every hour if necessary. Sam had picked up the extension and both he and Tom were exhorting her along the same lines Faith had.

She hung up, drained her glass, and then remembered: She had totally forgotten to tell Faith that Seth hadn't done any work since Memorial Day.

It would just have to wait.

Chapter 3

No one claimed the body.

After the medical examiner finished the autopsy and established that the cause of death was most certainly due to multiple stab wounds, the state police let it be known that whoever wanted to was free to take Mitchell and hold whatever last rites deemed fitting and proper. The remains were transported to the back room of Durgen's Funeral Home in Granville, pending the wishes of the near and dear.

Those wishes were still pending at the end of the week, by which time Donald Durgen had sensibly opted for cremation. Aside from the obvious reason, Donald told his brother and partner, Marvin, "We don't know how long we're going to have Mitch's company. Could be quite a while, and you know we need the space." He conscientiously labeled the cardboard box and placed it next to their tax receipts from 1980 to 1985. If someone wanted to come along and pay for an urn, why then they'd be only too happy, but for the moment, Mitch would stay filed.

That Mitchell Pierce had been stabbed to death with a hunting knife did not make the investigation any easier. On Sanpere, hunting was not merely a sport but a passion, and in many cases, a necessity. Finding a household without a hunting knife would be as surprising as the use to which this particular one had been put. Far in advance of opening day, knives and guns were honed and oiled, stories told and stretched. The winners of the state moose lottery, those fortunate individuals who got the chance to track a really big creature, were targets of envy for weeks.

But the fact remained: No one seemed to be in a hurry to claim any kinship with Mitch. He seemed destined to remain at Durgen's, not even perched by the one window in the room where his spirit would have had an unobstructed bird's-eye view across the harbor to the old granite quarries on Crandall Island and straight out to Isle au Haut, rising from the sea in the distance—with its Mount Champlain resembling some sort of Down East version of Bali Hai. Durgen's was one of the best vantage points in Granville.

Pix was expressing her surprise at Mitchell's lack of earthly ties to Louise Frazier who had called to remind the Millers about the Frazier's annual Independence Day clambake on Sunday.

"The police have tried to track down a relative or even a close friend, but so far no luck. There's *got* to be somebody. It's really very sad. I told Sam we ought to bury him and hold a small service. There's plenty of room in the plot, and I don't imagine mother would mind. I can't stand thinking of him on some shelf at Durgen's for eternity, but Sam is sure someone will turn up. He told me to wait."

He'd also told her that there was no way Ursula was going to let a nonfamily member eavesdrop on their conversations in the next life, particularly when they had been careful to avoid revealing more than where to replace a two-by-four in this. Pix was sure her mother would be more accepting, but Sam convinced her to let things lie for the moment.

"It is odd," Louise agreed, "but Mitchell was a loner. He seemed to know everybody—and he certainly knew a lot about everybody; he was a wonderful gossip—but I can't ever remember his having a good friend. Nobody lived with him whenever he was on the island, although he lived with plenty of people."

It sounded illogical, but Pix knew what Louise meant.

"He was certainly adept at mooching a place to stay when he needed one, but when he was working on a house and living on the premises, you're right: He was always alone. He lived with other people only when he couldn't live in the house. The time he was restoring that barn in Little Harbor, he lived with one of the Prescotts."

"And didn't he board with John Eggleston once?"

"Very briefly. I don't think he was there a week before they quarreled and John threw him out. I'd forgotten that." Pix made a mental note to talk to John. A former Episcopal priest, now a wood sculptor, he might have evoked some revelations of a confessional nature from Mitch before things went awry. It would be interesting to discover what had happened to cause the heave ho, although it would no doubt turn out to have been something like Mitch's using John's towel or drinking milk from the carton. In Pix's experience, this was usually why roommates parted ways—nothing dramatic, just irritating little everyday things that piled up to actionable proportions.

Pix continued: "Jill told me that Earl told her the state police have been trying to find out about Mitch's past from his tax returns and Social Security. It seems everybody has a paper trail. He was born in Rhode Island, but his parents are dead and there were no siblings. His permanent address was a post office box in Camden. They got all excited when they went over the court records—you know, he's been sued a number of times. They found a lawyer's name and got in touch with him, but he says Mitch never told him anything personal, just hired him by the case. Never, apparently, made a will, either—at least not with this guy. Now they're going over his bank records, seeing whom he may have written checks to and if he had a safety-deposit box anywhere. The last place he was living was a rented room in a house in Sullivan, and there wasn't much in it except a few clothes and a whole lot of paperback mysteries."

"It does seem amazing to us. We're so embedded in our families, our relationships, and yes, our legal affairs." Louise laughed. "What I'm saying is, people like us don't often think of people like Mitch—someone with no roots."

Louise came from a large South Carolinian family, bringing with her to Maine softened speech, a penchant for drinking iced tea all year long, and an endless supply of stories about various family members. She had a tendency to talk of the living and the dead in the same tense, so Pix was never sure whether Aunt Sister, who dressed all in white and spent fifteen minutes every day of her life with slightly dampened bags—which she fashioned herself from silk and rose petals—on her closed eyes, was still alive or had passed on. Surely, however, Cousin Fancy, who saved the sterling from the Yankees by burying it in the family plot, moving Grandaddy's stone to mark the spot—merely for the duration, you understand—was no longer rustling along the sidewalks of Charleston in her hoop skirts.

Pix accepted Louise's invitation, hoping that Sam would be able to be there with her. He liked to help Elliot prepare the pit. It was an old-fashioned clambake always held in Sylvester Cove, with half the island in attendance. She offered to bring her usual vat of fish chowder, her grandmother's cherished, but not particularly closely guarded, recipe—unlike some she could name, she told Louise, both women having tried unsuccessfully for years to get Adelaide Bainbridge's recipe for sherry-nutmeg cake. Pix had tried not so much because she wanted to make it, but because of the principle of the thing, and besides, her mother would like it. Louise wanted it because it was a favorite of Elliot's.

Pix always thought of the Fraziers as ospreys, the large fish hawks that were once more returning to the islands, building their enormous nests on rocky ledges, high atop spruce trees, and occasionally even balanced on a channel marker. Ospreys were birds who mated for life. She'd told her theory to Sam, who agreed, commenting that Elliot was actually beginning to look a little beaky as he got older. Whatever the name or the comparison, the Fraziers were a devoted couple.

Louise accepted Pix's offer of the chowder gratefully. "Timing at clambakes is so unpredictable, and people always get hungry before we uncover the pit."

After she hung up, Pix thought she'd better put in a quick call to Faith before Sunday to ask her advice about making a large quantity of chowder. Usually, she simply quadrupled or quintupled the recipe, but working at the catering company had heightened her sensibilities. Maybe there was some special proportion known only to dedicated cooks or foodies. She wished the Fairchilds could come up for the Fourth of July festivities on Sanpere, which actually started the weekend before. The day itself would begin with a parade in Sanpere Village, followed by children's games in the elementary school playground, before moving to Granville for first the Odd Fellows Lobster Picnic, then later the Fish and Fritter Fry run by the Fishermen's Wives Association on the wharf. The day ended back in Sanpere Village, with fireworks over the harbor at nightfall. But Faith was catering four different functions and couldn't get away.

Pix would miss the Fairchilds, but it might be best if they weren't around until the whole business with Mitchell Pierce was cleared up. She reminded herself to call Earl and see when Seth could start work again. She presumed they'd been over the site with magnifying glasses, tweezers, fingerprint powder, and whatever else it was they used to find clues. They'd taken both her and Samantha's sneakers away on Sunday, so examining footprints was one activity, although it had been so dry that the slightest breeze would have long since blown away any traces in a cloud of dust.

All right, she told herself briskly. Call Earl, call Faith, get out chowder recipe, make shopping list, pick up Mother at the Bainbridge's, where she is lunching, stake tomato plants, set out beer-filled tuna cans to kill slugs, pick up Samantha at work . . . She got a pencil and made a list. Pix had lists everywhere—in her purse, in her pockets, on the wall, on the fridge, tucked into books. She'd told a friend once, "My life is one long list," and the friend had replied, "I know—and the list is never done." It had depressed Pix at the time and it depressed her now. She decided to take the dogs outside and do the tomatoes first.

The exercise and the fresh air lifted her spirits immediately and she stood up and stretched. It was a long one. Pix was not her given name, but an abbreviation of the childhood nickname "Pixie," bestowed by her doting parents when she was a wee mite of two. At four, she had shot up to the size of a six-year-old, but the name persisted. And as she grew older, she was thankful to whatever fate had been responsible for that brief petite moment. As a name, Pix was vastly preferrable to what was on her birth certificate, Myrtle—for her father's favorite aunt and her horticulturist mother's favorite ground cover. In retrospect, Pix was grateful Mother hadn't opted for the Latin and chosen Vinca Minor instead of little Myrtle. When Aunt Myrtle died, she left her namesake a cameo, a diamond brooch, and some nice coupons to clip. Everything but the cameo had long since been converted into a hot-water heater, braces for the kids, and, one particularly tight winter, antibiotics for the dogs, the cost of which had led Pix seriously close to fraud as she considered listing them under their given names of Dustin, Arthur, and Henry Miller on the family's health insurance.

After all, what was in a name? Pix, like most people, seldom remembered she even had another one, unless she received a notice for jury duty or her mother was particularly annoyed with her. Her mother! She dropped her tools, ran into the house, hastily washed, and dashed out to pick Ursula up. It wouldn't do to be late.

Samantha, on another part of the island, stopped for a moment to look about. It was bright and sunny—a little too warm for Maine. They still hadn't had any rain. She'd been working for several days and was beginning to get the lay of the land.

Maine Sail Camp consisted of a number of small rustic wooden cabins plus a large dining hall that doubled as a recreation center scattered over a sloping hill ending at the shore with a large dock and boathouse. When not actually on the water, campers could still see it and the sailboats that were the focus of each encampment. In addition to the sailing lessons, campers were instructed in nature lore, swimming, and the all important crafts of lariat making and pot-holder weaving. The oldest campers were thirteen; the youngest, seven. An invisible but impenetrable wall ran down the middle of the hill separating the boys' from the girls' cabins. There were campers whose parents and even grandparents had attended Main Sail. Reunions were nostalgic affairs and camp spirit was actively encouraged. A tear in the eye when singing "O Thou Maine Sail of My Life" was not viewed amiss. Jim Atherton, the director, was the embodiment of a Maine Sail camper. He lived, breathed, and now ran Maine Sail.

He had told Samantha her first day the camp wasn't just a camp but a state of mind. Kids returned year after year, not simply for the sailing and all the rest but for the "experience." Samantha had noted that he seemed to be too choked up to put it into words. Finally, he'd told her, "You'll have to feel it for yourself."

Mostly what Samantha was feeling was tired. She was responsible for teaching ten of the youngest children beginning sailing, which was going to involve everything from knot tying, to reading the water, and finally to putting a tiny hand to the tiller. Then she had to race up to the kitchen and help serve lunch, cleaning up afterward. She'd thought it would be fun to work with Arlene, but so far, they were much too rushed to do more than exchange a quick greeting in passing. Arlene stayed on with the crew to prepare dinner and clean the cabins. She told Samantha that if last year was anything to go on, the counselors would be much worse pigs than the kids. The kids had to keep their own bunks tidy. There were no such rules for the staff.

Today was as busy as the earlier part of the week had been. Samantha raced up the hill to the dining hall, swinging open the screen door, then letting it close behind her with a bang when she saw the kitchen crew surrounding Jim, all talking at once.

"Now, now, let's not get hysterical," he said, "There are mice all over the place. You know that. We'll put out some more traps."

Mabel Hamilton, Freeman's sister-in-law and the cook at the camp for so many years that local people thought of Maine Sail as "Mabel's Place," spoke above the din. Everyone quieted down.

"We've all had mice in our kitchens. I found one poor little fellow suffocated in a sack of flour once, but what we have not had until now are three mice with their heads cut off laid out on the counter along side a carving knife."

Samantha had moved next to Arlene. "Did you see them?" she whispered.

"Yeah, it is so gross."

"I think we should call Earl." Dot Prescott's voice was firm. Everyone nodded. Dot was in charge of housekeeping and, like Mabel, had been at the camp forever.

Jim tried a jocular approach. "The police! Over a few dead rodents!" He laughed. It didn't work. A sea of tightly shut lips faced him. Mabel and Dot stood directly in front of him, feet planted solidly on the worn pine floorboards, arms folded tightly across their ample bosoms.

"All right, all right, I'll tell Earl. Now, can we clean the mess up and feed the hoard of hungry kids who will be streaming through that door in less than thirty minutes?"

Everyone returned to the kitchen. Mabel scrubbed the counter, muttering angrily to herself. "I don't like it. Not one little bit. Have half a mind to . . ." No one learned what Mabel was going to do with half of her mind, although all hoped it wouldn't be the lobe with the recipe file. She was far and away the best cook on the island. She suddenly stopped and addressed them in a louder and determinedly cheerful voice. "Let's forget about this now. It doesn't do any good to think about such foolishness. Probably a prank somebody thought would be funny."

Samantha wasn't sure. She also didn't think it should have been cleared away until Earl had had a chance to look at it, but no one was asking her, and she didn't feel she knew anyone except Arlene well enough to offer an unsolicited opinion. Besides, she was a kid and they were mostly grown-ups.

She had been unable to keep herself from looking at the gruesome sight. The tiny creatures were neatly laid side by side in a row, with their gory heads tidily set above each carcass. Samantha had seen dead mice before, even a mouse who had met its demise in a trap, but this precise carnage was worse than all the rest put together.

She watched as Mabel scoured the carving knife. Mitchell Pierce had been killed with a hunting knife. Carving knifes. Hunting knives. It suddenly seemed that there were an awful lot of knives in the news on Sanpere. She felt a bit dizzy and shook her head.

"Sam, are you okay?" Arlene was loading bread into baskets. The diet at Maine Sail leaned toward a carbohydrate overload. Today's entrée was macaroni and cheese. Dessert was bread pudding. There was a salad, though, lemon Jell-O with shredded carrots and mayonnaise dressing on an iceberg lettuce leaf.

Samantha nodded. "I'm fine. It's just creepy, especially after Sunday."

Arlene nodded knowingly and put an arm around Sam's shoulder. Since she'd started going steady, she'd begun to adopt a kind of big-sister attitude that Sam wasn't sure she totally liked.

"It is creepy, but I know who did it, and he's a harmless creep, believe me."

"You know who did it!"

"Well, I'm almost positive. It's got to be Duncan, of course. He's like stuck in the third grade or something, and I bet he thought this would be a really great joke on us and Jim. He hates it here. Maybe he thinks if he does enough weird stuff, they'll send him away. They should send him away all right—to the loony bin. It would serve him right."

Samantha hadn't given much thought to Duncan Cowley, whom she had yet to meet. Given everything she'd heard, though, Arlene's theory made sense. Samantha was willing to bet this had occurred to her employer, too. It certainly would explain why he wanted to make light of the incident.

She was about to ask Arlene to tell her some more about Duncan when one of the doors to the kitchen opened and a woman walked in. It wasn't the way her mother walked, Sam immediately observed—those purposeful strides meant to get you someplace. This walk was more like a glide. A dancer's walk. A beautiful walk.

The woman had very short, very fair hair that hugged her head in a silken helmet. Her eyes, or her contact lenses, were turquoise blue.

"It's Valerie," Arlene said in a low voice, "She's so awesome. Dunc had to have been switched at birth. He just can't be her son."

Valerie Atherton was speaking to Mabel Hamilton, then came over to the counter where the two girls were working.

"You must be Samantha Miller. I'm Valerie Atherton." Her voice was as smooth as the sea on an dead-calm day when you sat in the boat anxiously watching the drooping sail for a hint of tautness. Nothing was taut about Valerie, except her trim body and unlined face, shadowed by a large straw hat with a big red poppy pinned to the brim. Sam's mother had three hats: a floppy white sun hat with something that was paint or rust on it, a black hat for funerals, and a yellow rubber rain hat that made her look like the old salt on the package of Gorton's fish sticks.

"Hi." Samantha, star of the debate team, lead in the junior class play, searched for some other words, something that would make an impression on this witty and urbane woman, a woman Arlene worshiped. Sam had heard so much about Mrs. Atherton, she felt she already knew her—her clothes, her car, her cat, Rhett Butler. Valerie hailed from the South and what was a hint in Louise Frazier's speech was a full-blown answer in Valerie's.

"Hi," Samantha said again, now ready with a remark. "I'm Samantha Miller."

She met Arlene's eyes and turned scarlet with embarrassment. Someone else might have said, "I know. I said that, stupid," but Valerie appeared to find it new and delightful.

"I just adore your grandmother and your parents. It's lovely of you to be helping us out this summer. I hope you'll come by the house real soon. We can't show it off enough. It was in such bad taste to build such a big place and we have no excuse, except we all seem to take up so much space and if the house was any smaller, Jim and I would probably end up getting a divorce, so really we're helping to change those terrible statistics about failed marriages."

Mabel Hamilton, who'd been beaming since Valerie came into the kitchen, burst out laughing, "I have to remember this. Maybe if I tell Wilbur it's to save our marriage and set a good example for folks, he will finally winterize the porch so I can have my sewing room."

Samantha's cheeks were back to their normal color. She didn't know anyone who blushed as much as she did; it was annoying, so immature. She realized Valerie had entirely changed the mood of the kitchen and gotten everyone thinking of something else in a very short time.

Valerie perched on one of the stools and asked Mabel if she could have a bowl of the macaroni and cheese. "It's my ultimate comfort food." She was looking at Samantha, so Sam nodded and finally found some words. "Mine, too, along with chocolate pudding and whipped cream."

"And warm applesauce," Arlene suggested. Soon everyone was listing their favorites—mashed potatoes, cinnamon toast, tapioca—until Mabel brought the reverie to a halt with her own candidate—sardine sandwiches.

"Ugh! That's more like bait, Mabel," Dot said. She was about to elaborate when they heard the trample of little feet, many little feet. Samantha and Arlene jumped up to take the huge trays of steaming food out to the tables, where the kids helped themselves family-style. But first Jim asked for quiet. Samantha expected some reference to the mouse incident: "If anyone has any information"—the old "Put your heads down on your desks and I won't tell who raises a hand" kind of thing. Yet he didn't mention it. Instead, he recited from Tennyson's "Crossing the Bar," his voice growing slightly husky at "Sunset and evening star/And one clear call for me!" Jim started every meal with some inspirational nautical quotation. The man must have spent years memorizing them all. Sam was curious to see whether he recycled them each session or whether there would be a new one every day. Irreverently, she wondered whether he had picked today's quote as a tribute to the mice.

She stood near the wall on one side of the dining room, ready to refill platters and the pitchers of milk and water that were set in the middle of each table. She took the opportunity to study Jim. He didn't seem to be Valerie's type. He dressed invariably in L. L. Bean khakis, the camp T-shirt, and, of course, Top-Siders. He was handsome. Days on the water had bleached out his light brown hair and given him a good tan. His eyes were clear and blue. He always looked as if he'd had a good night's sleep. But there was nothing exotic about him, nothing special. He didn't have any style. Samantha found herself searching for the exact words that would sum up her employer. Jim Atherton was . . . well, he was just so straight.

As she'd groped for the definition, Jim's antithesis appeared at the dining room door: black/white, ying/yang, right/wrong, you say *either*—all rolled up into one. It had to be Duncan. A nudge and a whisper from Arlene confirmed it. Samantha watched as Jim Atherton's gaze, which had been sweeping steadily across the room at regular intervals like the beam from the old Eagle Island lighthouse, rested on his stepson. There was no mistaking Jim's look of dismay. He concealed it hastily and walked toward the young man.

"Duncan. Hello. Are you hungry? Take a seat. We're still on the macaroni and cheese." Jim made the mistake of resting his hand on the boy's shoulder. Duncan shook it off with disdain. Arlene whispered, "Cooties" in Samantha's ear. Sam had to bite her lip to keep from laughing. Duncan *had* looked childish.

Duncan Cowley inhabited that curious limbo between childhood and adulthood, called, depending on the speaker, "the best years of your life," "the process of self-actualization," or "teen hell." To stake out his own particular territory in this strange land, Duncan had chosen to dress all in black. Today he wore a Metallica concert T-shirt under an unbuttoned black denim shirt, black jeans, and black high-top L.A. Lites, untied and without socks. A black leather bracelet complete with lethal metal spikes completed the ensemble.

"His parents should make him smell his shoes for punishment," Samantha said, adding, "I thought only elementary school kids wore those shoes that light up. You're right. What a loser."

Without a word to his stepfather, Duncan made his way to

the kitchen, his shoes indeed flashing tiny red spots of light as he walked. The girls turned to the wall. It was the kind of thing that could send them into uncontrollable fits of the giggles.

"And he stinks, too! What is that smell?" Samantha gasped.

"Musk and B.O."

"Poor Valerie." Samantha was in total sympathy with his mother, something that would have astonished some of her Aleford friends. But then, she wasn't in Aleford, and besides, Valerie wasn't like a regular parent.

At dinner that night, Samantha couldn't stop talking about the Athertons. She and her mother had taken big bowls of chili down to the deck by their own boathouse. Life with Samantha was turning out to be very relaxed, Pix thought as she reached for a tortilla chip straight from the bag. She hadn't even bothered with a bowl and she pushed thoughts of what Mother—and Faith—would say far from her mind. Instead, she concentrated on a cold Dos Equis—Faith would at least approve of the beer—and on what Samantha was saying. Obviously, the girl was in love.

Had Pix's own besotted crush on their neighbor, Priscilla Graham, been as boring, and even slightly irritating to Ursula? Pix sighed. If she was going to have to listen to paens to Valerie every night, she'd better lay in some more booze. What made it worse was that Valerie was a pretty fascinating creature and Pix liked her. She also knew, though, that in terms of types of women, she, Pix, was somewhere in Julia Ward Howedom, while Valerie inhabited the realms of Carole Lombard and Claudette Colbert, women who could and did wear satin.

"You have got to see him, Mom. He wears an earring, but not one like normal people—it's a notebook ring. I don't even want to think about how he got it through!"

It was an unappetizing thought, Pix agreed. Her mind swerved to the current fashion that bestowed normalcy on male earrings and she laughed aloud. She liked the freedom today's kids had to dress the way they did, although she still wished Samantha would cut her hair. In Pix's day, the most outré thing one dared do was wear one's Pandora cardigan buttoned up the back instead of the front.

"What are you laughing at?"

"Nothing in particular. I was just thinking about how differently teenagers dress now compared with when I was growing up."

"Your kilts and kneesocks? Your Weejuns? Your circle pin?" Samantha teased her.

"Someone told me circle pins were coming back. I always used to get so confused about which side to wear it on that I never wore mine much—one side meant you were a 'nice' girl and one meant the opposite. The middle meant something, too, but I can't remember what."

Now Samantha laughed. "Where would you have put it?"

"None of your business." Pix was not the type of parent who believed in revealing all to her children, especially before they had passed through the particular stage.

"Do you really think Duncan put the dead mice on the counter?" Pix was ready to move on to another topic. This had been the first thing Samantha had blurted out to her mother when Pix picked her up. Pix knew there could be no possible connection with Mitchell Pierce's murder, but it was another unsettling event in a place usually devoid of such things.

"I don't know. It's no secret he hates Jim, hates the camp, maybe even hates his mother for bringing him here. Arlene says he only has a couple of loser friends, mostly younger kids who are together not because they particularly want to be, but because nobody else likes them. They all wear a lot of black and listen to mope rock, that kind of stuff."

"Mope rock?" This was a new one, but Pix had grown to expect unrelenting novelty after raising one adolescent. The temps and mores changed at roughly the speed of light.

"Yeah, The Cure, New Order. I mean, I like them sometimes, except it gets a little much—tormented souls, desperate love. It's depressing."

"I think these were the kids who used to write poetry and try to get their parents to let them take the train down to Greenwich Village in an earlier day."

"Beatniks! I read about them in my American history book."

Sometimes children could make you feel very, very old with merely a few well-chosen words.

"I've read about them, too," Pix countered. She picked up her empty bowl and glass—she had taken the trouble to pour the beer from the bottle—and stood up. It was still light and she hated to go indoors, but she told Samantha, "I really have to call Faith. The kids should be asleep by now."

"I can't wait until they come. I miss seeing Ben and Amy. By August, they're going to be all different. Amy probably won't even remember me." Samantha had gone straight from passionate involvement with horses to small children, and now, it appeared, to soignée thirtysomething women, as well.

"I'm sure the Fairchilds can't wait to see you, either," Pix assured her, silently adding, Especially Faith.

"So what's going on? No more bodies I trust." Faith felt she could be flippant. If another corpse had turned up, in their well, say, surely Pix would have called her at once. Besides, she knew every nuance of her friend's speech. From the moment Pix had said hello on Sunday, Faith had known something was disastrously wrong on Sanpere. Tonight's greeting had been cheerful, everyday Pix.

"No, not human ones, anyway." Pix hadn't intended to start the conversation by telling Faith about the mice, but here it was.

Faith's reaction was similar to Pix's. "It seems unlikely that the two events have anything to do with each other, except proximity in time, and the use of knives. But why three mice? Were they blind?"

"I imagine they weren't taking in any movies," Pix said. "I've tried to think of a connection with the rhyme, but Valerie Atherton isn't a farmer's wife, nor are you, and there aren't any other wives involved."

"That we know of," Faith reminded her.

"That we know of. Besides, if it was meant to illustrate the nursery rhyme, their tails, not their heads, would have been cut off."

"Maybe the person has a bad memory and thought it was 'cut off their *heads* with a carving knife.'"

This actually made sense. Pix often misremembered childhood ditties, much to her mother's dismay. Her mother was supposed to be in the time of life when one's gray matter retreated into the shadows. Ursula's was a veritable Costa del Sol.

"What kind of mice were they?" Faith asked.

"Common field mice, I suppose. They're all over the island, you know."

Faith did not know and wasn't sure she was grateful for this new information.

"Not white mice, the kind kids keep as pets?"

"Samantha didn't say, but I don't think they were; otherwise, she would have mentioned it."

"Well, it is odd. Let me know if anything of a nursery-rhyme nature occurs again. There isn't anything in Mother Goose about a body in the basement, is there?"

"Probably. Some of the rhymes were pretty violent. I'll ask Mother."

"Speaking of violence, what's happening with the investigation?"

Pix told her everything she knew, including Mitchell Pierce's present whereabouts.

"I agree with you. It is sad. And it certainly gives new meaning to the phrase 'on the shelf.' If no one has claimed him by August, he should be interred someplace on the island. Tom can do the service," Faith said, cavalierly offering her spouse. "If relatives or friends haven't turned up by then, they would be unlikely to later."

"As soon as they calculate his estate, they're going to advertise—not the amount, of course, although Mitch couldn't have had much—just that you could hear something to your interest. If this doesn't bring someone forward, nothing will—or there's no one to be brought. I'm not saying it well."

"You're saying it wonderfully. Why, I don't know, but the whole thing reminds me of the time I went in the backyard and saw this man scattering ashes on the rosebushes. It must be the ashes," Faith added parenthetically.

"You never told me about this!" Pix exclaimed, surprised at the incident and even more at the fact that she hadn't known about it.

"It was shortly after we were married, and I didn't know you as well then as I do now. I probably thought you'd be scandalized, because I was furious with him. I mean those were our roses! He could at least have had the decency to ring at the front door and ask permission. It turned out that he was a former parishioner who was passing through and just happened to have his aunt Tilly in the car and thought she'd like literally to be pushing up roses."

"Her name wasn't really Tilly."

"Possibly not. I don't remember. Of course I ended up feeling sorry for him. He finished his sprinkling and I gave him something to eat. I think it was some leftover blueberry tarte."* Faith's food memory was flawless.

"I want that recipe, remember. We're going to have a bumper crop this year and the wild strawberries in the meadow are already ripe. I should have plenty for jam."

*See recipe on page 287.

"Don't make me jealous. I wish I hadn't accepted all these jobs for the Fourth. I'll never do it again."

Pix got her chowder advice; it wasn't complicated, simply good old multiplication. Faith suggested she might like to sprinkle fresh dill on top, but Pix told her this was a chowder purist crowd, eschewing even oyster crackers.

Faith then asked Pix's advice on how to stay sane while Amy was determinedly learning to walk, reeling around the house on feet that looked too tiny to support any kind of movement, let alone something as complicated as standing erect unaided.

"I want to give her knee and elbow pads, plus a helmet. Ben never went through this self-destructive phase. Sure he pulled himself up on things a lot, but he basically just sat, then started walking when he was about fourteen months."

"You just don't remember. It's a merciful forgetting. All that falling down."

They talked and laughed about the kids some more. Pix had yet to receive one of the stack of self-addressed stamped postcards she had sent off to camp with Danny. She had wanted to do the same with Mark but dared not. She'd have to pray for collect calls. She told Faith about Samantha's Valerie worship, was reassured—and realized she needed it—by Faith's own loyal remarks as to Pix's superiority, despite her lack of a subscription to *Vogue*.

"It wouldn't hurt to put on a little lipstick occasionally, though. I know what happens to you in Maine. Squeaky-clean is not all that intriguing. And leave a fashion magazine or two around the house with your cow-manure manuals or whatever you're reading these days."

"I'd rather have manure on my roses than what's on yours," Pix retorted.

"That was years ago. Besides, they've bloomed like crazy ever since."

It was very difficult to get the last word with Faith. Pix said good-bye and went to bed but not to sleep. They were showing movies at the old Opera House in Granville again and Samantha had gone with a group of friends.

As she lay listening for the sound of a car door, she thought about putting up another trellis in the garden for morning glories, across from the one that now sported a lush purple clematis. Building. House building. Earl wasn't sure when Seth could get back to work again.

Bang. Samantha was home. Pix turned out her light and was almost startled into wakefulness by remembering.

She'd forgotten to tell Faith what she still didn't know— that Seth hadn't done anything at all since May. Forgotten to tell her *again.*

The Sanpere Stitchers, which was what the Sewing Circle had decided to call itself about twenty-five years before, was meeting at The Pines this month. Many island routines were disturbed by this sacrosanct meeting. Louella closed the bakery for the afternoon; Mabel Hamilton left a cold dinner for the camp; and Dot Prescott's daughter went over to fill in for her mother. Anyone in residence at Adelaide and Rebecca Bainbridge's bed-and-breakfast would find the doors locked. A note affixed to the shiny brass front knocker announced their return at five and suggested a long walk or drive to Granville until then.

When the ladies convened at her mother's house, Pix's life was not her own for about twenty-four hours. She wasn't a member of the group, although they graciously allowed her to sit in when it was at Ursula's. Membership was a closely guarded affair, bestowed infrequently and only to women of a certain age and level of skill. The Sanpere Stitchers were very proud of their handiwork, and their annual sale in August to raise money for the Island Food Pantry was sold out by ten o'clock.

Pix's role began the night before with a call from Mother.

"You remember, dear, that tomorrow is Sewing Circle at my house, don't you?"

Since Ursula had managed in subtle and not-so-subtle ways to work this into the conversation every day since last Friday, Pix did indeed remember. It was written down on several lists.

"Yes, of course, and I'll be there early to help. I know you want my big coffee urn. Is there anything else you need?"

"Not really. Gert has things under control. She's been baking since Tuesday and cleaning since *last* Tuesday. But it occurred to me that you might bring some savories—a cheese spread, some crackers, you know the kind of thing. Perhaps arranged on a nice plate with some grapes, for those who don't want just sweets."

Pix developed a bowline in the pit of her stomach. Mother wasn't talking about a Wispride spread or Cheez Whiz. Her reputation was at stake.

"I'll see what I can do," she promised, vowing to call Faith as soon as Ursula hung up. This was an emergency.

Faith, knowing Pix's culinary expertise, gave her two very simple recipes* and told her to go to the foreign-food section, one shelf, at the IGA and pick up some Carr's water biscuits and Bremer wafers.

"Basically, these are cream-cheese spreads. For the first, blend some of the goat cheese from the farmers' market with an equal amount of cream cheese. That goat cheese by itself is too crumbly. If you don't have any, it's Mrs. Cousins who makes it, and you can go to her house. Try to get the kind she puts herbs in. For the other spread, take some of the green-tomato chutney you put up last year—you must have some left; you made vats of it—and mix it into the cream cheese. Don't make it too gooshy; taste it as you go along. Then put each in a pretty little bowl and decorate the top with a nasturtium or some other nonlethal posy from your garden. Put them on a platter and arrange the crackers and grapes around the bowls with more flowers."

The next morning, Pix stepped back from her creation and

*See recipes on page 285.

was tempted to take a picture for Faith. The platter looked beautiful—and tasty. Julia Child, watch out. She decided to go early to mother's and show off.

"Isn't that lovely!" her mother exclaimed. One of the nice things about Ursula was that she expressed her appreciation, even if it was for something she herself could have done with one hand tied behind her back, especially in earlier years. This was a woman who still gathered her grandchildren and their friends together at Easter to make the sugar eggs with the frosting scenes inside from scratch. "Gert, come see what a good job Pix has done."

Pix usually felt about twelve years old on Sewing Circle days. Today it might be ten.

The ladies started arriving promptly at one o'clock, bearing work bags and projects, some to display; some to complete. Pix scurried around fetching chairs and even a footstool or two for those who needed them—like Adelaide Bainbridge. She was an immense woman and said the blood ran better in her legs if her feet were up. She took up two spaces on the couch, further claiming territory as she spread out her work. There was a tiny corner left to sit in and she called over to her sister-in-law, seated in one of the multitude of Boston and Bar Harbor rockers, "Rebecca, there's plenty of room here and I need you to thread my needles. My eyes aren't what they used to be," Addie explained to the group. Rebecca obligingly gathered her things together and squeezed into the space. Fortunately, she was spare and lean, with elbows exposed in the warm weather that looked as sharp as the needle she was now threading. She had brought Ursula an old-fashioned, beribboned nosegay—pale pink sweetheart roses mixed with dried sea lavender surrounded by lily of the valley leaves. It graced the table now in a small white pitcher Pix had found, perfect for a tea party.

Louise Frazier had been voted into the group some years ago and after giving Pix a warm hug sat down on the other large couch next to Mabel Hamilton and pulled out a child's sweater with brightly colored crayons worked on the front. "I have just got to finish this today," she said, needles clicking away. "The sale is only six weeks away and I have two more to do!"

After appropriate praise was given for various articles, the talk turned to how many raffle tickets each member had sold for Adelaide's quilt.

"It's so good of you to give it, Addie. The summer people are buying chances like crazy and now that the inn is displaying the quilt, even more people will want tickets," Dot said.

Adelaide Bainbridge was one of the island's celebrities. Fame had come late in her life. She now admitted to seventy-nine and friends politely ignored the fact that this admission had been made several years ago, as well. She'd started quilting as a child, taught by her mother to while away their time on one of the small islands off Sanpere. Adelaide's father had been a lighthouse keeper in the days before automation replaced the families who faithfully tended the beam. Pix always pictured Addie as one of those lighthouse keeper's daughters in old storybooks, battling through the storm to keep the light burning while Papa lay tossing with fever at her feet. If her childhood had been lonely on the island with only her parents for company, she never said anything. She seemed to have learned how to do an enormous number of things well from her mother—the art of housekeeping, reading and ciphering, and sewing.

Her quilts had become collector's items, depicting elaborately appliquéd scenes from her childhood and island life. A few of the recent ones were more abstract—colorful shapes suggestive of trees, waves, birds, and fish. Some of the quilts were in the permanent collections of museums. No shrinking violet—her appearance alone claimed center stage—Adelaide enjoyed being the Grandma Moses of the quilting world. Just when people thought her head couldn't get any bigger—an entire article in the *Ellsworth American*—"Good Morning America" included her in a special about Maine.

She lived with Rebecca, or rather Rebecca lived with her, moving into the large white nineteenth-century farmhouse after her brother James, Adelaide's husband, died. That was thirty years ago. Rebecca was the perfect handmaiden, basking in Adelaide's glory. No mean quilter herself, Rebecca had already contributed two quilts to the sale, a Double Wedding Ring and a Log Cabin. Now she was turning out an endless number of counted cross-stitch Christmas ornaments, hunched over her work, looking even smaller than she was next to Adelaide's bulk. The two were the island's own odd couple. Adelaide ran the household and was totally down-to-earth and practical, despite the fits of fancy her quilts represented. Rebecca drifted through the day with her head in the clouds—and occasionally her purse in the refrigerator or the garden implement she'd last been using set on the table in place of a fork.

Pix knew what she was supposed to do at these gatherings and announced that the coffee was ready. People filled their plates and she was gratified to see the cheese spreads disappearing. They put their handwork aside and sat back. Pix and Gert passed around more goodies.

"My word, but these are tempting, Ursula, how did you find the time to do all this?" Mabel asked.

Credit where credit was due. "Oh, Gert and Pix did most of it." Her self-deprecating smile hinted at the possibility that she might have sliced a lemon or two and put out the milk.

The talk drifted away from the sale to what was uppermost on every islander's mind these days—Mitchell Pierce. Most people were regarding it as an isolated incident, so it wasn't stirring up anyone's fears. Talk about it tended to the matter-of-fact.

"And the police don't have any leads? You'd think someone would have seen something." Adelaide Bainbridge declared emphatically after consuming one of Gert's cream puffs in two bites.

No one seemed prepared to respond. All eyes turned to

Pix. She was certain that they knew as much as she did but supposed her discovery of the body conferred some sort of mantle of expertise.

"I'm sure the police have leads that we don't know about. Mitchell hadn't been seen on the island for some time, so they're concentrating around Camden and Bar Harbor. As for seeing something, anyone could have landed on the Point at night—or even driven out there without being noticed. There were no signs of a struggle, so they are probably assuming the murder occurred someplace else. If you were lucky and no one was picnicking, you could even get away with bringing in a body in broad daylight."

"And Seth hadn't started working out there yet," Gert added.

"I know." Pix still found it hard to keep the irritation from her voice whenever she thought about it. If Seth had stuck to his promised schedule, or what Pix had assumed was promised, the foundation and basement would have been poured and the murderer would have had to find someplace else for the body. Yet with Seth's mother sitting across from her, hard at work on a smocked baby's dress, Pix couldn't give vent to her true emotions.

"Poor Mitchell, he was a likable soul," Louella said.

"But he swindled you out of all that money!" Pix's emotions found an outlet.

"I know, I know, still I'm going to miss him." It was the first real expression of mourning Pix had heard. "It hasn't been easy to make up the loss, but he intended to pay me back, I'm sure. He simply didn't have it."

"Well, he'd have it now if he could've taken it with him," Ursula commented dryly, "Seems like there's quite a fortune in his bank account in Bar Harbor—close to half a million dollars."

This was news, and for an instant the ladies were too amazed to comment, then everyone spoke at once.

Mother has been holding out on me again, Pix thought, and

after I slaved away all morning concocting gourmet cheese spreads for her party!

Ursula's voice cut through the fray. "I found out just as you were all arriving and haven't had a chance to tell anyone." She gave her daughter an apologetic look. "Nan Hamilton called to say she'd be late and told me Freeman had heard it from Sonny, who picked it up on the police band."

This was an impeccable source, and the obvious question was voiced by one of the Sanfords, "Where in this world would Mitchell Pierce get all that money?"

It was what Pix was asking herself. Less than a year ago, he was skipping town to avoid his debts and now he was on easy street—or would be if alive. Either he'd been restoring houses at breakneck speed up the coast or he'd been branching out into some other lines of business. The multitude of coves and inlets on the coast brought to mind several illegal possibilities.

Jill offered a suggestion. She was younger than the other members, but she had come so often with her aunt, who had raised her, in days gone by that when the aunt died, it seemed only right to ask Jill to take her place. "He did sell a lot of antiques and maybe he came across something really valuable."

"That's possible," Pix agreed, "but the police would have discovered that by now."

"How do we know they haven't?" Jill asked.

"Well, if you don't know, no one on this island does," Dot teased her, and Jill obliged by turning red.

"Has anybody claimed him yet?" Serena Marshall asked. "Because when they do, you march right down, Louella, and get your money back." Serena was partial to Court TV. Cable had changed the landscape of the minds of islanders forever. "They have to settle his debts from the estate."

Everyone nodded and they moved away from the topic of Mitch to the consideration of a new member.

"She hasn't lived here that long, but she does beautiful work and they are year-round now."

Pix assumed they were talking about Valerie Atherton. She said Samantha was enjoying her work at the camp.

"Oh no, not Valerie"—Mabel laughed—"though she'd liven things up. I don't believe that girl has ever even threaded a needle in her life. We're talking about Joan down to the inn." Joan Randall and her husband, George, owned the Sanpere Inn. Smiles of the "silly old Pix" variety crossed some lips and Pix lowered her age to five. She loved these women—but one at a time.

"I don't see why we shouldn't have her," Louise said. "There's a space open." Everyone grew silent for a moment as they remembered their friend who'd died the year before. "Joan's eager to join and she's a gifted quilter, although a bit shy about her talents. I've seen her quilts. In some of them, she's taken the traditional patterns and given them a new twist by using contemporary fabrics. She has a wonderful sense of color."

It was agreed that Joan would be the newest Sanpere Stitcher and informed of this signal honor as soon as possible so she could contribute to the sale.

The afternoon drifted on. A lot of coffee was drunk, some gossip conveyed, and a surprising amount of work accomplished. The only note of discord had been struck when Adelaide misplaced her scissors and, finding that her sister-in-law was sitting on them, chewed Rebecca out in no uncertain terms, "I do believe you are getting scattier by the minute, Rebecca! You know you put cream that had turned in the gravy last week." Rebecca appeared not to hear her and just went on working. It was something she'd grown adept at over the years. The other women ignored Addie, too. They'd also heard it all before.

After the last woman left, Ursula looked about at the wreckage of half-filled cups and crumb-laden plates and said, "Don't you wish we could leave all this until tomorrow?" Unfortunately, Gert had had to leave, as it was her evening to do for the Bainbridges. Besides Ursula, Gert seemed to do for most of Sanpere.

"Why don't we? Come to my house for supper and leave everything," Pix suggested. She had no problem with it, yet she was sure what her mother's response would be.

"Getting up and seeing a pile of dirty dishes in my living room would be worse than seeing a . . . well, let's just say would be unpleasant."

Pix knew what her mother had intended, but she didn't agree. Seeing a body would be far worse. And she, Pix, should know.

It didn't take as long as they thought to clean up. Ursula turned down Pix's offer of supper. "Maybe it's the noise, but all I ever want on Sewing Circle days is a boiled egg and early bed."

Pix kissed her mother good-bye and headed home. She felt like talking to Sam and hoped her husband would be around. She'd always thought it was one of life's little inequities that when a man was left on his own, he was showered with dinner invitations—the poor thing. When Sam was out of town, kids home or not, no one so much as offered her a casserole.

Samantha was in the living room reading. Pix was glad to see it was Alice Hoffman and not Martha Stewart—this after Samantha's remark the other evening that their soup bowls didn't match. It had never come to her attention before, and the bowls had been around as long as she had. She'd be tying ribbons around their napkins next.

"How was your day, sweetheart?"

"I like the teaching part, but it's boring standing around while they eat, then it's a big rush to clean up. The kids are great, except it's kind of sad."

"What do you mean?"

"Well, some of them really don't want to be there, although I think they kind of like me."

"They're probably just homesick. Most kids are that way at camp in the beginning."

"I know. I remember Danny sending you all those cards to come get him, then when you finally broke down and went, he wanted to know what you were doing there."

Pix remembered the incident well. Danny, or their unexpected little dividend, as she and Sam called him in private, was predictably unpredictable in all things.

"But these kids have been sent to camp for years, even though they're so young. It's like their parents want to get rid of them," Samantha continued.

"Maybe their parents need to have a program for them. If both are working, a child can't simply stay home."

"I know and I think that's true in some cases, but there's one little girl, Susannah, who's so sweet, and I know her mother isn't working. She said so. And then there's this boy I'm kind of worried about. He's really mad at his parents for what he calls "dumping" him at camp while they're on vacation."

"It's hard to know what's going on in other people's families." With that understatement, Pix went to make some supper for the two of them, after which she had a delightful and foolish talk with her husband, reminiscent of all the talks of all the other summers.

"Dad thinks he will be up on Sunday," Pix happily told Samantha. "And he can stay on through the Fourth."

"I'd better make myself scarce," her daughter teased her. "I know what you two are like."

Pix was still not used to the idea that her older children knew their parents had and enjoyed sex. "Oh, Samantha, don't be silly. Daddy wants to spend as much time as possible with you, too."

And it was true. Sam was taking the thought of his daughter's leaving for college in the not-too-distant future even harder than Pix.

The phone rang and Samantha grabbed it, but this time it was for her mother.

"Pix? It's Jill. What are you doing tomorrow? Valerie and I

are going to go antiquing over in Searsport and toward Belfast if there's time. Could you join us? Valerie says prices are especially low because of the economy, and since it's still early in the season, things haven't been picked over. We'll leave after breakfast. I have someone to cover the store then.''

"I'd love to. I have to be home in the afternoon to make chowder for the Frazier's clambake, so the morning is perfect for me," Pix answered. "I'm looking for a night table to go in the guest room at home, and in any case, it's always fun to poke around.''

"Plus, Valerie knows so much about everything. Whenever I go with her, I always learn new things—and she's very good at dickering. I can never find the nerve.''

Pix had always been amazed that Jill had found the nerve to open and run her store. She was extremely quiet and shy. Both Pix and Faith thought Jill was beautiful—what was called in another day a "pocket Venus"—tiny but perfect, with thick, silky dark brown straight hair falling to her shoulders. Her attire betrayed the fact that she spent winters off-island working in Portland. The outfit she'd worn today at the Sewing Circle—a hand-painted turquoise tunic over a gauzy white accordion-pleated skirt—hadn't come from the Granville Emporium, where it was still possible to find printed shirtwaist dresses circa 1955. Tom and Sam both said "attractive" was as far as they would go in describing Jill, thereby confirming Faith's oft-stated notion that men knew nothing about female pulchritude.

The next day, Valerie met them at Jill's. Pix had offered to drive, but Valerie had a van and there was always the possibility they might be carting home something big. Jill hoped to get some things for the store—small folk art items and thirties jewelry had proved especially popular.

"Hop in," Valerie called out cheerfully. She was wearing work clothes—jeans, turtleneck, sneakers, each discreetly emblazoned by Lauren.

The first place they stopped was a barn. The sign outside promised TRASH AND TREASURES. Jill had found some alphabet plates at a procurable price there earlier and wanted to look in again. Pix walked through the door feeling the tingle of excitement she always did at an auction, a yard sale, any place that offered not just a bargain but a find.

Jill started sifting through boxes of costume jewelry and Valerie was climbing over dressers and bedsteads to examine an oak dining room set. Pix strolled through the musty barn. There was a pile of *Look* magazines next to a windup Victrola. Tables were filled with a mixture of fine cut glass and gas station giveaways. She was slightly taken aback to see the kind of tin sand pail and shovel from her childhood behind locked doors with other toys of various vintages. Maybe hers was still in the attic at The Pines. At the end of the aisle, there was a heap of linens, and her heart began to beat faster when she saw there were some quilts in the pile. She started to sort through them. Motes of dust floated in the strong light from an adjacent window.

Some of the quilts had suffered a great deal of damage, but one was remarkably well preserved. Left in a trunk or used only for company, it was the Flying Geese pattern, done in shades of brown and gold. The triangular "geese" were several different prints—some striped, some flowered. The setting strips were muslin and elaborately quilted. It was a real scrap quilt and Pix fell in love with it. There were occasional touches of bright red, perhaps flannel, and the handwork was exquisite. She took it and two of the damaged ones that she thought could be repaired to the front of the barn.

"How much for all three?" she asked the owner. "Some of them are very badly worn."

"Came out of a house over near Sullivan. Nothing that went in ever left until the party that owned it departed in a pine box." He seemed to find this very funny. Pix had heard about these untouched houses before.

"What's your price?"

"Two hundred dollars," he said firmly.

Pix almost gasped. The man obviously didn't know what quilts were bringing. She held on to her senses and countered, "A hundred and fifty."

"We'll split the difference, deah. How about one seventy-five—plus tax."

Pix agreed. She wasn't about to lose her quilts. She paid him and ran over to Jill, who had a fistful of Bakelite bracelets.

"Look what I got!" Pix kept her voice down, but it was hard.

"Quilts! How wonderful. I'll pay for these and then let's go where I can see them properly."

They called to Valerie that they'd be outside, then spread the quilts on the grass by the van. The Flying Geese quilt looked even better in the sunlight against the green grass.

"Pix, it's gorgeous," Jill enthused.

Pix was elated and bent down to look at the stitching again. That's when she saw it. Close to the border, just like the other one. Two crossed blue threads.

Two crossed blue threads just like the ones on the quilt that had served as Mitchell Pierce's winding-sheet.

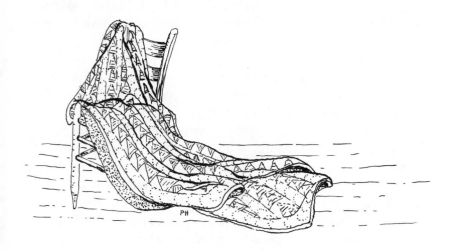

Chapter 4

Pix was so startled that she grabbed Jill's arm.

"It's the—"

She started to speak, then stopped abruptly. She hadn't told anyone except Earl about the mark, a mark that had come to represent a hex in her mind. He hadn't seemed very interested. Pix quickly decided to change course.

"It's the best quilt I've ever found. What a treasure!"

Jill did not appear to find Pix's overt enthusiasm odd. Quilters were known for their passion.

"It *is* beautiful. You are so lucky. I could probably get three or four hundred dollars for it, maybe more." She sounded wistful. "What about the other quilts, what are they like?"

Pix was suddenly eager to examine them for more marks. They spread them out in a row.

"What a shame! This quilt is almost perfect, only some wear in the corner. But that could be repaired. What's the pattern?"

"I'm not sure. Some variation of Pinwheel. This one is Irish Chain, though, and it will take some work, but I think I can replace the parts where the fabric has disintegrated."

Pix wanted to go back to the pile of linens to examine them further. For all she knew, the blue cross-stitches could be a kind of laundry mark, but it was strange to find them in exactly the same place on both quilts.

"Shall we see what else we can turn up? Valerie seems to be engaged in mortal combat with the owner over that dining room set, so we might as well look around some more."

Jill commented, "Mortal combat with velvet gloves. When I was leaving, I heard her tell him, 'My, what lovely things you've got here. I have so many people asking me to find antiques for them, I just *know* I'm going to be coming here all the time.'"

Pix had to laugh at her imitation of Valerie's accent—Down East meets Down South. It was a curious encounter.

Happily, Jill wanted to look at the linens, and Pix led her to that corner of the barn. They sorted through the stack of mismatched napkins, huck hand towels, and tablecloths, turning up the two badly tattered quilts Pix had previously spotted. Pix shook out each one thoroughly, ostensibly looking for holes. There wasn't a blue mark to be seen. Jill decided to take some of the monogrammed guest towels.

"People don't care whose initials they are so long as they have them. It adds a touch of class to one's powder room."

"I'll have to remember that if I ever have one," Pix remarked. The downstairs half bath off the kitchen in the Miller household always seemed to be filled with the kid's overflow from the bath the three shared upstairs. In the past, it was dinosaur toothbrush holders and whatever toothpaste manufacturers had dreamed up to entice kids to brush—sparkles, stars, exotic flavors. Now it was hair gel and hot combs. The towels, while not actually on the floor, were always in disarray, except for the first five minutes after she put out clean ones.

With her mind torn between a vision of what a home inhabited by two reasonably tidy adults would look like and how dreadful it would be not to find mud-covered cleats in the living room anymore, she wandered toward the big open barn door.

At the front of the store, Valerie was writing a check and arranging to come back later for the dining room set. She didn't want to stand around and wait while he unearthed it all. When the owner's back was turned, she shot Pix a triumphant glance and winked.

Outside as she looked at the quilts, she softly crowed, "Golden oak, never restored—perfect condition and everything my client wants, even the lion's paw feet on the table. It's not my taste, but at the moment it's delicious. He said he was happy to get rid of it, wants the room!" She picked up the corner of the Flying Geese quilt to examine the stitching. "It looks like you made a steal, too, Pix. This is gorgeous. You sure you want to keep it? I have just the place for it. I wouldn't sell this one."

"And neither would I, thank you," Pix said gleefully. Somehow it added to the sweetness of the coup to have a professional's approval—and envy.

"Ladies, the morning is young. Let's get going!"

By lunchtime, they were ready to quit. The shops had begun to merge together into one antique haze. Valerie had picked up some yellowware bowls and pitchers. "These used to go for a song, but now that everyone has a country kitchen, or a modern one that has to be accented with a few old pieces, the prices are up. Still these were good buys." Pix did not find her night table. What she did find was an elaborate Victorian wire plant stand perfect for the second-floor landing in her house in Aleford. She might even bow to convention and put a Boston fern in it.

Jill had found several more small items, including an old doll made from a clay pipe that she knew would appeal to someone. Also a cigar box full of old hat pins. Her find for the day was an elaborately carved picture frame, a sailor's valentine. The picture was gone, but the wood was in perfect shape.

"Who do you suppose looked out from here," Valerie mused, "his sweetheart, his mama? We'll never know."

"Maybe his dog," Pix suggested. That would have been her choice. She'd see what price Jill put on the frame. Dusty's face would look perfect surrounded by the intricately carved wood, the same golden honey color as her fur.

They decided to stop for lunch at Country View, a stand on the way back to the island that overlooked a large cow pasture and blueberry fields. The view changed with the seasons, green and yellow now with a few contented Swiss Browns in clover, their tails swinging like pendulums at the flies. Pix had a sudden image of a chirpy cuckoo emerging from a yawning pink mouth on the hour.

Happily munching fish sandwiches—and the fish was so fresh—Pix realized she'd be up to her elbows in haddock and cod for much of the afternoon. She wasn't going to get any gardening done, but at least the chowder was foolproof. No anxiety there. She'd made it dozens of times before.* And it had to be made the day before so the flavors could blend. If she put it off until the morning, it would still taste delicious, but at the first bite Ursula would go into her old "Can you look me straight in the eye and say that?" routine, asking, "When did you make this chowder?" She might even call her Myrtle. It had happened before.

Over their coffee and thick wedges of the pie made at the stand, apple today, Jill brought up the subject of Mitchell Pierce.

"Did you know Mitch, Valerie? It's funny. I hadn't thought about missing him until someone mentioned it at the Sewing Circle yesterday. But he was a part of life here—both his good and bad sides. And, of course, the whole thing is so disturbing." Jill did seem to be extremely disturbed. She was picking

*See recipe page 283.

at the handle of the paper coffee cup, reducing it to shreds. And several of her cuticles were ragged. Pix had never seen her display any nervous gestures. Jill was normally as imperturable as a china doll—and just about as easy to read.

"I've met him," Valerie replied, "but I didn't know him. I saw him at a few shows and bought things from him once or twice. He sold me that sweet little collection of fans I had framed to hang in my bedroom. We'd planned on having him down to the house sometime. Jim says he was quite the storyteller. The two of them were friends, but we've been so busy with the move and the house, there hasn't been much time for anyone."

Pix was tempted to tell them about the cross on the quilts and see whether they had any idea what it could mean. Valerie, especially, might know if this was a common mark on antique quilts. But again, she decided to do as Earl had advised and keep quiet.

"I hate to break up the party. It's been so nice to get away—and with grown-ups, too—but if I don't make the chowder, I really will break up a party. Louise is counting on it."

"I'm taking some of Louella's pies. I don't dare try to cook any of my southern specialities for Louise."

"Well, I'm bringing festive plates and napkins from the store," Jill said. "Louise knows the size of my kitchen—and the extent of my culinary expertise. Dinner guests are lucky to get a hamburger. I need Faith to give me a few lessons."

This was encouragingly domestic, and Pix longed to give Jill a little more of a nudge altarward. "There's a wonderful house for sale on the crossroad. The last owners put in a new kitchen and the back has an orchard that slopes down to one of the long inlets from Little Harbor." She could picture Jill, rosy-cheeked and smiling, hanging up her wash near the old apple trees, a pie keeping warm on the stove for Earl's return. "And Faith likes nothing better than teaching people how to cook. Dismal failure though she's been with me, she keeps trying."

But Jill wasn't biting. "How could I afford a big house like that? Besides, it's so convenient living over the store."

Pix sighed. Maybe another time.

The first thing Pix did when she got home was spread out the quilt in the living room. It had not diminished in effect, yet she found herself with a definite feeling of unease as she stood looking at it. The blue threads—but what else was nagging at her? It was too cheap. Why had the dealer let it go for so little?

She thought about it all the way over to Sonny Prescott's lobster pound. Sonny dealt in all kinds of marine life, besides those succulent crustaceans. Pix had already ordered the cod and haddock for the chowder. The mixture of the two fish, as well as the use of slab bacon instead of salt pork gave the Rowe family chowder a distinctive flavor. They also put in more onions than most recipes called for.

Hearing the car, Sonny stuck his head out the bait shed doorway and yelled, "I'm over here." Pix followed him in. He'd been close to the only other murder investigation on Sanpere in recent memory and Pix wondered what his thoughts might be on Mitchell Pierce's death. Among others, Mitch had boarded at Sonny's one winter, so he knew Mitch better than most.

"I've come for my fish," Pix said. The smell of the bait, decomposed herring, was overwhelming, but it didn't bother her. It was one of those smells you got used to in childhood and never noticed again. She vastly preferred it to all those perfume samples magazines and catalogs were including in their glossy pages with increasing eye-watering and nose-itching frequency.

"Be right there, deah. Got to get this ready for Jeb Sanford." Sonny supplied fishermen with bait, fuel, and whatever else was needed. In turn, they sold their catches exclusively to him.

While she was waiting, Pix left the shed and sat at the end of the pier, dangling her legs over the side. She'd known

Sonny since they were both teenagers and had occasionally "borrowed" a dinghy from the yacht club to row out into Sylvester Cove to watch the sparkling phosphorescence magically drip from the oars, a mirror image of the mass of brilliant stars shining overhead. What else Pix and Sonny might or might not have done in the way of canoodling was between the two of them, but they always had a special smile for each other. Sonny came and sat down next to her, the huge package of fish fresh from the boats tied up and set behind him.

"I cleaned it for you. Save you some time. It's for chowder, right? The Fraziers' clambake?" Sonny probably knew the social plans of every inhabitant on the island for the holiday just from the orders that had been placed.

"Yes, and I'll be peeling potatoes until midnight. I've been dreading cleaning all this fish. You are truly a godsend. What would I ever do without you?"

Sonny grinned. "Let's not find out." They sat for a while looking at the boats moored in the cove. There were some beautiful yachts from farther down the coast. From behind Barred Island in the distance, one of the windjammers sailed into view.

"Is it the *Victory Chimes*?" Pix asked.

Sonny nodded. "Funny to think these were workboats, hauled lumber, whatever else was traded. Now they're hauling rich tourists who want to experience the good old days— cramped sleeping quarters and plenty of hard work to sail the things. Me, I'd like to take one of those cruises Kathie Lee advertises. That would be some good time."

Pix laughed and asked if he'd heard what the weather was going to be for the next couple of days.

"Same as it's been. Good for vacations and good for me; not so good for the crops or fires. Heard they had a big one up to Baxter State Park," Sonny observed.

"My garden is going to shrivel up and die." There was that word. Pix had used it on purpose. "Like Mitchell Pierce."

They looked at each other.

"If you hadn't have gone out there, no one would ever have found him. Seth was fixing to pour this week."

"I know. It's scary. Who do you think wanted Mitch out of the way so badly?"

Sonny had to have a theory. He did about most things and he did about Mitch.

"I figure he must have gotten in over his head somehow with the antiques or maybe the cars. He was a trusting soul for a crook and not a real good judge of character. This time, he put his faith in the wrong man."

"Crook!"

"Come on, Myrtle," Sonny was virtually the only person who used her name in everyday conversation. "The man was running scams up and down the East Coast. Where do you think he got all those fancy cars?"

Mitch had a fondness for vintage sports cars.

"Saved up?"

"Touch one of those fenders and like as not you'd burn your fingers."

This was food for thought: a stolen-car ring.

"Lot of talk about a car wash place in Belfast that really laundered the vehicles. Mitch was a regular."

"And the antiques?"

"Fakes. Don't look so surprised. Just because he could tell a good story and did a nice job for your mother doesn't make him a member of the choir. People are not always all of a piece like you."

Pix wasn't sure whether this was a compliment or not. She suspected something in between. Oh, for a bit more intricacy.

"Not that I'm suggesting you change. I like you just the way you are—especially those long legs of yours." Sonny stood up and eyed them, exposed to full advantage in Pix's denim shorts. For an instant, they were teenagers again, ready to take off for a picnic on Strawberry Island, a little knoll off Prescott's Point. Pix was suddenly acutely aware that Sonny was divorced and her own husband was almost three hundred miles away. She paid for her fish and left with a pleasant sense of having been tempting and tempted. The fact that she was absolutely and totally in love—and loyal—to her husband made it all the more enjoyable.

At home, she began the mammoth task of cutting and chopping, running what Sonny had said about Mitch through her mind as she alternately was drenched in tears from the onions and splattered fat from the sizzling bacon.

Maybe there would be a chance to talk to Earl in private at the clambake tomorrow. Jill said he was coming, although he'd probably be called away just as they were uncovering the lobsters. There were going to be about fifty people of all ages at the party, and Pix found large gatherings often offered more opportunities for intimate conversation than small ones. Two people strolling off to gather driftwood for the bonfire were much less likely to attract anyone's notice than say two people disappearing from a group of eight at a dinner party.

She decided to call Faith and have her give Sam a book that Pix had about identifying quilts, so that he could bring it up. Sam would never find it himself, and Faith wouldn't stop until she did. Pix was absolutely sure it was in the stack of books by her bed, in with the cookbooks in the kitchen, or down in the basement in a carton waiting for more book-shelves. The quilt looked authentic, yet it was possible that it was a fake. Using the book, she could date it. Which would mean what? That she had been swindled? The man hadn't said it was an old quilt. Maybe the quilt on Mitchell Pierce's body wasn't old either, but what would that matter? It did some-how, though. She was sure. She took her cleaver and whacked the head off an enormous cod Sonny had missed when he cleaned the fish. She thought of the mice. She thought of Mitch. The cod stared at her, glassy-eyed. She came to her senses. Chowder, rich, fragrant fish chowder. She tossed the head into a pot for stock and beheaded the other cod she found with aplomb. These were fish, not French aristocrats, and she was definitely not a murderess.

"Anything I can do to help?" Samantha's voice was a welcome alternative to the sound of tumbrels.

"Perfect timing. Could you peel these potatoes?"

"Mother! There are mountains of them," Samantha shrieked.

"Well, just do as many as you can and I'll help when I get the onions done and the rest of the fish cut up."

Samantha had spent the morning at The Pines. She often bicycled over to see her grandmother. They had a very special relationship. Pix wondered what they found to talk about, but they shared a love of the outdoors and it was Ursula who had started Samantha on the first of her many collections—seashells at age three.

"Granny's helping me with the mosses," Sam told her mother.

"I thought you'd given the project up."

"Of course not, after all that work last summer!"

"This wouldn't have anything to do with the fact that Arlene is otherwise occupied, would it?" Pix was curious to know how Samantha was taking Arlene's defection.

"Not really. Besides, she and Fred aren't married. She is allowed to go places without him." Samantha cut the sarcasm in her voice and admitted to her mother, "It's true, I miss her, but with her job, we wouldn't see each other that much, and she does like to spend time with her boyfriend. Otherwise, why bother having one?"

Pix decided to change the subject.

"I bought some beautiful quilts this morning antiquing with Jill and Valerie. One is especially lovely. It's on the couch. Take a break and go look at it."

"You didn't tell me Valerie was going. I thought it was just Jill! What did she buy?"

Correctly surmising Samantha meant Valerie and not Jill, Pix gave an account of the morning.

"She has got such perfect taste. We should hire her to do our house."

"But our house is done."

Samantha raised an eyebrow, clearly indicating that a decorating scheme that had evolved simply because that was where things had happened to land did not represent interior design in her opinion.

"How about my room, then? We could send her pictures. I'm sure she'd have some great ideas."

"Some expensive ideas,"

Pix heard it inside her head before it was said: "Oh, Mother!"

Samantha, happy for an excuse to leave the potatoes, went to look at the quilts.

"The one with the triangles is really beautiful, Mom. We should hang it on a wall here or at home."

"That's what I was thinking." Pix went into the other room and the two of them held the quilt out.

"What's that blue cross on the bottom?" Samantha moved her thumb to indicate the threads.

"I have no idea," Pix replied truthfully, but something in her voice betrayed her.

Samantha looked her straight in the eye—and where she had picked up this trick, Pix didn't like to think. "Come on, Mom. What aren't you telling me? You are such a bad liar."

"And you're a good one?"

"Don't try to change the subject."

Pix realized that the proximity in which they were spending the summer would make keeping secrets difficult. "I don't know what it means. Probably nothing. It's just that there was a cross like this one on the quilt out on the Point, too."

"Nothing! It could be a major clue!" Samantha was excited, yet after they discussed it some more while finishing the chowder preparations, both women were forced to agree that if it was a clue, they were without one.

The chowder was simmering and Samantha had gone off to the dance at the Legion Hall. It was an island institution, a mixture of ages, groups, and most especially music—everything from "Like a Virgin" to the Virginia reel, with a stop at "a one and a two and a three" in between.

She'd called Faith, who had then called back to say she'd located the book and placed it in Sam's car just before he left. That was at six o'clock. He'd arrive, like Samantha, before midnight. Pix told Faith about the discovery of the quilt and the second mark.

"Perhaps both quilts belonged to the same family," Faith suggested.

"Sullivan!" Pix was annoyed she hadn't made the connection before. "The man said the linens had come from Sullivan and that was where Mitch was living before he was killed."

"It does seem like more than a coincidence. What you need to do is figure out if your quilt is authentic and talk to Earl."

Pix was tempted to say she'd already planned this very course of action, but instead she thanked Faith for getting the book and told her she'd be in touch soon.

"I know," her friend said before she hung up.

Pix never minded being in the cottage alone. It was so familiar and felt so safe that she thought of it as a kind of shell. Now she curled up inside, actually in one of the big over-stuffed armchairs in the living room, with a mug of Sleepytime tea and the latest issue of *Quilter's Newsletter Magazine*.

The first car door slam was her husband's. She'd dozed off but awoke instantly at the welcome sound and was at the door. He dropped his suitcase and held her tightly.

"I wish I could have come up right away. It has to have been a hellish time for you both."

After a moment, she leaned away and told him, "It honestly hasn't been too bad. Everyone is more puzzled than alarmed, and it's easier because none of us was really very close to Mitch.''

"He was an interesting son of a gun, though. Remember the night he came and played the mandolin at the Hamiltons and he and Freeman got to trading stories. I don't think I've ever laughed so hard in my life.''

"That was a great night.'' It had been many years ago, before Danny was born. That reminded her. "Did you stop at Chewonki and see Danny?''

"No, I did not.'' Seeing the look on her face, Sam took both his wife's hands. "First off, it was late and I would have interrupted the evening program, thereby embarrassing him for the remainder of his summer, and second, he likes, even loves, his old man, but at home. Chewonki is his turf, a parent-free zone for Danny. Don't worry, sweetheart, he'll be back before you know it and expecting you to do everything for him just as usual.'' It was not entirely a frivolous observation and they'd had this conversation before—many times before, inserting Mark or Samantha for Danny.

"Are you hungry?'' Pix asked, hoping Sam would want only a drink and maybe some crackers and cheese. She had some of the chutney spread still left from Friday's Sewing Circle.

Sam saw the look on her face. He had not stopped to eat, but he couldn't do it to her.

"Not very, how about a drink and maybe a few crackers or whatever you have around.''

Pix beamed. Why wouldn't Jill—or Earl—want to get married?

In bed, Pix found having someone to keep her company while she listened for Samantha to come home did a great deal to diminish the anxiety. Also, they were busy telling each other all the things that had happened in their respective worlds since they'd last been together. Atypically, more had been going on in Pix's than Sam's.

He did not seem to think the quilt marks meant much. "It was probably a common way to mark where something else was going to go—the name and date, as you suggested. Or maybe it was part of the basting that didn't get removed." Sam had watched his wife complete several quilts and was quite knowledgeable about how they went together. Sam was the type of man who liked to know the way things worked. This had led him to medical school, but the discovery that he fainted with great regularity at the sight of an abundance of blood curtailed his career, although not his interest. He still read *The New England Journal of Medicine* and the *Harvard Health Newsletter* in between briefs.

Slam—music to the ears of parents of teenagers, just as the cessation of noise was for the parents of toddlers. Samantha was home safe and sound.

Pix reached up to turn out the light.

"No, I want to say hello. I'll be right back." Sam threw on his robe, a well-worn Black Watch plaid flannel one he kept hanging on the back of the door, and went downstairs. He had missed his daughter and wanted to tell her so. He also wanted to tell her that a quarter after midnight was the thin end of the wedge on a twelve o'clock curfew. Pix had enough to cope with this summer without Samantha's coming in just a little bit later every Saturday night.

The weather continued unbroken and the Millers awoke to gorgeous blue skies and almost balmy weather. Too balmy, Pix thought as she got dressed. It wasn't supposed to be this hot on the coast of Maine.

Sam was already gone, having offered as usual to help Elliot get the clambake ready, no small task and one Pix suspected the men relished for its complexity and the opportunity to dig in the sand. After constructing a pit unpleasantly reminiscent of what she and Samantha had stumbled across the previous week, they would line it with rocks and pile driftwood, plus anything else that would burn—charcoal if there wasn't enough wood—on top. The fire had to heat the rocks for at least five hours. Otherwise, when they threw the wet seaweed on, there wouldn't be enough steam to cook the lobsters, clams, corn, chicken, and sausage that would be layered on top. The Fraziers' clambake was famous for its authenticity and had become a Fourth of July tradition. They always seemed to be able to find room for more guests and it had grown each year from humble beginnings to the kind of quintessential red-white-and-blue photo opportunity that politicians running for office dream about.

Pix and Samantha were going to church. After last Sunday, Pix was not about to skip it, even though she relished the clambake preparations as much as her husband did. She was not a superstitious person, yet something told her she'd enjoy the day a whole lot more if she'd bent a knee in a pew rather than hauling rocks.

Sam returned before they left. He wanted to get more wood from their cove.

"We'll be back at noon to change," Pix told him, "and then I promised Louise I'd help her bring things to the beach, so I'll see you there." She kissed her husband good-bye. He returned it somewhat absentmindedly and she knew his thoughts were on hot rocks and rockweed, the "snap, crackle, and pop" seaweed, the kids called it, because of the sound it made beneath your toes and when squeezed between your fingers.

"I'll get rid of this load of wood, then change cars with you, so take both sets of keys." It wasn't that he didn't like her driving his Porsche—he allowed it because he knew he should. It was that he didn't want coleslaw, chowder, and whatever else was going to the clambake to be stowed on his particular leather-covered backseats.

"Don't worry, Daddy, we'll take good care of your baby," Samantha teased him. "Can I drive?"

"Don't even joke," her father replied.

Pix enjoyed the short trip across the island to the small

white clapboard church where they worshiped. It was nice to drive a sleek, jazzy machine that sped forward instantly at the slightest pressure on the gas. Maybe she should trade her Land Rover in. It was such a symbol—Pix, the trucker, the transporter of men, women, children, animals, and all their worldly possessions. It would certainly be nice to have an excuse: "Sorry, I can't pick up twenty watermelons for the school picnic. They won't fit in the car," and so on.

"Mom, what are you thinking about? You have the funniest expression on your face."

"Do I? I was thinking maybe I ought to get a new car, something smaller."

Samantha shook her head. "Your car is always loaded now. If it was any smaller, you'd have to get a trailer. Make Daddy let you drive his more. I wish *I* could. It must be a blast," she added longingly.

They stopped outside the church and hurried in, sliding next to Ursula just as the bell in the steeple began to toll.

"Such a perfect day for the clambake," Ursula whispered. "I figured Sam would be with Elliot, but I was beginning to wonder where you two were."

At one o'clock, Pix was helping Louise set up. Sam had started a smaller fire, let it burn down, and placed a grill on top for the huge pot of chowder Pix had made. They lugged it over and gingerly set it in place. Sam took off the cover and inhaled. "Sweeter than all the perfumes of Araby. I believe this is going to be the best ever. Why don't I get a cup and give it a try?"

"You say the same thing every year!"

"That's not true. I don't remember ever comparing your chowder to perfume before."

"Possibly, but the rest. Anyway, by all means get a cup. You know me—a bottomless sink for reassurance when it comes to cooking."

Sam got a cup and ladled some out. He took a heaping spoonful. "It's . . . well, how can I describe it?"

"Good or bad?"

"Superlative."

Pix heaved a sigh of relief. He always said *superlative*, too, but it was comforting to hear. The perfume simile was new, though: "All the perfumes of Araby." Wasn't it "Arabia"? *Macbeth*. Lady Macbeth scrubbing at her hands. She wished he'd picked something else.

It was impossible to forget that only a week ago on such a day as this, a corpse had turned up. As people began to arrive, struggling with food, sports equipment, and small children, she wondered whether the guilty one walked among them. She had to put it out of her head. Sonny Prescott had provided the most logical answer. Mitch had gotten in with the wrong business partners.

"Pix, Pix, could you help set these out?" Louise always became mildly flustered at the start of the clambake. She was nervous that the food wouldn't cook until it was too dark to eat, although the rare years when Elliot had miscalculated and they did eat late, nobody had minded a bit. Eyeing what Louise had provided and others were bringing, Pix thought the problem would be finding room to eat anything else when the tarp was taken off and the fragrant layers of food exposed.

"There's enough to feed an army here!" she said, gesturing to the tables they'd constructed from planks and sawhorses, then covered with red-checked oilcloth.

"Good," a voice behind her commented, reaching for a deviled egg—Louise's great-aunt Lily Sue's prized recipe.

It was Earl, and Jill was by his side, Pix noted happily. They were carrying paper plates, napkins, and other necessary objects. For the next hour, Pix was busy ladling out her chowder, which was disappearing fast. The party was in full swing. The volleyball net had been set up and there was a ferocious game of over forties versus unders going on. The younger children were exploring the shore, climbing over the rocks, oblivious of the sharp barnacles and other hazards that threatened their bare feet. Samantha and some of her friends were with them. Arlene and her boyfriend had put in an appearance, politely tasted the chowder, then left for the Prescott clambake. There were time-honored functions occurring all over the island and the problem was not having enough time, or room in one's stomach, to visit them all.

The actual day of the Fourth was so crammed full of activities that years ago, islanders had started celebrating early with their family picnics, usually clambakes.

Seth Marshall had also dropped by with his parents. He didn't partake of any of Pix's chowder. Maybe he was saving room for the next clambake. And maybe he was avoiding her. The crime site was still sealed off by the police, so this was unlikely. But when she waved him over to ask him how quickly he could start once the police gave the word, he was so engrossed in conversation with Jill that he appeared not to see Pix's gestures. Overseeing the Fairchilds' cottage could be more work than she had envisioned. The first, almost overwhelming task was proving to be getting it started.

Pix reached up to mop her brow. Her T-shirt was beginning to stick to her back. It was getting unpleasantly hot, especially standing over the chowder. She was glad she'd worn her bathing suit under her clothes. The cove was on deep water, which explained why the yacht club had selected the spot roughly eighty years ago—a yacht club that consisted of a venerable equipment shack, some moorings, and a few life buoys with SANPERE YACHT CLUB stenciled on them. Some people were already in the water, and Pix was amused to see friends who expressed amazement at the Millers' tolerance, even enjoyment, of the cold temperature, bobbing about and calling others to join them.

The Athertons had arrived laden with pies and Valerie and Jim promptly joined the volleyball game—on opposite sides of the net, Pix noted. She glanced around. Duncan, who she recognized from Samantha's description, was at the other end of the beach. It was hard to see him. He was sitting high up on a granite ledge at the point where it met the woods. His somber attire blended into the shadows of the trees. A figure of melancholy, a figure of gloom. Of doom? A mouse killer. Pix firmly shoved back all the morbid thoughts that persisted in crowding into her conscious mind and joined the volleyball game—on the over-forty side. Away from the chowder fire, she felt ten degrees cooler, and giving a good hard thwack to the volleyball felt terrific.

During a break, Sam brought her a cold beer. "Who's that guy with the Bainbridges?"

Pix turned to look. Adelaide was settled into a monstrous lawn chair with all sorts of cushions, rugs, and satchels strewn about her. Rebecca was pressing sunblock on her. "You know how you burn, Addie."

"Oh, can't you let a body be? I'm fine. You'd think I was a two-year-old." This last comment was made to the man Sam had wondered about.

"I think he's staying at their bed-and-breakfast. I've seen him in the post office. But it would be odd for them to bring one of their guests to the Fraziers' clambake. I'll ask Louise."

Pix walked over to her hostess, keeping the unknown visitor in view. He was very slim, attractive, with dark closely cropped curls and a small neatly trimmed beard but no mustache. His clothes were appropriate and looked expensive. His jeans were pressed. Faith would be able to tell the brands and how much he'd paid instantly, but all Pix could determine was that his shirt might be silk. He'd knotted a raspberry-colored cotton sweater about his neck and there wasn't a drop of perspiration evident anywhere on his body. Pix's own damp hair told her what she looked like. After her swim, she'd get the fresh shirt she'd left in the car and put it on. Looking at this guy was having this kind of effect on her. He was tan and the only jewelry he wore was a watch. Maybe if she got closer, she could see what kind. Faith always said that you could tell almost everything about a person by his or her watch and shoes. Pix looked down. He was barefoot. Her own feet were clad in serviceable white Keds.

Louise was drinking a glass of white wine, not a good sign. "I don't know when we'll be ready to eat," she announced. "I've decided not to let it bother me, though." Her tone belied her words.

"Good, you shouldn't worry about a thing," Pix reassured her emphatically. "Everyone is having a marvelous time. And besides, what have we been doing since we got here? No one would leave hungry, even without the lobsters and clams. But they'll be ready soon, so we won't have to find out."

"You're right. Some years it just takes longer than others." She put down her glass and picked up one of Aunt Lily Sue's eggs from a carefully shaded area on the table. "Don't you just love the Fourth of July celebrations? It's my favorite holiday. When I was a little girl, we'd have big picnics like this. Of course we didn't bury our food in the sand."

It must have been something more than mystifying when Louise met Elliot and first heard about a Down East clambake.

"By the way, do you know that man who came with Addie and Rebecca?" Pix asked.

"Haven't you met Norman? He's been here for two weeks now. That's Addie's beau." Louise smiled.

"Beau!"

"Well, perhaps not strictly speaking, but he does dance attendance on her—and on Rebecca, too. He's an antiques dealer from New York City and he's taking a working vacation, he told them. They're to keep his room available for a month and he comes and goes."

New York City—that explained the clothes and the good haircut. Pix was trying very hard in what she hoped was the second half of her life—and look at Mother, so it was not impossible—to cultivate a more open mind about certain things, one of them being New York City. She now had a dear friend in Faith, who had actually been born and raised there. In fact, truth be told, she might even prefer it to Aleford and Boston, although Pix was always careful never to ask outright. She didn't want to know for sure. Try as she might, the name New York City did not suggest the Statue of Liberty or the Empire State Building, but fast living and danger. Whenever she was there—and they dutifully took the children, as well as making one or two adult forays—she felt like a rube who would leap at the chance to buy the Brooklyn Bridge before she knew what she was doing.

She looked over at the Bainbridge group, appraising Norman in light of this new information.

He certainly seemed to be enjoying himself. Whatever Addie had just said had sent him into peals of laughter. He'd been sitting on a blanket literally at her feet and got up now, walking toward the table with the drinks.

"Addie says he told her she's the most interesting woman he's met in years. Every time he goes off-island, he brings something back for them."

"I'll bet he just wants to get her quilts cheap," Pix said skeptically.

"No, he doesn't sell anything made after 1900. He told her he liked her work, but they're not his 'thing.'"

"Then, what do you suppose he sees in her?"

"We all take Addie for granted because we know her, but she *is* a great storyteller. Elliot thinks Norman is writing a book. Most people are. And Addie is a great source."

The afternoon wore on. Pix took a swim, which felt heavenly while she was in the water, but without a shower to wash off the salt, increasingly itchy later, even under her clean dry shirt. She sat down with her back against a log cast up on the shore by one of the winter storms and glanced around to check on her family, a reflex. Ursula was in deep conversation with John Eggleston, whose bright red beard and hair blended well with the shade his face had taken on during the day. What on earth could they be discussing? Was Mother going to take up wood sculpture? Pix would not be surprised. Sam was poking at the mound with Elliot. They might have been considering a Viking tomb, given the intensity of their expressions. And Samantha was . . . walking toward her.

Samantha sat next to her mother, leaned back, and stretched her long legs, almost as long as Pix's, out, wriggling her toes in the sand. The two considered the view for a moment before speaking. This one from Sylvester Cove was every bit as good as the one from The Pines, or the Millers' cottage, or just about anywhere else on the island Pix could name. Today there were dozens of sailboats, crisp white triangles against the dense green outer islands and the deep blue sea.

"I love the Fraziers' clambakes," Samantha said, "but not when the weather is like this. We might as well be home, it's so hot."

Pix nodded. She considered another beer, then decided to wait. Others had not waited and the laughter and talk was noticeably louder than it had been earlier. Some of the children were getting whiny. It was definitely time to eat. A sudden onslaught of sand fleas sent Pix and Samantha flying from their seats.

"At least it's not blackfly season," Pix said. Nothing came close to that. They'd all worn beekeeper's hats when they'd tended the graves on Memorial Day. It had been a strange sight.

A possible discussion of "annoying insects I have known" was sharply curtailed by the noise of a loud disturbance farther down the beach. It was moving toward them.

"It's that jerk Duncan!" Samantha said as she moved closer. Pix followed, out of curiosity and to get away from the fleas.

"I'm speaking to you, young man! Don't you walk away from me!" It was Valerie. Her face was red, and as she'd been wearing a fetching sun hat since she arrived, it wasn't from a burn. She was absolutely furious.

"Fuck you!" Duncan answered, and kept walking.

"I saw that beer can in your hand! Don't you lie to me!"

Duncan stopped and turned to face his mother. "So what? Only grown-ups can get wasted?" He said this last in the jeering singsong tones of a small child. Pix marveled at Valerie's self-control. Sure, she was yelling, but had Duncan been Pix's son, she would have had him by the arm by now and marched him straight to the car.

Jim appeared. He'd been swimming and was dripping wet. It magnified his rage—a bull from the sea.

He stood next to his wife.

"Don't you *ever* talk that way to your mother again! Where do you get off using words like that? Now, I've had just about all I'm going to take from you. Get in the car. You're going home."

"Home?" Duncan screamed. "You call that 'home'? Your home maybe, not mine!"

Valerie stepped forward and put her hand on his arm. "Now Duncan, let's calm down. . . ."

He pushed her away rudely and she went sprawling in the sand. Everyone on the beach froze for an instant, including Duncan. He stared at his mother and seemed about to reach for her before noticing Jim virtually foaming at the mouth.

Duncan took off, the tiny red lights of his sneakers blinking frantically in the late-afternoon light.

"Let him go," Valerie said to her husband. "He needs to be alone." She brushed the sand from her white pants, adjusted her hat, and said to everyone with a big smile, "I apologize for my son. In his case, adolescence really is a disease. I only wish there were shots for it."

People laughed and Jim let out what seemed like the breath he'd been holding since confronting his stepson. He hugged Valerie and echoed her sentiments. "My parents always said someday I'd get mine the way they got theirs from me, and boy, were they right!"

"I don't believe it." Samantha said. She and Pix were on the fringes of the group.

"About Jim, you mean?"

"Yeah, I don't believe he was ever the way Duncan is. And he's definitely not the type who got in trouble when he was a kid. More the kind other parents wanted their kids to be like."

Pix was not unduly surprised at her daughter's analysis. Samantha was a good judge of character.

"I agree. Plus, I happen to know for a fact Jim was an Eagle Scout. But I think you're being a little hard on Duncan. He may feel like the odd person out in that big house. And he must miss his father terribly. Then, the move couldn't have been easy."

"I guess it's because I like the Athertons so much. I wasn't thinking of it from his point of view. It's hard to be sympathetic, but you're right. What if Daddy died and you got married again and made me move from Aleford, although coming to Sanpere wouldn't be so bad." Samantha was working out a whole scenario. "Except no matter who you picked, it wouldn't be Daddy."

"Who wouldn't be Daddy?" Sam appeared at his daughter's side.

"Mom's next husband—that is, if something happened to you and she remarried," Samantha added hastily, seeing her father's startled look.

"I thought you were going to be faithful to my memory," Sam said to his wife. "Now I find out you're getting hitched when I'm barely cold in the ground."

Whether it was the heat, the sand fleas, the scene with the Athertons, or something altogether different, Pix suddenly felt a sense of deep despair. She didn't want to joke about Sam's demise. She didn't want to talk about death at all.

"Samantha, why don't you and your friends see if you can find Duncan. He may want someone to talk to." Pix had not liked the look of fear and anxiety on the boys's face as he'd run off. "He's probably up in the ledges at the other end of the beach. I saw him sitting there before."

"You're right, Mom, but I think he'd be more apt to talk to one person than a bunch of us. I'll go."

She ran off. Sam looked at Pix. "What's going on?"

"I don't know. I wish I did. It's probably just me. I got tired all of a sudden."

At that moment, Elliot began to bang on the lid of Pix's now-empty chowder pot with the ladle.

"Hear ye, hear ye! Gather round!"

Elliot, normally a reticent and mild-mannered man in his late sixties, assumed an entirely different persona at the clambake. He wore an apron that proclaimed him "The Clam King," a gift from a partygoer some years ago and now indispensable garb, as was his broad-brimmed straw hat decorated with small plastic clams, lobsters, and various seashells bearing absolutely no resemblance to reality.

People crowded near to the pit, knowing that before they would get their hands on a lobster or an ear of corn, they'd have to listen to Elliot's traditional clambake speech.

"Some of you have heard this all before," he started.

"Many times before," a friend called out, and everyone groaned.

Elliot continued undaunted.

"When my friend Sam and I dug the pit and lined it with rocks this morning, getting everything ready for you sleepyheads who were still snoring away, we were continuing a tradition that goes back to the first summer people to come to Sanpere—the Abenaki Indians. Along with all the other useful things Indians taught the early colonists, they showed them how to cook in the sand this way. I always like to remember them—we could be eating at the site of one of their clambakes—and say thank you before we tuck in."

"Thanks, Abenakis," a little girl shouted, and everyone laughed. She buried her head in her mother's skirt in embarrassment.

"Now, I'm not quite done yet. At the risk of being accused of being sentimental—"

"Risk it, Elliot." This, much to Pix's surprise, came from her own mother.

"Thank you, Ursula, I will. I'd like to make a toast to all of you good people, who mean so much to Louise and me, and also, as always, to absent friends. Finally, in the words of Sean O'Casey, 'May the very best of the past—be the worst of the future!'" He took a swig of beer, handed the bottle to his wife, took the first stone anchoring down the tarp covering the steaming pit, removed it, and flung it into the sea. It resounded appropriately with a loud splash. Everyone cheered and rushed to help uncover the steaming food, packed in cheesecloth parcels.

Pix stayed close to Sam. "I love Elliot's toasts." Things were beginning to be all right again.

"And I love you," he said, kissing the tip of her nose. "Now let's eat." Definitely all right.

Perhaps because they had been waiting so long for the food or because the various potables that had been imbibed created an atmosphere of heightened enjoyment, one and all declared the food the best ever. Pix knew she was a mess. She'd dripped melted butter down her chin as she'd consumed her lobster and clams. Her fingers were sticky from the chicken—Louise always charcoal-broiled it a bit first—and corn. Above all, she was full—and there was still dessert. She and Sam were sitting on the blanket she'd brought when Earl and Jill strolled past laden with lobster carcasses and clam shells.

"Come and join us," Pix called.

"Just as soon as we dump this stuff," Earl answered.

She'd have to go see Earl down in Granville at the combined post office, town hall, and office of the law to get him alone and talk about the blue quilt marks. Although her appearance at the tiny hole-in-the-wall that served the needs of justice on the island would immediately cause talk. She'd better call him. Now she might just try to steer the conversation to antiques, quilts in particular, perhaps, and fakes. She was feeling comfortably sated and the demons disturbing her earlier were gone. She didn't want to waste the opportunity. Earl was right here and she hadn't made much progress in her investigation so far. Faith would no doubt have had the whole thing sewn up by now—but maybe not. Pix sat in the growing darkness waiting for Jill and Earl's return. Elliot had lighted his huge bonfire and a few people were playing guitars. It was a lovely scene. She was content to wait.

Samantha had not been able to find Duncan at first. He wasn't in plain sight and she walked deeper and deeper into the woods before she found him, curled up in a fetal position on a bed of pine needles.

"Duncan, it's me, Samantha Miller. I'm a friend of Arlene Prescott."

He didn't move for a second, then slowly sat up and eyed her warily.

"You work at the camp. I've seen you. Did they send you to get me?" He spat the words out.

Assuming he meant Valerie and Jim, Samantha answered, "No, I just thought maybe you'd like to talk to somebody. You seemed pretty upset." He was so antagonistic that she'd begun to wish she hadn't been the good little Samaritan her mother expected and had stayed down on the beach.

"I'm not going back."

"It's a long walk." She almost said *home*, then quickly changed it to *the house*.

"So what." He leaned against a tree and put his arms behind his head. He was pathetically skinny and short for his age. Samantha hoped for his sake that he would grow a few inches this summer and maybe start to work out. It would certainly make life easier if he looked a little more attractive.

She decided to give it a try. "I know a kid whose mother

died last year—cancer. It was really terrible. Anyway, I wanted to say I'm sorry about your dad. I know how my friend feels, and she didn't have to move."

Duncan looked as if he was going to cry. His face got all screwed up, then he opened his eyes wide and shook his head. The ring in his ear wobbled. Samantha noticed that the hole was red and angry, obviously infected. Now completely grossed out, she decided she'd done her duty and turned around to return to the party.

"Hey, are you leaving?"

"My parents might be wondering where I am," she lied, "and besides, the food is almost ready and I love lobster cooked this way. You ought to try it."

"I don't eat fish—or meat," he added.

Definitely not getting enough protein, Samantha thought. She sat down beside him. He was so pathetic. "There's lots of corn. It's steamed in the husk. My dad brought it up from Boston, since there's no corn here yet. Come back and you can eat with us." It was worth a try.

"Why are you being so nice to me?"

She didn't have an answer ready.

"I don't know. I guess I feel sorry for you."

He nodded. She assumed he felt sorry for himself, too.

"Life sucks. Especially in this rinky-dink place."

"It must seem small after living in Richmond. That was where you were, right?"

"Yeah. Richmond was okay. The best place was where we lived before my real father died. Outside the city."

"There are a lot of good kids here, though. I've been coming every summer since I was born and I know everybody. You could come to the movies with us next week if you want." Samantha had no idea why she proposed this. Arlene would kill her.

"I don't need your friends. I've got plenty of my own." She should have saved her breath.

"Well, that's great. Now I'm going to go get something to eat before I starve." Enough was enough.

"Plenty of friends. We even have our own club."

"Club? That sounds like fun," Samantha commented perfunctorily. She was picturing a steaming red-hot lobster.

"Maybe you'd like to join." Duncan's tone was mocking.

Samantha resented the implication—that she was too good for his little club, or whatever.

"Maybe I would—and maybe I wouldn't," she said in as even a voice as she could manage. He really was irritating. She stood up to go. Duncan got up, too. He seemed to have sprouted during the conversation and stood only a few inches from her face. He had a sour smell and the skin on his face was oily. She took a step backward. He followed.

"Naaah, I don't think you could get in."

Suddenly, she had to know.

"So what do you have to do to be a member of your club?" she said slowly, moving away from him.

"You have to kill something."

Chapter 5

Jill and Earl had joined the Millers, bringing cups of fresh-brewed coffee for everyone. As soon as the sun had gone down, the air had assumed some of its more characteristic Maine snap and the sight of the steaming cups was a welcome one.

"You take yours with milk and Sam doesn't take anything, right?" Jill had an amazing memory. Pix could barely recall the preferences of her immediate family, let alone friends. This was why she made lists. But then, Jill might get lost on the intricate carpool routes Pix routinely negotiated without a second thought.

"Thanks," Sam said, "When I find the energy—which could be sometime next week—I'll make a pie run."

They talked about the summer. Jill bemoaned the economy; Earl bemoaned the increase in the island population—it doubled during these months—and Sam bemoaned the fact that he wouldn't be back again until August. It took a while for Pix to steer the conversation around to antiques.

"We had a good time with Valerie the other day exploring the antique stores in Searsport. She has a wonderful eye. Plus, having an expert along was insurance against getting duped by fakes. Have you heard much about antique fraud along the coast?" She addressed Earl directly, evidently striking a nerve.

"Have we! It's big business. I went to some seminars last winter in Augusta on this very subject. The Sheriff's Department has a special unit that does nothing else but deal with these scams."

"What kinds of things are being faked?" Pix asked in as idle a way as she could muster, aware that her mother had joined them, slipping quietly next to Sam.

"You name it. Toys are big." Earl started to warm to his subject. He must have been a star pupil. "One way is to make them from scratch, putting celluloid or bisque into molds from originals to imitate things that are popular collectibles, like Mickey Mouse figures. The modern ones are easy to spot once you know how—different colors, obvious brushstrokes, but even dealers get fooled. Especially if they're made by joining a new toy with an old one, it's called 'marrying.' "

"What do you mean?" Pix was glad to hear the word introduced, yet this sort seemed more likely to be headed for divorce.

"Well, you might have a part missing from an original and you substitute a fake, but often these two never left the factory together. Like Mickey in a car becomes Minnie at the controls. That sort of thing. Then they even forge Steiff buttons and insert them in the ears of new stuffed bears or other animals that have been made to look worn. Another thing we learned is that both fake and genuine toys are put into 'original' boxes printed by color laser to increase the values. The boxes are the easiest to detect. You just need a good magnifying glass, my dear Watsons. You should see dots, not the parallel lines the laser produces."

Pix remembered that Valerie had a whole battery of devices tucked into her jaunty Pierre Deux bag when they had gone off yesterday: a fancy kind of flashlight, a Swiss army knife with more than an extra blade and toothpick, plus a magnifying glass.

"This is amazing," Ursula commented. "I had no idea things were so sophisticated. Tell us more."

Pix looked at her mother. Ursula's face showed nothing other than sincere interest, but it was almost as if she was in on the plot. Whatever the motive, Pix silently thanked her for keeping the conversation going.

"Oh, I could talk all night about this," Earl said jovially, "There's nothing I hate more than a fraud, and these crooks are accomplished ones."

Jill, oddly enough, since antiques were a current and growing interest, did not seem as fascinated. "I'm sure we all do, but I think Louise is cutting the pies."

"Oh, she's barely started, and I can't eat anything yet, anyway," Pix said quickly. "Do tell us some more, Earl."

"Part of the problem is that some people pay such fool prices for things that even legitimate dealers get itchy. Take a painting, for instance. You might think it's old, but you get tempted to sweeten the pot a little by rubbing some dirt and grime on it, tucking it under the cobwebs you don't sweep away in the back of your shop for some tourist to 'discover.' A real con man—or woman—takes what he or she knows is a new painting, maybe even painted it him or herself, and does the same thing. Just now, the unit is getting a lot of calls about paintings—and photographs, fake tintypes and ambrotypes."

"What's an ambrotype?" Sam asked. "Is that anything like a daguerreotype?"

"Yup, daguerreotypes are older and they were more expensive. Ambrotypes used a glass plate to capture an image. And tintypes were obviously on metal. They were the most common, relatively cheap compared with the other two. The thing is that now all three methods can be duplicated using the old cameras or even doctoring a modern image with the right emulsions. So you get a friend to dress up as an Indian chief or a Civil War soldier—this is what people want—and lo and behold, in a few months you've made enough for that condo in Florida."

"I had no idea you were learning so much at those seminars," Jill remarked a bit tartly. "Do you think it has much relevance for law and order on the island?"

Earl frowned. Her tone was decidedly un-Jill-like.

"Maybe not, although what with everyone and his uncle putting some thundermugs in the shed and calling it an antiques store, it will probably pay off one of these days."

"Are you by chance referring to my decision to carry antiques?"

Pix was not happy with the turn the conversation was taking. Not only were they veering from the topic but it seemed that Jill and Earl were heading for a quarrel and about to topple off the top of the cake.

"Of course he isn't!" she said in what she hoped was a lighthearted tone. "We're just gossiping. It's fun to hear about how other people get fooled, so long as you're not one of them."

"Exactly." Ursula came to the rescue again. "Like the Pilgrim chair hoax."

"What was that?" Earl asked eagerly, slipping his arm around Jill in an attempt to make up—for what, he knew not. She sat stiffly but didn't shrug him off.

"This all happened about twenty years ago and it was big news. Our forefathers and mothers didn't have dining sets,— they were lucky to have a crude trestle table and a few stools, however there were exceptions. These few people, men, of course, had imposing thronelike chairs with elaborately turned spindles at the back and below the rush seat. You can see the one said to have belonged to Elder William Brewster at the Pilgrim Hall down in Plymouth. Sometimes the chairs are called 'Brewster chairs,' and nobody had to remind you to sit up straight in one. It must have been pure torture for them, and perhaps why they always have such sour expressions in the paintings. Now, where was I? Oh yes, in the 1970s, a Rhode Island furniture restorer concocted one of these chairs and aged it by, among other things, putting it in a steel drum with a smoky fire to get the right patina, if that's the right word, on the wood. He then allowed the chair to surface on a porch here in Maine."

"I *do* remember this story," Earl exclaimed, "Some museum bought it for a bundle, right? And now they have it on display as a fake next to one of the real ones."

"Yes." Ursula nodded. "The hoax worked and the restorer always claimed it was not his intent to make money, merely to point out how easy it was to fool even the experts, and you can believe him or not." Ursula's stern expression made her own prejudice clear. "It's in the Ford Museum in Michigan. I don't know if it's next to a real one, but they do have it on display with a note telling the real story—that it was still a tree in 1969."

Earl was off and running again. "Furniture can become an antique over night—a little ink spilled in a drawer or table and chair legs rubbed with a brick on the bottoms to simulate wear. Old furniture isn't that difficult to duplicate for a master furniture builder. You can age wood by just throwing it into the woods for a winter, and period nails are available—people collect those, too! But legitimate reproductions are marked as such, and they command a lot of money!"

"Yet not as much as originals," Sam said.

"There are still bargains to be had," Jill asserted emphatically.

"I know"—Sam laughed—"just look at what my wife carts home!"

Before they got back on the question of pie again—Pix had noticed Sam's eye turning in that direction—she squeezed in her last question. "Who's doing the faking mostly, and what kind of crime is it?"

"To answer your first question, we'd like to find out. Some of the rings have been broken up and they've included dealers, but it's also people who know nothing about antiques, except for the ones they're duplicating. It's a business to them, just not a legal one. Which answers the next part: Selling fakes is larceny. Transporting them across state lines is not a federal offense, however a phone call to set up the transport is—fraud by wire—and we got some guys that way. I guess I get pretty worked up about the whole business, because people come to Maine trusting that they'll find some nice old things here and instead they get burned by a few selfish, crooked individuals. And we haven't even talked about all the traffic in stolen antiques!"

"But we have talked enough about this business for one night. I for one want dessert." Jill jumped up and headed for the table with a seeming determination for pie that brooked no opposition.

"Sure, honey, I want pie, too." Earl joined her and Pix could hear him asking, "Now what's going on? What did I . . ." The rest of his remarks were inaudible, as was Jill's reply, but what all could see was that this time she did shake his arm away.

Pix and her mother looked at each other. Ursula raised one eyebrow. Even Sam, normally oblivious to the ins and outs of the relationships about him—his own was enough to keep track of—noticed and said, "I thought those two were an item. They don't seem very chummy tonight."

"A lovers' quarrel—or more like a spat," Ursula said. "I expect they'll iron things out. You and Pix do."

"Oh, come on, Mother, Sam and I never fight."

"Then you probably should."

It was hard to get around Mother.

With one accord, they all started walking toward the dessert table, discreetly waiting for Jill and Earl to get theirs and disappear in the darkness. At least, Pix thought Jill got a piece of pie. In the dim light, it was hard to see.

"Did I hear you talking about antiques as I passed a while ago?" asked a voice at Pix's elbow. It was the Bainbridge's guest, Norman, and he was returning for seconds, or maybe thirds, judging from the crumbs that lingered on what Pix assumed was his normally impeccable mouth.

"I'm Norman Osgood, by the way. I came with Adelaide and Rebecca Bainbridge."

The Millers introduced themselves in turn and while doing so, Pix reflected that it was never Rebecca and Adelaide, always the other way around. Was it Pix and Sam Miller? Or Sam and Pix? She thought they were getting roughly equal time.

"We were talking about antiques, or rather, fake antiques."

"Fakes. So unpleasant when one has been burned. I'm in the antique business myself and have been totally tricked on several occasions—once by a nice Russian lady from New Jersey who one would have sworn was directly related to the Romanovs, but in fact, all her trinkets might as well have been prizes from a penny arcade. Has one of you come across such artifice lately?"

Pix wondered whether it was her imagination at work again, but his query seemed to be couched in a rather probing tone. Why was he so interested? Merely because it was his business?

"No—at least not to our knowledge," she added. "But all of us are interested in antiques and we like to know what to guard against."

"Stick to reputable dealers and beware of bargains, that's my advice," Norman said.

Pix thought of her quilt with a twinge. It was too gorgeous. It *had* to be real. The pile had been in a dusty corner with more than a few cobwebs, but the whole barn had been like that.

"Of course, one does sometimes come across a steal. But that's pretty rare these days."

"What kind of antiques do you sell?" Pix asked.

"Early American furniture, some European; paintings before 1900; and clocks. I adore clocks."

"My mother was just telling us about the Pilgrim chair hoax. You must have heard about it."

"Oh, indeed. Such a scandal. Now I must rejoin my lovely hostesses. I believe Adelaide is getting tired. It's been quite a day."

Pix watched his elegant back retreat into the darkness. Up close, she could see some extremely attractive muscles of the rippling variety under his thin silk shirt. The man kept himself in good shape. It was hard to say whether he knew the story of the hoax or not. A real dealer would, no doubt. And he was a real dealer, wasn't he?

"It has been quite a day," Sam said contentedly, tucking into an enormous slab of strawberry-rhubarb pie. "I wouldn't miss this clambake for the world. Thank goodness we had a sensible jury."

"Obviously, since they found in favor of your client."

"That's what sensible means—and they did it quickly."

Pix looked at her own pie. She really wasn't hungry, but she began to eat it in a mechanical fashion that became less so as her taste buds awoke. It *had* been quite a day, and night. There had been that scene with the Athertons, then the talk with Earl and his tiff with Jill. She looked about the beach at the shadowy figures. Then there were all the things that might have gone on at the party that she didn't even know about.

"Let's get Samantha and start packing up ourselves. I want to check on the dogs." Dusty, Artie, and Henry tended to run amok at gatherings like this and so had regretfully been left at home. "I don't know why having this much fun should be so tiring, but it is," she added.

Sam nodded. "Something about the combination of sand, sun, and beer, I think. Where is Samantha, by the way?"

"I saw her with a group of kids by the bonfire a while ago. She was eating her lobster. I think I can still make her out. They're all singing old Everly Brothers songs with John Eggleston. That man has talents we've never suspected."

"I'll make them sing 'A Real Nice Clambake.' Louise always likes that. I think that *Carousel* was the sum total of her knowledge about Maine before she arrived here. It must have been a shock to find out that bait smelled and people didn't dance on the wharf."

Sam went off down the beach in the direction of the fire and Pix started to assemble the stuff they'd brought. She knew the Fraziers hired some of the local kids to help clean up each year, so she didn't feel she had to stay any longer. Ursula called out to her as she was making the first trip to the car.

"Pix, are you leaving? May I beg a ride? Then I won't have to trouble the Moores."

"Of course you can have a ride. I was planning to look for you. Sam is getting Samantha and they'll start back in his car." As she spoke, husband and daughter came up the path with the rest of the Millers' belongings. Sam's song suggestion had been successful and he was singing along from afar: "The vittles we et were good, you bet! The company was the same." His energetic performance contrasted with his daughter's lagging footsteps. She wasn't joining in, not even at her favorite part: "Fitten fer an angel's choir!" Pix was immediately concerned.

"Samantha, are you all right? You look a little wan. I hope you haven't picked up something from one of the campers, all those small children just loaded with germs."

Samantha was quick to squelch any notions her mother might have of bed rest and herb tea.

"Mother! I'm fine. There's absolutely nothing wrong. No bugs, no microbes of any sort whatsoever."

But she wasn't fine. Duncan's words continued to haunt her. She hadn't seen him come back to the beach and would be happy never to see him again. She needed to talk to Arlene.

If she wasn't home, she might be at Fred's house. The last thing Samantha wanted was her mother's eagle eye on her. She'd made plans for the evening while she sat staring into the flames of the bonfire, listening to everybody sing. Samantha didn't want to be watched at all.

Ursula came straight to the point as usual. "What are you up to, darling? All those questions to Earl about phony antiques. *And* Mitch sold antiques, among his other trades. You're trying to find the answer to his murder, aren't you?"

It was the time-honored parental ploy for asking questions—trapping one's offspring in the car. Short of turning the wheel over to her mother and walking home, there was no way for Pix to escape.

"Don't be ridiculous," she lied. "I'm just interested in the antiques business. You yourself said it was all 'amazing,' if I recall correctly."

"Hmmmm," her mother replied, which left the conversation hanging until Pix could stand it no longer and started talking again—another trick, and one Pix herself had used occasionally to her advantage with her own children.

"Anyway, I don't see how asking a few questions that may or may not relate to Mitchell Pierce's death can hurt anything."

"But it can hurt something—you, or dear Samantha, or Sam. We have all assumed the person who did this left the island after the terrible deed, yet it may not be so. I think you need to exercise some caution."

"Stop worrying, Mother. I'm not going to do anything foolish."

"I believe I've heard that before."

Mother could, in fact, be very irritating. Pix saw her into the house, kissed her good night, and then took great pleasure in driving as fast as she dared up and down the hills across the island to her own cottage.

Sam was groggily reading the latest issue of *The Island Crier* by an unlighted hearth.

"Honey," Pix asked immediately, "why don't you go up to bed? And where's Samantha? In her room?"

"Arlene and that pimply-faced boyfriend of hers came to get her for some kind of bonfire at his parents' camp. You know, where the Ames' are—down near the bridge. Bert Ames is taking everyone in turns in his outboard to look at the underneath of the bridge by moonlight, all very safe and sound. I said yes and reminded her when curfew rang."

Sam was feeling mellow and happy. Pix hated to destroy his mood. She ventured a tentative, "But Samantha did seem tired . . ."

"So she'll go to bed early tomorrow night or the night after. Besides, my little chickadee, this gives us a few precious moments alone, a rare thing, you may recall, these last twenty-plus years."

There was something to what the man said. Samantha was young and healthy. And so were her parents.

An hour later, Pix was stretched out next to her sleeping husband. The only sounds she could hear were his heavy breathing, the soft wind in the trees, a far-off bullfrog, and her own heart pounding insistently in her ears as she lay in bed wide awake.

Samantha Miller was not at Fred Ames's parents' camp. Neither was Arlene or Fred himself. They had put in a brief appearance for appearance's sake—not long enough for a boat ride, to Samantha's regret. She loved seeing the long arch spanning the Reach from all vantage points, especially gliding underneath through the water, looking straight up. The bridge—Sanpere's connection to the mainland. To the outside world. There were still some people on the island who wished it had never been built and blamed it for everything from teenage rowdiness to the increase in traffic on Route 17.

"I can't believe he actually said that!" Arlene was nestled

close to Fred in the front of his pickup. Like his father, Fred planned to be a fisherman as soon as he graduated from high school next June. Also like his father, he planned to marry his high school sweetheart shortly thereafter. Things looked good. He and Arlene had been king and queen of the junior prom, which virtually ensured a long and happy life together, Fred believed. If she still wanted to go to college, fine. He didn't care—just so long as she went as Mrs. Fred Ames.

Samantha was feeling a lot less frightened now that she'd told Arlene and Fred about the scene with Duncan. Sitting by the fire at the clambake, she'd decided she had to find out what he was up to. It could be nothing—or it could explain a lot of what had been happening lately. She had a feeling that after the fight with his parents, he wouldn't go home, but would gather his "club" together and do something. Arlene and Fred agreed. Fred had an idea where Duncan might be.

"There's an old cabin in the woods behind the camp that used to be a place counselors went on their days off in the olden times before Jim was the director and figured out it was the perfect place to screw. Maybe used it himself." Fred laughed. Arlene made a face.

"It's gross enough to think of adults doing it, without having to think of Jim Atherton as a teenager."

Samantha agreed and asked, "What about the cabin? Do you really think Duncan hangs out there? It's pretty near the camp. Wouldn't he want to get farther away?"

"That's what I've heard. Besides, the kid isn't old enough to drive. How far can he go? Though some of his loser friends are older and have cars. But I think he'd pick his own spot, something close to hand, and chances are he'll be there tonight. After what you described, he'd be nuts to go home. Doesn't spend much time in the mansion, anyway. My cousin worked on it and said Duncan's room was pretty cheesy compared to the rest of the place. Small and no Jacuzzi in the bath."

"Well, no wonder the boy's disturbed," mocked Arlene,

and they all laughed. It occurred to Samantha that she'd never heard Fred talk so much, and what he said made sense. Maybe Arlene knew what she was about.

"We can park on the road and go in the back way. I'm pretty sure I can find it."

"You sound awfully familiar with the cabin yourself, Frederick Ames," Arlene said.

"So, maybe we took some brews there once or twice on a cold winter's day," he admitted, "but we never hurt anything. The place was pretty well trashed before we ever found it."

He stopped the truck, got a flashlight from the glove compartment, and they started to walk silently through the woods. Samantha wasn't sure what she thought she would find, yet it seemed like a good idea at the time, and if she'd stayed at home doing nothing, she would have gone out of her mind. If nothing else, she'd provided Fred with some excitement for the night. He was as keyed up as if he was stalking a stag.

They almost missed the tumbled-down cabin. Evergreen boughs and fallen trees had been piled around it in an attempt at camouflage. In the dark, it was quite effective.

"Probably doesn't want his stepfather to notice it's still here when he's leading one of his hikes," Arlene whispered.

"Sssh." Fred put his hand over her mouth, expecting a kiss. The abruptness with which he pulled away told Samantha he got something else. Arlene was not easily shushed.

They crept up to the front of the cabin and could make out the door. It was closed and no light shone beneath it, nor at any of the windows.

"It doesn't look like he's here," Samantha said. She was disappointed.

Fred switched on the flashlight and they went up the steps. A board was missing from one and Samantha's foot almost went through. She grabbed at the rickety railing.

"Be careful. This place is liable to fall apart like Lincoln Logs," Fred warned.

They peered in the window, glass surprisingly still intact, unless Duncan had replaced it. It was pitch-dark and they couldn't see a thing. Fred shone the flashlight in and they could make out a heavy-metal calendar and a King Diamond poster on the far wall.

"What did you expect? Joey Lawrence? Come on, let's go in," Arlene said.

The door was open. It appeared the cabin had never been wired for electricity. There were lots of candles around, especially on a low shelf just above a small footlocker. A table with an ashtray filled with cigarette butts, a couple of dilapidated chairs, and a mattress with a sleeping bag on top completed the decor. There were more posters on the walls: Kiss, AC/DC, and one with a winged skull. Fred walked over to the ashtray and sniffed at the contents. "Marlboros, nothing else. If he's got a stash, it's someplace else. Like in that trunk over there."

The trunk had drawn Samantha's eye, too. So far, the room indicated perhaps a borderline unhealthy fascination with the occult and satanic music, yet nothing like upside-down crosses or inverted pentagrams to indicate the need for an emergency exorcist. Duncan seemed to spend his leisure time reading—not Proust or even *Catcher in the Rye*, but comic books. There was a stack of them next to the mattress. Arlene picked up a couple. "Look at this. The kid is really totally weird. I mean he's got *Ghost Rider* and *X-Men* mixed in with *Archies*. He doesn't know if he's six or sixteen."

Fred had flipped the two catches and was fiddling around with the center lock on the footlocker. It looked like the kind you took to camp, and maybe Duncan had, some summer in his past life. Samantha found it hard to imagine him as a normal kid in shorts playing capture the flag in a camp T-shirt.

"These things are pretty easy to open." Fred took out his knife.

"What's that sticking out from the side?" Samantha asked.

Fred pulled at it. "I dunno. Some kind of black cloth.

Maybe he has orgies or something here and they dress up." He inserted the knife into the lock and began to twist it open.

Samantha had a funny feeling about all this. It was one thing to walk through an open door but another to open someone's private property, even if that someone was Duncan Cowley. She was also not sure she wanted to know what was inside.

"He's coming! Let's get out of here!" Arlene had been watching at the window. "I can see his shoes! Come on, run!"

They flew down the front stairs and into the woods. Samantha could see Duncan's shoes blinking in the dark. He wasn't far behind them and he'd realized someone had been at the cabin.

"You bastard!" he screamed, "Come back here. I know who you are. You can't get away from me."

They ran until they reached the pickup and then were back on the main road in a few moments.

"That was close," Fred said.

They drove in silence for a while. The feeling of the dark cabin and what it might contain seemed to have invaded the thoughts of all three teenagers. Now that she was away, Samantha perversely felt she had to find out what Duncan was up to—even if it meant breaking into the footlocker. She reached over and grabbed Arlene's hand. It was as cold as her own.

"It was great of you guys to come with me, but I've got to get home or my mother will have a fit."

"Mine, too," Arlene said.

They pulled into the drive in front of the Millers' cottage and Samantha got out. "Tomorrow night?" Fred asked. In the beams of his headlights, Samantha nodded solemnly. Tomorrow night.

The phone rang early the next morning. Sam was asleep and Samantha had already left for work, taking her bike. Pix was drinking a cup of coffee, still in her nightclothes, out on the back deck. She dashed inside. Her hello was a little breathless. It had been the fourth ring; islanders were known to hang up after less, assuming no one was home or didn't want to be bothered.

"Mom!" It was Samantha and she was breathless, too. "Get over here right away! It's the sails! They're covered with blood and all these dead bats are lying around in the hulls!"

"Blood! Bats! My God, what's happened?" Pix could scarcely believe Samantha's words. "Samantha! Samantha!" The line appeared to have gone dead.

"That was Arlene." Samantha was back on the phone and her voice was marginally calmer. "It's not blood. It's paint, red paint. And the bats are plastic. But it *looked* like blood when the sails were raised and the bats were totally gross with red stuff coming out of them, so we all ran back here. I could have sworn it was real!"

"Darling, how dreadful!"

"Just come, okay?"

"I'll be there as soon as I can." Pix was already unbuttoning her pajamas. After she hung up, she raced upstairs.

"Sam, Sam, wake up! There's some trouble over at the camp. Someone painted the sails with red paint and they all thought it was blood, because there were bats in the boats that they thought were dead. But they turned out to be fake too." Pix was struggling for lucidity.

"Bats? What kind of bats? Baseball bats? Paint? Blood?" Sam sat up, rubbing his eyes. "What the hell is going on over there? Wait while I throw something on."

When the Millers pulled into the parking lot at Maine Sail Camp, they could see that Sergeant Dickinson had beaten them. They hurried down to the waterfront, where the entire camp was gathered. Samantha was in the center of a group of the youngest campers. Two were literally clinging to her. Pix was proud of the way her daughter was handling the crisis. Stroking one head while patting another, Samantha was saying, "It's just someone's idea of a stupid joke. A very, very bad joke and that's all. We'll get the extra sails and be out on the water in no time."

One of the children, a little girl, looked up at Samantha with absolute certainty that she would get an honest answer from this goddess. "Are you sure? So many spooky things have been happening—the mice and those other tricks."

Sam turned to Pix. "Mice?" he asked softly, not wanting to upset the scene further.

"I'll tell you later," Pix replied. "Another nasty prank." She wanted to listen. What was this about "other tricks"?

Jim strode over to them, obviously pleased at their presence.

"Sam, Pix. Good of you to come. Earl is down on the beach now and then he wants to search all the cabins. Clayton Dickinson is working here as handyman this summer. He's Earl's cousin, I believe, and is going to help him. The kids are understandably upset. Do you think you could give us a hand? We're going to gather in the dining hall and sing some songs. Mabel is getting together some cookies and milk. The counselors have been terrific, but the kids need some more adult reassurance."

"No problem," Sam replied, abandoning his morning sail with only a slight trace of regret. "Before you start your hootenanny though, I think you'd better talk about what's happened. There's the possibility that someone may have some information, but mostly you want to keep it all out in the open or you're going to have them jumping ship in droves."

"Don't I know it. One kid has already demanded to leave. His parents are on a barge in Burgundy, pretty unreachable, as he well knows, but he's stirring up the others."

"Is this one of Samantha's group? She said there was a boy who was pretty annoyed at his mother and father."

Jim nodded. "Geoff Baxter. He may have been too immature for such a long sleep-away session."

Pix went over to Samantha and began to help her move the

kids into the dining room. Sam went to another group. "Hootenanny?" Had her husband been listening to his old Pete Seeger records while the family was away?

The clingers were still clinging and Pix gently pried the little girl away from Samantha. Pix had the distinct impression that the campers around Samantha, and especially those who had commandeered each of her daughter's hands, were not so much scared as excited, despite appearances to the contrary. There was definitely something in the air. She made a mental note to talk to Samantha about it later—and also ask her how she liked being the object of such devotion. The crushes at Maine Sail were beginning to resemble some sort of food chain—beginning with Samantha's on Valerie.

"Now, listen to Samantha. She's right. It's just a rotten trick. What's your name?" The girl gulped, took a tissue Pit offered, and blew her nose. "It's Susannah." Obviously the effort was too much and she began to cry, adding the tearful protest, "I didn't do it. I don't know who did it!"

"Shut up, Susannah, and stop showing off." It was one of the boys in the group. "Nobody thinks you did it. Besides, you would never have the guts."

Pix was inclined to agree with him. Whoever had done it would have had to have nerve and some to spare. The sails had been fine the day before, Samantha said, so the deed involved getting up in the dead of night, raising the sails, painting them without leaving a trace of the evidence on one's person, then making everything shipshape before going back to bed.

It would have been very difficult for any of the campers—or counselors—to do without someone detecting his or her absence.

That left . . . Arlene supplied the name uppermost in everyone's minds, whispering to Pix as she swept by, several charges in tow, "It's just creepy Duncan again. If this doesn't get him sent away, I don't know what will." She was smiling.

In the cavernous dining room, the commotion was deafening and it took Jim several minutes to get everyone quieted down. During that time, Pix saw Valerie and Duncan slip in through the side door. Valerie looked furious. Duncan's mouth was set in a tight line. He looked as if he hadn't slept—or changed his clothes—for a few weeks. When Pix tried to read the expression in his eyes, all she could come up with was fear. If there was red paint on his body, it wasn't anywhere that showed.

"Campers, staff, I know how upset everyone is, and believe me, I feel it just as much as you do—more. Right now, what we need is to stay calm and do everything we can to help Sergeant Dickinson figure out who did this. While the kitchen crew gives us a little snack, we'll have a few songs and practice for the parade. I'm going to be in my office in case any of you wants to come to talk to me. If you want to bring a friend, fine. I'm prepared to treat this as a very bad joke—something that maybe seemed like a fun idea at midnight, to scare your friends the next morning. But I *will* find out who did it."

Jim Atherton was definitely displaying the nonpussycat side of his camp-director role this morning. Nobody but nobody messed with Maine Sail.

Samantha joined her parents. Pix took the opportunity to ask her a few questions as the group began to sing "There Was a Tree," volume increasing as they went along, until it sounded like any other camp group. All they needed was to be on a bus or tramping through the woods

"What did the kids mean by the other tricks?"

"Oh, those were just the normal things that go on in a place like this—salt in the sugar bowls, short-sheeting the counselors' beds—the ones who don't have sleeping bags—and cowpats in people's shoes."

Pix nodded. These were the typical perils of camp existence. "Nothing else? Nothing like the mice?"

"Not that I know of, though the kids have been saying they hear creepy noises at night—scary music, rustling in the bushes—but I'm pretty sure it's one or two kids wanting to get the others worked up."

"Now what is this about the mice?" Sam demanded. He really wanted to be sailing. It was a gorgeous day and through the window he could see luckier folk skimming the surface of the water just beyond the vandalized boats moored in the camp harbor. They did look pretty dreadful and reminded him of an ancient Greek myth, only those sails had been black. He shuddered slightly and put any and all implications firmly out of his mind.

They filled him in on the mice and he commented, "The sole connection I can see is blood and gore. Kids this age love it, but I'm damned if I can figure out how a kid could have done it."

"The Athertons were at the clambake all afternoon; someone could have snuck away then," Pix proposed.

"Except the whole camp was here practicing for the Fourth of July parade. The counselors have planned an elaborate routine where the campers flip cards as they march and sing, like at sports events. If someone was missing, it would have been spotted right away. You couldn't do that much damage in the time it might have taken to go the bathroom."

"Samantha's right, which leaves an outsider."

Samantha elaborated. "Which leaves Duncan. We know he had a wicked big fight with his parents. What better way to get even than try to get the camp closed down? If Jim can't keep this hushed up, there are a lot of parents who'll want their kids out of here. You know, 'Kid's Camp Cult Target'— that sort of thing.

"Duncan had plenty of time to do it while the rest of us were eating lobster—or he could have done it later after everyone was asleep." Or, she said to herself silently, he could have been coming from his painting party just in time to surprise us at the cabin.

"Well," Sam said, rubbing his hands together, "I don't see

that there's too much more we can do here." The group was lustily singing "One Hundred Bottles of Beer on the Wall" and it was time to leave—tide or no tide. "Why don't we go talk to Jim, see if anything more has turned up, and skedaddle." Skedaddle? Pix thought. What was happening to her husband's vocabulary. He definitely needed to be around his family more.

"I'll come, too. Are you staying, darling?"

"Mother! Of course! It's my job. Besides, I want to." Samantha went back to her post. The worshippers were waiting.

"It seems odd that little Susannah would have felt it necessary to protest her innocence," Pix remarked to her husband as they started across the ground, so heavily carpeted with years of fallen pine needles that their every footfall released a strong scent of balsam as they crunched along.

"Maybe she's the salt/sugar culprit. She has the perfect face for it—those big baby blues and that sunshine-from-behind-the-clouds smile."

Pix looked at Sam admiringly. "You would have made a good detective."

"Thank you, Mrs. Holmes. Now let's say good-bye and not waste any more of this beautiful day."

Outside the office, they could hear voices, raised voices.

"I tell you, young man, one more incident and you'll go. This is not a threat; it's a promise. You are not hiding behind your mother's skirts anymore. Of all the idiotic things to do, frightening some of the younger children half to death!"

"I didn't do it, I tell you!" Duncan screeched. "And I'm not going to any fucking military academy. Go ahead and send me. But you can't make me stay there."

"Duncan, Duncan, what choice do we have? Your behavior has been so odd lately." It was Valerie and she sounded as if she had been crying. "At least won't you see the counselor again?"

"I'm not the one who needs a shrink; you are! And this has

nothing to do with Daddy. Why can't you just leave me alone!"

"Fine." Valerie's voice was resolute, the voice of a woman who has come to the end of some sort of tether. "We will leave you alone—and you leave us alone. One more of these incidents and you'll be sent off. Maybe your grandparents will keep you for the rest of the summer."

"That's a laugh." Duncan sneered. "Don't forget what they said to you the last time we were there."

"That will be enough, young man, I will not have you address your mother in that tone of voice." The Millers were unable to move from their spot right outside the door—in Pix's case from outright curiosity; in Sam's because he was mortified they might be heard leaving.

"Don't you touch me!" Duncan's voice was frantic and what sounded like a chair falling over was followed by the more recognizable noise made when a sharp slap connects with flesh on some part of the body.

Head lowered, Duncan plunged out the door, past the Millers, oblivious to their presence. Pix could see two things: He was crying and an angry red handprint streaked across the left side of his face.

They waited a few seconds before Pix called out, "Jim, are you there? We have to be going."

"Come in; come in." Nothing was out of place.

"We've just had another scene with Duncan," Valerie admitted to them. "The last psychologist we took him to said it was all an extended grief reaction, but I'm beginning to think Duncan is milking it. At the moment, he is simply a pain-in-the-ass teenager, no ifs, ands, or buts about it." She laughed at her pun. "Excuse me. This has been a pretty awful morning."

Pix patted Valerie's shoulder. "I know—and if there's anything more we can do, give us a call."

"Thank you both for coming." Jim was a bit stiff. Pix knew he must be wondering how much they had heard—and seen.

"It will all sort itself out," Sam assured him. "Maine Sail

has one of the finest reputations of any summer camp in the country. Parents know this."

"I hope so," Jim said dismally. "I also hope I can keep it out of the papers."

As the Millers were on the point of leaving, Earl walked into the office. Pix sat down.

"You can let the kids back into their bunks. Nothing, not so much as a drop of red paint on anything. The only thing we've found with any paint on it is a rubber glove—the kind you use for dishwashing. It had washed up on the shore and its mate, the paint, and brush will probably float in, too. After being in the water for this amount of time, there's no way we can get any prints off it. We'll just have to hope there is a guilty conscience—or more than one—out there. I'm assuming the paint was down in the boathouse. There's a space between two cans of white primer."

"We use red paint for the waterlines and the names, so if you didn't find another can of it, that's where it came from," Jim said, then put out his hand for a hearty masculine shake. "Thanks, Earl, for all your work. I'm pretty convinced it was my stepson. We've been having a lot of trouble with him. You know that."

Earl nodded and gave them a sympathetic look. The first week in June, Duncan had been picked up for driving his mother's car without a license. He'd only made it down to the end of the Athertons' road when he had the bad luck to encounter Earl. Rather than get bogged down in the juvenile-court system, Earl had placed him on a kind of supervised probation of his own. Now when the boy saw the policeman coming, he tended to walk in the other direction, but not before giving Earl a look that spoke volumes—pretty unprintable ones.

"If you find out anything more, give me a call. I'll write it up, plus it will have to go in *The Island Crier*. Let's hope none of the eager beavers in the national press are reading 'Police Brief' these days."

"Thanks."

Pix knew what Earl meant. There had been a spate of quaint column fillers reprinting items from local Maine papers—examples of life Down East. The latest had a Sanpere dateline and purported to quote an island schoolboy's report on George Washington in its entirety: "George Washington was born off-island." True, that said it all, but the image of the life it represented was as faded as one of those daguerreotypes Earl had been mentioning—just yesterday?

"We have to be going." Ever so gently, Sam pulled his wife to an upright position. "See you."

They spent the afternoon sailing, and despite her every intention to forget the events of the morning for the time being, Pix kept seeing gobs of red dripping down the smooth white sails they passed.

Ursula Rowe sat on the front porch of The Pines trying to decide whether she should walk down to the beach or stay where she was and finish the book she was reading about Alice James. A few years ago, there would have been no question. She would have leapt up, taken her walk, and returned to read—or even taken the book with her. Now she eyed the ascent. First there were the porch stairs, then the sloping grass, and finally a line of low rocks that separated the beach from the dirt road leading to the dock. She sighed. It was too much, especially with no one around at the moment. It was all well and good to assert her independence when people were near, but she knew she was slowing down and there were things she just shouldn't attempt anymore. It was profoundly depressing.

It had all started with the car. She'd resisted the calls of common sense for several months, then when she'd backed over one of the lilacs her mother had planted for her when she first moved into the Aleford house, she'd called Pix and told her to come get the keys. For the first few days, she felt not only trapped but angrily dependent. Gradually, she'd become used to relying on friends, taxis—and Pix. Fortunately, the house wasn't far from the center of Aleford. The day Ursula couldn't walk to the library would be the day she took to her bed for good, she'd told herself dramatically. Now she knew she'd hang on to every bit of mobility she had, from house to garden, from bedroom to bath, as her world diminished.

The unchanging scene before her lifted her spirits. For all the waves knew, she could still be that little girl in braids chasing the foam as it swept down the wet sand. Yet this summer had not been a typical one. The murder of Mitchell Pierce hung suspended in the air, accompanied by whispered rumors, hints, accusations. She wished Pix would stay out of it, but knew she wouldn't. Children were so influenced by their friends. Pix was taking a leaf from Faith's book. But then Pix wasn't a child anymore and she, Ursula, wasn't really a mother—some other category. The magazines talked about role reversal and children becoming parents. Ursula hated that notion. Only it was true. She wasn't walking to the beach anymore without Pix to watch her. Retired mother? Perhaps, but when she thought about Pix and Arnold, named for his father, the fierce pangs of maternal love were not retiring in the least.

It would be good to see Arnold and his wife. What was the old saying? "Your son is your son until he takes a wife. Your daughter's your daughter for the rest of your life." Or was it "her life"? Some daughterly element in one's makeup that just kept on going along, even when the mother was gone? Had she felt this way about her own mother? She didn't think so. Her older sisters had assigned themselves caretaker roles early on and there wasn't much left for Ursula to do save visit from time to time—like Arnold and Claire. He was her son. She was proud of him, but it was a good thing she had Pix.

She thought about her conversation with John Eggleston at the clambake. "It's no loss to anyone I know or can imagine." She'd been surprised at the uncharitableness of the remark. She ought to tell Pix about it. The clambake had seemed like a kind of play. Perhaps it was because she knew that at eighty, she wouldn't be at too many more of them. She had tended to regard the day as several acts and many scenes one after another. Addie Bainbridge had been watching, too. Or maybe holding court was a better description. Ursula resolved to invite Addie and Rebecca for tea later in the week, after the Fourth of July festivities. Give Rebecca a break. Addie was inclined to ride roughshod over her. What could Adelaide's childhood have actually been like out at the lighthouse? It sounded idyllic, and reflecting on her own upbringing, one of seven, in a well-appointed but unavoidably crowded town house on Boston's Beacon Hill, Ursula thought how lovely it would have been not to have so many people to talk to all the time. That was what had always made The Pines so special. You could be alone.

She could still be alone. Except now she didn't want to be.

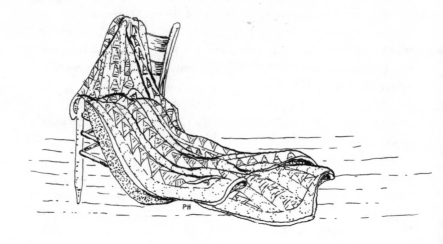

Chapter 6

A midnight curfew was a definite disadvantage to detective work, Samantha decided as once more she entered the woods behind Maine Sail Camp with Fred and Arlene. Fred had no curfew, of course, and Arlene's was a great deal more elastic than Samantha's own. Whatever Duncan and his friends were up to, Sam was willing to bet, things didn't get rolling until the wee hours.

This time, there were lights flickering in the windows of the cabin, just visible through Duncan's elaborate camouflage.

"Should we try to look through the back window?" Arlene whispered.

"Let's wait a while and see what they do," Fred suggested. "They may go someplace else. The cabin is pretty small."

They retreated behind a row of tamaracks and took turns watching.

"More kids are coming," Samantha reported. True to Fred's prediction, soon a group of about eleven teenagers came out of the cabin and headed straight for the tamaracks. Samantha froze in position after crouching close to the rough trunk, the sharp-needled boughs pricking her bare arms. Why hadn't she thought to wear a sweatshirt? The weather was still peculiar for Maine, up into the high eighties every day. She'd been shedding clothes, not adding them.

The group passed by without noticing anything. Samantha, Fred, and Arlene waited a minute before following. Once again, Fred was full of ideas. "There're only two places where they could be headed, the quaking bog and the old settlement quarry—unless they're planning to dispose of something or someone, which would mean the bog—I'll bet they're on their way to the quarry."

"What do you mean?" Samantha had never been to the bog, deterred all these years by reports of mosquitoes as large as robins and giant Venus's-flytraps.

"The suction—you put your foot down wrong and it takes two men to help you twist it and pull yourself out. People used to junk cars there before Earl came. And there's always talk, especially on Halloween, of what may be lying under the surface from years past."

"You know that's all nonsense," Arlene whispered angrily, "except about the cars. That's true. Stop trying to psych us out Fred. I'm nervous enough as it is."

Samantha had to agree with her and was glad the bog had been eliminated as the probable gathering place for the club.

Fred put out his arm to stop them. "See, they're turning left. That leads to the top of the quarry." The flashlights the group ahead of them was carrying did go left, darting like so many fireflies through the dark woods.

Samantha had been to the quarry. It was one of her favorite places—also her mother's and grandmother's. They picked blackberries there and then, later in the season, tiny tart mountain cranberries that appeared as conserve at the Millers' Thanksgiving table.

The view from the top of the quarry was spectacular—

straight out to sea across vast expanses of granite carved in huge blocks, like Brobdingnagian steps. During the day, you had to be careful not to walk into one of the crevasses where the charges had been set to blast the stone. At night, it would be treacherous. Was Duncan's club an elaborate game of chicken?

Fred stopped suddenly and led them up a granite ledge until they were directly above the group below. A fire had been lighted and everyone was drinking beer. Duncan was no-where to be seen. It looked like any other gathering of kids from Maine to California, eager to put themselves at a dis-tance from adult supervision. A few were smoking. One of the cigarettes was being passed from person to person—obvi-ously not tobacco.

"So, what's the big deal? They're partying," Arlene said. "Let's go home."

Samantha wanted to wait until Duncan came, and Fred agreed. It was at least fifteen minutes before they heard the music and saw him leap suddenly into the midst of his friends, dangerously close to the fire. He was wearing a black robe—it looked left over from someone's graduation—unfas-tened. They could see that he was stripped to the waist under-neath and had covered his body with symbols and lines done in red marker—at least Samantha assumed it was marker. He didn't seem to be oozing blood, but the effect was dramatic and she felt instantly nauseated. Everyone grew quiet and the words of an old Black Sabbath song filled the stillness from the tape deck he set down.

When the music stopped, Duncan began to chant "We are everybody and everybody is nobody" over and over. The group picked it up, some laughing a little—maybe because of the beers and the pot. A few of the guys stripped off their shirts and pranced unsteadily around the fire.

Duncan took out a chicken that looked like a roaster from the IGA and made a great show of slitting its throat—or rather, the place where the throat would have been if the head was still attached. Blood flowed; he must have stuck a sack of red-colored liquid inside.

"The asshole!" Fred whispered, "He couldn't even get a live chicken."

Samantha wasn't finding the scene humorous. Duncan's intent was the same as if the chicken had been alive—or if it had been something other than a chicken. She shuddered and gripped the granite hard with her hand to remind herself that this wasn't a movie. She wondered what would happen next. The kids below her looked so normal. She stared at one girl in particular: short dark hair, a striped tube top, and cutoffs—a typical teenager on a summer night. Maybe she wore a little too much makeup, especially the exaggerated black mascara around her eyes. But she wasn't typical. The whole gathering wasn't typical at all, and Samantha began to feel frightened. Duncan had somehow managed to tap into an unhealthy fascination shared by this group, and it was a vein better left unopened—and it might well have been if he hadn't come here to live.

The kids passed the chicken around. Solemn now, each smeared some of the "blood" on their foreheads. One girl almost broke the mood by declaring she was not going to touch something so gross, but the boy next to her did it for her, loudly declaring she was a wuss. The dark-haired girl fiercely told them to shut up. "You're spoiling it!" There was no question about her own dedication.

Throughout, Duncan watched intently. If the scene had not been filled with such potentially evil symbolism, Samantha began to think, it would have been pathetic. Duncan was pitifully thin and his chest concave. All the kids seemed to have spent more time indoors than out; and if they were robust, they were overly so—tending in one boy's case to obesity.

"Do you know everybody?" Samantha whispered to Arlene.

"Yeah, I'll tell you later. It's what we've been saying—loser kids. But sometimes it's not their fault, like Karen over there.

Her old man beats her pretty badly. Everybody knows it." It was the girl with the dark hair.

Now Samantha did want to leave and she poked Fred. They started to back away from the ledge.

"Let the games begin!" Duncan threw off his robe and turned on the music again, louder. He grabbed a beer, chugged it down, threw the empty can high into the air, and stripped off his pants. The beer can clattered down the rock and rolled off into the darkness.

"We are all and all is in us. Join with the darkness. Cast off your garments." He'd definitely been reading more than comics, Samantha thought. His language was getting positively gothic.

"Nobody wants to see your dick, Duncan," one of the girls said. "And besides, I'm not allowed to take my clothes off. My mother says so."

Duncan looked at her with scorn. "You are not a true sister of blood."

"I'm not a sister of anybody here. If you're going to get foolish, I'm leaving."

A few others stirred and Duncan appeared to weigh losing his audience against maintaining his noble position. He decided to go for the numbers and pulled his jeans back on. "All right. Let's go climbing instead." This appeared to find more favor. Armed with beers and smokes, they set off, teetering dangerously close to the edge of the quarry precipice.

"Someone's going to get killed!" Samantha started forward.

"No, come on. We'll make an anonymous call to Earl from the CB in my pickup. They're not going to stop because we tell them to," Fred advised.

The three climbed down to the woods below and went back to the truck as fast as they could.

"Assholes," Fred was muttering. "And Duncan's the worst. After we call, I want to see what's in that trunk of his.

Obviously, the black stuff was the thing he was wearing. He is really into it."

Sensibly, Arlene pointed out that as soon as Earl got the news, he'd be up at the quarry and they'd come running back to the cabin.

"Another time, then," Fred said.

Samantha wasn't so sure. The day had been filled with images of blood—intended images: the gory sails that greeted them in the clear light of the morning and the streaked faces around the flames in the dark of night. Another time?

She'd have to think about it.

The next morning Pix was putting away her chowder pot. She must have been more fatigued than she'd thought to have left it on the beach. Louise had dropped it off. As Pix was pushing it up onto the top shelf in the pantry, the lid fell, clattering to the floor and narrowly missing the side of her head. As she put the pot down and bent to retrieve the lid, she discovered a large Tupperware bowl had inadvertently been placed inside. She opened it up and found a few cookie crumbs. A piece of masking tape clearly marked BAINBRIDGE was on the bottom. The two women had brought a number of desserts to the clambake and this must have been an offering Pix had missed. The crumbs smelled delicious. She washed the bowl out and decided to go to the village to drop it off. Norman might be around and she could pick up some more information about fake antiques. She'd also like to get him alone to ask him about Mitchell Pierce. Mitch dealt with museums, and presumably a New York dealer in the know would be familiar with Mitch's name, even if there hadn't been any business transacted between them. She'd try him on Mother's Brewster chair story again, too.

Pix could not shake the feeling there was something that didn't quite ring true about Norman. She was trying hard to be objective about him and knew that a good part of her mistrust had to do with his Big Apple shine. Then too there were few strangers on the island. There were tourists and people who rented cottages for a week or so, but Norman—someone from away—had managed to insinuate himself into everyday island life to an alarming degree. Why, he'd even been at the Frazier's clambake! Things, especially socially, moved slowly on Sanpere and people waited a decent interval, say ten years, before expecting invitations.

Why was Norman here? She knew what was purported. There was that word again. It reminded her of Mitch. "Purported" activities. Norman and Mitch. Dealers in antiques. Norman had arrived on the island well before the murder. Where was he at the time?

There was a lot to work into a conversation.

Driving down Route 17 past the turnoff for Little Harbor, she wished Faith were around and resolved to call her later to talk about these misgivings. Pix turned into the Bainbridge's drive, stopped the car, and got out. The property had once included many acres to the rear and on both sides, but the land had been sold long ago, leaving the farmhouse and barn. The first thing to greet her was the sound of hammering. Curious, she followed the noise and discovered Seth Marshall and someone obviously working for him inside the barn, replacing a beam.

"Seth!" He dropped his hammer in surprise.

"Now, Pix, I have to keep busy. The police won't let me out there yet."

"But it could be tomorrow. Well, not the Fourth, but maybe the next day, and you'll be all tied up here!" She was livid. The Fairchild house was becoming a dream one, literally.

"I told Aunt Addie I would have to stop once I got the go-ahead on another project. Don't worry." Seth spoke soothingly and tried flashing an ingratiating grin. It made him look more like Peck's Bad Boy than ever and Pix was not mollified.

"I'll give Earl a call and see if we can get some idea of how

much longer they need. Goodness knows, they should be finished by now. I think you had better plan to start Thursday at
the latest.''

''Which means working here tomorrow,'' the other man
muttered angrily, stopping the rest of his complaint after a
glance from the boss.

''Thursday will be fine. Now, please, remember I want to
get started as much as you do.''

Pix certainly hoped so, said as much and good-bye, then
walked out into the sunshine and over to the house. ''Aunt
Addie'' indeed, although she could really be his aunt, or more
likely, great-aunt. The whole island was connected by ties of
varying degrees of kinship.

Rebecca answered the door—the back door, of course. A
bed of ferns had grown up over the front steps and Pix
thought it unlikely that the door with its shiny brass knocker
in the shape of an anchor had been opened since James Bainbridge had been carried out in his coffin. It would never have
done to take him the back way through the kitchen.

''Who is it?'' a querulous voice called out. ''Don't just
leave whoever it is standing with their chin hanging out! Invite
them in!''

Rebecca ignored Addie's remarks and reached for the Tupperware bowl.

''Oh, Pix, am I glad to see this. I couldn't remember where I
had mislaid it, but I knew I had it at the clambake, because I'd
filled it with butterscotch shortbread* that morning.''

She *had* missed something good, Pix thought, stepping into
the room. The Bainbridge's shortbread was another of those
secret family recipes.

''I'm glad I found it. It was in my chowder pot and I might
have put it away without opening it until next year, but the
top fell off the pot when I was putting it on the shelf.''

''The Lord works in mysterious ways,'' Rebecca said confi-

*See recipe page 286.

dently, then led Pix to the front parlor, where Addie was somehow managing to keep herself poised on the slippery horsehair Bainbridge fainting couch. Pix knew that it was a fainting couch because Adelaide had told her once, adding, perhaps unnecessarily, "not that it has ever been used as one." Oddly enough, today she did seem a bit under the weather. She wore a housecoat that made her look like a large pink-and-orange-flowered tea cozy. Her legs were stretched out and she apologized for wearing her bedroom slippers.

"The heat is some terrible for my circulation; I can't even get my shoes on this morning. I told Rebecca to order the next-biggest size, but she forgot and got the same as always."

"We could send them back. It wouldn't be any trouble."

"Well, it would be for me. What will I do for footwear while they're gone, I'd like to know?" She kept right on going: "And there must have been something I et at the clambake that didn't sit right—not that I think for a moment it was your chowder, deah," she added, looking Pix straight in the eye. The intent was clear. Now was the moment for Pix to confess to buying suspect fish and last year's potatoes. Pix stared right back. Nobody else had suffered from the chowder in the slightest and Addie's indisposition was more than likely a case of overindulgence. Addie was starting to catalog her major symptoms, such as severe diarrhea and stomach cramps, rather graphically when Rebecca tactfully broke in.

"Pix brought our Tupperware bowl back, the one we thought was lost at the clambake. It was in her chowder pot."

Adelaide beamed as if she'd recovered the family jewels instead of an airtight storage container. "It's hard to get good Tupperware nowadays and I won that at one of Dot Prescott's parties when she was selling Tupperware. I don't know who's doing it now."

Pix tried to steer the conversation away from plastics to antiques and Norman.

"It must be interesting having an antiques dealer like Norman Osgood as a guest." The Bainbridges always called their bed-and-breakfast customers "guests."

"Oh my, yes, he's been a treat. The stories that man can tell. We sit and laugh for hours."

Rebecca didn't look quite so merry, and Pix wondered whether she was included in these funfests.

"Is he around now? I had a question I wanted to ask him."

"No, he's off on one of his jaunts today. Be back in time for the parade tomorrow, he said. What's your question? I'll ask him for you."

Pix had been afraid Addie would say this and was now thankful she'd prepared a mythical inquiry about the best way to take care of an old Sheraton dresser her mother was giving her.

"Just keep it clean with a dust cloth," Rebecca advised, "if the wood is not too dry and the finish still good."

"And what do you know about the care of valuable antiques, Rebecca Bainbridge? I don't recall too many down in that shack you grew up in. No, Pix. I swear by Olde English and plenty of it. You can't go wrong there."

Faith could smell it had been put to good use in the parlor. She looked anxiously at Rebecca. It might have been that Addie had gone too far.

"Your own husband was raised in that 'shack,' Addie, and you're lying on Grandmother's couch this very moment. I guess we had just as many nice things as you did out at the lighthouse."

Pix was glad to hear Rebecca answering back. It didn't happen very often.

"You couldn't have had many, then," Addie one-upped her. "I slept on a cot in the kitchen and there wasn't a decent piece of furniture in the place. The only thing worth any money at all was the light, and that belonged to the government. Now where are my regular glasses? You've gone and fetched the wrong ones, as usual! Can't see a thing with these."

"Those are the right ones. Remember, you put a piece a tape on the frame so we wouldn't get mixed up. There it is, plain as the nose on your face."

Addie pulled her glasses off. "Can't see a danged thing. You must have put tape on both."

Before the fur could fly any faster, Pix made her farewells with promises to sit together at the parade the next day. The Bainbridge's lawn sloped agreeably down to Main Street and was a perfect viewing stand.

"And don't forget your mother!" Addie called after her.

As if I would—or could, Pix thought.

After leaving the Bainbridges, she felt a little betwixt and between. Sam was on a long cruise to Swans Island with a sailing buddy and Samantha was still at work. She thought she might pop in to Jill's store and pick up a baby sweater made by one of the women on the island that The Blueberry Patch stocked. One of Pix's cousin's children was having a baby, which would make Ursula a great-great-aunt and make Pix a what, a cousin some number of times removed?

Removed. She realized Mitchell Pierce's death had removed her from her normal embedded island feelings. She had the constant sense that she was on the outside looking in, not because she was from away but because there were things going on she couldn't quite make out. She had the illusion that if she could only squint hard enough, she'd be able to make out the shapes.

Jill was at the register. The store was empty.

"Hi, Pix," she said. She had been working on her accounts evidently and now shoved a large ledger under the counter. The cash register was an antique—and not for sale. It had been a fixture in the previous store to occupy the space, a cobbler's shop owned by Jill's grandfather.

"My cousin's daughter is having a baby soon and I want to send a sweater."

"Do they know what they are having? I always think that sounds so odd, but you know what I mean?"

"Yes, I do, and they don't, so the sweater had better be white or yellow."

After taking a pleasurable amount of time, Pix took her purchase to the front of the shop. It was always fun to buy baby gifts. A few years earlier, she used to toy with the idea of another bundle of joy herself, then remembered all the home-work supervision that would entail and opted to wait for grandchildren—a wait she fervently prayed would be a long one.

Earl had come in while she'd been in the back and was buy-ing a paper.

"How are you, Pix?" he asked, "Quite a business yesterday at the camp. Samantha was great with the kids. Really kept them calmed down."

"Fine, thank you, and thank you for saying that about Samantha. I'll tell her. She's always wanted to go into science, marine biology, but she's so good with people."

"Maybe she'll figure out a way to combine the two. Now I've got to go pick up something to eat at the IGA or I'll start to get malnutriated."

Earl looked anything but. Pix smiled. Jill didn't. Hadn't they patched things up yet?

The next exchange made it clear they hadn't.

"So, I'll see you about eight?" Earl asked.

"I'm afraid I can't make it tonight. Maybe another time," Jill answered. The time, from her expression and tone, could possibly be well into the new century.

"Okay." Earl flushed and left quickly.

Pix was tempted to ask what was going on, but Jill did not look as if she'd welcome inquiries into her personal life at the moment. She rang up the purchase and Pix was soon out on the walk planning a dinner party with a few friends, mainly Earl and Jill—soon.

She got into her car and noticed Earl was parked next to her. It was the perfect time to tell him about the mark on the quilt, if he was not too distracted by his own affairs of the heart. But Pix doubted it. Work was work. The notebook would be out in no time, just the way it had the day before at the camp. When they'd arrived, it was the first thing she had noticed. There was Earl standing before the bloody red sails, calmly writing down each and every word.

He was at his car soon, carrying what she knew to be one of the IGA's Italian sandwiches—bologna, salami, and cheese on some sort of large hot dog roll. It also had green peppers and onions if those were to hand and a drizzle of Italian dressing, hence the appellation.

"Earl, have you got a minute? There's something I've been meaning to tell you. It's probably nothing, yet I thought you should know."

The notebook came out. He clicked his pen.

Mercifully, they were parked behind the post office. They might be news, but not big news, particularly if she spoke fast. She explained about finding the mark on the quilt she'd bought—a mark identical to the one on the red-and-white quilt.

"I know you told me. It's a blue cross, right? Like this?" He drew one on the pad.

"Yes, maybe a bit smaller. I wouldn't have noticed it on the one around the body if the quilt had had more colors. Then in the one I bought, it just seemed to jump out at me."

"Do you have any idea what it could stand for?"

"It could be some kind of family laundry mark. Both quilts may have come from Sullivan. I mean, that's where the antiques dealer said the quilt was from, and Mitch was living in Sullivan when he died. The red-and-white one may have been taken from his room."

Earl agreed. "That makes sense. Although I'm not sure

148

what kind of link there could be. He hadn't been in his room for some days before he was killed, according to his landlady, but she admitted he could have been there one of the times she was out doing errands.''

"There's another possibility. Much as it pains me to realize I may have been duped, I think the quilt I bought could be a fake. The price was suspiciously low. I have a book about dating quilts and I'm going to go through it to try to establish when mine was made. If it's a modern one, as I suspect, the mark could be a way whoever was faking the quilts kept track of which were real and which weren't.''

Earl looked at Pix admiringly. "Good thinking. Obviously, we don't want it spread around, but we're pretty sure Mitch was involved with one or more of the antique scams. Unfortunately, he was also involved in some other tricky businesses, so the field is pretty broad." His face fell a bit.

He continued: "So that's why you were asking all those questions on Sunday.''

"Yes," Pix admitted.

"Look, I'd like to photograph the mark and see how it matches with the one that was wrapped around Pierce's body. I've got my camera in the trunk. All right if I come over and take a picture now? I'll be able to send it to Augusta right away. They may also have something in their files about it.''

"Sure," Pix agreed. She was excited. They were beginning to get somewhere. Maybe.

As Earl got into his car, he called over to her, "By the way, since you're turning out to be so interested in detective work, how about finding out why my girl is giving me the cold shoulder?''

Pix was sorry to disappoint him. "I'll try, but I'm sure it's nothing much. You two have been together a long time.''

" 'Nothing much,' " Earl was uncharacteristically sarcastic. "Do you think the fact that she had dinner with Seth Marshall last night might mean something? The entire island and half the mainland saw them down at the inn.''

Pix did not have an answer.

Nor did she have an answer shortly thereafter when she spread out the new quilt on her living room floor.

"Where is this mark?"

She looked. Then looked again.

It was gone.

"I felt like a fool. Fortunately, I thought to get one of Samantha's magnifying glasses and I showed him where the holes were. There had definitely been something sewn there."

The first thing Pix had done after the police car had pulled away from the house was call Faith. She was at work.

"But this proves that the marks mean something." Faith was excited. "Why am I stuck down here making blueberry pies and coleslaw, not to mention a cake in the shape of an eagle some patriotic soul has ordered, while you're having all the fun!"

Pix thought of Mitch and the incidents at the camp. It wasn't exactly what she'd call fun, but Faith tended to view life a bit differently.

"I wish you were here, too. Sam has to leave after the parade. He's got a client coming in early Thursday morning. It must be someone important, because it's not like Sam to miss the fireworks. Since he's been here, I've realized how nice it is to have another adult around. Samantha is wonderful company, but she's at work or off with her friends. In fact, I think she's doing too much. She looked terrible at breakfast—as if she hadn't slept a wink, but she says she's fine."

"Well, what did you used to tell your mother? Speaking of whom, she certainly qualifies as an adult. Why don't you get her to come over for a while? No, that's not right. That's not what you need."

Faith knew her so well, Pix thought. Much as she loved her mother, it would not provide the ease she was seeking.

"Even before we got here, I asked her to come until my brother arrives. I don't like to think of her alone in that big house, but she wants to be on her own, and when we're her age, we'll be exactly the same."

"I should hope so. Now, back to the quilt. Obviously, nothing else in the cottage was disturbed or you would have said so."

"Right, and yes, I did leave the door unlocked as usual. There's nothing of value here, and it's such a nuisance for Samantha to carry a key. I have one with my car keys, but I can't remember the last time I used it."

These New Englanders, Faith thought to herself. The unlocked door represented their trust in humankind and belief in a certain way of life: "Come in; it's off the latch." And she knew Pix would still keep her doors unlocked even now. What would it take? Faith hoped Pix would never find out.

"I've been doing some detective work for you in between shucking corn for corn pudding and the like. There was an article on quilt making in the paper. You remember that controversy about the Smithsonian's decision to reproduce some of the quilts in their collection using overseas labor? That's what it's about mainly, however it started me thinking. These new quilts could be made to look old, particularly if they are unmarked. I think the Smithsonian ones have an indelible tag on the back, but a lot of mail-order companies and department stores offer quilts. I doubt they're all labeled so conscientiously. Anyway, I mailed the article to you and you should get it by Thursday."

"It's pretty easy to spot some of the reproduction quilts, even if they are made by hand, because the stitching is uneven and there are fewer stitches to the inch. Handmade quilts, like the one I got in Pennsylvania last year, have ten to twelve stitches."

"What about this one? How many does it have?"

"Ten in most places, more in a few others."

"But it could still be a new one made to look old."

"Yes, and that's what I have to do now—figure out for sure if it's a fake. Then I can tell Earl to have an expert look at the one the police have. I also thought I might do some more antiquing and see if I turn up any more marked quilts."

"So what else is going on up there—or I should say down there?"

Pix had patiently explained to Faith her first summer on the island what Down East meant. The term dated from the days when the coastal towns of Maine were part of an active exchange of goods with the port of Boston. Timber, quarried stone, and of course fish were sold to purchase manufactured goods from Massachusetts. Since the coast curves eastward as it heads north to Nova Scotia and since the prevailing winds from Boston to Maine are southerly, a sloop sailing before the wind, downwind, from Boston to Bangor was headed down east. Pix made Faith learn it until she was letter-perfect, but although she was sure she had the words right, it had never made a whole lot of sense to Faith. Up was north and down was south. And Maine was north.

"The clambake was great, but the weather's been much too hot."

"It's the same here. Thank goodness this place is air-conditioned. It's a relief to come to work. The parsonage may self-ignite, it's so stuffy—even with fans going. Tom's afraid the window frames are too fragile for an air conditioner, but if the heat keeps up, I will personally pay to have the old ones ripped out and new ones put in, never mind the blasphemy. I know God allows New Englanders to be very cold in the winter and very hot in the summer because they prefer to suffer in this way, but I'm tired of taking the kids to work or to a movie when I want them to cool off!"

Pix felt a twinge of guilt. She was on the Parish Buildings and Grounds Committee, which, among other things, saw to the upkeep of the parsonage. No one had ever raised the notion of air conditioning. The Millers had never had it, and Faith was no doubt right—some of Pix's fellow committee members would definitely classify it as wickedly self-indulgent.

They talked a bit more, then Faith let out a shriek. "Got to go! Amy's at the pies!"

With a vivid picture of a toddler smeared from head to toe with blueberry pie, gleefully licking her hands, Pix hung up. She was on her own.

She spread the quilt out on the floor and opened her book, *Clues in the Calico* by Barbara Brackman. It had been bedtime reading the last few nights. She leafed through it, then set to work. First, she considered the fabric: lots of small-figured calicos, some shirting material. The abundance of brown-colored triangles indicated a pre-1900 quilt, a time when this was a very popular color. It wasn't used much again until the 1960s and was still favored. She took her scissors and turned the quilt over, snipping a piece of thread, then pulling out a few stitches. With a fine needle, she unraveled it and looked at the strands through Samantha's magnifying glass—Six-ply. That meant post-1860. She was narrowing the date down. Maybe the quilt was genuine after all and she had scored a terrific coup. She teased a bit of the batting from between the top and backing and rubbed the fibers between her fingers.

Her heart sank. It was very cleverly done. The thickness of the batting mimicked what would have been used earlier. But they did not have polyester in the late 1800s. It could be an old top newly quilted. With that optimistic thought, she turned the quilt over and spread it out again. On hands and knees she looked at each and every triangle and at one fabric design in particular. It appealed to her, as it had when she bought a yard of it herself last year.

Pix closed the book and carefully folded up her quilt, laying it across the back of the couch. She stroked the fabric. No question, no question at all: The whole thing was as phony as a three-dollar bill.

The Miller family was quiet at dinner that night. Pix had set the table, rather than eat on the deck, in honor of her husband's presence and also as a nod to the gracious living à la

Valerie Atherton that Samantha continued to espouse. They had cold blueberry soup, a big salad with fresh crabmeat, rice, sweet red peppers, and plenty of lettuce. There were some of Luella Prescott's rolls and ice cream for dessert. Nothing was even remotely connected with Pix's having to turn on her stove.

"This is good, Mom. Did you make it?" Samantha asked, tilting her bowl to get the last of the soup.

Pix was tempted to reply, "No, the fairies left it on my doorstep," but chagrin at her culinary reputation and the soft glow of the candles she'd put on the table tempered her reply.

"Yes, I did." She paused. "Faith gave me the recipe."

Sam and his daughter both laughed and Sam said, "The important thing is that you made it and we're eating it. You have many other talents."

Which were? Pix waited for him to go on. When he didn't, she got up to get the salad. Samantha followed with the soup bowls—the unmatched ones.

"I was at the Atherton's house today. Jim asked me to take some mail over to Valerie that had come to the camp by mistake. You should see it. It's like something from a magazine."

Jim and Valerie, it had come to this.

Oblivious to her mother's lack of interest, Samantha prattled on and on about the house: the two-story fieldstone fireplace—"And Valerie selected every rock herself"—the artwork, the Italian leather couch, apparently large enough to accommodate Michelangelo's *David*—if he could sit, of course. Pix felt increasing giddy as she listened to her daughter repeat the tour Valerie Atherton had given her. Simpler to put it on video.

"Salad's ready. Get the plates, will you?"

Samantha placed the three plain white ironstone plates on the table. One had a tiny chip.

"Get another one, Samantha, and put that one aside, please," Pix said grandly. She'd stick it back in the pile when Samantha was otherwise occupied.

* * *

The Fourth of July was supposed to be sunny and it was. The sky was supposed to be blue and it was. The Millers were supposed to be sitting on lawn chairs brought from home, waiting for the parade to start at 10:00 A.M., and they were. The only thing that felt odd to Pix was that she didn't have any children to remind not to run into the street or get overheated. Samantha was lined up with the camp at the far end of Main Street, waiting to march, and of course her other two were far, far away. Not even a postcard or a call yet. Such was a mother's fate.

Her own mother was on one side, Sam on the other. Various friends and relatives of the Bainbridges, as well as the B and B guests were strung out in a line. Pix waved to Elliot Frazier, who was perched with the other judges in chairs set up on the porch roof of the old Masonic Hall. It was the ultimate viewing platform. Louise was down on the ground next to Ursula.

"I think Elliot agrees to judge every year just so he can go up on the roof," Louise said. "The view must be magnificent."

"Where's Adelaide?" Ursula asked Rebecca, who was coming down the lawn carrying a big pitcher of cold lemonade and some cups. It was already hot and she was greeted enthusiastically.

"She'll be along. She's feeling a little poorly this morning. Must be the humidity."

Pix didn't wonder Adelaide was suffering. With all the extra weight she carried, this weather must be brutal.

John Eggleston appeared, chairless, and plopped down at Pix's feet.

"Am I in your way?"

"Not at all. It's good to see you."

Pix had always liked John, despite his being odd, even for a place that tolerated a wide range of differences in human nature. It wasn't merely his appearance, his shoulder-length wiry red hair and bushy red beard made him unique, especially since there was usually sawdust, and occasionally wood shavings, in both. Nor was it his reluctance to discuss his past life, although Pix knew that as a priest he had served a large church somewhere in the South. She'd also learned something about why he left, but not from him—rather, from Faith. There were lots of people who came to Maine to start fresh, leaving certain doors firmly closed. In his present incarnation as wood sculptor, John's talent was enormous and widely recognized. He received orders for carvings from all over the world and specialized in religious objects. The last time she'd been in his studio, he was working on a huge menorah. "I did not lose my faith," he'd told her once, "just my head."

But what made him unusual was his unpredictability. You never knew what kind of mood he would be in. Pix had seen towering rage and quiet gentleness. The kids on the island flocked to him for advice and it was only with them that he seemed able to maintain his equilibrium. Pix thought of these younger people as his new parish. Arlene had told the Millers many stories about the help John had quietly given to one or another child. Today he seemed mellow and gave Ursula a big smile. She was a favorite.

"What's the theme this year?" he asked her.

"I believe it's storybook characters, but I think it's being interpreted rather loosely in some cases. I know the Fishermen's Wives Association has constructed a lobster boat, and I can't think of a book to go with that."

Ursula was managing to look completely cool in a crisp white blouse and navy skirt. She'd tied a red silk scarf around her neck in honor of the day. A sunshade was clipped to the side of her chair and its resemblance to a parasol lent Mrs. Rowe a timeless air.

"It's a new book, Mother, based on a true story. Two twenty-pound lobsters got caught in a dragger's net and ended up way down in Rhode Island. They were sold to a seafood dealer and eventually went on display in some fish store in Philadelphia. Somewhere along the line, someone named them Bob and Shirley. Anyway, people got upset seeing them in the tank and wanted the owner to set them free. They were flown back up here and released!"

Ursula was laughing. "I want to read that book! Of course, if they'd been caught in a trap, they would have had to be released right away, since they were oversized. But this way, they got to do some traveling."

"It's starting!" someone called out. The crowd along the parade route had grown considerably. The high school band was playing "It's a Grand Old Flag" and another Sanpere Fourth of July was marching along its invariable course. First came the kids on their decorated bikes. Pix remembered how excited she'd been as a child to thread crepe-paper streamers through the spokes of her Schwinn, then ride grandly with the others at the head of the parade. Except for the color scheme and crepe paper, today's bikes looked radically different, although two or three were relics obviously handed down by a previous generation. After the bikes came the school band.

"Isn't that Arlene's boyfriend?" Sam asked.

Pix nodded. Fred had been completely transformed by his drum major's uniform, gold braid dripping from his shoulders and sparkling in the sun as he solemnly raised and lowered the baton. It was a very important position. Fred was class president, too.

"Nice kid," John commented. "I guess he'll be the fourth generation to lobster from Ames Cove, although things have certainly changed since his great-great-grandfather used to go out with nothing more than his traps, buoys, a compass, a watch, and a hank of rope with a weight on it to tell him how deep the water was around the ledges."

"It's simpler now," Sam said, "and safer, yet some of the romance is gone. I think it every time I see the plastic buoys, instead of the old wooden ones they carved, and the new traps."

"The new traps weigh less, same with the buoys, and both don't require the kind of upkeep as the old ones. But I'm with you, aesthetically—maybe even practically. Sonny Prescott told me the other day he's not so sure all the new computers are helping the industry. Makes it too easy, and God knows these waters are being overfished enough." John seemed to be off and running on a favorite topic and Sam was ready to join him, but Pix didn't feel like hearing about the demise of the island's fishing economy today. She wanted to enjoy her lobster at the noon Odd Fellows Lobster Picnic without worrying about the cost of bait and later at the Fish and Fritter Fry she didn't want to think about the growing scarcity of clams. As her friend Faith Fairchild was wont to say, "Denial ain't just a river in Egypt."

"Look at the children. Imagine making all those lobster costumes! Aren't they precious!" The lobster-boat float had to be a major contender for Most Original. The boat itself was a miracle of construction, papier-mâché over chicken wire, and the red-clad children gleefully wriggled about its hull snapping their "claws" at the parade viewers.

Barton's lumberyard sponsored a huge float with Mother Goose figures and the cannery had opted for Alice in Wonderland. Sonny Prescott drew a big round of applause as Robert McCloskey's Burt Dow, Deep-Water Man, dragging his double-ender, *The Tidely-Idley*, complete with rainbow stripes, set on wheels behind him.

"He must be roasting in all that foul-weather gear; they'll probably give him Most Foolish for that alone," Sam commented.

"More lemonade, Pix?" asked Rebecca.

"Yes, thank you, but let me help you." Suddenly, Pix realized she'd been so intent on the parade, she'd forgotten about Rebecca, who was dispensing lemonade and now cookies in the hot sun. "Does Addie feel any better?"

Before Rebecca could answer, Norman Osgood, coming toward them from the house, beat her to it. "She says she's fine.

Just wants to be left in peace—that's a direct quote—and she'll see everybody later." He took the pitcher from Rebecca's hands and started pouring. "I brought your hat," he said, and plunked an old leghorn—her grandmother's?—on Rebecca's head. Handy man to have around, Pix thought. He was beginning to seem more like a member of the family and less like a guest all the time.

"Oh, Norman, thank you," Rebecca gushed. "This is so much better." She turned to Pix. "It's my gardening hat; actually, it was Mother's. The straw makes it light."

Pix was off by one generation, yet, who knew where Rebecca's mother had picked it up. Rebecca's garden was one of the showplaces of the island. She did put in some vegetables, at Addie's insistence, but they were behind the house. In front and on the sides were Rebecca's borders, plus an old-fashioned cutting garden. Her roses never suffered from Japanese beetles and her delphinium, in intense blues and lavenders, had been known to stop traffic during the tourist season.

"Look, it's Samantha! Samantha!" Pix called, and was rewarded with a brief acknowledgment. The campers, singing lustily, dressed in immaculate Maine Sail Camp T-shirts and crisp pine tree green shorts marched in perfect synchrony, stopping opposite the judge's platform to flip their cards to form a perfect replica of Old Glory. They then crouched down so the crowd could see and flipped the cards again, displaying for all the message: HAPPY FUCK OF JULY, SANPERE ISLAND! written on the hull of a sloop with yet another flag for its sail. The prankster had struck again. A gasp went up from the crowd and the judges all stood up simultaneously like puppets on strings, peering down from the roof. The children knew something was wrong, and predictably, Samantha's adorers moved in her direction. Jim, attired like his charges in the camp uniform, except with long pants, was shouting, "Put the cards down! Put the cards down!" Ranks broke and the campers raced for the bank parking lot, parade's end, to the strains of "Anchors Aweigh" as the band played valiantly on.

"I can't believe Duncan would do this. Not after what happened on Monday!"

"Why do you assume Duncan did it?" John asked. Pix was struck by the protective tone in his voice.

"Well," she wavered, "he seems to be very angry at his parents and there have been a number of incidents at the camp, unpleasant things happening."

"Yes, I know," John said impatiently, "but that doesn't necessarily mean it's Duncan. Lots of kids fight with their parents and don't chop the heads off mice."

"Whoever did it, it was a horrible thing to do. They've been working on the parade routine for days!"

The old fire engine, bells ringing and crank-operated siren blaring, was bringing up the rear of the parade. It effectively put an end to any conversation, and Pix, for one, was glad.

She stood up and stretched, trying to recapture the mood of the day. "Anybody going to the children's games? Why don't we walk up and leave the car here," she added to her husband.

"Darling." He kissed her earlobe, "You don't have any children in the games anymore. We don't have to go and watch our progeny dissolve in tears when the egg rolls off the spoon or the balloon breaks when they try to catch it and they get soaking wet. There are other things we can do. Things at home. Grown up things."

Pix blushed. She couldn't help herself. Mother was here.

"I know, sweetheart, but the camp will be there. I'm sure everyone is quite upset, and Samantha may need help."

"All right, we can check in, however I doubt Samantha needs or wants us. She's doing a fine job on her own, and remember, I have to leave straight from the picnic."

Pix remembered. She went to thank Rebecca and say goodbye to everyone. Ursula was going to the picnic with the Fraziers.

"Go home with your husband and help him pack, Pix," her mother said with a very amused look in her eye.

Saying good-bye to Sam had been hard. He would try to get up again for a long weekend, but the likelihood was that they wouldn't see each other until August. She didn't want to think about it. They'd checked in with Samantha at the games and the kids were not as upset as Pix had feared, especially since the judges had awarded them the prize for Best Walking Group. Everyone was studiously ignoring the incident, except for some of the younger campers who were still giggling. Samantha's sidekicks, Susannah and Geoff, were among the worst. They would get in control, glance at each other, and burst out laughing again. Pix watched in amusement herself at her daughter's struggles to be firm with the two. Samantha had told her that their initial homesickness had quickly given way to a friendship based mainly on a mutual love of corny "Knock, Knock" jokes and mischief.

Jim and Valerie were overseeing the three-legged races, laughing just the right amount as they partnered unlikely combinations—fifteen-year-olds with five-year-olds. Everyone seemed to be having fun. Duncan was nowhere in sight. Samantha's camp duties ended after the Odd Fellows Lobster Picnic and she told her mother not to worry, which Pix correctly interpreted as meaning mother would not see daughter until midnight. She was tempted to extend Samantha's curfew—it *was* a holiday—yet the girl was still looking pale, quite unlike her usual hale and hearty self. Pix wondered whether anything was wrong—unrelated to health. Samantha had seemed preoccupied for the last few days. Of course with everything that was happening, this was a reasonable response. But Pix's motherly intuition was picking up more, her antennae were twitching. She'd try to talk to her daughter later. Maybe the two of them would drive to Ellsworth for dinner and a movie tomorrow night. She needed to get her in the car for a good long drive.

Pix spread her blanket out on a choice spot on the library hill overlooking Sanpere Harbor and waited to see who would join her for the fireworks. They were due to start at 9:00 P.M. and it was 8:30 now. You had to arrive early to grab a good place. Her mother had decided to forgo the fireworks this year, as she had for the last two years. The first summer she'd declared she was going to bed early and had seen enough fireworks to last the rest of her life had Pix ready to check her mother into Blue Hill Hospital for a thorough examination. Ursula loved fireworks—or so she had always claimed. "It's the beginning of the end," Pix had told Sam mournfully. "First fireworks, then she'll stop going out of the house altogether." Sam had reacted less dramatically. "Just because your mother doesn't want to sit on the damp ground with hundreds of people chanting *ooh* and *aah* while they get cricks in their necks plus kids running around throwing firecrackers, waving sparklers in everyone's faces, doesn't mean she's cashing in her chips." And of course he'd been right. But Pix didn't like things to change.

Well, her mother had made it both to the Lobster Picnic and the Fish and Fritter Fry. Few Rowes would miss the chance to eat lobster, dripping melted butter and lobster juice all over themselves and their neighbors at the picnic tables the Odd Fellows erected especially for the occasion in the ball field each year. Some of the older people always reminisced about the days when lobster was so cheap and plentiful that they would beg for something else. Ken Layton, Sanpere's resident historian, would remind everyone that around the time of the Civil War, lobsters, regardless of weight, were two cents apiece—and they pulled in bigger lobsters then. It had all happened again this year and Sam had managed to eat two lobsters, since he was going to miss the Fish and Fritter Fry, but Pix had stopped at one to save room.

She lay back on the rough wool blanket, an old army blanket of her father's, and gazed up at the dark sky. You never saw so many stars in Aleford and certainly not even a quarter in Boston! She felt as if she were peering into a big overturned bowl and the milky white constellations were tumbling out above her. The fireworks would have some competition. It was even a full moon.

Just as she was beginning to feel a bit sorry for herself, no kith nor kin by her side, Jill came and sat down.

"Do you have enough room for me?"

"I have enough room for ten or twelve of you," Pix said, sitting up. "Sam had to go back early and Samantha's off with her friends."

"What a day! Business hasn't been this good in years." Jill was clearly excited. "People stuck around after the parade and I even sold the lobster-pot lamp that one of the Sanfords made. It's been sitting in the store for years."

Pix knew the lamp well. She had threatened to give it to Faith more than once and vice versa. Not only had the resourceful craftsman wired the pot buoy but he had attached netting, cork floats, and, as the pièce de résistance, a whole lobster that glowed when the lamp was turned on. The plain white shade had been lavishly painted with yet more bright red crustaceans.

"That's great, especially about the lamp." Pix laughed.

"Don't worry," Jill said, "you can still have one. He's bringing another one up tomorrow! If I'd known, I might have been able to sell them as a pair!"

"I doubt it. When you buy such an object, you like to think it's one of a kind."

"The only thing about being so busy was that I didn't close for lunch or dinner. I missed the picnic and the fry." Jill sounded very disappointed.

"I think I ate enough for both of us," Pix said. "And everyone at the parade and in your shop must have gone down to Granville for both. I've never seen so many people! Mabel

Hamilton told me they went through three hundred pounds of potatoes, a hundred and sixty pounds of fish, twelve gallons of clams, fifty pounds of onions, and goodness knows how much else for the fry!"

"That's wonderful. All the profits go to the scholarship fund for kids from fishing families, which really helps the island. Those women are amazing. Think of all that peeling."

But Pix was not thinking of peeling potatoes or any other vegetables. She was thinking of what Earl would say. Seth Marshall was standing next to them, obviously waiting for an invitation. Jill gave it.

"You said there was room, didn't you, Pix? Why don't you sit down, Seth." The woman actually patted the blanket. It wasn't that Pix disliked Seth. It was just not the way things were supposed to be. And come to think of it, Seth wasn't exactly flavor of the month.

He appeared to realize this and eyed his hostess a bit warily as he sat down.

"You do know we're pouring tomorrow," Seth said.

"Yes, Earl told me this morning. I'll be there at seven. That about right?"

"You don't really need to be, unless of course you want to," Seth added hastily.

With the start in sight, Pix was feeling generous. "Don't worry, I'm not going to hang around all the time. I just want to see the foundation go in and call Faith." It was the least she could do.

"No problem," Seth replied.

Pix sighed. She had the feeling she'd be hearing this phrase often in the weeks to come. And Seth was also sitting awfully close to Jill. In the moonlight, his resemblance to to one of Captain Kidd's mates was even more pronounced. Maybe Jill found him romantic. Pix thought him hirsute—and suspect. She started to think what he could possibly gain from Mitchell Pierce's demise—she'd never been happy with Seth's explanation for being at the site—when a long shadow fell across the blanket.

"May I join your party?" Norman Osgood asked. Pix was delighted. She might have the chance to work in some of her questions, although with Jill and Seth around, it might be hard to steer the conversation toward Mitchell Pierce. Jill had made it plain that she didn't want to hear anything at all about the subject whenever Pix had referred to the event.

"Are Addie and Rebecca watching from their lawn?" Pix asked.

"No, Addie is still not feeling well and she needs Rebecca. I suggested they go over to the Medical Center or at least call a doctor, but Addie won't hear of it."

"According to my mother, neither lady has ever had any contact with the medical profession," Seth said.

"That's amazing." Norman was astonished. "At their ages. Not even tonsils?"

"If they did have them out, the doctor did it in the kitchen, and since that meant a boat trip in Addie's case, it might never have been done."

Norman was still shaking his head when the first rocket went up and they all said "Aah."

A huge golden chrysanthemum shape filled the sky and the petals dropped slowly toward the sea, leaving trails of golden sand. The show was spectacular. The finale was positively orgasmic and the cries of the crowd grew louder and louder as bursts of color and sound exploded overhead. Then suddenly, it was finished and only smoke hung in the air like dense fog.

Norman sighed happily. "That was wonderful. I love fireworks, especially over the water. I was in a boat on the Hudson for the Statue of Liberty display in 1986. Sublime, but this came close."

"Have you lived in New York City all your life?" Pix asked as a way of starting her inquisition.

"No, my dear, I haven't, however you'll have to wait for the tale, which is a lengthy and enthralling one. I told the Bainbridges I'd be back as soon as the show was over, and I am a little concerned about Adelaide. She hasn't been eating, and you know how she enjoys her table."

Something must be wrong indeed, Pix thought. "Please call me if there's anything I can do. Maybe my mother could convince her to call a doctor."

"I doubt that the Almighty Himself could convince Mrs. Bainbridge to do anything she didn't want to do, but if I think otherwise, I'll call. Thank you."

Pix had the peculiar feeling that Norman had become closer to the Bainbridges than she was—two people she'd known all her life.

Seth picked up on it, too. "Who do you think is adopting who?"

"I'm not sure," Pix said. "Maybe it's mutual."

Jill jumped up and said she was exhausted after her busy day. "All I want to do is collapse." Pix said good-bye to them both and slowly began to fold up her blanket as she watched the crowd disperse—as she watched Jill and Seth go into The Blueberry Patch together.

Duncan Cowley was lying on the mattress in his secret cabin, staring up at the rafters. Long-ago inhabitants had carved their names and various epitaphs into the wood. He'd painted over the ones on the walls in disgust at such sentiments as "Maine Sail Camp. I pine for yew." He was disgusted tonight, as well—and angry. What a bunch of pussies. They knew how important the full moon was and still his friends had deserted him for some stupid fireworks.

The cabin glowed with the candles he'd lighted. He looked at his watch. It was still too early. He closed his eyes yet knew he wouldn't sleep. Restless, he got up and went over to the trunk.

He'd just have to do it alone.

It was a long wait until midnight. Pix had been tempted to call Faith but didn't want to bother her. If she was home, she'd be weary after working the holiday. She hadn't had a chance to tell Faith about the blood red sails at the camp. Amy had diverted her mother's attention just as Pix had remembered she hadn't mentioned the incident to Faith. She'd call tomorrow. Telling Faith what was going on was making things clearer, or, if not clearer, making Pix feel better.

She did call Sam, to make sure he'd gotten home all right. She missed him more than ever when she hung up. Finally, she got into bed with the latest issue of *Organic Gardening* and tried to get interested in mulch. When Samantha did get home, just before the stroke of twelve, Pix called out to her daughter to come say good night.

"Weren't the fireworks awesome? The best ever." Samantha had clearly had a good night. Pix felt less worried.

"Truly awesome," she agreed. "Whom were you with?"

"Oh, the usual people—Fred, Arlene, their friends. How about you?" Samantha sounded slightly anxious.

Oh no, Pix thought, don't tell me Samantha is starting to worry about poor old Mom. The way I do, a still-deeper voice whispered.

"We had quite a crowd on the blanket. I was by the library. Jill, the antiques dealer who's at the Bainbridges, some others." Pix didn't care to get more specific. Samantha was hoping to be a junior bridesmaid at Jill and Earl's wedding.

"That's nice, Mother." Her daughter actually patted her hand. "Now I see you've got your usual exciting bedtime reading, so I won't keep you from it a minute longer."

"Don't you patronize me. And where's my kiss!" Pix grabbed Samantha for a hug. Sam had given them all magazine subscriptions last Christmas: *Organic Gardening* renewed for his wife, *Sassy* for his daughter, and the *Atlantic Monthly* for his mother-in-law. There they were in a nutshell.

Pix drifted off to sleep. Maybe this was a new way to categorize people. She'd have to talk about it with Faith—*The New Yorker*, obviously. And who else? Valerie Atherton, *House Beautiful*, without question, and Jim, *Boys' Life*. Jill? Not *Modern Bride*, not yet anyway.

She thought she was still thinking about magazines, then realized that dawn was streaking across the sky outside in shades of burnt orange and magenta. The phone was ringing. She grabbed the receiver in a panic. Nobody called this early. It was just over the edge of night.

"Pix, Pix, are you awake?"

It was Mother.

"What's wrong? What's happened? Are you all right?" Pix ignored the obvious question. Of course she was awake.

"I want you to get over to the Bainbridges as fast as you can. Addie's dead."

Pix was momentarily relieved. "Oh dear, Mother, what sad news, yet I suppose with this weather, her age and all that weight, it—"

"Rebecca found her on the floor of her bedroom with an old quilt Rebecca's never seen before wrapped around her—a red-and-white quilt."

"I'll be there as soon as I can."

Chapter 7

Once when Mark Miller had been about nine years old, he had inveigled his mother into trying out the new tire swing at the school playground. Somehow, Pix had gotten her feet caught in the rim and for what seemed like a giddy, reeling eternity was unable to stop or get off. The world whirled around. She was almost sick and momentarily terrified. As she pulled into the Bainbridge's drive and opened her car door, she felt as if she was back on that swing.

Rebecca opened the door before Pix could knock. The sight of the grief-stricken old lady, pathetic in a worn flannel robe, her gray hair untidily sticking out in clumps around her face, brought Pix soundly back to earth. She put her arms around the woman and hugged her hard. "I'm sure there's some explanation for all this. Maybe Addie had a quilt you didn't know about, felt cold, and got up to get it." It didn't sound especially plausible, but it was something to say.

Rebecca shook her head. Tears had been filling the soft

wrinkles of her cheeks ever since Pix had arrived and obviously for a long time before that.

Pix looked around the kitchen. Ever since she'd driven up, she'd had a sense something was wrong besides what was so obviously wrong, and now she knew what it was: No one was around. Where was Earl? Where were the B and B guests? The Bainbridges had countless relatives all over the island. Where were they?

Rebecca followed her glance. "Your mother thought I should call Earl, but I just couldn't, so she said she'd do it. I couldn't call anybody except her."

Ladies like Rebecca and Adelaide did not get involved with the police. Well, they were involved now. Pix wondered when Rebecca had discovered the body. But first things first. Rebecca appeared to be in shock.

"Let me make you some tea. Are you warm enough?"

It was already stifling hot again, but Rebecca was shivering. Pix took a jacket from one of the pegs inside the door and put it around Rebecca's thin shoulders. From the size, it must have been Addie's.

"Tea." She managed only the one word and Pix took it as a yes. After a moment, Rebecca finished the thought. "I was on my way to make our morning cups when I went in to check on Addie. She's been poorly lately and I wasn't sure she was awake or, if she was, whether she'd want any." Rebecca sighed heavily. Pix could imagine what would have ensued if her sister-in-law had awakened Addie or brought her a cup of unwanted tea. Yet Addie had been Rebecca's main job in life for so many years, now what was she going to do?

"And there she was, all wrapped up like some kind of parcel. I went over and pulled that strange quilt down. It was her feet first. Then I found her head and she wasn't breathing." Rebecca broke down completely and sobbed noisily. What was taking Earl so long? Pix wondered frantically. She wanted to get Rebecca over to Mother's. Ursula had obviously called her daughter first so someone would be there to take care of

Rebecca, but the best thing of all would be to get her with her old friend. Pix debated waking Norman. He had become so close to the two old ladies. She decided to let Earl handle things and put a mug of tea with lots of sugar in Rebecca's hand. The warmth of the liquid seemed to steady her. She stopped crying to take a few sips.

"Why don't you go up and say good-bye? They'll all be here soon and you won't have a chance."

It was exactly what Pix wanted to do, except she hadn't wanted to leave Rebecca, and it wasn't really to say good-bye.

"Are you sure you'll be all right?"

Rebecca nodded and patted Pix on the hand. There seemed to be a lot of that happening lately. "You're a good girl. Now run up quick. I'll be fine here."

Adelaide's bedroom was a large one in the front of the house. Pix darted up the stairs, glad the rag runner was there to muffle her steps. She wasn't sure how many of the rooms were filled and she didn't want anyone waking up right now.

She turned the old glass doorknob slowly—Rebecca had already obscured any prints—and went in. At first, the room looked empty. The big old four-poster that had been in the family for generations had obviously been slept in, but no one was there now.

Then she saw the quilt. Rebecca had covered the body again. It was so close to the bed as to be almost underneath. Dark red patches in a spiral pattern stood out sharply against the white muslin background, which, as she bent down, she realized was not completely white. There was a second spiral, the material white, with the tiniest of red dots. Dots like pin-pricks.

But there was no sign of any blue thread—in a cross or not.

Pix stood up to steel herself. She looked around the room. There was no sign of a struggle. Addie's comb and brush, along with several bottles of scent, Evening in Paris vintage, were arranged neatly on the embroidered dresser scarf gracing the top of the painted Victorian dresser that matched the rest of the furniture in the room. Her quilting frame and the quilt she'd been working on were in one corner, next to a chest filled with sewing supplies. When Pix was a child, Addie had let her play with the button box kept there. Pix suddenly realized she *did* want to say good-bye. She'd been forgetting this was Addie, her friend. She got down close to the body and pulled back the quilt—at the end she'd have expected the feet to be, after Rebecca's description.

It was horrible, and a more lengthy good-bye would have to wait for the funeral service. Rebecca must have assumed Pix wouldn't uncover the body. Adelaide Bainbridge had died in great agony. Her face was contorted in pain and there was a foul smell of vomit. Pix jumped up and headed for the door. This was definitely a police matter.

She almost collided with Earl on the stairs. He put a finger to his lips, so it was obvious he didn't want the whole house roused yet. He also made it plain from a look of annoyance she'd never seen directed at her before that he wasn't pleased with her presence at the scene—or upstairs, at any rate. She passed him quickly.

"What will they do now?" Rebecca asked tremulously as Pix reentered the kitchen.

Pix took the mug for a refill and decided to make herself some tea, as well. Her legs were trembling and it was all she could do to answer Rebecca.

"I'm sure Earl called the state police. They'll probably be here soon. They'll take pictures of everything and ask everyone who's here a lot of questions." She tried to keep her voice steady. It was going to be a bitch was what it was, but she couldn't say that to Rebecca Bainbridge with her companion of many years—and the object of the investigation—lying dead upstairs.

"I hope we can have the funeral tomorrow. Reverend Thompson will do a beautiful service, I know, and Addie liked him so much better than Reverend McClintock, although I never minded him myself. It was the candles on the altar that did it. Addie stopped attending after that until he left." Rebecca was speaking calmly, even affectionately. Pix decided to try to keep her going on the same track. Now was not the time to suggest that a funeral tomorrow was extremely unlikely.

It was the calm before the storm. The state police and the coroner arrived in two cars and the guests were roused. Pix was kept busy making tea and coffee. Norman Osgood seemed to be in almost as bad shape as Rebecca. Besides Norman, there was a couple from Pennsylvania and a young woman from California. The Californian was in the small downstairs room off the parlor the Bainbridges used when they were crowded. She was excited by the drama of it all, she told them breathlessly, bemoaning the fact she was such a heavy sleeper that she had missed everything. Pix was a bit puzzled by this last remark, then realized the woman believed if she had only managed to wake up, she could have caught the perpetrator single-handedly. The perpetrator. The whole thing was insane. Someone going around killing people and then wrapping the bodies in quilts? A lunatic? A serial killer? Who could possibly want to get rid of Adelaide Bainbridge? Pix needed to get to a phone. She had to call Faith.

It was going to be quite a while before she would be able to chat with anyone except the police, she soon realized. First, they questioned Rebecca. Earl thought it might be a good idea for Pix to come with them, since Rebecca was unable to let go of Pix's hand and had sent an imploring look his way. The older woman had been bewildered by all the activity and had sat in a rocker in the kitchen, shrinking away at the arrival of every new stranger.

Adelaide had been sick for a couple of days, she told them, and was no better or worse the night before when she, Rebecca, had looked in on her before going to bed at about ten o'clock. The noise of the fireworks had kept them up a bit later than usual, Rebecca explained, and Addie had been a bit put out. Addie had first felt ill Sunday night after the clambake. They had both assumed it was something she ate, then when it didn't go away, just a touch of summer sickness.

"Summer sickness?" Earl stopped writing for a moment. It was a new one to him.

"You know, the heat and some kind of bug. There's a lot going around." Rebecca seemed surprised that she'd had to explain.

"And she didn't go to the Medical Center?" he asked.

"No, Addie didn't hold much with doctors. Said they'd only send her up to Blue Hill for a lot of expensive tests or tell her to lose some weight, which she already knew she needed to do and wasn't going to." She seemed to be repeating the words verbatim.

"And you didn't hear anything during the night?"

Rebecca shook her head and started to cry. "If only . . ." She couldn't finish. They waited for her to compose herself, which she did, finishing her sentence with "I had" and adding, "There was a bathroom off her room, so even if she was up in the night, I wouldn't have heard her in the back where I am. Sometimes I hear the guests, but after they all came in from the fireworks, I didn't hear a thing until this morning."

"And what was that?"

"Oh, the first birds and a cricket or two. It was still dark. Addie and I have always been early risers."

Pix knew this to be true, but she hadn't known just how early. It made the Rowes, who carried some sort of puritanical gene that made sleeping beyond seven o'clock physically impossible, look like layabouts.

"When you opened the bedroom door, what did you see?"

"Nothing."

"Nothing?" Rebecca was getting flightier as the questions went on, what with birds, crickets, and now this.

"There was no one in the bed or in the room. I thought she was in the bathroom and so I went in to call to her. I didn't want to wake the others, of course. They do like their sleep.

174

Why, we had a couple here last summer who didn't get up until noon every single day!"

Earl tried to lead her back to the matter at hand.

"You didn't see her, so you called to her at the bathroom door?"

"Oh no, I didn't get that far. Why, you couldn't miss seeing that quilt, and I had no idea Addie was in it until I pulled it off and then it was her feet first and I knew right away she had passed, because they were so still." The tears were running down her cheeks again.

"And you're sure this wasn't one of her own quilts or a quilt that's been in the house."

"Oh no, not a red-and-white one. Addie didn't like them. Said they looked too plain. Hers had lots of colors," Rebecca added admiringly.

"But isn't it possible the quilt was one someone else made and it's been in a drawer or trunk for a while?" Pix gave Earl credit. He knew the ways things happened in these entrenched families. She was sure there were things in the trunks in the attic at The Pines that neither she nor Mother had ever laid eyes on.

"No," Rebecca said firmly. "We cleaned out everything last fall and there isn't a trunk or drawer in the house and barn we didn't go through. Got rid of a lot of rubbish. Made some money from it, too. What people will pay for worthless junk never fails to astonish me."

And that appeared to be that. Earl took Rebecca back to the kitchen and left her under Norman's care. Another state police officer was chatting with the guests. Her grandparents had come from the western Pennsylvania town where the couple had lived all their lives and they were having a grand time playing "What A Coincidence!" and "Do You Know?"

After Rebecca was settled, Earl returned and said to Pix, "So your mother called you first?"

"Yes, I think she wanted someone to be with Rebecca as

soon as possible and I'm not that far away. I'd like to take Rebecca over to Mother's when you're finished. It must be very painful for her to be here."

Earl was shaking his head. "First, Rebecca doesn't call me, then your mother waits God knows how long." He was taking it altogether much too personally.

"They're old ladies. Even a policeman they know as well as you is frightening at a time like this. I'm sure nothing was hurt by the slight delay."

The state police officer looked tired.

"We understand you went upstairs after you arrived." His tone indicated it wasn't clear whether she'd be indicted or not.

"Yes. I wanted to say good-bye." Pix had the grace to lower her eyes.

Earl was getting impatient. "Look, we have to talk to the rest of the people. Pix, what do you make of all this business with the quilts? Beats me how there can be any connection between Mitchell Pierce and the Bainbridges. I doubt he ever did any work for them. Addie wouldn't have trusted him."

"I didn't see any mark on this quilt. Of course I wasn't in the room long and most of it is wrapped around the body. But I agree. I can't see a connection. Although"—she was thinking out loud—"Rebecca just said they sold a lot of things from the barn and attic. Maybe they sold some of it to Mitchell, except I don't know what that tells us."

"Good thinking." Earl was scribbling hurriedly.

"Isn't it possible that a woman her age might forget about a quilt or two?" the officer asked. "There seem to be enough quilts in this house to cover half the beds in the county."

Pix had thought of this, too—and Rebecca was definitely absentminded—but the fact that the quilts around both bodies were the same colors had to be more than a coincidence.

"It's possible—maybe even more than possible. I don't see any reason why you shouldn't take her to your mother's after we ask her about who they sold the stuff to. We'll go over there if we need her for anything. And where are you going to be?"

Pix was glad Earl wanted to stay in touch. She was sure he'd tell her if there was a cross on the quilt and maybe what had killed Addie when he knew. It was hard to believe from the expression on the woman's face that the death had been a natural one.

"After I leave mother's, I want to go over to the camp and tell Samantha what has happened. She's probably wondering where I was this morning and I don't want her to hear the news from someone else. Then I'll go home."

"Okay, but no details at the moment. I know you know how to keep your mouth shut."

Pix thought Earl intended this as a compliment. It also meant she was forgiven for going upstairs. The state policeman was not so cordial. He didn't even look up as she left the room.

Rebecca was still in her night things, but it didn't take her long to change. She seemed relieved to be going to Ursula's. Pix had phoned her mother while Rebecca was getting ready to say they were on their way and admonished her to keep quiet about what had happened.

"It's a little late for that, dear. Half the island has seen the police cars in the drive. Gert told me that when she got here an hour ago and of course I had to tell her Addie was dead. I didn't mention the quilt, but it will get out soon enough. These things always do."

So much for shielding Samantha, Pix thought, but she resolved to stop by the camp, anyway.

Driving Rebecca over to Mother's, Pix was struck by the normalcy of the day going on all around her. Vacationing families were beachcombing alongside the causeway. Someone was taking advantage of the influx of holiday visitors and having a yard sale. The UPS delivery truck barreled past in the opposite direction and old Mr. Marshall sat on his front porch overlooking the brightly painted Smurfs, flamingos, posteriors of fat ladies in bloomers, and other tasteful lawn ornaments that he made for sale in his woodworking shop out back.

"Mother says you're to stay as long as you want," Pix said.

"I know, it's very kind of her, but I don't like to be away from my garden. In this weather, I have to water twice a day. Addie always loved my roses." She was breaking down again. "Now I'll be putting them on her grave."

There was a lot Pix wanted to ask Rebecca. She'd said there hadn't been any strangers around this summer—except for the guests, whom of course they didn't know until they'd been there a while—when Earl had asked her. But Pix wanted to ask about Norman and also whether the Bainbridges had sold anything to Mitch. This last, she was able to work in. Rebecca had quieted down again by the time they turned off the main road. The Pines was at the tip of a small peninsula and often there was water on either side of them. The view of Eggemoggin Reach was spectacular at this point. Today it was filled with sailboats, moving slowly. There wasn't much more wind offshore than on. Pix had a sudden desire to be on one, cruising gently toward the Camden Hills, watching the granite shore meander along below the tall evergreens. Sailing always bordered on voyeurism: a house at the end of a private road exposed for all to see, occupants of that special beach no one else had ever discovered forced to share the secret.

Rebecca was looking with an appraising eye out the window at the postmistress's flower garden.

"So, you and Addie had a real turnout last fall. I'm hoping to do the same with Mother at The Pines this summer. We have no idea what's up in the attic."

"Not in the heat, deah," Rebecca said anxiously. You won't make your mother go up there now."

"Of course not. Only if it cools down." And besides, Pix added to herself, I've never been able to *make* Mother do much of anything.

"We may find there are things we want to get rid of, too," she continued, "Who did you get to take yours?" Surely this was subtle and gentle enough. Pix felt a little guilty probing someone in the extremes of grief.

"It was Addie's idea." Typically, Rebecca was answering some other question. "She had a horror that after she was gone, people would be going through her things. You know what it's like at those auctions."

Pix did. She'd been to plenty of estate sales where Grandmother's letters to Grandfather were heaped in a box lot with the odd buttonhook and mismatched cups and saucers, but it had never struck her until now how awful this would be if you'd known the people. She resolved to winnow out her own mementos ruthlessly.

"But Addie wasn't planning on having an auction." Pix tried to keep Rebecca going.

"Mitchell Pierce was interested, you can imagine. Addie met him in the IGA and told him she would sell him some things if he wanted."

It worked.

"What kind of things did he buy?"

"Rubbish. Addie got a good price. Do you know he gave us one hundred dollars for an old yellow painted shelf that's been in the barn ever since I can remember? It was fly-spotted and even had a chip out of the top!"

Pix recalled an article in the paper about the skyrocketing value of country antiques, particularly those with their original paint. It sounded as if the Bainbridges had been well and truly snookered.

Rebecca's next remark confirmed the impression. "He took all the junk. There were some dirty old blanket chests. One even had the top off. And he wasn't even interested in our Wallace Nuttings. I was beginning to think *we* knew more about antiques than he did."

Pix pulled the car alongside the dock into the grassy area

that served as their parking area. "Well, I'm glad to know all this and that you were able to make some money out of it. Did you do anything special with it?"

The last question popped out from she knew not where—and it was none of her business.

Rebecca didn't seem to mind, answering directly for once. "Oh nothing special. Addie just liked having money. 'A heavy purse makes a light heart,' she used to say."

Along with several thousand others, Pix thought.

Ursula and Gert were waiting on the porch and as soon as they saw the car arrive, Gert ran down the steps to help Rebecca into the house. She was in good hands and Pix left soon after. She decided to head straight for the camp, although the fact that she had rushed out of the house so fast that she hadn't brushed her teeth or properly dressed—she'd thrown on a sweatshirt of Sam's with the sleeves cut off and a pair of shorts over her underwear and was glad she'd remembered this much—was beginning to bother her.

It was lunchtime and she walked into the dining room, where she soon spied Samantha pouring milk for a table of younger campers. She caught her eye and Samantha came straight over.

"Oh Mom, it's so sad! What will Rebecca do now? She'll be so lonely."

"Why don't we go outside for a minute. I'm sure it will be all right."

Samantha nodded and they walked toward the waterfront. The sails were sparkling white again—the extra sets. The red paint had turned out to be latex and those were being cleaned, so there was no great loss. Apparently it hadn't been the marine paint they used for the waterlines. Pix was sure that Jim was relieved. It wasn't the money so much as the waste. She put her arm around her daughter's shoulders and they sat down on the dock. Samantha seemed extremely shaken by the news.

"How did you hear?"

"Gert called Dot and she told us. Is it true that the police are there and there's something funny about the way she died?"

"The police are there, but it's not altogether clear whether anything's wrong. She was not in the best shape, avoided getting medical advice, and probably had a million things wrong with her that she didn't know about. You know how short of breath she was. She could barely walk down and back to her own mailbox."

"I know. It's just . . . well, after the other thing, everyone's saying there's a killer loose on the island."

Pix drew her daughter close. "We can't leap to conclusions like that. There doesn't seem to be anything to connect the two events at the moment, except that both people died."

And the quilts. But she didn't want to burden Samantha with that knowledge yet; besides, she was supposed to keep her mouth shut. A word to Samantha meant a word to Arlene, another Prescott, and it would be simpler to print up announcements and drop them from a plane over the entire island.

"It's not only Mrs. Bainbridge. Everything's still going crazy at camp. There was a dead seagull on the dining room porch this morning when the breakfast crew arrived. None of the kids saw it, thank goodness. Arlene said it was horrible."

"But these things happen—probably an injured bird who just happened to end up there."

"With its throat cut?"

Now Pix was shivering. Knives. Too many knives.

"Are you sure?"

"Yes, and Arlene thinks it's Duncan again. I mean after what we saw—" Samantha stopped abruptly.

"After you saw what?" Pix had to know. This was obviously what Samantha had been keeping from her.

"Mom, I promise I'll tell you, but I can't now. I have to get back. The kids are very jumpy. They swear there's a ghost around, although I think that's some of the older campers trying to scare the little ones."

"How are your two imps?"

"Not exactly happy campers. Kids are so weird, Mom. One minute everything is fine, the next they're imagining all sorts of gruesome things, especially these two. I think maybe they *are* too young to be here. Anyway, all this is going to affect them for a long time. Susannah leaps a foot in the air if someone startles her, and she and Geoff are always off by themselves. At the moment they're feeding each other's fears. I can't even get them to tell their stupid jokes."

Kids are so weird. The understatement echoed through the long tunnel of maternal memory. You never know, until you're there, Pix thought. Samantha was arriving sooner than her mother had.

"It's Parents' Weekend soon, isn't it? Maybe we should bring them to our house for a day, since they won't have visitors."

"That would be really great, Mom. They need to be with the dogs."

Pix understood. There was nothing more therapeutic than a good roll in the grass with an overly affectionate golden retriever.

"I've got to go, and I'm sure you want to get home and change." Samantha clearly did not approve of her mother's choice of outfits.

"Honey, I was in a rush. I just grabbed what was on the chair."

"That's all right. I understand." To avoid more hand patting, Pix grasped her daughter's paw firmly in her own and pulled her to her feet. They walked back toward the car together and were saying good-bye when, as luck would have it, Valerie came out of the director's office, a vision in a short Adrienne Vittadini brightly patterned sheath with a matching scarf tied carelessly around a broad-brimmed chapeau.

"Pix! I just heard about Adelaide Bainbridge. Come over to the house and tell me what happened. What a tragedy!"

Pix hesitated. She was curious about the fabled abode, but she wasn't really dressed, or even combed sufficiently, and she wanted to get home to call Faith. She hadn't reckoned on Samantha's reaction. Samantha clearly regarded an invitation to the Atherton's "Million Dollar Mansion" as a command performance for those fortunate enough to be asked. She actually poked her mother in the back.

"Well, perhaps for a minute. I have to get home. Mother may be calling. Rebecca is over at her house."

Valerie smiled brightly. "You come, too, Samantha, unless you are needed here."

Crestfallen, Samantha admitted she should be inside helping with lunch.

"Another time." Valerie turned to Pix and said just loud enough for Samantha to hear and swoon, "You have the most precious thing for a daughter I ever did see." Valerie occasionally lapsed into the Kappa Kappa Gammanese expressions of her college and deb days in the real South.

"Thank you. We like her," Pix replied, then realized it sounded a little snippy and added, "We're going to miss her terribly when she goes off to college."

"You're so lucky having a daughter," Valerie commented wistfully as they went down the path connecting the Atherton's house to the camp. "But then, you have sons, too." Her voice was full of commiseration. Pix was tempted to say they had never put them through the kind of hell Duncan seemed to be inflicting on his parents, yet it seemed inappropriate to gloat, and Danny was still young. Pix was loath to make any predictions—or say anything out loud—that might jinx things.

Valerie led her into the huge living room with teak-paneled walls soaring to a cathedral ceiling. The shape of the room—it swept forward, following the lines of the bluff on which it was

183

situated—and all the wood made Pix feel as if she was in a boat, a very spectacular boat, and that must have been the architect's intent. She admitted inwardly that she was indeed envious. The house *was* gorgeous. Every plate-glass window framed a spectacular view. One set looked straight out to sea, another to the cove. Jim's boats, including the souped-up lobster boat he'd recently purchased, were picturesquely moored there. It looked like July on a Maine-coast calendar. The fireplace was as stunning as Samantha had described. Pix noticed a large photo on the mantel of a handsome smiling man with his arm around a much younger, and happier, Duncan. Valerie followed her gaze. "My first husband, Bernard Cowley. Duncan looks a bit like his father. I wish he could act like him. Buddy was a saint. I don't think I'll ever stop missing that man. Of course," she added quickly, "Jim is just about the nicest thing on two feet I've ever met, but you never get over something like this, and Jim understands."

"It must have been a terrible time for you and your son."

"It was—and if I hadn't met Jim, I don't know how I would have survived. Coming here was just what I needed and I know Duncan will settle down." Valerie did seem genuinely happy, more so than Pix had noted recently. Maybe things were going better with her son. Certainly it would be hard to be depressed in these surroundings. Most of the furniture in this room was modern, with a few well-chosen antiques: a softly burnished cherry card table, a child's Shaker chair, and an enormous grandfather clock, the sun and the moon slowly changing places above a stately schooner on the face. Scattered about in what Pix was sure was not a haphazard fashion were old brass navigational devices, a collection of Battersea enameled boxes, and other conversation pieces.

"Now tell me about poor Adelaide while I make coffee. I think there are two of those devastating muffins from that bakery in Blue Hill left. I swear Jim and Duncan devour whatever goodies I bring into this house like a swarm of locusts."

Pix begged off. The locusts could feast on her devastating

muffin. She really had to get home, so she quickly gave a brief account of Adelaide's death.

"I didn't actually know them well, but Jim and his family had," Valerie said. "Poor old lady. She did kind of let herself go, if you know what I mean."

Pix looked at the svelte figure gracefully draped across the leather couch before her and did indeed. Valerie Cowley Atherton would never let herself go. Pix saw her twenty years hence with face as smooth as plastic surgery could make it, body as trim as aerobics and a diet of lettuce and Perrier would supply.

She left and promised to return for a full tour of the house. "It's beautiful, Valerie, and everything you've done is perfect."

"Thank you." Her hostess flashed a well-satisfied smile. "I've always wanted to live in a modern house. Buddy's family, bless their hearts, would have a conniption over this place. The Cowleys are an old family and they never let anyone forget it. You can't imagine the inconvenience they put up with in order to stay authentic!"

Pix laughed. She had often heard Faith on the same subject with regard to New Englanders. She hoped the heat was breaking in Aleford, although it wasn't here. She still felt guilty about the question of air conditioning at the parsonage.

"I can imagine. I'm afraid in my family, we may tend in this direction ourselves. Thank you for showing me the house. I'll take a rain check on the coffee."

"Bring Sam. We'll make it something else and all go into the hot tub," Valerie called after her. Pix waved good-bye. You'd have to put a gun to Sam's head to get him to disport in that kind of revelry.

A hot tub sounded particularly unappetizing at the moment. A cold shower would be more like it. The temperature was up over ninety again. No one could remember such a long stretch of searing hot days.

But everything, including bodily comfort, took a backseat

to her most important task; she was rewarded by Faith's an-swer on the second ring. What was more, Ben was at a friend's house and Amy was napping.

Faith was shocked at the news. "I know who Addie Bain-bridge is. She's the fat one who runs the bed-and-breakfast and makes those incredible quilts, right? Her sister—what's her name again? She lives with her."

"Yes, except it's her sister-in-law. She's a Bainbridge, too, Rebecca. They've lived together for over thirty years."

"Oh, the poor thing. What will she do now?"

"Her main worry at the moment, besides getting Adelaide buried, is keeping her garden watered, so I think she'll be all right. She's got something to focus on. Then, too, she may not really be taking it all in. Rebecca's always been a bit scat-terbrained and it's become more pronounced recently."

"Totally gaga?"

"I wouldn't go that far, definitely bordering on eccentricity though."

"Well, so are most of the people I know, including you. There's nothing wrong with that, but what is going on up there? I think I'll pack up the kids and come this weekend. There has to be a connection between the two quilts. Let me know as soon as you find out whether there's a mark on the latest one and what killed her."

"I will—and it would be lovely to have you here." At least Pix thought it would be, wouldn't it? A tiny voice was whis-pering that these were *her* murders, but she valiantly ignored it.

"The only problem is, we promised to go to Tom's sister's for a big family picnic, since everyone couldn't get together on the Fourth, and you know how they are about these things."

Pix did know, having listened to Faith lo these many years. Fairchild gatherings were sacrosanct, as well as invariable. They were a family that celebrated—birthdays, major holi-days, and then their own specific South Shore rituals: First

Spring Sunday Raft Races on the North River, All-Family Autumn Touch-Football Saturday, and so forth. Faith's own family had tended toward less strenuous fetes, such as taking the children to the tree at the Metropolitan Museum of Art or shopping for Easter dresses at Altman's, followed by lunch in the store's Charleston Gardens restaurant. Pix wasn't sure what her own family did all those years, because they were much too busy.

"Maybe you can come up the following weekend." Things should certainly be sewn up by then, which brought her back to the quilts.

"I told you the quilt I bought is a fake, right?"

"No, but I know you've suspected as much. Have you heard about the one found with Mitchell Pierce's body?"

"No, Earl hasn't said anything. They'll probably send the one around Addie to Augusta for testing, too. By the way, the Bainbridges sold Mitch a lot of antiques, things they thought were worthless, although I'm sure they were anything but. Maybe Addie discovered that she had been swindled, but that would mean she'd be angry at Mitch, not somebody at her. But she might have had a reason for wanting him dead, except I can't imagine her killing him. In fact, it would have been a physical impossibility for her to transport his body, let alone dispose of him in the first place."

"Could the sister-in-law have helped?"

Pix was stunned. "Rebecca! God, no. I don't think she even swats flies."

"I think what you need to do is sit down and make some of your lists. You're so good at that. You know the kind they do in all those British detective stories. There's got to be some link you're missing."

Pix had been thinking all morning that she hadn't exactly been bringing the organizational skills that propelled her to the fore of every cause in Aleford to bear on this situation. It wasn't just making some lists, although that might help. She planned to sit her daughter down as soon as she came home and find out what she knew. And the same with Mother. It wasn't going to be easy, but somebody had to do it.

"I'm going antiquing again," she told Faith, full of plans and energy now. "Maybe Jill will come along. I want to find out if there are any more of those quilts around. Perhaps the police can trace them. We'll go up toward Bar Harbor—and Sullivan."

"That's where Mitch was living, right?"

"Yes. Maybe I should talk to his landlady. I could pretend I was looking for a place for a friend to stay."

Pix was learning fast, Faith realized with a twinge. If she wanted to be any part of this, she'd have to get up to Sanpere as soon as possible. Damn the Fairchild fun and games, she thought guiltily.

Looking out the window over her struggling squash vines to the imperturbable line of firs beyond, Pix wished life on Sanpere would return to normal. She told Faith about the paint on the sails, adding, "And don't say a word about red sails in the sunset."

"It never crossed my mind," Faith lied. "It's more red and white, though."

Pix hadn't thought of that. Things were becoming more complicated by the minute.

Amy was waking up. Faith heard soft little coos that would soon become bellows of rage. She told Pix, who remembered the scenario all too well.

"Call me as soon as you find out anything more."

"I will," Pix promised. "Oh, one last thing." She couldn't hear the baby yet, so Faith had a few seconds more. "Jill and Earl have apparently split up and Jill has been going around with Seth Marshall."

"That's a surprise. Seth is all right, but he's not what I would call husband material. Who left whom?"

"Jill, according to Earl, and he's as puzzled about it as I am. Jill is very touchy this summer. I haven't felt that I could ask her what's going on."

"*Definitely* invite her to go on your little jaunt."

Pix laughed and suddenly perversely wished Faith were on Sanpere.

"Talk to you soon."

"Bye-bye."

As soon as she put the phone back in the cradle—it was an old black dial phone that no one wanted replaced—she remembered she had completely forgotten to tell Faith that Seth had planned to pour the foundation today. Maybe she'd go over there with Samantha before dinner. At the moment, she wanted to get to work. She felt more like her old self now that she had a plan. The tire swing was receding into past memory.

She couldn't talk to Mother so long as Rebecca was there, but she should call to check in. Gert answered. Her mother was napping and Rebecca was sleeping, too. Earl had sent Dr. Harvey from the Medical Center over and he had given her a mild tranquilizer. The police had roped off the Bainbridge's house and the guests had moved on, leaving addresses, except for Norman, who was now staying at the inn. Norman. It occurred to Pix that he probably would have given his eyeteeth for some of the rubbish the Bainbridges had disposed of so blithely last fall. She wondered why Addie had gotten it into her mind to clear things out then—intimations of mortality, or simply wanting a heavier purse? And for what? She made quite a bit of money with her quilts and it wasn't as if she was a lavish spender. If she'd traveled as far as Ellsworth in the last ten years, Pix would be surprised, so Paris or cruises to the Caribbean were not the incentive.

The last thing Gert told her was that Addie's body had been taken away for the autopsy and the police hoped to be able to release it for a funeral by Saturday or Monday at the latest.

It was horrible to think about. Pix went into the kitchen and made herself a tuna-fish sandwich, taking the time to toast the bread. She grabbed a pad of paper, poured some milk, and went out on the deck to get to work.

Samantha came home just as she got to the fourth heading

for the columns she'd neatly folded: "Suspects." The others were "Who Benefits?"; "Causes of Death"; and "Quilts."

"I'm out here on the deck," Pix called. "Come join me. There's tuna fish if you want a sandwich."

Samantha came directly.

"Well, wasn't it fabulous?"

Pix was tempted to tease her daughter and ask what was fabulous, but obviously the subject was too important.

"*Fabulous* is exactly the right word," she told her, "and I was even a little jealous. The view is spectacular and the house is in exactly the right spot."

" 'A little jealous,' the view! Oh, Mother, what about the fireplace, the furniture, and that rug! Valerie had it woven to order when she couldn't find one the right size with the colors she wanted."

Pix remembered the rug. It went from dark to light blue, with every possibility in between. It looked like the sea and the sky in every conceivable light. But what she wanted to do now was talk to her daughter about what she wasn't telling dear old Mom, not discuss Grecian versus Roman shades or any of the other fine points of interior decorating. She decided to be direct; besides, she couldn't think of another way.

"You started to say something about Duncan at the camp and told me you'd explain later. It's later now."

Samantha saw the look in her mother's eye and knew she meant business. Any attempt at avoidance would mean being nagged for days. It was best to get it over with. She plopped down in one of the canvas sling chairs from the fifties that her grandmother had happily donated and told her mother everything about Duncan, starting with the conversation in the woods during the clambake.

Pix was aghast. "The boy is clearly disturbed. He needs help. We have got to tell his parents."

"Mom, Arlene says they've taken him to a million shrinks. I'm sure they know he's got problems. I mean, look at the way he treats them."

"But I doubt they're aware of his 'club.' " Pix was torn. She really didn't know what to do. Jim Atherton's response had been so harsh. She hated to think she might be responsible for the boy's being struck again—or sent to the military school, which appeared to be the next course of action. And she really wasn't acquainted well enough with Valerie to gauge her reaction. John Eggelston had come to Duncan's defense. Maybe the best thing would be to talk to him.

Samantha was speaking. "It's like I feel sorry for him and hate him at the same time. I don't want to get him in trouble, but maybe you're right."

"Don't say *like*," Pix said automatically. "Why don't I tell all this to John? He knows Duncan and he also seems to know a lot about teenagers."

Samantha brightened. "That's a great idea. Maybe he can talk to all three of them together. He's done that for some other kids who are having problems at home here."

Duncan Cowley disposed of, Samantha wanted an update on what was going on at the Bainbridges. Pix gave her the PG-13 version and soon Samantha headed for her room to write letters to Aleford friends. There was a lot to tell.

Pix went to the phone to call John. She was more disturbed about Duncan's behavior than she wanted Samantha to know and the sooner someone talked to the Athertons, the better. As she dialed, she realized Duncan had to be added to the list of suspects. He was clearly drug-involved and might have graduated from mice and poultry to larger game.

John answered immediately. He sounded cheerful.

"Hello, Pix. I just sent off a large piece to a congregation in Australia."

"Congratulations."

"And I accept them. I've been working on this altarpiece for several months. Now, what can I do for you?" John was not one for idle chitchat.

He was completely quiet as Pix related what Samantha had told her.

"And I don't know whether I should talk to Valerie and Jim, try to talk with the boy first, or what. You know him better than we do and I thought you'd have an idea about what would be best to do."

"Poor Duncan. He has never been allowed to grieve properly for his father. He feels responsible, you know. They were caught in a terrific storm and had all been taking turns at the helm—or rather, Bernard and Valerie were. Duncan was sitting up with his father to help him stay awake while his mother got some rest. The child became exhausted himself and agreed when his mother suggested he sleep for a while. That's when Bernard Cowley was washed overboard."

"How horrible!"

"I knew Duncan was fascinated with certain aspects of the occult. It's a way to make himself feel powerful, but I didn't think it had gone this far."

"The whole thing is terribly sad. I'm sure his parents will understand."

"Maybe and maybe not. Jim is a pretty straight arrow and I'm sure any suggestion of witchcraft will have him on the phone to that school he's always threatening Duncan with. Not that I blame Jim. He walked into a pretty hopeless situation. There was no way Duncan would ever have accepted him."

"But we can't simply ignore this and hope it goes away. Some night, one of the kids is going to get hurt or worse up in the quarry."

"I agree. I'm not suggesting we ignore the matter. Let me handle it. I'll talk to Valerie in private without getting too specific. This worked after Duncan took her car earlier in the summer. The main thing I'll do is start seeing more of Duncan. I've been so involved in this commission that I haven't had time for him these last months. He likes to come to the workshop. I'll go see if I can round him up right now. I have the feeling it won't take much to start him talking. We've talked a great deal about the supernatural before. I've lent him some books, so he won't think it odd if I bring it up."

Pix felt relieved, although she would have thought the Hardy Boys or, since the boy was interested in other worlds, perhaps Tolkien, more appropriate for John to have suggested.

"Thank you so much, John. And let me know how things go."

"Thank you for telling me." He'd been speaking in a serious tone of voice and now it took on almost a warning note. "You've had a pretty full plate and I'm sure it hasn't been pleasant. And then there's this business with the Bainbridges. I hope you're not getting too involved."

"Involved?"

"Like that friend of yours—Faith. There are things about the island better left alone. I know you summer people think it's paradise, but paradise had a dark side, too, remember."

Pix was stung by his remark: "summer people." She'd thought they were better friends, and even his closing words did not mollify her.

"I just don't want anything to happen to you. I care about all the Millers deeply. You know that. Bow out, Pix. Bow out."

"Don't worry. Nothing is going to happen. I'll let Samantha know about what we're doing and if either of us finds out anything more, we'll let you know."

She hung up feeling much less satisfied than she had earlier in the conversation. She walked back out to the deck and picked up her list. How well did she know John, anyway? Loaning books about the occult and supernatural to Duncan? John was a very colorful, at times charismatic figure. He had a great deal of influence over the youth of the island, most especially Duncan Cowley, it seemed. Maybe too much? And what kind was it exactly? Mitchell Pierce had stayed with

John. She had to find out why Mitch left. She put it on the "To Do" list.

With Samantha occupied with her own writing tasks, Pix got out the folded paper and started to fill in the columns. Under "Suspects," she decided to list everyone, no matter how far-fetched, starting with Mitchell's death. There weren't many. Duncan Cowley, the knife wounds were suggestive of some sort of ritual slaying. Seth Marshall, just because he had access to the spot and could pour the foundation when he pleased. John Eggleston, because he might have nurtured some sort of grudge since Mitchell had lived with him or because Mitchell had found something out about John during that time. Norman Osgood. These *were* far-fetched, but she had to put something down. Osgood might have had some kind of falling-out with Mitch over antiques. Last, she wrote down Sonny Prescott's suggestion: unknown partners in crime. Of course, others could be known ones, yet as she jotted down this final possibility, she was forced to admit it made the most sense.

Now Adelaide—If, in fact, she had been murdered. The only thing pointing toward foul play was the quilt. She went over to the "Who Benefits?" column. Adelaide may have left at least part of her estate to her nieces and nephews. Seth Marshall was a nephew. She wrote him down. Who else? Norman Osgood again? Although if he was hoping to do a book with her, that wouldn't make sense. But he was there. Maybe Addie had found out something about him. She wasn't known for her reticence. Pix considered the other bed-and-breakfast guests and reluctantly ruled them out. Unless they were seriously deranged people, which the police were no doubt checking, she couldn't come up with any motives.

She listed Seth under "Who Benefits?" with the initials A.B. after his name. She couldn't think of any way he would benefit from Mitch's death, unless Mitch was blackmailing him. Mitch a blackmailer: It was a thought. He had been charming and eminently likable, but if desperate for money, he might have done anything. He certainly hadn't shied away from other crimes. Except he hadn't been desperate for money. He'd had a huge bank account and it was the result of what? As Jill suggested he might have made a killing—strike that phrase—a huge profit from the sale of something. Then again, he might also have been blackmailing someone, or more than one person. Pix sighed. She wasn't getting anyplace. Maybe you had to be in a large English country house staring out the window at the hedgerows. But at least she had a list. She'd get Mother to find out about Addie's will. Rebecca surely must know.

"Causes of Death." Mitch was stabbed and Addie's was unknown at the moment. She'd like to call Earl, yet she had a feeling she'd do better to wait. It was certainly too soon to know anything and she thought he probably wouldn't take kindly to being hounded right now. She remembered the look on Adelaide's face and the stench. The woman had obviously been violently sick and the police might have found further signs in the bathroom—all of which pointed to poison of some kind. Addie had been sick for days and Pix recalled the graphic account of her symptoms. What did one have to do with the other? Was her illness merely a coincidence? Poison. This made absolutely no sense. Things like this didn't happen on Sanpere.

Then there were the quilts, two red-and-white quilts. Three quilts, including Pix's purchase with the disappearing mark. She *would* call Earl later to find out whether there was a cross on Adelaide's. It would be impossible to sleep otherwise. She also wrote down *sails*. As Faith had pointed out, they were red and white, too. Sails were made of cloth, so were quilts. Quilts and sails. Sails and quilts. Mitch had been wrapped in Drunkard's Path. Could there be some connection between the name of the quilt pattern on Addie's and her death? Pix closed her eyes and concentrated on remembering the spirals she'd seen that morning. She drew a square at the bottom of the page and filled it in as best she remembered: two pinwheel shapes, the tiny dotted fabric alternating with the red. She'd go through her quilt pattern books after supper and try to find the name.

It wasn't much of a list, not up to her usual standards. But it was a beginning. She went to the bottom of the stairs and called to Samantha to come for a walk with the dogs. They all needed to get out.

For once, Samantha was staying home. After an early supper of toasted cheese sandwiches and tomato soup, one of the Miller family's favorite repasts, the phone rang. During the course of a lengthy conversation, Pix heard Samantha tell Arlene she was tired and ask her how about the following night. The phone rang again as Pix was getting out her quilting books. It was Ursula. Rebecca had agreed to stay the night, since Earl had promised to water the garden. So that's where he was, Pix thought. She'd been trying to reach him.

She started to ask her mother about Adelaide's will and how big the estate might be, but Ursula cut her off, obliquely indicating Rebecca had attached herself limpetlike and was at Mrs. Rowe's side every waking moment.

"I understand completely. Poor Rebecca! I know you can't say anything, but could you find out if she has any further thoughts about where that quilt might have come from? And perhaps see if she knows what the provisions of Adelaide's will are?"

Even though her mother would not be able to comment at length, Pix had expected a note of disapprobation to sound in her reply—Pix was prying—but Ursula said in an even tone, "Good idea, dear. I'll do that."

It amounted to approval. Addie's death had changed things and it might just be that Mother was on the trail, as well.

It was much too hot for a fire in the fireplace, but they sat in front of it, anyway, Pix with her quilting books and Samantha curled up on the couch with E. B. White. She was rereading *Charlotte's Web*, as she did every summer.

Charlotte had finished saving Wilbur's life the first time and Samantha stood up and stretched. She really was tired, yet that was not why she'd put Arlene off until tomorrow. Fred wanted to go back to Duncan's and check out the trunk. He was convinced Duncan was responsible for what was going on at the camp, including the dead gull. Arlene also hinted that Fred thought Duncan might be responsible for the other bizarre things happening on the island. "Fred's good and steamed," she'd told Samantha. Samantha was afraid he might be right and she, too, thought they'd better look around the cabin some more, but she just couldn't handle it after everything that had happened today. She'd known the Bainbridges all her life and Addie had always been nice to her. At the moment, all Samantha wanted to do was read about Charlotte, Wilbur, and Fern until she fell obliviously asleep.

Pix found the pattern shortly after midnight. It had become an obsession. Samantha had long since gone to bed. Pix, though, remained wide awake and when the design jumped off the page at her, she was jolted into even-greater consciousness. Her mother's earlier words regarding Mitchell Pierce's killer came immediately to mind. Whoever was responsible was not simply evil, but nasty.

The name of the pattern was End of Day.

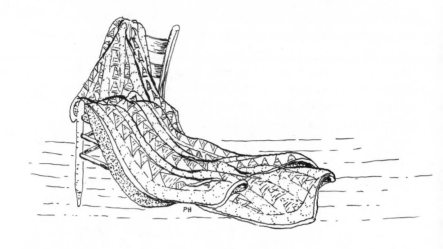

Chapter 8

The next morning Samantha left for work after a big breakfast of sour-cream pancakes and fresh strawberries. Pix had picked the first ones in the garden, thankful the heat hadn't ruined what looked to be a bumper crop.

As soon as her daughter was out the door, Pix piled the dishes in the sink and went to the phone. As she dialed, it struck her that she was spending an inordinate amount of time on this instrument—especially for Sanpere. Other summers when it did ring, it was usually for one of the kids, and she seldom made many calls herself.

Earl was in his office, as she had hoped. He'd recovered from whatever feelings of pique her actions at the Bainbridge's had engendered and said he didn't see any harm in telling her no cross of any color had been found on the quilt surrounding the corpse.

"Now whether the quilt's an old one or not, I can't tell you, because I don't know. The other one wasn't, though."

Pix was grateful for this confirmation of her suspicions.

"I thought I might do some more antiquing," she told him. "Maybe head up toward Bar Harbor. I'm hoping Jill will come along." Pix had thought of asking Valerie, too, but decided that a third person would provide a further excuse for Jill to avoid talking about her love life.

"Well, say hi from me, that is if she remembers who I am."

Pix returned to what was obviously a more cheerful topic. "Do you have the results of the autopsy yet?"

"So far, all I've heard is heart failure."

"Then it may not involve any foul play?"

Pix was finding comfort in phrases like this. The alternatives were overly specific.

"Not necessarily. Could be something was given to her to cause the heart attack. But could also be she was due."

Pix hung up, feeling better than she had for days. No mark on the quilt and the possibility that death was from natural causes. Addie's weight and eating habits—she disgustedly referred to salads and the like as "rabbit food"—definitely put her at risk. And as for the quilt, it was no doubt one Rebecca had simply forgotten about.

Next she called Jill.

"Oh Pix, I *would* like to go. It's so horrible about Addie. I can't think about anything else, and if I don't get out of the shop today, I think I'll go insane."

Pix was surprised at the intensity of Jill's reaction. She hadn't realized the two women were so close. Maybe Jill was some kind of niece, too.

"But I don't have anybody to cover for me. I can't afford to just close up. There are still so many tourists in town. Would you mind waiting while I try to find someone?"

"Of course not. Too bad Samantha's working at Maine Sail, but she does get through after lunch. We could go then if you don't find anyone sooner."

"That would be great. I'll call you in an hour if not before to let you know what's happening."

Pix was not in the mood to sit by the phone. "If you don't get an answer here, call me at The Pines. I want to see how Rebecca is." And maybe get a few words with Mother, she added to herself. She also wanted to drive out to the Point on the way and inspect the foundation. There hadn't been any time yesterday to make sure Seth was doing as he had promised.

Seth and his crew were taking a break when Pix drove up. Nobody jumped up to greet her, but she didn't care. The sight before her eyes was greeting enough. The foundation and basement floor for the Fairchild's house had been poured and the tart smell of fresh concrete filled the air. It was more fragrant to Pix than any number Chanel.

Seth did come over to her as she walked the perimeter of the house, inspecting the job intently.

"It'll be smooth as a baby's bottom. Don't worry," he said.

"I'm not. It looks fine." Pix believed in credit where credit was due.

"We're working on the stairs to the beach today. If the weather holds, we should be able to strip the forms and start framing the floor by Thursday, maybe even Wednesday. The wood's already cut and Barton's is holding everything for me—nice number-two Douglas fir."

Pix nodded. Maybe this wasn't going to be Mr. Blandings' dream house after all. Maybe Seth would come through.

"The family is some upset about Aunt Addie. Don't understand why Earl had to get all hot and bothered. There was no need to get Augusta involved. Gorry, we'll be lucky to have the funeral by Labor Day." Seth sounded extremely annoyed.

Pix's recent well-being vanished.

"He *had* to call the state police. Rebecca never saw the quilt before—and it was a red-and-white one, just like the one here." She had been consciously trying not to recall what had recently lain beneath the surface of the ground now covered by the gray concrete.

"Rebecca doesn't know the color of the blanket on her

own bed once she's out of it. No, Earl had no right to ship Addie off for them to cut up. He's been watching too much TV. This is Sanpere, not New York City."

Seth had bent down and picked up a stick. He was poking the ground ferociously with it as they walked. Pix made sure to keep well to one side.

She could understand why Adelaide Bainbridge's relatives might be upset, but surely they wanted to find out what had happened. She made a mental note to ask Ursula what she'd heard about their reactions through the island grapevine.

Pix tactfully changed the subject. "It's going to be lonely for Rebecca in the house now, but I suppose she'll keep running the bed-and-breakfast."

"Well, she may not be there for long," Seth stopped stirring up the dust with the stick and gave it one final shove, driving it into the soil. "She has life tenancy under Addie's will, unless she's found unable to be left on her own, and that seems pretty certain."

"Where will she go and who will get the house then?" If you didn't ask, you didn't find out.

Seth did not seem too concerned about Rebecca's future and Pix realized that of course Addie was the relation and Rebecca merely a distant in-law to some one of Seth's parents or grandparents.

"Probably a nursing home on the mainland or maybe one of the Bainbridges in Granville will have her. The house will be sold and the whole kit and caboodle gets divided in equal shares."

Given what Addie's quilts sold for plus the value of the lovely old house and barn, it would add up to quite a caboodle, Pix figured.

She had the answer to one question at least.

Seth Marshall, unaware that his name had just been starred under two columns, called to his crew to get back to work.

"I'd love to chat with you some more, but I wouldn't want you to think we were wasting time." He smiled warmly to soften his sarcasm. It almost worked. He really was attractive, particularly at the moment, stripped to the waist because of the heat, his skin glistening slightly with sweat. Maybe Jill was tired of good old Earl and wanted a fling with bad old Seth.

"I have to get going, anyway," she said. "If Jill can find someone to cover the store, we're going to drive up to Bar Harbor." She decided not to get too specific about what she intended to do. She needn't have bothered to be circumspect.

"Yup, so I hear. Going antiquing, right?"

Pix's mouth dropped. He laughed. "Heard it on the CB just before you drove up. Jill's got one of the Ames kids. I heard her asking her dad if she could do it."

"There are no secrets on this island," Pix remarked.

"Oh, I don't know about that," Seth said as he walked toward his crew, the sound of their hammers ricocheting in the still air. "I'd say there were plenty."

Doris Ames was sitting at the register reading the latest issue of the *National Inquirer*, and from the speed at which she was chewing her gum, Pix suspected the story was more racy than some of the fare: MOM SELLS KIDNEY TO BUY FURNITURE or SPACE ALIEN BABY FOUND ON MOUNT EVEREST MEDICAL DR. SAYS NOT HUMAN.

"Oh, hi, Mrs. Miller. Jill has been trying to get a hold of you. She's upstairs."

"I'll go on up, then. How's everything with you this summer?"

"I can't complain. Making good money and don't have to work days." Pix remembered that one of the Ames girls was waitressing at the inn, which was only open for dinner, and it must be Doris.

"I hear the food is even better than last year."

Doris made a face. "It's too fancy for me. I like to recognize what's on my plate. I eat at home before I start."

Pix laughed. "Well, maybe some of it is an acquired taste." She decided to take Ursula and Samantha to the inn soon, all three of them having acquired a taste for any and all good food.

Jill had a snug little apartment over the store. Pix walked up the outside stairs and knocked at the door. Hearing no reply, she pushed it open, stepping inside. She could hear water running and Jill had obviously decided to take a quick shower while waiting for Pix.

"Jill," she called loudly, not wanting to startle her when she emerged, "It's me, Pix."

"Oh great," Jill replied above the noise of the spray. "I'll be out in a minute. I just had to cool off."

The apartment was divided into two large rooms plus bath. The front room was Jill's bedroom and the larger back room served as living room, dining room, kitchen, and storage for the overflow from the store. There were several large boxes in the corner by the door, but this wasn't what caught Pix's eye. She was struck by the change in the room's decor since she'd been there last summer. Jill had been buying a great many antiques over the course of the year and the Goodwill finds spruced up with paint and fabric that had previously filled the room were mostly gone. An Early American cupboard with open shelves on top stood against one wall, behind a trestle table and chairs from the same period. Pix walked over to take a closer look. She wondered whether Jill had gotten the things from Mitch. Spying a pumpkin pine stand that would make a perfect bedside table, she also wondered whether these things were for sale. She tripped on one of the uneven floorboards and her hip bumped into the corner of the cupboard. Jill's apartment had originally been used for storage by the cobbler's shop below and the floor had never been finished off. One of the cupboard doors flew open. Pix bent down to close it, rubbing her hipbone, which, with little cushioning, smarted sharply.

She didn't close the door; rather, opened it wider. The shelves were filled with various items: some wonderful folk art carvings, especially one who looked like one of the prophets; miniature furniture—the kind that used to be carried around as samples; and several patchwork quilts. The shower was still running. Pix was sure Jill wouldn't mind if she looked at the quilts. At least that's what she told herself. Her self also wondered what they were doing up here instead of down in the store, where they would certainly attract buyers. For that matter, all the things in the cupboard would. Perhaps Jill was saving these things for herself.

Pix careful removed the top quilt and opened it up. It was an appliqué sampler quilt, every square a different wreath or bouquet and intricately quilted. The quiltmaker had used red, green, yellow, and white. It was museum-quality. The shower stopped and Pix started to call out her appreciation, but her words froze in her throat as her eyes moved down to the lower corner. Moved down to a tiny, barely perceptible blue cross.

She folded the quilt up and quickly put it back, latching the cupboard securely. When Jill came out, she found Pix sitting in a low rocker by the window reading this week's *Island Crier*.

"The parade pictures are wonderful. Sonny is going to love the shot of him as Burt Dow," she said brightly—too brightly.

Driving across the bridge to the mainland with Jill at her side, Pix was in a quandary. Should she come right out and ask Jill about the quilt and the other antiques? She probably should have done so immediately, but she wanted to take time to reflect. What could it possibly mean? That Jill had unwittingly bought a fake quilt—or wittingly? It was the latter possibility that was keeping Pix's tongue securely tied. Was Jill somehow connected to an antiques scam? At this point, Pix was certain it had been one of Mitchell Pierce's activities. Had they been in it together? She had certainly gotten antiques from him. This would explain Jill's recent attitude toward Earl, and perhaps her new alliance with Seth. Supposedly, Seth had learned everything he knew from Mitch. Did that include how to construct old from new?

The blue crosses were no laundry mark, as she'd speculated to Earl. They must be an indication to those who knew that these quilts were not the real McCoy. Had Jill seen the mark on Pix's quilt when it was spread out on the ground and later come into the house and removed it?

Jill was talking and Pix realized with a start that she hadn't heard a word the woman had been saying. She forced herself to concentrate. Jill was suggesting where they might go.

"There's that barn right outside Blue Hill as you head up the hill toward the fairgrounds. I found a wonderful bamboo easel at a very reasonable price last spring. Why don't we stop there first, then go farther up the coast?"

"Sounds fine to me," Pix answered. Anything was fine at this point, when her main worry was how she was going to get through this trip without coming unglued.

The barn door was firmly shut and they didn't have much luck in Ellsworth, either: no quilts to examine and nothing else tempting. Pix knew why nothing appealed to her, but Jill seemed just as restless and disinterested. Maybe she had simply needed to get away because of Addie's death and the antiquing was an excuse. Whatever it was, neither had bought anything by eleven and Pix suggested they drive straight to Beal's in Southwest Harbor for an early lunch. A big bowl of their chowder consumed at the pier while looking across the water at Acadia's Mount Cadillac was exactly what she needed to soothe her troubled mind, and perhaps it would do something for Jill's too. Pix had noticed that whenever Jill wasn't speaking, her fingers were finding their way to her mouth and her cuticles looked red and sore.

Many of the tables at Beal's were already full. In tacit assent, they took their food to the one farthest away from the groups noisily cracking open the lobsters they had picked out of the tank.

A cool breeze was coming off the harbor and for a while they sat in silence consuming the delicious chowder thick with clams. Pix was in no hurry to get back into the car. Eating gave her something to do and think about other than what was pressing most on her mind.

"Coffee and pie?" Jill asked. Beal's was known for their blueberry pie.

"Sure, we came all this way. We can't leave without pie."

More silent enjoyment followed, or rather, Pix thought, more silence. The pie was as good as ever, yet it was beginning to turn to ashes in her mouth. She had to say something to Jill—Jill, who had been a friend for years.

"Maybe—no, probably—it's none of my business, but you know how much we care about you, both of you. Do you want to talk about what's gone wrong with Earl?" Pix decided to start with this trial balloon to gauge Jill's reaction before attempting to discuss such matters as antiques fraud and breaking and entering, although Jill had always been free to walk into the Miller's unlocked house whenever she pleased.

Jill frowned. "I don't know why everyone thinks something's wrong between us. Goodness, if you don't happen to be climbing all over someone every minute of the day, the whole island assumes you've broken up, and of course it's not true. No one's bothered to remember we both have jobs. I've been busy and Earl's been even busier with all that's happened. We haven't had time to see each other."

She jammed a large forkful of pie into her mouth. Some of the juice dripped onto the front of her gauzy white blouse.

"Damn," she said, rubbing at it with a paper napkin, which only made it worse. She seemed close to tears. It didn't seem the moment to mention Earl's remarks or the fact that Pix had been there herself when Jill had turned her swain down the day after she was spotted dining with another. Nor was Pix inclined to raise anything else. They finished eating quickly, paid, and got into the car.

"Are you game for some more or do you want to head back?" Pix asked, hoping Jill, like she, had had enough.

"Let's keep going. Doris can stay until she has to go to work at the inn." Jill's chin jutted out. "Besides, I haven't had any luck yet."

Nor have I, Pix thought dismally.

They retraced their steps and went into a large antiques shop in Trenton. It was one Pix had frequented before, but Jill said she had never been there. They walked in and the owner greeted Pix warmly. The shop was free of cobwebs and dust. Everything was shown to its best advantage. It was quite a contrast and at the moment a welcome one. When Pix asked about nightstands, he said he thought he had the very thing and led them into another room. There were several customers browsing and one turned at the sound of their voices to greet them. "Pix, Jill! I never expected to see you two playing hooky again so soon." It was Valerie, and contrary to her earlier impulses, Pix was delighted to have a third wheel. This day out with Jill had begun to seem like a week.

"It was a spur-of-the-moment thing. I'm still looking for a table for my guest room and Jill was able to come along."

Not wanting to keep the owner waiting, Pix followed him to what was in fact "the very thing," except not the very price. Even with some friendly dickering, she knew it would be way out of her range. Valerie and Jill joined them. Pix said she liked it but would have to wait for something less expensive.

"It *is* a lovely piece," Valerie commented, "Are you sure you're not going to take it?"

"Yes. Saying no to this price tag, besides saving my marriage, gives me something to keep looking for this summer."

Valerie was on her hands and knees, examining the chest from all angles.

"Take your time, ladies," the owner said, "I'll be in the front of the store."

"Do you have any quilts?" Pix asked before he left.

"I have a crib quilt and a nice quilt top from the thirties but nothing else at the moment. Good ones are getting harder and harder to come by. The market in general has been hurt by the foreign imports that look old—and also by the fakes."

What it her imagination or did Jill give a sudden start?

"I'm a quilter and very interested in all this," Pix told him. "How do you spot the fakes?" It was too much to hope that he would say they were marked with a little blue cross, but she might learn something.

"It's very difficult, especially now that the fabric companies make so many reproduction fabrics. I look at the stitching, examine the material, and mostly consider the source. I get pretty suspicious when someone comes in with an armload of quilts they just happened to find in an old trunk that hasn't been opened since goodness knows when in Grandmother's attic."

"They aren't marked in any way, then?" Pix felt her investigation was going nowhere and she had to ask.

He laughed. "That would make it easy, now wouldn't it? No, they aren't marked. Do you want to see what little I have?"

Pix did and so did the others.

"I think I'll take the stand, if you're absolutely sure you don't want it," Valerie said.

"Absolutely sure. I can visit it at your house."

"Anytime."

The crib quilt was precious, Valerie declared, and that was the word for the price, too, Pix thought. She wasn't really interested in crib quilts—not for a long time to come—but she did like the quilt top with its bright 1930s prints. It wasn't particularly unusual. Someone had simply machine-pieced the rectangles together, yet it was someone who had had a good eye for color. Pix figured she could tie it rather than quilt it and have an attractive cover for Samantha's bed in Sanpere. If Samantha didn't want it, Pix would keep it for her own room. The price was reasonable and her spirits lifted.

"Do you have time to head up to Sullivan?" she asked Jill. "And can you come with us?" she added to Valerie.

"That's going to be a little far," Jill said. "I can't cut it too close with Doris or she may not want to help me out again."

"Why don't you ride back with me?" Valerie suggested. "There's only one place I want to check in Surry and it won't take long."

"Thanks," Jill said. "Then I won't feel like I'm spoiling Pix's fun."

Pix felt a major stab of guilt. How could she suspect such a nice person? And instead of talking to her about Addie and Jill's feelings about the death, Pix had pried into her private life, upsetting her further. Certainly she did not look any better for the outing. If anything, she seemed more perturbed. Pix was tempted to call it a day herself and drive Jill home.

But at this point, she was compelled to keep going, even though she didn't have the slightest idea where Mitchell Pierce had lived in Sullivan. A quick stop at the post office should take care of that. Mitchell Pierce—it had all started with him, Mitch and antiques. Antiques—and antiques dealers—were cropping up regularly.

She paid for her quilt top and impulsively asked the owner, "Did you ever have any dealings with Mitchell Pierce?"

"Everybody in this business had dealings with Mitch and most of us wish we hadn't, however I don't want to speak ill of the dead. You do know about that, don't you?"

"Yes, yes, I know," Pix said. But not enough.

She waved good-bye to Jill and Valerie and drove north to Sullivan. Without Jill, her mind raced from subject to subject, trying to figure out a way to link Mitchell, Addie, Jill, Seth, Duncan, and John, plus God knew who else, together in one pat solution. As she pulled up in front of the Sullivan post office, she was sure of only one thing: She needed to talk to Faith.

She had prepared what she hoped was a plausible story on the drive. It was hard enough to pry information from taciturn Mainiacs without the complications of whatever oaths postal employees swore. Not that this ever seemed to bother the ones in Aleford, who considered return addresses and what was written on a postcard public information.

"Hi," she said in as self-confident a voice as she could muster, and it wasn't half-bad. "I'm looking for someone named Mitchell Pierce. I understand he lives here."

"Lived" was the laconic reply from the other side of the counter.

"You mean he's moved?"

"You might say."

Pix waited, then, when that appeared to be the full extent of the reply, asked, "Do you have a forwarding address for him?"

"I have my ideas, but I'd rather not say."

Just as she was beginning to wonder whether she was dealing with yet another would-be "Bert and I," the recording of classic Down East humor, her informant turned inquisitor.

"Why are you so interested in Mitchell Pierce?"

The story came out smooth as a new dory down the slip into the water. "Mr. Pierce took some old things my mother wanted to get rid of on consignment. He told her they might be worth something, especially the quilts." Pix planned to mention quilts whenever possible. "He gave her a receipt and his phone number and said he'd be in touch, but that was over a month ago and she hasn't heard a thing. The number must have been wrong, because a recording says it's no longer in service."

Maybe it was the word *mother* or the tale itself, but it unleashed a veritable fountain of information.

"He's dead. Guess if you want to find out what happened to your stuff, you'd better talk to the police."

"Police?"

"Mitchell got himself planted in somebody's cellar hole down to Sanpere. It's a police matter. And I wouldn't hold out any great hopes of finding your things."

"Oh dear, what am I going to tell my mother?" This last bit was genuine enough. "Isn't it possible that they could still be in his house?"

"I doubt it. He boarded with the Hardings just up the road. Didn't have a place of his own."

"Well, I'm glad I came. At least we know now why we didn't hear from him. Thank you for all your help."

He nodded in acknowledgment.

It was nice to find some humor in all this, Pix thought as she started the Land Rover. Faith was going to love the post office story.

The Hardings had thoughtfully painted their name in white on their mailbox, which jutted out into the main road. It was a neat little house, the upper story painted bright yellow, the bottom dark brown, the shutters white. The yard was filled with machinery in various states of repair, several pot buoys, and broken traps. Whatever Mr. Harding did, it wasn't fishing. She knocked on the back door, noting the bright pink and purple petunias that grew profusely in the planters made from old tires on either side.

An elderly woman in a flowered housedress with a bib apron covering most of it answered.

"Yes?"

"Are you Mrs. Harding? I got your name at the post office."

This appeared to be vetting enough.

"Yes, I am. Why don't you come in, deah, and sit down? It is too hot for man or beast today. I told Virgil—that's my husband—that he was to stay in the shade as much as possible and keep his hat on. He's bald, you know, and bald people have to be very careful not to get burned. He won't let me put any of that cream I got from Marge Thomas. She sells Avon. Anyway, Virgil says he doesn't want to smell like a perfume factory, but it has no smell I can make out. Those summer people work him to death, cutting the grass, weeding the garden. He caretakes now, you know."

This, Pix thought, profoundly grateful, was going to be a piece of cake.

She told her story again—or rather, tried to. Mrs. Harding—"Call me Bessie, deah. Everybody does, even the grandkids"—tended to use Pix's every word as a jumping-off point for one of her own tangents. But after hearing about the priceless antique garnets—necklace, bracelet, earrings, *and* ring—Mr. Harding's mother had owned and which were promised to her, Bessie, but just because Mother had lived in their house, Mr. Harding's brother's wife, "who was no relation at all" claimed everything and she, Bessie, did not get so much as a button of her own mother-in-law's who also happened to be a second cousin, Pix was able to get on with her story.

Once Mitchell Pierce's name was mentioned, Pix didn't have to do anything else.

"I know he was no better than he should have been, but I liked the man. Always paid his rent on time and sometimes he'd come down here to the parlor—that's where we watch TV—and sit with us. Played that mandolin of his. A couple of times, he'd bring a bottle of something, not that Mr. Harding and I are drinkers, though we do enjoy a nip of something now and then. I don't know what he was doing down on Sanpere in a basement, but the whole thing is very sad and we miss him. That man could make you laugh from here to Christmas."

"Do you think it's possible he may have left some of Mother's things here in his room or maybe someplace else in the house? Mother is particularly concerned about her quilts. He said they might be valuable."

It was the longest remark she'd been able to make so far.

Bessie shook her head. "He never did keep much here. Told me once that he put his wares—that's what he called them—over to Ellsworth in one of those storage places people rent. Why on earth, I can't imagine. If you don't have room for what you've got, then you've got too much, is what I say.

Somebody else is in his room now, a real nice man who's working at Acadia this summer. We don't see too much of him, though, and of course he can't tell a story the way Mitch could. I think he's from New Jersey or one of those places."

Pix made one last try. "So you never saw any quilts—or other antiques—that Mitch might have taken on consignment or bought?"

"No, deah, and I'm real sorry for your mother. The only quilt Mitch ever brought into this house was the one he gave me last year for my birthday. I was some surprised. Don't know how he knew, but he come into the kitchen right after breakfast—I always gave him breakfast when he was here—and gave me the most lovely quilt. It's too nice to use, so I keep it on a rack in the parlor. Do you want to see it?" Bessie had a sudden thought. "You don't think it could be one of your mother's? I mean, with this talk about Mitch being a little crooked and all."

"Oh no," Pix hastened to reassure her, speaking with the conviction the absolute truth gives. "It couldn't be. It's only been a little over two months that he's had ours."

She followed Bessie into the parlor and stood to one side as the woman spread the quilt out for her to admire. Pix made all the right comments—and once again she was speaking the truth. The quilt was beautiful, intricately worked, the colors lovely. And Pix ought to know. She'd bought the twin of it a week ago—the twin, even down to the tiny blue cross at the edge.

It was difficult to get away from Bessie Harding, but after drinking two glasses of iced tea and promising to drop in again if she was ever up that way, Pix got in her car, waved good-bye, and backed out of the drive. Bessie watched her go, then ran to the mailbox calling after the car, "I never did get your name, deah! What was it again?" Pix turned onto the main road and headed south. The car windows were rolled down, but she missed Bessie's last words.

The sight of the bridge from the mainland to Sanpere always gave Pix a feeling of well-being. A welcome-home feeling. She drove up the steep incline and looked at the sky overhead. She felt inches away from the heavens on the top of the bridge. As a teenager, she and Sonny had climbed to the uppermost crossbar of the bridge a few times before their parents heard about it and forbade them to ever do such a crazy thing again. Still it had been wonderful, swinging your legs into nothingness and seeing all of Penobscot Bay at your feet. She let the car coast down the other side and reminded herself to mention, as she did each summer to her children, that the top of the bridge was strictly off limits.

She was eager to talk to Faith but decided to stop at The Pines before going home. She had spoken with her mother earlier to tell her about the planned excursion and see whether she needed anything in Ellsworth, it standing in relation to Sanpere roughly as, say, Paris to a French village on the Atlantic Coast. Mother had wanted for nothing and told Pix that Rebecca was fine, sitting by Ursula's side as she spoke and sipping a cup of tea.

Tea, or rather, iced tea again, sounded good. It was a long drive from Sullivan to Sanpere and Pix was tired. She needed to recharge before calling Faith and trying to figure everything out.

She walked into the living room, surprised not to see her mother and Rebecca on the porch.

"Hello," she called. "Mother, where are you?" She walked through to the kitchen and saw the two women in the garden vigorously attacking anything that wasn't supposed to be there.

"You have to keep at it every day," Rebecca was saying, "They really do grow up over night."

Ursula was about to reply when she saw Pix. "Will you excuse me for a moment, Rebecca? I have to talk to my daughter." Pix liked neither the expression on her mother's face nor the tone of voice in which she had said "my daughter." What have I done? she wondered.

She wasn't in the dark for long. Mother pulled her unceremoniously up the back stairs into the kitchen and plunked her down on a chair.

"Myrtle Rowe Miller! What have you been doing? What could you be thinking of going up to Sullivan like that!"

Mother was definitely clairvoyant. The word *witch* did not even occur to Pix.

She was stunned. "How did you know where I was?"

"Earl called. The Sullivan post office thought they should report to the state police that someone was asking about Mitchell Pierce. They called Earl, who knew, of course, from the description it was you. There was no answer at your house, so he called here to see if I knew whether you were off-island. It was quite embarrassing."

"I'm sorry," Pix mumbled, "It seemed like a good idea at the time." And still does, she thought defiantly. She was sorry she had upset her mother, but some prices had to be paid.

"You're to call Earl immediately. Now, you must be exhausted, all that driving. Would you like a cup of tea?"

She was forgiven.

"After I call Earl." Sometimes virtue was its own reward, and besides, she might get a cookie.

She went upstairs to call, since Rebecca might run out of weeds and Pix didn't want her activities known by any more people than she could help.

He answered on the first ring. "Now before you get mad at me, let me tell you what I found out," she said, hoping to distract him, which she did.

"We knew he had the storage place. It was clean as a whistle, but this business with the quilts seems to prove he was involved in antiques fraud."

"Does this mean you'll have to take Bessie's quilt?" The

woman had been so proud, Pix was sorry to be responsible for having it impounded or whatever they called it when they seized evidence.

"Yes, but she'll get it back. It's her property, unless at the end of this mess we find out differently."

"No one has stepped forward to claim the estate yet, right?"

This would have been big news on Sanpere.

"Not so far, but it hasn't been very long."

It just seemed long.

Pix was about to hang up, grateful that she had avoided a talking-to, when she remembered Jill's protest. "Oh, by the way, according to Ms. Merriwether, any problems between the two of you are a figment of the public's imagination. She and you have simply been too busy to see much of each other lately."

"Oh, is that it? Better than nothing, I suppose." From the way he spoke, it sounded much better.

Rebecca and Ursula were sitting in the living room. "It's too hot on the front porch. The sun has been beating down on it all day," her mother explained.

"If you don't mind, I think I'll lie down for a while. I can't understand why I'm so tired all the time," Rebecca said.

"I'm sure you'll feel better soon," Pix reassured her.

"Thank you, deah, but I know one thing. I'm not going to feel any better until we can have a proper Christian burial for Addie." Her voice broke. "It's not fair to do this to her."

Pix went upstairs with Rebecca and spread the afghan she requested over her, despite the warmth of the room, tucked up under the eaves as it was.

"I like to lie here and look out the window at the water," she told Pix drowsily. "I could never see it from my bedroom in the back, but Addie could."

The woman was almost asleep. Pix left, closing the door. When she went back downstairs, her mother was in the kitchen pouring iced tea, adding sprigs of mint she must have just cut in the garden.

"In all this commotion, I forgot to tell you Faith called. It seemed every call was someone looking for you. She said for you to call her back as soon as you could."

"I wonder what she wants?"

"I have no idea. She didn't mention anything to me." Mrs. Rowe smiled. Let the girls have their secrets was its implication.

Pix didn't feel like going back upstairs and so called from the kitchen. She got the answering machine and left a message.

"Still too hot for the porch?" she asked her mother.

"Yes, but not the backyard. Let's sit there."

They took their glasses and a plate of sugar cookies out back. There were chairs and a small table set out under a large black oak surrounded by a bed of lilies of the valley. They weren't in bloom now, but the columbines that had sprung up among them, managing to get just enough sunlight, were lovely.

"It's because I worry about you," Ursula said. "That's why I was angry."

"I know, but I wouldn't put myself in any danger." Pix suddenly thought of all the things she was responsible for, starting with her family. Well, she certainly hadn't been in peril. Half the state of Maine knew where she was every minute.

"It's just this terrific need to know what happened—maybe because I found the body. I can't not try to find out whatever I can," she told her mother.

"I understand. An enormous wrong has been done, two wrongs if, as we suspect, Adelaide was killed, too."

"You don't think she died of natural causes? A heart attack?"

"It may have been a heart attack, but I don't think it was natural. However, I could be wrong. I hope I'm wrong."

"Did Earl say anything more about the autopsy?" Pix realized she'd forgotten to ask him.

"He said they're not finished doing their tests. Rebecca wants very much to go home, although she's happy enough here. But the house is still sealed."

"This whole thing has been terribly hard on her."

"Yes, I suppose it has."

Pix told her mother what Seth had said about Addie's will.

"I haven't felt right about asking Rebecca so soon, but I'm not surprised. The whole show was always Addie's and James's, her husband. You wouldn't really remember him. Besides, he was sick at the end of his life. But he and Addie were well matched—two very strong-minded people. He was First Selectman for years. His people hadn't farmed for a long time, so he fished, yet buying the house in town set them apart from some of the others. Rebecca had lived in the house, taking care of her parents until they died, then moved out when James inherited it. She lived in Granville and worked at the Emporium until Addie asked her to move back in to help take care of James. After he died, she just stayed. But it was always James and Addie's house, even though Rebecca had lived there for most of her life."

"I hope she can stay at least for a little while. I get the feeling she'd like to move into Addie's big front bedroom with the view."

Her mother nodded. "I'm sure she would."

"What about the quilt? Has Rebecca said anything more about it?"

"I did ask her that, only she insists she's never seen it before and that if it had been in the house, she would have known about it. I suggested maybe the antiques dealer staying there had purchased it and left it for Addie to look at, but she said it wasn't the kind of thing he bought."

"That's true. Remember, he told us he was interested in clocks and furniture at the clambake." An image of Ursula deep in conversation with John Eggleston earlier that same day came into Pix's mind and she remembered she wanted to ask her mother some questions about him.

"Which reminds me, what were you and John talking about so earnestly over your lobsters?"

If her mother wondered at the abrupt change in subject, she did not show it. She was working on a pair of mittens with sailboats on the back for the Sanpere Stitchers Fair and her needles continued to click rapidly. Pix had worn similar mittens in her youth, ones with kittens, ice skates, and once her flower namesake done in purple on green. Pix was a fair knitter herself, but her mittens tended to be utilitarian solid colors, as the Miller children scattered them all over Aleford while sledding, making snow forts, and skating on the old reservoir.

"We were talking about changing one's occupation in midlife. He was expressing some amazement, and contentment, with the way the Lord had worked things out for him."

There didn't seem anything untoward here.

"What about Mitchell Pierce? Did John mention him to you or have you heard why Mitchell moved out?"

"It was foolish to think those two could ever have lived together. They were both much too stubborn, but that wasn't what happened. John caught Mitch using his tools without permission and went through the roof. It seems he's very, very particular about them—the same way an artist would be about his brushes, I imagine."

"What was Mitchell making?"

"That, I cannot tell you. You'll have to ask John. I do know he was very upset, because Mitch had waited until John was asleep, then went out to the woodworking shed. It may have been the subterfuge that bothered John most."

Woodworking in the dead of night, a fake quilt for his landlady: It all sounded very much as if Mitch had been in the business of making and selling forged antiques. But had John realized this, too?

Or had Mitch found something in John's shed? Something John didn't want him to know about?

Pix wanted to go home, make herself a drink, and stretch

out in the hammock. There was a pizza in the freezer and she could make a salad for their dinner. It was the utmost effort she could envision, and she knew Samantha wouldn't mind.

As it turned out, she didn't even have to do that much. Samantha called as she was about to leave to tell her she was going out with Arlene. Fred was helping some relative move and he'd let his girlfriend have his car. Samantha and Arlene were looking forward to Girls' Night Out: dinner and a movie in Granville. Pix gave her consent, said good-bye to her mother, and went home.

She poured herself a drink, put the pizza in the oven, and tried to decide whether she had enough energy to wash some lettuce for a salad. She didn't. She grabbed a handful of carrot and celery sticks to munch on instead and prepared to head for the hammock until the pizza was ready.

They kept only a small portion of the lawn mowed, so the kids could play croquet and badminton. The rest they left to its own devices, watching the cycle of wildflowers and grasses change over the course of the summer. Now the meadow was filled with white daisies, purple vetch, and hawkweed, yellow and dark red against the green. Pix stretched out in the hammock and looked up into the sky. The air was cooler as dusk approached. She gave herself a swing with her foot and balanced her glass on her chest. The phone rang.

She leapt from the hammock, setting the drink down on the grass, and sprinted for the house. Fortunately, Faith did not hang up.

"I figured you'd be out doing something energetic in the garden or digging clams at the shore. Whatever."

"Actually, I was lying in the hammock."

This did not sound like the Pix Miller she knew, Faith thought. When her Pix Miller indulged in contemplation, it was usually paired with something else—taking the dogs for a run or a ten-mile hike with Danny's Boy Scout troop. Things must be seriously out of kilter on Sanpere.

"What I have to tell you may help put some of the pieces together—or confuse things further. I'm not sure."

"Tell me. Tell me!"

"A few days ago, I called a friend of mine who has an antiques shop on Madison Avenue. She knows everybody in the antiques world, nationally and internationally. Anyway, right off the bat, she hadn't heard of Norman Osgood, which was pretty surprising. But she said she'd check her professional directories and ask around. She called me back today, and the man does not exist. She didn't even find him in the Manhattan phone book!"

"Faith, this is amazing. What made you think about checking on Norman?"

"You kept saying something wasn't quite right about him, and I trust your impressions absolutely."

"I'll let Earl know right away. Obviously Norman Osgood is an alias. If they can find out who he really is, we may have found the link between the two murders." And the murderer. She couldn't bring herself to say it out loud, even to Faith. The murderer? He'd been sitting on her blanket watching fireworks two nights ago.

"So, you actually think Adelaide was murdered?" Faith asked.

"Yes, and what's more, so does Mother."

"No question, then." Faith sighed. She knew how Pix and the whole Miller-Rowe clan felt about Sanpere Island, and now it would never again be the unsullied Eden it had been.

Pix told Faith about her trip to Sullivan and what she'd found at Jill's.

"I can't see Jill being involved in this—fake antiques, murder. Besides, she was close to the Bainbridges, wasn't she? And isn't she in that sewing group of your mother's? I believe it's an unwritten law in these societies that one lady does not bump another off."

"It does seem improbable, but I saw the quilt with my own eyes, and she *has* been behaving strangely this summer."

"True, if you're engaged in any sort of criminal activity, the last person you want for a fiancé is a cop."

They talked a bit more, particularly about the possibility that Mitch and Norman, or whoever he was, had been in business together.

"All those buying trips Norman made off the island—maybe he was meeting Mitch. And staying with the Bainbridges—that could have been to swindle them out of more things. Addie must have found out something. Oh dear, it's too dreadful to think about."

"Forget the Fairchilds and their traditions! I'm coming up this weekend!" Faith felt she belonged with her friend—and besides, things were heating up.

"No, you go. Plan to come up the following one. Arnie and Claire will be here by then and I'm giving a party for them."

Faith correctly sensed that Pix was more thrown by the idea of cooking for the party than solving any multitude of crimes.

"If you change your mind, call. We won't be leaving the house until ten."

"I will—and have fun."

"*Fun* is not the word we're looking for here, but I'll have something. Mosquito bites and sunburn maybe."

They laughed and said good-bye.

Pix had to cut some burned edges off the pizza and it was pretty crusty. She'd completely forgotten about it while talking to Faith. It tasted fine with the scotch she'd retrieved from the lawn, only one small ant having invaded the alcohol. She might not be hitting all the food groups, but it was exactly the kind of supper she wanted.

Afterward, she cleaned up, taking a mere merciful three minutes, and called Earl. He wasn't around, so she left a short message for him on the office machine to call her back, which he did an hour later. He did not seem unduly surprised at the news she had uncovered about Norman. Maybe he was getting used to having her for a partner, she thought somewhat smugly. Well, Faith had John Dunne, a detective lieutenant with the Massachusetts State Police.

She went to bed early and tried to read while she waited for Samantha. So, Norman Osgood wasn't an antiques dealer and might not be Norman Osgood, either. Who and what was he?

Samantha and Arlene had gone to the early movie and at nine o'clock found themselves in a booth at the new pizza restaurant near the cannery, consuming a large pie with everything on it but anchovies.

"Who eats those things? Why do they even bother putting them on the menu?" Arlene asked.

"My father loves them," Samantha said, making an appropriate face. "He says our tastes are not as refined as his."

"Yuck!" Arlene popped a stray piece of pepperoni in her mouth. It had taken her a few years to work up a taste for that.

"What do you want to do? When do you have to get the car back to Fred?"

"I'm supposed to pick him up at his cousin's around ten-thirty. He's going to be ready to leave, I'm sure. They've been working since early afternoon."

The girls gave their full attention to the food before them for a moment. It was disappearing fast.

"It's great having a place where you can get real pizza on the island. Gives us somewhere to go, too."

The restaurant was jammed and the crowd at the door was eyeing their booth longingly—and in some cases, aggressively.

"Let's go," Samantha said after catching one particularly beady eye.

"Yeah, I'll take the rest for Fred in case he's hungry, although his aunt and mother sent over enough food for an army."

They got in the car and Arlene started the engine.

"Are you thinking what I'm thinking?" she said to Samantha.

"Will Fred be mad if we go without him?"

"No, I told him we might. He just wants to know what's in the trunk. He doesn't care if he's there or not. I don't think he likes to go into the cabin, anyway. He told me if he sees the stuff Duncan has around again, he might be tempted to smash it to pieces."

"Maybe it's better he doesn't come, then."

Arlene turned the car down Main Street and drove up the steep hill by the old Opera House, where the movies were shown now. In an earlier era when Granville had been a boomtown because of the granite quarries and fishing industry, Nellie Melba and other stars had tread the boards.

They parked the car by the side of the road again and made their way to the cabin with no difficulty. It was dark. Fred had left his flashlight in the glove compartment. With it to guide them, they went back up the tumbled-down stairs and pushed open the door. It was much as before—the bed mussed, some dirty clothes in the corner, the candles placed about. Samantha had come armed with several bobby pins.

"I'll try to open it and you stand guard."

She directed the beam of light on the lock and wiggled the bobby pin around, trying to press down on the catch. The first pin snapped and she tried another with greater success.

"It's open!"

Arlene came quickly to her side and they raised the lid slowly.

A heavy smell of incense made Samantha sneeze. The black robe was on top and they lifted it away apprehensively. Underneath were some books, magazines, and several large photograph albums. There were also more clothes.

"This is really weird. Why would he keep his clothes locked up?"

Samantha thought she knew why and she found she had a lump in her throat.

"These aren't his clothes. They're his father's. Look at this Nautica sailing jacket. It would be huge on Duncan."

At the bottom of the trunk was a box with a man's watch, some cuff links, and a bunch of birthday cards—all from Duncan to Dad.

"And the albums are probably full of pictures of him," Arlene said. "I can't believe it, but I'm actually feeling sorry for the creep."

The albums did have pictures, starting with Duncan as a baby and his young parents, smiling and looking straight into the camera with the confidence they would all live forever that a moment like this brings.

"Let's put it back. It's too sad."

"Sssh," Arlene said, and grabbed the flashlight, clicking it off.

Samantha heard it, too. Someone had jumped off the porch and was running into the woods.

They went to the window, but all they could see were some tiny red flashing lights disappearing into the darkness.

"Let's get out of here before he comes back!"

They hastily put the things into the trunk, trying to remember exactly where everything had been. Some of the books were about the supernatural, but the magazines were mostly back issues of *Hustler*. As Arlene refolded what must have been Mr. Cowley's gown from some graduation, something fell from the pocket and onto the floor with a clunk. Samantha trained the light on it.

It was a hunting knife.

"Should we give it to Earl?"

"Let's ask Fred. But I'll tell you one thing, I'm not leaving it here." Arlene took off the tank top she was wearing over her shirt and wrapped the knife in it.

They closed the trunk and returned to the car through the woods, much faster than they had come.

It was almost 10:30. They had been at the cabin much longer than they had thought.

"Look, just drop me at the end of my road and go get Fred."

"Are you sure?"

"So long as I have the flashlight, I'll be fine. I'd probably be fine without it, I've walked this road so many times."

"All right, but I'm calling your house in a little while. I want to be sure."

"That's very sweet, but be real. What's going to happen to me?"

"Do you want to take the knife?"

Samantha shuddered. "No thank you. And tell Fred that I think we should give it to Earl as soon as possible. Tonight. I think I should tell my mom about it, too."

"Yeah. I'm sure he'll agree. Why do you suppose Duncan didn't come in and blast us for being there? The last time, he yelled his head off."

"Maybe he planned to come back with his friends and ambush us. Or maybe he didn't know who or how many we were."

This first alternative left Samantha feeling distinctly shaky.

They were at the end of the Miller's road. Arlene stopped the car.

"Good-bye. I hate to do this, except I'm late already—"

Samantha cut her off. "Don't be silly. Go! It was my idea. If Fred is nice enough to let us have the car, the least we can do is get it back to him on time. He's probably imagining all kinds of things, from crumpled fenders to dropped transmissions."

Arlene laughed. "Talk to you later."

The moon was waning yet still quite full and bright. Samantha switched the flashlight off and decided to jog home. It was beautiful and the familiar sight of the dark trees on the opposite shore as she passed the first inlet comforted her. But who would comfort Duncan? The trunk and the candles above it were a virtual shrine to his dead father. She imagined him slipping his skinny arms into the sleeves of that familiar jacket, trying to recapture some of the warmth and security those other arms had provided. She thought about her own father and what would evoke him most. His handkerchiefs, she decided. Big white squares of the finest cotton. When she was sick with a cold, her nose raw from Kleenex, she used those. They smelled slightly of the drawer where he kept them—a drawer filled with years of Old Spice soap on a rope sets given to him by his kids. She felt tears pricking at her eyes and stopped to speak to herself sternly. "Your father's not dead, Miss Samantha Miller. Get a grip, girl." She laughed when she realized she'd said it out loud. She started jogging again, her mood elevated as she brought her knees up and down. She was almost home.

She was almost home before she realized that she wasn't the only runner out that night. Someone dressed in black streaked by her and knocked her to the ground. She screamed, felt a sharp pain on the back of her head, and had time for just one impression before losing consciousness.

Lights. Small, red twinkling lights.

Chapter 9

The phone was ringing. Pix swung her legs over the side of the bed, shoved her feet into her slippers, and ran downstairs. It must be Samantha needing a ride home.

"Hi, Mrs. Miller," Arlene said cheerily. "I know it's a little late, but can I speak to Samantha?"

"Isn't she with you?" Pix's chest tightened and her heart began to pound.

"You mean she's not home yet! I left her off at the end of your road about half an hour ago."

Pix dropped the phone and raced up to Samantha's room, calling her daughter's name. She had to be there. Pix hadn't heard her come in. Obviously, Samantha hadn't wanted to bother her and had gone straight to bed. Even as Pix opened the door, she knew none of this was true. The room was dark and the bed still neatly made.

Pausing only to grab her keys from the kitchen counter, she picked up the phone and told Arlene to call the police—and the ambulance corps. Then she got in the car and started slowly down the road, searching on either side for Samantha.

The moon was bright; if it hadn't been, she would have missed her. Samantha was lying under a tree, partially concealed by a stand of large ferns. A few feet farther on, the ground dropped off to a ledge of jagged granite rocks, now nearly covered by the incoming tide.

She ran to her, calling, "Samantha! Samantha!" But there was no answer. She was sobbing as she reached her daughter, carefully putting her arms about her. She was warm and Pix could feel her soft breath on her mother's cheek. She was alive.

"Samantha! Oh dear God, please help us!" Pix had no idea what her child's injuries might be, so she dared not move her, but knelt next to her, cradling her, burying her face in her daughter's sweet-smelling hair. The night air was warm, yet Pix had never felt so cold.

She held her daughter's hand and felt for her pulse. It was steady. Samantha's eyelids fluttered.

"Samantha? Can you hear me?"

"Where am I, Mom? What's going on?" Samantha's voice started as a whisper, then got stronger. She looked about her in agitation. "My head hurts. It was Duncan. His shoes. I saw his shoes. Duncan hit me." She reached her hand to the back of her head and pulled it quickly away.

"Mom, I'm bleeding! I'm scared! Do something!" She began to cry.

"The ambulance will be here soon. Try to stay still." Pix had not seen the blood. She lay down next to her daughter, with her arm over Samantha's body to keep her calm. Where was the ambulance! With her other hand, she grasped Samantha's hand, wet with her own blood, tightly.

"Sssh, honey, don't worry. Everything's going to be all right."

But it wasn't.

After what seemed like several hours, she heard the ambulance siren and tears streamed down her face in relief. Earl was right behind them. He ran toward them.

"What happened?" he asked as the rescue workers rapidly assessed Samantha's injuries.

"I don't know! Arlene Prescott called and said she'd dropped Samantha off at the end of the road. When Samantha wasn't in the house, I came to look for her. She said it was Duncan. She saw his shoes!" The rescue workers were wrapping Samantha in a blanket and moving her onto a stretcher.

"She's had a concussion; we're treating her for shock," one of the squad said. "And she has a scalp wound that's going to need some sutures, but nothing seems to be broken. You want to ride with her?"

Pix climbed in the back of the ambulance for the drive over the bridge to the mainland. Samantha seemed to be sleeping. Pix was on one side, a corps member, bless him, on the other.

Duncan Cowley had attacked her daughter. Intending what?

At the hospital, Samantha was taken away before Pix could get out of the ambulance. Earl had been following and gave her a hand.

"I've been in touch with the state police and they're going down to the island to question the boy and his parents. You know she's going to get the best care possible here. I know how hard it is, but she's young and healthy. Everything's going to be fine, Pix."

Pix did not trust herself to do more than nod and let him lead her into the waiting room, where a nurse promptly put a cup of coffee loaded with sugar into her hand. Arlene and Fred were already there. For a moment, Pix was in the peculiar position of having to comfort Arlene when what she was feeling was anger. Why hadn't she driven Samantha to the door!

"I shouldn't have let her walk home," Arlene wailed.

Fred looked at Pix and told his girlfriend to be quiet. "No

one's blaming you. Now stop bothering Mrs. Miller." Arlene took a mighty gulp and calmed down.

Then they waited.

Someone at the nurse's station offered them more coffee, but Pix didn't want any. The cup she had drunk was making her feel jangly. She had called Sam soon after they'd arrived and he was waiting by the phone. She wanted him by her side. Hospital waiting rooms. She thought of all the hours she had spent in them: her father's last illness, a friend's mastectomy, Sam's ulcer, Danny's broken arm. No one talked except in occasional hushed voices. Each was totally absorbed in the thoughts being directed toward the room you weren't allowed to be in.

She knew, as Earl had said, that Samantha was going to be okay, but the nature of the attack—and all that blood—was taking her down these dark corridors in her mind.

Then, as it happened in hospitals, the time stretched out beyond anxiety into boredom, and finally numb fatigue.

Arlene suddenly got up. "The knife! I forgot all about the knife. It's in the car."

"What knife?" Fred asked.

"The one in Duncan's trunk. Thank God he didn't have it with him."

Earl tuned into the conversation. He'd been off with Jill on the long white sandy beach out at the Point.

He came over to them and said, "You better tell me all about it—and keep your voices down. We don't want to worry Mrs. Miller."

If Pix noticed that Earl and Fred left soon after, it didn't really register, nor did Fred's return alone. Earl walked in later. What did capture her immediate attention was the entry of a man in a white coat.

"Mrs. Miller?" Pix jumped up, for once unaware of the picture she presented. It was an odd one in these wee hours of the morning—she was in her pajamas, with Earl's jacket over them.

It was a young doctor, as most of them seemed to be these days. "Your daughter would like to see you." He was smiling.

"She's going to be all right?" Her tears flowed freely. Earl, Arlene, and Fred gathered close.

"Yes, though she's going to have a very large lump on her head and we had to do a little embroidery on her scalp—not much. The ambulance crew said from the way she was lying, she struck a tree root or a rock when she fell, which knocked her out cold. Samantha says someone pushed her and it must have been with some force. We also did a CAT scan and I don't see anything to be concerned about. We do want to keep her over night to be sure, but she's a very healthy specimen and should be just fine."

The news was overwhelming.

"When can I have a few words with her, Doctor?" Earl asked. "There seems to be an assault involved and we need all the information she can give us."

"If you keep it very brief, I don't see why you can't do it now. But"—he looked back at Arlene and Fred—"that's all. The best thing for her now is rest. She was pretty shaken up."

They nodded solemnly.

"Tell her . . . well, tell her I'm sorry and give her my love. And I'll be here as soon as she can have visitors."

Pix gave Arlene a hug, her recent anger totally vanished. Samantha had been dropped off at the end of the road, as had all of them day and night, hundreds of times.

The sight of her daughter in a hospital bed threatened to unhinge her, but Pix took a firm hold of herself—and Samantha.

"I have to call Daddy right away. He's waiting. Then I'll be right back. Earl wants to talk to you about what happened. Do you feel up to it?"

"They gave me something to make my head stop hurting

and I feel a little dopey, but I can tell him what happened. It was so quick, Mom." Samantha gave a little sob. "Duncan must really hate me!"

"Don't think about it, sweetheart. He's a very, very troubled boy."

As Pix was leaving to get Earl, the nurse came in. "You have a phone call, Mrs. Miller. You can take it out here."

Pix followed her and soon heard her husband's familiar voice. She told him what the doctor had said. "I just wish you were here, even though she's fine."

"Well, I will be in about three and a half hours tops."

"What!"

"I couldn't simply sit home. I'm a little south of Portland and will be at the hospital as soon as I can. Nobody's too concerned about speed limits at this time of night. If I do get stopped, I'll have them call Earl."

"Please be careful, darling." Pix was thrilled that he was on his way, but one Miller in the hospital was more than enough.

"Don't worry, I will."

She hung up and went back to Samantha's room, where she intended to spend the night.

Earl had finished questioning her.

"We'll let you know what happens with the Athertons. Duncan must have been upset that they were in his cabin and he blamed Samantha. But why he didn't confront her, I don't know. Usually, he just yells. I never expected violence." Earl's lips were tight. "He's been trouble since he arrived and we've been too soft with him. Not this time."

"In his cabin?" Pix had missed the story so far.

"I'll let Samantha tell you. The doctor told me I had five minutes and they're up. Take care of yourself, Pix. I'll be by in the morning." He gave her a quick hug and left. Before the door closed, she ran over and told him, "Sam is on his way." Earl nodded. "I'm sorry this happened. Samantha's a terrific kid. Now you get some rest, too."

Samantha was barely conscious, but for different reasons than earlier. She had heard the last part of their conversation, though.

"Daddy's coming?"

"Yes, he'll be here in a couple of hours."

"Good. I bet he wants to beat the shit out of Duncan."

Pix did not deny it. She wanted to do it herself.

The next morning, things were not so clear. Duncan Cowley had been at the nine o'clock movie that did not get out until past eleven. Two friends swore to it and Wendell Marshall, who manned the ticket booth, distinctly remembered selling him a ticket.

"It's hard to forget a kid with a hoop in his ear and green hair," he'd told Earl. Duncan had apparently streaked his locks with some sort of dye for the evening out. Now in the hard light of day, it looked pretty pathetic as he sat in Earl's office uneasily flanked by his parents. The state police had come to the house the night before and Jim had still not shaken off his indignation at his stepson for being the cause of their visit.

"In all my years on Sanpere Island, the police have never had to come to my house for any reason whatsoever. Now we want some answers here and we want them fast."

Earl thought this was his line, but he let it lie.

"Duncan," he said to the boy in a milder tone. The kid looked like he'd been through the mill. "We just want to know what happened. No one's accusing you of anything."

"Be real," the boy shouted. "You're never going to believe a fucking word I say, so why don't you go ahead and lock me up!" Earl wondered where Duncan had found the energy. Since he'd come in with Valerie and Jim, he'd sat slumped over in the chair, dressed as usual in black and smelling of stale beer and cigarettes. He was probably hungover from the night before. When the police had not found him at home, they'd driven around the island, turning their flashlight beams into a number of cars and soon locating Duncan in the backseat of one, trying to hide a six-pack under his scrawny frame.

Earl was pretty tired, too. This was the second time he'd talked with the Athertons and the boy himself. Duncan's denial and alibi had left Earl in a dilemma. He'd been asking around. There were only a few other kids who had the same shoes, mostly summer people. Those things cost a fortune. But in light of Duncan's alibi, he'd have to track down every pair and owner. As alibis went, it was a pretty good one. Patrons who got up in the middle of the film, obscuring the sight of those behind them, did not go unnoticed or unremarked on Sanpere. The only possibility was that Duncan had bought a ticket from Wendell and then immediately went out by another door. Could he have been so furious at Samantha that he'd plotted the attack ahead of time, even providing himself with an alibi? Of course his friends would lie through their teeth for him. At the moment, Earl was trying to find others, less loyal, who might have seen him in the audience. The whole thing was complicated by the group's penchant for the same style and color of dress. He'd have to hope Duncan was the only one with the nifty hairdo.

The boy claimed that he had not even known Samantha and Arlene had been in his cabin. He seemed pretty upset about it. Until Jim told him to shut his mouth and keep it shut, Duncan had tried to turn the tables, inveighing against the two girls. "They're the ones you should get. Trespassing. B and E. That's private property!"

Earl didn't say anything about the knife the girls had taken away. The night before, he'd taken it to the police station in Blue Hill for the state police to pick up. He hadn't heard anything since.

After a further wearying hour, Earl sent Duncan home with Jim and Valerie to what he was sure would be house arrest. Duncan cast an odd look back at the sergeant and Earl had the distinct impression that Duncan would have favored the one and only cell down the hall from the office—mostly used to store stationery supplies for the town hall.

Valerie had sat tight-lipped and grim throughout the ordeal. She seemed to have erected a wall between herself and the rest of the world. She was dressed in a simple blue-checked skirt and white blouse, no hat, no makeup. At one point, Duncan turned to her and said, "Why would I want to do anything to Samantha Miller? I don't even know her." Valerie just shook her head in utter defeat.

Earl walked out with them to their car. "Thank you for coming in."

"A rotten business," Jim said, "a sorry mess. Samantha's one of the best sailing instructors we've ever had at Maine Sail." He glared at Duncan.

An old pickup came roaring down the street—it needed a new muffler—and screeched to a halt next to them. John Eggleston, his hair a mess of disheveled fiery locks, leapt out and ran toward them.

"I just heard. Please, let's sit down and talk about what happened before anyone goes off the deep end."

During the long wait the night before, Pix had filled Earl in on everything Samantha had told her and had also mentioned her conversation with John. And John had, in fact, been in touch with Earl, asking him to keep an eye on the old quarry. Earl had touched on some of this with Duncan and the Athertons.

"You've done enough harm here! All your little talks! We know about the kinds of 'literature' you've been recommending and you may be hearing from my lawyer." Jim had apparently already dived in.

John stood for a moment, openmouthed. "Too late," he muttered, "too late."

He stood with Earl, watching the family drive away.

"I was hoping they'd let the boy stay with me for a while until things cool down."

"I doubt there's much hope of that. One way or another, Duncan Cowley is going off this island."

It was almost dark when Pix woke up. She lay still for a moment. Sam had thrown a light blanket over her. The heat was finally breaking. She looked out the window at the familiar line of pines pointing to the boathouse and shore. The outcroppings of pink granite were faintly visible, or maybe it was because she knew they were there that she could see them. She could hear Sam and Samantha talking in her room down the hall. Pix felt warm and safe. She stood up and draped the blanket around her shoulders, trailing it like a queen's mantle as she went in to see her daughter and husband.

"Mom, Daddy's cheating!" Samantha laughed. They were playing Uno.

"That's nice," said Pix. "What do you want for supper?"

Samantha was still in a good mood three days later, but was beginning to get restless. She had been showered with attention in both tangible and intangible forms. The campers had all made cards for her. Susannah and Geoff had created three gushing ones each. The Fairchilds had sent a basket of yellow roses, baby's breath, and daisies—not the kind the Millers gathered in big bunches from the meadow to weave into crowns or set about the house in a variety of containers, but perfect daisies with huge yolk yellow centers and every creamy white petal perfect. No tiny holes as evidence that some creature had rested there. Gert Prescott left two lemon meringue pies. Ursula brought a beautiful conch shell Samantha had long coveted.

Valerie dropped by to leave a tiny porcelain box with the words FORGET ME NOT surrounded by the flowers on the lid. She tried to say how sorry they were to Pix, but Pix, feeling very uncomfortable, cut her off, thanking her and adding,

"Samantha is fine, thank God, and maybe Duncan will get the help he needs now."

That you all need, she finished silently.

Sam had stayed until Monday night and he and Pix had spent a great deal of time talking together and with Earl about what to do. In the end, with Samantha's approval, they decided not to press charges. It wasn't because of lack of evidence but, rather, because they felt that Duncan might only become more withdrawn and disturbed if caught up in the juvie system. Both Pix and Sam had been very moved by Samantha's description of what the boy kept in his trunk. Earl spoke to the Athertons and they were going to find an appropriate residential school with a summer program—not the military one—for their son as soon as possible. Depending on how he did and what those working with him said, they'd decide whether he would return home in the fall or stay.

Sam had left reluctantly, trying up to the last minute to get his wife and his daughter to go back with him, but neither woman wanted to budge.

"I'm not going to let her out of my sight," Pix told her husband, "especially at night. Earl doesn't think she's in any danger. Duncan will be leaving soon, and we can't run away."

Sam agreed intellectually, yet his gut told him otherwise. "I'll be back Friday night." Pix wasn't going to argue with that.

Adelaide Bainbridge's funeral was Tuesday morning.

Pix and Samantha had driven out to The Pines to get Ursula. Rebecca had been picked up earlier by a contingent of Bainbridge cousins feeling pangs of familial obligation: "Poor old Becky."

Samantha had had plenty of company since she'd returned home from the hospital Saturday morning, none more constant than her grandmother's. Pix knew her mother would be terribly shaken by what had happened and she was right.

Today, Ursula opened the door to Samantha, who was running up the steps, the only evidence of the attack and her slight concussion hidden by her hair. To all intents and purposes, she was fully recovered, but the pain in the older woman's eyes was fresh. Pix was struck anew by how much her mother seemed to have aged since Saturday. There were dark shadows and lines that Pix had never seen on Ursula's face before. When she spoke, it was not in her usual timbre. The volume had been turned down and the treble increased.

"Mother, are you sure you want to go?" Pix asked. "They'll be so many people at the service, no one will miss us."

"Of course I want to go—and Rebecca would notice, for one. Besides, I couldn't miss Addie's funeral. I've known her for so many years."

Pix thought her mother would say this and she resolved to get her away as soon as possible after the graveside service.

As they drove across the causeway back toward Sanpere Village, Pix again noted the happy vacationers on the beach and out in their boats, enjoying the typical Maine day. The heat spell had broken and normal July weather was back. There was a good stiff breeze on the water, turning up small whitecaps. The sun shone just enough for comfort and a few hardy souls were swimming.

"I'm glad it's not so hot today. The idea of sitting through the service wondering who was going to pass out, maybe even me, is distinctly unappealing."

Samantha laughed. The idea of her mother passing out in any situation seemed pretty far-fetched—but then, she had been in no shape to judge on Friday night.

"Addie could never take the heat, even when she was thin."

"*Addie was thin?*" In Pix's memory, Adelaide had always been a substantial woman.

"Oh yes, she was thin—and very pretty—when she was young. She could have had her pick of any number of the boys. My brother, Tom, used to talk about the beautiful lighthousekeeper's daughter. She'd come over for dances and such, but even then she tended to be outspoken. He thought she'd probably boss a man to death."

It hit Pix that they were on their way to a funeral. So much had been going on that she'd been viewing the morning's activity as a kind of respite, especially since the medical examiner had ruled the death due to heart failure, plain and simple; nothing to do with quilts, crosses—or knives. Samantha had told her about the knife they'd found. She would have to ask Earl about it.

"Rebecca must have been mistaken about the quilt," she said to her mother, who was sitting up straight in the seat next to her, holding her purse in gloved hands. "I hope it's not a sign that she's beginning to deteriorate."

"I don't think Rebecca Bainbridge's going downhill any faster than the rest of us—but she may have made a mistake with the quilt."

Pix looked over to exchange a smile with her mother about the downhill remark, but her mother's face was shut up tight.

The whole island was crowded into the simple white church that sat high on a hill facing out to Penobscot Bay where Addie had worshiped, off and on—mostly on, of late.

The Sanpere Stitchers all sat in one pew, immediately behind Rebecca and the rest of the family. Pix reached for Samantha's hand and gave it a squeeze. She had told her daughter she didn't need to come but had been happy when Samantha wanted to be there. Pix was still not ready to be separated from her, even for an hour or two. She looked around the church, flooded with sunshine from the clear long, glass windows that framed the bay above the plain altar and that on the sides offered a view of the woods on the left, the cemetery on the right. Soon Adelaide would join her husband, James, there. The stone with both their names had been in place for many years, merely waiting for this last date to be carved on its polished granite surface.

Pix looked down the row of faces in her pew: Nan Marshall; Gert, Dot, and Louella Prescott; Mabel Hamilton; Louise Frazier; Jill Merriwether; Serena Marshall; and others. These island women held the community together in so many ways, a root system like the evergreens and ground covers that kept the thin layer of earth on top of this inhabited rock from washing off into the sea. The women were all subdued but showed no outward signs of grief. It was Addie's time. And she had had a long life, not like some: Louella's grandson, lost diving for urchins; Mabel's daughter, killed in a car accident. Pix saw Jill bow her head suddenly. In silent prayer? What—or whom—was she thinking about? Ursula's head was unbowed and her face appeared swept clean of all expression, except to one who knew her as well as her daughter did. Something was troubling Mother. The slight lowering of her eyebrows, the barely perceptible tightening of her lips. Pix looked at her mother's lap. Her hands were clenched together, thumbs locked over each other. Not in prayer. She had been upset about the attack on Samantha and the death of her old friend, of course, but was there something else? Mother was remarkably good at keeping things from people. Pix resolved to find out what was bothering her, even if it took the rest of the summer.

She gave a surreptitious glance over her shoulder as they stood for a hymn. The church was indeed packed. Norman Osgood was in one of the rear pews, solemn-faced. Seth was also in the rear. He seemed perfectly at ease in his unaccustomed formal garb, a well-cut dark suit. Pix wondered why he wasn't up with the rest of the family. Had to get back to work quickly?

They sat down and the minister began his eulogy. Rebecca began to cry audibly. She was going home today, she'd told Ursula. She'd been able to go back ever since the final report from the state medical examiner's office, but at Ursula Rowe's urging, Rebecca had decided to stay at The Pines until after the funeral. Would she move to the front bedroom right away? Pix wondered. Or would she stay in the small one in back until a decent period of mourning had passed? And what would the family do? Surely not turn her out immediately. Pix hoped the force of island opinion, mainly the formidable force of the Sewing Circle, would prevent that from happening.

She realized she had barely listened to the service. She was agitated, too. The world was topsy-turvy and the sooner she could get her feet firmly planted on the ground, the better. One death was resolved, but the other was not.

They all filed out of the church in silence as the organist played Adelaide's favorite hymn, "Abide with Me." Then they buried her.

"Mother, you cannot keep me locked up like some princess in a tower! I want to get back to work. They need me! And nothing could be safer. I'm surrounded by hordes of little munchkins every minute I'm there. You can drive me over and pick me up. I won't even go to the bathroom by myself, I promise. But you've got to let me leave. I'm starting to go nuts here."

The argument had begun the night before and had not been resolved by bedtime. Now, the next morning, Samantha was up bright and early, perched at the foot of her mother's bed, picking up where she had left off. Pix hadn't slept well. She knew Samantha would have to resume her schedule sometime, but why did it have to be today? She'd hoped to keep her close to home for another week at least to make sure she was all right.

"I'm fine," Samantha argued. "The doctor said I could go back to work when I felt up to it, and I feel great. This is *your* problem, not mine. Would it make you feel any better to follow me around the whole morning?"

"Yes," Pix answered immediately, "it would."

"Oh, Mother!" was Samantha's annoyed reply as she noisily stomped off to her room.

Pix knew she was beaten and she also knew that she had to let her daughter go. Much as she wished to, she could not keep Samantha wrapped in cotton wool for the rest of the summer—or the rest of her life. She followed her down the hall.

"All right. But I drive you there and back. Plus, if you get tired or feel anything out of the ordinary at all, you call immediately. I'll be here all morning." Sitting by the phone.

Samantha flung herself at her mother and gave her a big kiss. "I love you, Mom. Now we'd better hurry. I don't want to be late."

Well, at least it was Mom again.

Samantha felt like a bird let free from its cage. She darted into the kitchen to say hello to everyone before meeting her group down by the waterfront.

"It's great to have you back, Sam. I didn't think your mom would let you out so soon," Arlene said after giving her friend a big hug.

"Desperate situations call for desperate measures. I had to get tough. Would you believe at the last minute she wanted me to bring the dogs? Like they would really protect me. And can you imagine how nuts the kids would be!"

They laughed and Samantha went down to the waterfront, where she was greeted with enthusiasm, Susannah dramatically throwing her skinny little body straight into Samantha's arms. "You're okay! I thought I'd never see you again!"

Susannah could be headed for a career on the stage, and living in Manhattan as she did, this might come to pass, Samantha thought. The little girl seemed constantly to be playing some sort of role. Geoff was hovering nearby. Samantha quickly got her group together and they started for the boats. The kids had been quick learners and she was taking them out on the water two at a time while the others practiced knot tying and studied the sailing manual. She'd allowed them to pick their own partners, figuring they'd work best with someone they liked. Geoff and Susannah had chosen each other and were the fourth pair to go with Samantha. She kept quiet and let them set sail. They started off fine, but soon the sail was luffing and the boat almost at a standstill.

"All right now, what do we do?" Samantha asked.

"We did it on purpose, Samantha," Geoff said. "We have something to tell you." His voice was firm and serious.

Susanna had less control, or more theatrics. "It's our fault that you got hurt."

"What!" Samantha said in amazement.

"Well, not exactly our fault," Geoff explained, "but we kind of feel that maybe if we'd told you what we'd been doing sooner, then it might not have happened."

"What *have* you been doing?" Samantha asked sternly.

"Your getting hurt was like a punishment to us." Susannah was off and running. Geoff interrupted her.

"Let's just tell her." He turned toward Samantha. "It started because Susannah and I were really pissed off at coming here. Maybe we kind of hoped we'd get caught and be kicked out."

Samantha got a sinking feeling in the pit of her stomach. The mice. She looked at the two cherubic faces in front of her.

"You're not telling me you put those dead mice in the kitchen are you?" she gasped.

"Yuck! No Way!" said Susannah. "Although it did make things more fun."

Geoff continued patiently. "We did all the other stuff—the short sheeting, the spoiled milk, the salt in the sugar . . ."

"Not the paint!" Again Samantha leapt to the worst.

"No, not the paint. We like sailing. But," he had the grace to lower his head slightly, "we did screw up the parade."

"And God punished us," Susannah declared solemnly. "He let you get hurt and you're the most decent thing here. Besides you, Geoff," she hastened to add.

"God doesn't work that way, but we'll talk about that some

other time. What we have to do now is tell Mr. Atherton what's been going on."

Geoff and Susannah's expressions clearly indicated they would rather face their Maker.

"Do you think he'll send us home?" Geoff asked.

"I thought that's what you wanted?"

"Only at first, then doing stuff was fun because everybody was getting so crazed at everything else that was going on. This is the best camp I've ever been to."

Susannah nodded agreement.

The idiots, Samantha thought as she headed the boat back to shore and proceeded to give them a talking-to that would have made her mother proud.

The rest of the group was waiting for them on the dock with puzzled expressions on their faces.

"What was taking you guys so long? There's a good wind today. Why couldn't you come about?" one of them asked. "We're going to be late for lunch."

"You all run along and I'll put everything away. Tell Mr. Atherton that Geoff and Susannah are helping me. We'll be there as soon as we can."

As they stowed the gear, the two children chattered happily like the reprieved felons they were. Samantha, the godess, didn't hate them. She had barely yelled.

Samantha was preoccupied. So it hadn't been Duncan who had spoiled the parade.

But that still left everything else.

After lunch, Samantha called home with the news. Her mother had been surprised, amused, and ultimately sympathetic.

"So, I'm going to take them to Jim now and then I'd really like to spend the afternoon here. The counselors can use my help and I hate to leave the kids like this. I won't stay any later than five and you can pick me up at the Athertons' house, where I will stay absolutely put. I left without my paycheck

Friday, Jim told me. I didn't know I would be getting one so soon and it's at the office over there."

"As long as you're not too tired, but swear that you'll get someone to walk you over."

"All right, but I'm only doing this to make you happy."

"Could there be a better reason?"

"Mother! I've got to go."

Jim reacted to Susannah and Geoff's confession almost absentmindedly. Samantha could only assume that his problems with Duncan overshadowed everything else, even the sabotage of the Fourth of July parade, one of Jim's favorite camp events. "The jewel in the crown of summer," he called the fancy formations they dreamed up each year.

Chastised and chastened, the two children were released to their counselors. They would have to apologize to the whole camp. Jim would also inform their parents and he was firm. He didn't think he could accept them as campers again. Still, he told them they could write and plead their case this winter.

"He was really fair," Samantha told Arlene at the end of the day as her duenna escorted her through the woods to the "Million Dollar Mansion." "Maybe if he treated Duncan the way he treats the campers, things wouldn't have gotten so messed up."

"Dream on! The guy is wacko. He's responsible for those stitches in your head, remember."

"I know." Samantha stopped in the middle of the path. "But something has to make someone like that."

"You are too good. Remind me to call Mother Teresa and tell her to move over. Duncan is pond scum, pure and simple."

Samantha had to laugh at Arlene's choice of imagery, from Mother Teresa to pond scum.

"All right, I agree."

Arlene waved good-bye as Samantha knocked at the front door. Valerie opened it immediately. She was expecting her.

"Come in. How are you feeling? Are you sure you should be back at work so soon?"

"You sound like my mother," Samantha said. "I'm fine and I was beginning to get stir-crazy."

"Come on upstairs. Your check is in my office."

Samantha followed her up the spiral staircase, made by one of the last practitioners of this art in the state.

The only thing that distinguished the thoroughly feminine boudoir Valerie ushered Samantha into as an office was the Macintosh on a pale green-and-white sponge-painted table underneath one of the windows. Beside it was a daybed covered by a billowy white spread and piled high with pillows. Samantha imagined how lovely it would feel to lean back into that down sea of rose chintzes and white eyelet. The rug was covered by more roses, woven against a dark green background. In contrast to the rest of the house, the walls were not painted off-white, but papered in a sage stripe with a Victorian frieze of lilacs above. Two wicker chairs with plump cushions—you wouldn't have marks on the back of your legs from these—sat on either side of the French doors leading to a small secluded balcony overlooking the cove.

"I like to sunbathe there," Valerie said, following Samantha's eye. "I let myself go in here. I do spent quite a bit of time in this room. Jim hates it. Too much froufrou, he says," and she laughed.

"Well, I love it. I'd give anything for one like it!" Samantha enthused, forgetting her insistence two years earlier that Pix get rid of any and all vestiges of flowers, dotted swiss, and ribbon from Samantha's bedroom.

Valerie was rummaging around on the table, pulling open the drawer in the middle.

"Your check must be in Jim's study. Why don't you admire the view. I'll be back in a minute."

Samantha dutifully sat in one of the chairs. It was as comfortable as it looked. The phone on Valerie's desk rang, then stopped. She must have answered it downstairs. Samantha stood up and walked around the room, admiring the primitive still lifes that hung on the walls. Next to a plant stand with an arrangement of wax fruit and flowers never seasonal mates in nature, under a large glass dome, there was a closet door. Feeling slightly guilty, Samantha decided to open it after first listening carefully to make sure Valerie wasn't coming up the stairs. She just had to see what kind of leisure wear Valerie kept here—Victoria's Secret or Laura Ashley? She giggled and wished Arlene was with her. She'd die when Samantha told her.

She quietly turned the intricately embossed brass doorknob.

The closet was huge, but instead of the negligees, tea gowns, and whatever that Samantha had expected, there was nothing except a large antique armoire. It had an ornate lock but no key. The closet smelled strongly of potpourri and Samantha sneezed. She reached into her jeans pocket for a tissue. She didn't have one. Yet, there was something else there. Down at the bottom was the key she'd found over two weeks ago, that sunny day when she and Mom had taken the dogs for a walk to see how the Fairchild's new house was coming along—a sunny day that seemed to have had its start in another life.

All of a sudden, she felt nervous. She held the key in her hand. It had been so warm, she hadn't been wearing jeans much. This was the first time since that long-ago Sunday she'd had this pair on.

It was an ornate key, like the lock.

Before she could change her mind, she put it in, turned, and heard the click as the doors opened. When she saw what was inside, she laughed in relief. A whole shelf of plastic Mickey Mouse figures, old ones. There were also some folk art carvings of animals and one of a figure that looked like someone from the Bible. On other shelves were piles of quilts. This was obviously where Valerie kept her finds.

Samantha closed one of the doors and bent down to make sure the quilts didn't get in the way. She reached under a bunch to ease them farther into the chest and immediately pulled back, as if she'd put her hand into a blazing fire instead of a stack of linens. She closed the other door, pocketed the key, shut the closet door fast, and sat back down, looking straight out to sea. Her heart was pounding, her cheeks blazing.

There had been a neat little blue cross stitched on the binding of each of the quilts. They lined up like little soldiers. The crosses again. There had been one on Mitchell Pierce's quilt. There had been one on the quilt her mother had bought, a quilt her mother had told her was a fake. Should she tell Valerie? What should she do? She put her hands up to her cheeks to try to cool them down. They felt ice-cold against her blushes. She took a deep breath. Valerie was coming.

"The view is really something. I could stay here forever," she said in as normal a tone as she could.

"I hope you don't have to, dear." Valerie's tone wasn't normal at all. Samantha twisted around in the chair.

Valerie might have brought the paycheck, but she had also brought an extremely lethal-looking gun, which she was handling with ease, pointing it directly between her employee's big brown eyes.

"I have to run. I'm already a bit late picking Samantha up, but she's waiting for me at the Athertons' house, and it's certainly no punishment for her to revel in Valerie's company amid Valerie's perfect taste. If anything, she'll probably 'Oh, Mother' me for getting there too soon."

Faith laughed—while she still could. Amy, happily playing next to her adored Mommy on a water-filled mat, complete with floating spongy fish, would no doubt put her through this sometime in the future, as well.

"All right. I just wanted to check in and hear about the funeral, though this one sounds pretty tame." Faith and Pix had attended a more dramatic service on the island several summers ago—one that people were still talking about.

"Yes, poor Addie. Poor Rebecca. But I suppose their lives have been happy ones, if not bursting with excitement. And Adelaide really did make a name for herself in the quilt world."

"Hmmm," Faith was ready to move on back to the living, especially her own life. "If Tom can get away early, we'll be up Friday night. Do you think Seth will have started the framing by then?"

"He said he would, and even though it's been cooler, we haven't had any rain, so the foundation should be dry soon."

"I can't wait to see it—and you, and Samantha."

"Likewise, I'm sure."

The two women hung up. Faith reached for Amy. "Your first trip of many to Sanpere Island," she told her child, who listened intently and replied with a string of appropriate nonsense syllables. Was it just because she was a mother that Faith thought she could discern the words *wanna go, wanna go?* Well, I want to go, too, Faith reflected. With the amount she was spending calling Pix, it might have been cheaper, and more sensible, to have shut down the company and gone up in July in the first place. Besides, although things seemed to have settled down on the island, she knew she wouldn't feel easy until she saw Pix and especially Samantha for herself.

"You'll like it there." She continued to hold a one-sided conversation with her child, a situation she'd eventually gotten used to with Ben. In his early days, she'd felt as if she was talking to a cat or some other domesticated pet. "It has icy cold water, lots of bugs, no place to eat, no place to shop, nothing much to do." And they were building a house in this Shangri-la.

Pix knocked loudly at the Athertons' front door and, receiving no reply, knocked again. Perhaps they were on the deck in the front of the house. She walked around, didn't see anyone, and went back to the door. She knocked yet again, then did what she normally did in Sanpere: walked in. She could hear Valerie's voice coming from upstairs.

"It's me, Pix," she called from the bottom of the spiral. Taking the silence for an invitation, she went on up. She was curious to see more of the house. At the top of the stairs, she saw an open door and through it Valerie's back. She entered the room. "Sorry I'm a bit late . . ." Her apology was cut short first by her initial impression of the decor—it was fit for a little princess, or an aging romance writer—then by the gun.

"What's going on! Samantha, are you all right?"

"Shut up and sit down in the other chair."

Pix was so stunned that for a moment she couldn't move. It was simply too much to take in all at once. Valerie?

"Move!"

She moved.

Samantha had been similarly turned to stone. She had hardly moved a muscle since Valerie had entered the room; even Pix's arrival did not cause more than a flutter of an eye-lash. Every thought she had directed her to keep still and stay alive. Her mother reached for her hand and she grabbed it, but did not shift her gaze or open her mouth.

Valerie, however, was talking to herself nonstop. Tapping her foot in annoyance yet maintaining a steady aim, she sat down on the daybed, incongruously surrounded by lace.

"Everything was perfect! Mitch was out of the way. We'd heard Seth tell his crew that they would be pouring the foundation after they finished the work at the camp. Perfect!" She was fuming. "Mitch, the old lush. Couldn't keep his mouth shut *and* he thought he should get more money. For what? I ask you." Pix correctly assumed this was a purely rhetorical question, especially since Valerie did not even pause before continuing her tirade. "So he could make things look old. Big deal. There are plenty of people to take his place—or who could have taken his place." If looks could indeed kill, Pix would have been effectively demolished and the gun superflu-ous. "But *you* had to start playing Nancy Drew. Still, that didn't get anywhere, and I was home free. I had even gotten rid of Duncan, so life around here could be a little more peaceful. I thought we were all going to have a lot of fun to-gether. You haven't been a good friend at all!" She was pout-ing now.

The woman must be absolutely mad, Pix thought. She was talking as if Pix had done her out of an invitation to the Mag-nolia Ball or some such thing at the same time as she was con-fessing to murder! What else could the references to Mitch being "out of the way" and "pouring the foundation" mean?

The initial shock had passed and Pix was never one to sit meekly by.

"Valerie, put that gun down before someone gets hurt. I have no idea what you're talking about and you're upsetting Samantha—and me." Pix grasped for an out. "Did you think she was an intruder?" It was pretty feeble and she quickly fol-lowed it with some soothing words in as warm a voice as she could manage, "And what's this nonsense about our not being friends? You know that's not true."

If Samantha was surprised at her mother's sudden gift for bold-faced lying, she didn't show it.

"Now, Pix"—Valerie shook the gun like a chiding finger—"friends help friends, and you haven't helped me one little bit. I was all ready to settle down in my beautiful house for the rest of my life, but that's all spoiled. And you're to blame. Now, I have to think what to do."

Pix offered a suggestion. "Why don't we just forget that any of this happened and we'll go home."

"I said I was thinking! Shush!"

Samantha squeezed her mother's hand and Pix obeyed. She felt a sudden bleak stab of despair.

The spiral staircase did not muffle footsteps. Pix listened with a lifting of her heart as the sounds continued, mounting quickly to the second floor. Jim threw open the door.

"I don't have much time. I have to be back for my nature group after dinner."

So much for any hope of rescue. The Athertons were definitely a team.

"Her mother just barged in. Came to pick her up. As I said on the phone, I saw her go into the closet on the monitor in your den. Somehow she had a key to the armoire." Valerie looked away from Jim, to Samantha. "And where did you get that key, young lady? How many other times have you been snooping around our things!"

Samantha opened her mouth, but words did not come out. She thought she might be sick.

"Answer me!"

"In the woods. I found it in the woods out by the Fairchilds' new house," she whispered.

"Mitch must have had it in his pocket and it dropped out when we were carrying him," Jim said meditatively. He might have been mulling over the answer to a crossword-puzzle clue.

Meanwhile, Pix was trying to piece it all together. Samantha must have stumbled across something incriminating in the closet, something no one was meant to see. Pix had heard that along with their gold faucets and bidets, the Athertons had a state-of-the-art surveillance system. Yet it was the innocent caught by the guilty in this case.

"Jim, Samantha merely came over to get her check. I'm sure she didn't mean to pry into anything, but you know how teenagers are." She was sure her daughter would forgive her. "There doesn't seem to be any harm done, so why don't we simply stop this. I'd like to go home."

"And I wish I could let you go, but we can't." Jim sounded genuinely sorry. "You may not understand all that is happening now—I know you wouldn't lie to us; you're too good a friend—however you'll figure it out later and have to tell Earl. Then where will Valerie and I be? No, I'm afraid it's too late."

There it was again. The friendship thing. Well, friends didn't aim guns at friends in Pix's book. She couldn't think of anything to say and decided to keep quiet and concentrate on how she and her daughter were going to get away from these two lunatics. She was trying to replace all her fear with anger and it was working.

"It doesn't matter if we make a mess in here, because we're going to have to leave the house in any case." Valerie was speaking matter-of-factly. "So, why don't we kill them both now and get rid of the bodies after dark?"

"What!" Pix couldn't help herself.

Jim seemed a bit taken aback also.

"Honey, I'm not so sure. I mean, I've known Pix for simply ages, my whole life, in fact."

"So what? You knew Mitch—and Buddy, for that matter."

Buddy? Bernard Cowley! They had killed him, too!

"But not closely. I only met Buddy once or twice, remember, and of course he really did drown, albeit with a bit of help from you. Pix is another matter. Our parents used to play bridge together."

"Oh, well then, that changes everything." Valerie spoke with heavy sarcasm. "Why *don't* we let them go, then?"

Jim put his arm around his wife's shoulder in a gesture of affection. "Now, don't go getting all huffy, sweetcakes. I know we can't let them go, but I don't like the idea of having their deaths on *my* hands. We'll figure something out, don't you worry."

Pix had the feeling she was watching a strange combination of Ozzie and Harriet and Bonnie and Clyde.

"Look," he continued, "we'll tie them up and you can keep on eye on them. We can't go anywhere until after dark, anyway. And now I really *do* have to get back. The kids will be waiting. We're going to look at slides of seabirds."

The camp, Jim's beloved camp.

"Jim," Pix asked, "how can you give up Maine Sail? It's been a part of your family all these years. You love it. It's in your blood. Do you want to say good-bye to it forever?" Pix thought if she talked like Jim, she'd have a better chance of getting through to him.

He did indeed look downcast. "I know. There's always been the sad possibility we'd have to cut and run. That's why I got the new boat, biggest diesel engine Caterpillar makes. I was going to enter the lobster-boat races next month." He nodded his head toward the cove, where it bobbed in the water not far from the sloop. "Maine Sail was the most important thing in my life until I met Valerie, and you're right, I will miss it. But, Pix dear, there are other places and I'll have another camp. Of that, I'm sure. Don't you worry. Now, why don't you come with me? I think we'll have to separate you." This last was in a sterner, "caught talking after lights out" voice.

Separation—it was what Pix was afraid of, Samantha, too. "Mom!"

"No." Pix stood up and pulled Samantha into her arms. "I'm not leaving my daughter's side." She hoped Jim's parents had been lucky at cards.

He sighed. "Oh all right, you can stay together. Give me the gun, honey, and get some rope from the basement. Here's a thought. Maybe we should lock them in the wine cellar? It would be quicker."

"Yes, and why don't we give them some of the Baccarat so they can enjoy a glass or two." Valerie was still bitter.

"I doubt they would wish to imbibe now, Val. Besides, Samantha is underage. No, we best leave them here. They might break one of the bottles."

Nuts, completely nuts. The words echoed in Pix's head as she waited for Valerie's return. When Jim had mentioned the wine cellar, she'd had a thought. There was always the possibility that someone delivering something—the handyman at work, or maybe Gert Prescott coming to clean—would see the odd procession through the huge plate-glass windows, but they couldn't court even this slim chance.

"All right. That should do it."

Valerie dumped enough hemp to tie up the *Queen Mary* at her husband's feet and took the gun firmly in her own hand.

"Good, good," Jim said as he started to wind the coils around Pix, finishing with what she knew must be very efficient knots. After all, the man taught the art.

"Oh, by the way, my love, I almost forgot." He gave a sharp yank to tighten the rope around Pix's wrists. It dug painfully into her skin and she winced. "Sorry, Pix," he said, then continued to address his wife. "As I was saying, Samantha was very clever and got two campers to confess to some of the pranks that have been occurring. Apparently, they were angry at being here and wanted to get sent home or that's how it started anyway. It actually is rather funny. *They* were responsible for the parade! Here we thought it was Duncan all this time."

Valerie did laugh. "That *is* one on us, but it helped to tarnish his reputation. I probably didn't need to paint those sails—the mice and maybe the bird would have been enough with the parade. I ruined a perfectly good pair of pants for nothing."

"I do wish you had consulted me before that one." The change in Jim's voice was a grim reminder of the way he behaved when pushed to anger. "What if it hadn't come off? Those sails are custom-made for us."

"If you had known, you wouldn't have been so convincing, sugar. Now I thought you were in a hurry."

"What can I be thinking of?" He hastened to bind Samantha.

The job done, complete with handkerchiefs over their mouths, he kissed his wife good-bye and ran down the stairs, but first he took Pix's car keys from her purse, apologizing. "We mustn't leave the car parked out front. Sorry."

Jim gone, Valerie had clearly had enough of the Millers' company and told them, "Now remember, my parents didn't play games with yours and I'm in no mood for any games with you. I can see everything that goes on in here, so don't try anything." She closed the door hard.

Trussed up like the proverbial Thanksgiving bird, Pix thought this virtually impossible, nor was she planning on giving any indication like rolling over and futilely trying to cut the rope by rubbing it on the slick paint of the desk leg. Valerie alone was as dangerous as a well full of copperheads. Pix could hear her now: "Oops, sugar, the gun just kind of went off." Her well manicured hands seemed able to support any number of deaths.

At least she was lying close to Samantha. Now she inched still nearer. Her daughter had tears in her eyes and Pix could almost smell the fear coming from her body. Every maternal nerve ached to comfort Samantha. She clenched her teeth, unclenched, and miraculously the handkerchief loosened. She tried it again. And again. Soon she was able to talk.

"Clench and unclench your jaw. I've been able to loosen the gag," she whispered.

Samantha went through similar contortions and after a while was able to whisper back, "What are we going to do? Are we going to die?"

"No. Don't even think of it." Pix wanted to distract Samantha. "Now tell me what happened? What's in the closet?"

"Oh, Mom, there are stacks of those quilts. The ones with the blue X's—and more shelves full of a lot of other antiques."

"What kinds?"

"Toys mostly—plastic Mickey Mouse figurines. Also some wooden carvings of animals. Oh, and one of a figure. It looked like John the Baptist or someone like that from the Bible."

Mickey Mouses. Pix could hear Earl's voice explaining just how they were faked. And the folk art, folk art similar to what was at Jill's.

Mitch and the Athertons' business partners in marketing fake antiques—deadly partners for Mitch. They had killed him and used one of the phony quilts to bury him in. She'd been right. The marks indicated which were real and which were copies. They'd gotten sloppy about removing them. And Samantha had opened the door.

"But what did she mean about Duncan? And Mom, she killed her own husband!"

"I know, darling, it's beyond belief. Poor Duncan. All this time he's felt responsible, and really his mother was just waiting for him to go to sleep so she could push Bernard overboard." Pix shuddered. It was getting cooler as the sun dropped steadily toward the horizon. Obviously, it hadn't been only Jim who couldn't stand the sight of Duncan. Valerie wanted him out of their lives, too, yet didn't want public opinion against them. Hence, Duncan the incorrigible. Duncan may have attacked Samantha, perhaps pushing her harder than he intended. Pix was ready to give him the benefit of the doubt, considering his parents. But the rest had been manufactured by them out of the boy's own unhappiness and depression. What a thing to do to a child!

She wouldn't have to bother asking Jim why he did it, though. She thought of his wine cellar, the boats, all the expensive video toys, this whole "Million Dollar Mansion." He may have been partly motivated by the love of a bad woman, but the real answer was the old tried and true "for the money." What he had inherited and what he made from the camp had evidently not been enough. The Athertons were all set to live the good life—until the Millers happened along.

Pix looked around the room. Even if she could get free of her bonds, there was nothing even remotely resembling a weapon, unless you were up for a pillow fight.

They'd have to untie them enough to walk—that is if they were going to move them, and Pix was afraid they were. Left in the house, they might be found too soon and raise the alarm.

"Mom, can you think of anything? What would Faith do?"

Pix was stung. So far as she knew, Faith had never been

bound and gagged. She'd probably do exactly what Pix was doing–try to keep her circulation going. She decided to ignore her daughter's remark.

After a while, Samantha asked timidly, "What time do you think they'll come back?"

"They said at dark. The sun set at eight-nineteen last night." Pix did know some things. She continued to parade her expertise. "I'd say they'll come back around nine. They're obviously planning to leave by boat and they'll want to get a good start. This is deep water, so they don't have to consider the tide."

"Which gives us less than three hours."

"I'm afraid so."

"And no one to miss us. Arlene was leaving for Ellsworth straight from work with Fred. They knew you wouldn't let me go. How about Granny?"

"I spoke to her this afternoon, so she wouldn't expect to hear from me again. I asked her to come over tonight, but she said she was tired and wanted an early night."

"If Daddy calls, he'll think we went somewhere for dinner."

"And I talked to Faith just before coming over. That's what kept me."

Pix gasped, but Samantha quickly reassured her. "Even if you'd been on time, it would have been too late. She didn't have the check upstairs. The one thing that would have saved us was if the phone hadn't rung. Then I wouldn't have done such a stupid thing and opened the closet door. She must have been talking to Jim."

"Earl would have no reason to think it odd if we weren't home." Pix continued the litany with decreasing hope.

"And there's no one else."

"Only us."

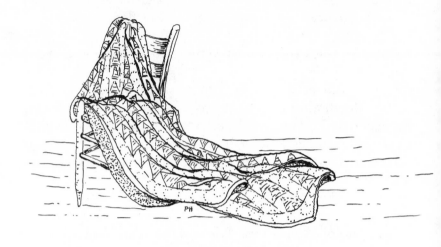

Chapter 10

The Athertons came back at 9:30.

When Valerie had first left the room, Pix had not been anxious for their return, but as dusk fell, her muscles and her nerves were crying out for some sort of change. And what that might be was something she had been speculating about for hours—silently. Samantha was calmer and had even dozed off at one point. Pix had felt drowsy herself, yet she dared not shut her eyes. She heard them before she saw them, rapid footsteps on the stairs.

The door opened and with a flick, light flooded the room, blinding Pix temporarily with its abrupt brightness. She could see how frightened Samantha was now. Her eyes were wide open, pupils dilated, like a fawn teetering about on the road, caught in the beams of a car's headlights.

"I still say we should take the silver service," Valerie was whining.

"We'll buy another. It's not that special and it weighs too

much. We'll be lucky to make any speed at all with everything you've packed." He bent down and untied Pix's ankles. The pain was intense but bearable. She knew she could walk. The question was, could she run? He helped them to their feet and said, "Get going—slowly in front of us, and don't try anything. Any noise and I'll shoot you both."

So much for Pix's plan to scream her head off the moment she was outside. They didn't know the gag was loose. With the way sound travels over water, the whole island would have been alerted. Only no one would be able to get there in time.

She started to head for the spiral staircase.

"No, the other way."

They filed down the hall past doors to rooms whose decor Pix could merely imagine. She had no doubt that had Jim not been around, Valerie would pull the trigger in a moment just because she was having to leave her fabulous house. And given her treatment of husband number one, Jim ought to be looking around a great deal, Pix thought ruefully. Her hands were tied behind her back and she gave a little wave to Samantha. Jim didn't want to leave two bodies behind. Pix was convinced they would remain alive, she told herself fervently. The question was, where?

They marched through the kitchen and out the back door. It was very dark. The moon had not risen yet and Pix stumbled on the stairs. If she broke a leg, would they shoot her?

"Down to the dock," Jim ordered.

As they left the house, lighted up like a Christmas tree to indicate occupancy, Pix wondered what they had done with her car. Another thought struck her. What had they done with Duncan? He was still on the island as far as she knew.

They reached the dock. Jim's Boston Whaler was pulled up.

"We're all going to take a little boat ride," he said. "Honey, you get in first." Pix was pretty sure he didn't mean either of them. Valerie slid by them awkwardly. She was struggling with a heavy canvas bag that she must have picked up on their way out. She was dressed for the voyage: heavy pants, jacket, and a kerchief tied over her hair. Pix gasped in surprise. Not at Valerie's outfit, but at what she was wearing on her feet—running shoes with twinkling red lights that flickered on and off as she got into the boat.

It hadn't been Duncan at all.

Why hadn't Pix tripped her, pushed her body straight over the side—this monstrous woman who had knocked Samantha to the ground, leaving her injured, with no more compunction than she would have felt swatting a mosquito? It was all Pix could do not to yell out every filthy name she had ever heard. But even if they didn't kill her, they would surely tighten the gag, and if she had sent Valerie sprawling into the sea, Pix herself might have followed her.

No, there was absolutely nothing she could do.

They got in the boat. If she had been in the mood, Pix would have been amused at the sight of a large wicker picnic basket—a few bottles of the bubbly and other assorted goodies for a midnight feast on the bounding main? Valerie set her bag next to it with a defiant look at her husband. The silver after all?

"We should be in Nova Scotia before dawn," Jim said with obvious pleasure, anticipating the trip. He was where he was happiest—on the water.

"Duncan won't be back until late—if he comes here at all. He'll probably sleep in his moldy old cabin as usual."

"I liked that 'good mother' touch." Jim chuckled. "How he wouldn't be seeing his friends for a while and you wanted to treat them all to pizza and the movies. Here, you steer. I've got to change my shoes."

Valerie took over. She was in a boat, steering a boat. The phobia, like everything else, had been fake.

Jim sat beside Pix companionably. They could see Valerie at the helm, shifting her feet every once in a while, causing the lights in her shoes to flash. Jim chuckled. "Technology. What next? Shoes that talk or sing? Sorry about Samantha, incidentally. Valerie must have pushed her a bit harder than she'd planned. We had merely intended to give you a scare so you'd stop sticking your nose into things. We hoped Samantha would see the lights and assume it was Dunc. It all worked out perfectly."

Depending on one's viewpoint. Pix was reaching the boiling point.

She saw they were headed for a small island that she knew belonged to the camp. It was a long way from shore. They used it for overnights, teaching the kids survival skills. Now it appeared it would test Pix's own. Valerie cut the motor and eased the boat into shallow water. Jim jumped out, pulling them farther onto the beach. The hull scraped along the rough sand, then all was quiet. The only sound was that of the waves gently breaking to either side.

"Last stop," Jim said heartily. He reached in the boat and picked Pix up, depositing her more or less upright on the sand. Samantha was next.

Pix had never noticed how strong he was. She'd never noticed a lot of things about Jim.

"Toss me the rope, Val. I won't be a minute." He pulled a gun from his pocket. "Okay, up the path."

Pix couldn't imagine where he was taking them, and although the night was still warm, she felt a cold sweat break out. Was it really going to be the last stop? Behind her, Samantha moaned.

They walked to a clearing in the middle of the island. Some summer's campers had built a lean-to and it was this that was apparently their destination.

"Get in and lie down. Let's not make things hard. I do so wish you two had not become involved. Believe me, I hate doing this," Jim said as he began to expertly bind Samantha's feet together again.

Pix thought about trying to kick the gun from his hand. She could do it easily, though with her hands behind her back, it would gain her nothing. Every plan she had devised had come to nothing. She had failed miserably. But she would not cry, she told herself angrily. She would not let the bastard see her cry.

He finished with Samantha and went to work on Pix. In a moment, he was standing up.

"Well, good-bye, I guess. There's really nothing else to say."

A few minutes later, they heard the boat start up again. Mother and daughter started talking at once. "Mom, they're gone!" "Are you all right?"

They were almost giddy with relief. They were alive. But, Pix soon realized, taking stock of the situation, not in good shape.

The island was uninhabited, and tied securely the way they were, there was no way they could attract attention tomorrow morning from a passing boat. When the Athertons didn't turn up at the camp and it became apparent that Pix and Samantha were also missing, a search would be made, yet it was unlikely that anyone would think to come here. There were countless islands of varying size dotted throughout Penobscot Bay. It could be days or even weeks before they were found.

Jim wasn't going to be directly responsible for their deaths. Obviously, he'd come up with a plan that effectively kept them out of the way while the Athertons headed for the Canadian border and still kept his hands clean. Pix could almost hear him explaining it to "sweetcakes," "That's all we need, a few hours. If they're found, fine. If not . . ."

If not . . .

"Samantha, we *have* to try to cut these ropes with something. Can you stand up?"

"I don't know." She strained to bend her knees and get into a sitting position. "It's no use. He's tied our hands and feet together."

"Maybe I can untie the knot. My fingers are free."

Pix rolled over to Samantha and began to pick at the knot at her ankles. Her fingers soon began to ache and she wished she hadn't kept her nails so short. Manicures didn't last long gardening.

"At least one of us has to get down to the shore and start yelling. There's always the chance that a boat could have pulled into the cove for the night. Distract me. Sing. Anything." The pain and frustration were intense.

"All right. What shall I sing?" Samantha mind's was suddenly blank. She and Mom had rather different tastes in music. The latest from the Indigo Girls would not do much to speed the process. "I know—what you and Daddy used to sing to me when I couldn't get to sleep." Her voice started out shakily and got stronger, "Hush, little baby, don't say a word. Papa's gonna buy you a mockingbird."

By the time Papa had purchased the sixth horse and cart, Pix had undone the knot and Samantha's feet and hands were no longer tied together. She stood up.

"Look and see if there are any nails in the wall or anything sharp you could use to try to undo mine." Pix did not want her daughter to suffer the way she had; she knew her fingers were bleeding from the rough rope.

Samantha hopped around the lean-to. The moon had risen. It was past eleven o'clock.

"Here's a bunch of nails. They must have hung stuff on them. I'll try to get one with my teeth."

"Be careful!" All those years of orthodontics, fluoride treatments, sealants. She watched Samantha hop back toward her with a rusty nail in her mouth and kneel by her side. Samantha dropped the nail to the floor and deftly picked it up, starting in on the knot, looking over her shoulder the same way her mother had.

"Boy, are we going to be stiff in the morning."

"Yes," Pix agreed, stiff, but not stiffs.

"All right, it's your turn."

Pix started to sing. This time Mama bought.

After what seemed like hours, Pix was somewhat freed also and they gingerly made their way down to the shore. Coming through the trees, the ocean with the moon streaking across it like a beacon was a welcome sight. Pix had almost fallen in the woods and now she fell on purpose, rolling over and over toward the shoreline, well away from the ledges. She closed her eyes as the hard rocks pressed into her body, then opened them when she reached the smoother sand. Samantha followed her and they began to call, "Help! Help! Please, someone help us!"

They decided to take turns, then figured they might as well wait until morning. No one was within earshot. Pix once more lay as close as she could to her daughter. The wind was picking up. It was getting colder. Even if they could free themselves, it was too far to swim to the mainland through the frigid waters. Pix reassured Samantha. It offered a measure of comfort for herself, too, despite the disbelief of a quick rescue steadily rising like the tide.

"Don't worry, everything will be all right in the morning. Why don't you close your eyes."

"I don't think I can sleep."

"Hush, little baby . . ."

Before she could get very far into the lullaby, Pix thought she heard the sound of an oar or a paddle. She lifted her head. Wishful thinking. Then the sound came again, more distinctly.

"Yoo hoo! Pix? Samantha? Where are you?"

It was Mother.

* * *

The three women and Duncan made a somewhat outlandish grouping as they sat on the deck of the Athertons' house waiting for Earl. Neither Pix nor Samantha had wanted to go inside, so Duncan had fetched blankets for them to wrap around themselves and a bottle of brandy and glasses at Mrs. Rowe's suggestion. Pix was drinking from the Baccarat after all. The teenagers had Cokes and were steadily devouring a bag of potato chips. Although hungry, Pix herself did not feel like eating anything from this particular larder.

Warm, the brandy seeping into her weary bones and bloodstream, Pix wanted her mother to tell the story again—and again—just as a child with a favorite book. Like most other parents she knew, she had more quotations from Doctor Seuss and Margaret Wise Brown to hand than Shakespeare.

"You actually have Duncan here to thank more than me," Ursula said.

"I know," Pix answered, and gave the boy yet another hug. Since her mother had climbed out of the canoe and deftly cut their ropes with the Swiss army knife she always carried, Pix had been doing a great deal of hugging.

"I knew something was weird. They had been treating me like shit—excuse me." Duncan flushed and looked at Ursula. "I mean, they had been yelling at me and saying I was never coming back here, then suddenly Mom gives me some money and tells me to take all my friends out." He shook his head. "She's been real jittery all summer and it's been worse lately. I thought because of what was happening at camp, and"—he lowered his voice—"because of what they thought I was doing."

Pix was indignant. "We owe you an enormous apology!"

"Don't worry about it. I probably would have thought it was me, too. Like who would have thought Mom would go out and buy the same shoes? They're for kids."

Pix pulled the blanket closer around her. The wind was picking up and it seemed they might finally get the rain they'd been waiting for all these weeks. It could come. The Fairchild's foundation was dry. Even if Seth couldn't work for a few days, the ground was so parched, it would be worth it.

The deck they were sitting on seemed another island and time was suspended, making it difficult for her to decide to move. Behind them the house was still illuminated, a gaudy backdrop to the dark landscape on either side. The waning moon shone across the water and the stars were out, mixing with clouds moving across the sky in an ever-increasing number. The air was fresh. Tilting her head back, Pix drank it in gratefully.

She realized she hadn't been listening to the conversation, and Duncan, uncharacteristically, was continuing to talk.

"So I go to my friends, 'Let's blow the pizza, get snacks, and see the early movie.' I wanted to check out what was happening. I came back here alone. All the lights were on, but no one was home. They weren't in the office at camp, either, and all the campers and staff were in their cabins. Mom's car was in the driveway and when I looked in the garage, Jim's was there, but yours was, too. It didn't make any sense. You couldn't have all gone somewhere together, unless someone else had picked you up, but you didn't seem to be that kind of friends, anyway. I decided to call your house. I was going to hang up when you answered so you wouldn't think I was a jerk. When you didn't answer, I began to get this funny feeling. I couldn't call Earl. We aren't exactly buddies. So I thought of your grandmother. She seemed okay."

Ursula took up the tale. "I couldn't imagine who was calling me at such an hour. Duncan wanted to know if you were there and of course you weren't. I told him I'd be right over." What Ursula did not say was that she knew immediately something was very very wrong. It was a summer out of sync and the disappearance of her daughter and granddaughter had to be serious. She stopped at their house to make sure and found it dark, completely empty.

"It's amazing what we can do when our adrenaline gets

going," Pix marveled, thanking God that she had not know at the time her octogenarian mother, who had not driven for years, was racing from The Pines across the causeway to the Athertons in the dead of night in her venerable "Woody"—a 1949 Plymouth Suburban wagon.

"Fortunate that I had just had the car serviced for Arnie and Claire to use while they're here. Anyway, Duncan had been doing some investigating of his own while I was on my way. When I arrived, he told me there were many things missing from the house—valuable things—and the lobster boat was gone; the Whaler was at the mooring. I called the police, then decided to take the canoe out. Duncan had found some rope and your purse on the floor in one of the rooms upstairs and we were both convinced that you'd been taken someplace under duress."

Pix liked her mother's choice of words—a quaint way to describe the terror that she and Samantha had just suffered.

She looked at the group. It was very late and they were all in one stage or another of extreme exhaustion.

"I think we'd better go home, especially because it seems a storm is on the way. I know Earl was coming here, but surely the state police have been in touch with him and told him we're all right. He'll know we went home—and all of us are sticking together for the rest of this night, anyway."

When Duncan had reached Earl, the sergeant had immediately launched a search of the area around the camp, including the quarry, calling back to tell the boy to stay put with the Millers if they turned up at the house.

There was one more thing Duncan wanted to say. Everyone was being so nice and he felt guilty. "I didn't think Mrs. Rowe should go out in the canoe like that, but I don't know how to paddle one, and she was pretty insistent."

Mother had won the Women's Singles Canoe Trophy at various events on the Concord River for more years than Pix could remember and had been paddling the Penobscot since she was a child. And "pretty insistent" was definitely a euphemism.

"She's very good at it, in fact, she'll teach you." Samantha thought it was time Duncan had some new interests and she fully intended to take her rescuer under her wing, if he would let her.

"That would be great," he said, then mumbled, "except I don't know if I'll be here."

Pix had studiously been avoiding any reference to Duncan's parents. It did not seem the moment to break it to the boy that his mother was a murderer, including of his natural father, and that both Jim and Valerie were involved in larceny up to their shirt-pocket emblems. Seeing him on the dock, as soon as they were within shouting distance, they'd called to him to phone the state police and get the Coast Guard to stop Jim's boat. Other than this, all mention of their captors had been moot.

"But Granny, why did you go to the island?" Samantha asked the one question that had not yet been answered. Pix felt foolish not to have thought of it. Why indeed?

"It was the only place that made sense. Their boat was gone. If you were still alive, and I believed you were, they had to put you someplace, but it couldn't be close to the camp. So, I simply started paddling along the shore, then out toward sea. Plus, I heard you shouting."

Sgt. Earl Dickinson was surprised and happy to see a group of laughing, obviously healthy friends as he drove up. Someone had been in time.

"Start throwing things overboard!" Jim shouted to his wife.

"What?" She couldn't hear him above the gale-force winds and rain that had greeted them farther out to sea.

He motioned with his hands and spoke louder, "Get rid of some of this stuff. We're too heavy."

"Are you crazy?"

He left the cabin, went to the back of the boat, and started tossing bags into the water. Valerie fell upon him, screeching, "My boxes! My collection of Battersea boxes! What are you doing!"

He slapped her hard across the face. "Shut up! I'm going to try to make for shore. We can't ride it out and we're not exactly in a position to radio for help."

She began to cry. "I'm scared, Jim."

"So am I. Now, do what I said and come back under cover." They were both soaking wet.

She threw the wicker hamper over the side and then the silver. We can always buy more, she told herself. We can always buy more.

At the wheel, Jim reached for a handkerchief to dry his face and found Pix's car keys in his pocket. She won't be needing these, he thought, and lobbed them in a long arc into the churning water. Then he turned the boat toward land, looking for a safe harbor.

The raging storm hampered the Coast Guard's search for the next few days. It was not until the sun broke out on Saturday that some children found a life buoy with the name VAL 'N JIM washed up on the shore—along with an empty wicker picnic basket.

"It's a great party," Faith Fairchild said to her friend, Pix. They were sitting side by side on the back steps of the Millers' house, watching a variety of activities. A large convivial group—with Pix's brother, Arnie, at the center—continued to consume lobsters at the large picnic table. "Frankly, at my age I'd rather have a talking frog" was obviously the punch line to a very funny joke. They all burst into laughter. Sam, who had once again made a mad dash for his loved ones, arriving early Thursday morning, started to tell one of his.

"He never gets this one right," Pix told Faith, "but he laughs so much while he's telling it that everybody laughs with him, anyway." Faith nodded. As far as she was concerned, the world was divided into people who could tell jokes and people who couldn't. Totally unable to remember even the most sidesplitting gem, she didn't even try, and kept to strictly off-the-cuff.

Another group was playing croquet. Pix watched her mother tap some poor person's ball miles off course, recalling that even when they were children, Ursula had played to win. "Otherwise, you won't learn," she'd explained with triumphant sweetness. Claire, Arnie's wife, had obviously drunk from the same well. Her ball hurtled through a hoop, smashed into another, which she briskly sent into the tall grass. Claire had been out for a long bicycle ride and still wore her black Lycra biking shorts with a bright periwinkle blue oversized linen shirt. She was one of those petite, nicely-put-together women who always made Pix feel much taller and much clumsier than she actually was—like Alice after eating the first cakes. Pix never knew what to do with her hands and feet when someone like Claire was around. Pix had assumed that in middle age you'd stop caring about what other people thought of you. Supposedly, it was one of the perks. She was still waiting.

The children were all over the place. Samantha and Arlene had immediately taken command of the Fairchild offspring, to Faith's unabashed delight. They seemed to be playing a game that involved a great deal of running and screeching, with little Amy riding piggyback and the dogs racing at their heels, barking happily. Duncan was with them. There had been no sudden transformation. He still wore a black concert T-shirt and black jeans, but his hair was clean and he and Fred were joining the game with every appearance of friendship.

There had been no word about the Athertons, other than the finding of the life buoy, and they were assumed lost. Duncan's paternal grandparents had been notified and were only too happy to have him come live with them. Pix did have a passing thought as to when they'd seen him last, but it seemed that they had always disliked Valerie intensely, especially after their son's death, when she'd contested his will, seeking to prevent certain bequests, among them a trust fund for Duncan. The Cowleys had told her they didn't care to see her anymore and she had retaliated by keeping Duncan from them, never allowing the boy to visit. He was living with John Eggelston at the moment and John was going to take him south the following week. John had been the one to break the news of his mother's probable death to Duncan. He'd told Pix the boy had pretended indifference at first, saying he'd never really loved her, since she'd never loved him. Then he'd sobbed for hours. Looking at him now playing like the child he still was in part, Pix hoped he would find what he needed from his grandparents. At any rate, it would certainly be an improvement.

"It *is* a good party, if I do say so myself," Pix said tritely and complacently. "What could be easier than lobster, especially when my guests brought almost everything else?"

Ever since Faith and family had arrived on Thursday, leaving Aleford as soon as they heard of Pix and Samantha's ordeal, Faith found she was happiest right by her friend's side. First, of course, she had to hear about it all. Then she realized she simply wanted the reassurance of physical presence.

"Do you think people are ready for dessert?" Faith had made a tableful of blueberry tartes with the succulent wild Maine blueberries now in season.

"Not yet. Arnie's still oozing butter and charm." Pix looked at her brother fondly. He'd been sticking to her side, too. He was reaching for a thick wedge of the corn bread* Louise Frazier had brought. She insisted that this treasured family recipe from the Deep South went perfectly with Down East fare. And she was right.

"Now that the rain has stopped, we can get a better look at the house. Do you want to drive out after everyone leaves?" Pix remarked. "It should also be a beautiful sunset." The Fair-

*See recipe on page 284.

childs had bravely faced the storm yesterday, but after driving out to the Point, they didn't even attempt to get out of the car. "These weren't drops; these were tidal waves," Faith had told Pix. "Wonderful climate."

"It is." Pix had stoutly defended what she thought of as her native clime. "Think how hot it is in Boston. I'd rather have rain, and especially fog, any day." Maine without its occasional soft, dense gray fogs molding land and sea alike into new shapes was unthinkable.

"I'd like to go out, especially for the sunset, and you can tell us what it's all going to look like."

Pix was a bit shamefaced. "I do feel that I should have been after Seth sooner. You might even have had the roof by now."

"Pix! No grades, remember? Did I tell you or did you tell me that life is not a final exam? Except maybe finally. Never mind. How you can possibly think this is your fault is totally absurd. Next, you'll be taking responsibility for what the crazy Athertons did!"

"Absolutely not!"

"Absolutely not what?" It was Jill—arm in arm with Earl, Pix noted with pleasure.

"Too complicated to explain," Faith said.

"Speaking of which . . ." Earl gave Jill a surprisingly piercing look.

She drew the word out, "Yes, I suppose now is as good a time as any. I do need to talk to you, Pix."

Faith stood up. "I'll leave you to it, then, and rescue the long-suffering teenagers from my adoring progeny." She didn't really mean it, and fortunately Jill said, "Oh you don't have to leave, Faith. It's not exactly a secret." Faith resumed her place, aware that good manners often paid off.

Jill sat down on the lawn. Earl stretched out next to her. She was finding it hard to begin, pulling at tufts of grass beside her until Pix began to worry seriously she'd have to reseed.

"You know I started carrying antiques at the end of last

season and stocked even more this year. They've been doing very well and I've made more money at the store than ever before."

"That's wonderful," Faith said. Pix had told her about Jill's cupboard, not exactly Old Mother Hubbard's, and she wanted to keep the young woman's turgid flow of conversation moving.

"Not really. You see, almost all the antiques I bought from Mitch were fakes—and these were the bulk of my stock."

No one said anything.

"I didn't know it when I bought them, of course. I should have been suspicious, since they weren't as expensive as similar things I'd priced at other dealers', but I thought he was giving me a good deal because he liked me. Then there began to be all this talk about phony antiques after his death. I got scared. If he was involved in something, I might be charged as a receiver. And I'd sold a good many. I had to be sure what I had were fakes for sure, so I began to go up to the library in Bangor and read whatever I could. I also talked on the way up and back to some dealers, without saying why or giving my name."

"And here we were spouting off about it at the clambake." Pix was sympathetic.

"Yes. I know it was wrong. I should have told Earl in the first place, but . . . well, I just didn't. Maybe I didn't want him to know what I'd done. No, make that definitely—I didn't want him to know what a fool he had for a girlfriend."

Earl put his arm around Jill. She didn't shrug it off and she continued speaking as she leaned toward him, "Once I was certain, I took everything from Mitch out of the store and put it all upstairs."

Faith gave Pix's hand a knowing squeeze.

"Despite Mitch's giving me a break, I was still out a lot of money and I couldn't afford the loss. I simply didn't know what to do, so I decided to talk to Seth."

"Why Seth?" Faith asked. Earl looked a little grim.

"I've known Seth all my life and I knew I could trust him. He was a good friend of Mitch's, plus he hears things." Faith finished her sentence silently for her: Things an officer of the law might not.

"And I thought he might know where the fakes had come from and maybe I could get some or all of my money back. I knew Mitch couldn't be making quilts, though he probably was manufacturing the furniture and the wood carvings. Seth was furious. If Mitch hadn't already been dead, Seth would have gone after him himself. He told me he'd do a little investigating on his own."

"What did he turn up?" Faith had assumed the role of chief interrogator. It was fun—so long as you were sitting in the afternoon sun at a backyard Maine lobster fest.

"Nothing much. We both suspected Norman Osgood, the antiques dealer who was staying at Addie and Rebecca's. Seth followed him when he went off-island a couple of times, but all he did was go in and out of antique shops, just as he said he was. We couldn't have been more wrong." She looked at Earl, who was grinning broadly.

"Norman Osgood is an undercover agent investigating antiques fraud. He's tickled pink that you, Pix, your mother, and Samantha somehow managed to crack a ring he's been following up and down the entire East Coast for a couple of years. The Athertons fortunately did not think to erase their computer files and Norman has been having a field day."

"I was right!" Faith exclaimed, "He wasn't a dealer!"

It was Jill's turn again. "I finally told Seth I'd have to tell Earl, what with the whole island talking about us, and besides, I missed him. That's when Seth had the idea that I could sell the fakes, just not as antiques. He helped me label every piece as a reproduction—indelible ink on the quilts, marks burned into the wooden pieces. They're very good copies and I have a big sign—'Genuine Fakes, Guaranteed to Fool Your Friends.' People think it's some more Maine humor, like the sign Wally Sanford has had outside his store for years—'Clams

Dressed and Undressed.' It's true, and so is mine. I've already sold two quilts and one of the carvings since I put them out yesterday."

Such being the joys of confession, Jill went with Earl to join the croquet game, an almost-noticeable weight lifted from her lovely shoulders.

"Is there anything left?" Faith asked.

"What do you mean?"

"Are all the loose ends tied up? Anybody not accounted for? Clues left dangling? Red herrings?"

Pix realized her friend was indeed much more adept at all this than she was.

"I think so." She leaned back against the gray shingles of the house.

She thought about her list. The columns with "Suspects"; "Causes of Death"; "Who Benefits?"; and "Quilts." Duncan, Seth, John, Norman—all eliminated. Sonny Prescott had been right all along: unknown partners in crime. Except they had known them, especially Jim.

"It's pretty clear that Valerie was not overly maternal—or wifely. But what an actress! I can hear her now speaking about Duncan's father—he was 'a saint' and so forth. She wished Duncan could be more like him. Maybe Duncan was like him and she hated them both. You should have seen her horror at the sails and the bloody bats! As soon as I heard it was latex paint, I should have known it was one of them. But Jim—an Eagle Scout! And the camp, it was like his child, wife, everything all in one."

"Until he met Valerie, my dear Watson."

"Now, don't be so patronizing. Just because you want to be Holmes, I don't have to be the poor dense doctor."

"My point is, don't underestimate the power of good old sex," Faith said.

"And in this case, the seduction of good old money."

"I'm sorry about the Watson crack," Faith apologized.

Appeased, Pix said, "Jill's cleared up the last question I

had. It must have been Valerie who came in and clipped off the X from my quilt. Which just about does it, I'd say."

"They never did find the weapon that killed Mitch?"

"No. Earl thought it might have been the knife the kids found in Duncan's trunk, but that turned out to be a special limited edition one belonging to Bernard Cowley. The knife had never been used for anything. And now, how about dessert?"

"Yes, but it's so hard to move. I could sit here in the sun for the rest of the day. Look at the kids. They are having a ball. Fred seems very nice, and I'm sure he and Arlene will be model parents, unlike some of the rest of us." Fred was showing Ben how to climb the apple tree.

"Look, Arlene is wearing bell-bottoms! I should have saved all those clothes I wore in the sixties," Pix commented.

Faith disagreed. "You did the right thing. Trust me."

Pix was cutting the tartes and Faith was putting everything on another table that had been set up out of the sun. Earlier, Samantha had picked a large bouquet of wildflowers and put them in an old white ironstone pitcher filled with water. Faith added a few roses from Pix's garden and several stalks of delphinium. She placed it on the dessert table now with the tartes and several large bowls of fresh strawberries. Pix had provided whipped cream and sugar, although preferring her berries straight. These were so full of flavor, they didn't need anything, even the crème de cassis Faith favored when she got tired of them plain. This never happened to Pix.

Arnie and Claire had apparently cleaned out Louella Prescott's entire stock of cookies—chocolate chip, oatmeal, and hermits—and surprisingly the Bainbridge's butterscotch shortbread. Apparently, Rebecca was not the one who hoarded the secret recipes. There was hope of sherry-nutmeg cake yet.

Pix was arranging the cookies on a large blue willow platter.

Ursula had come in to get a sun hat and see whether her daughter needed help.

"These are the most delicious cookies. I hope Rebecca will give me the recipe, too," Pix said, eating one that had conveniently broken in the box.

"I'm sure she will, dear." Her mother gave her a quick kiss, something that had become a habit of late.

Her daughter and grandaughter safe and sound, her beloved son in residence, Ursula should have been in clover, and she was—almost. But Pix thought she could still detect a wrong note in her mother's voice. She started to ask her about it when Faith came in with the empty tray to get the rest of the things.

"Everyone's already at the desserts. Tom says it's Maine air. Gives him an appetite. And this from a man who has consumed two lobsters, coleslaw, and untold pieces of corn bread all in the recent past!"

As soon as she left, Pix said to her mother bluntly, "Tell me what's bothering you." When he mother did not reply at once, Pix suddenly realized it was always when the Bainbridges' name came up that Ursula seemed perturbed. Could her mother miss Adelaide to such an extent? They had been close but not the best of friends. Addie. Faith had been talking about putting the last pieces in place. Surely the picture was complete. The card table could be cleared for another puzzle or tucked in a hall closet to make room for other activities. Wasn't it time to put everything away?

"Does it have to do with Addie? Are you worried about Rebecca? Oh, Mother, surely you don't think the Athertons killed Addie, too? I always thought the quilt was too much of a coincidence! She must have discovered what they were doing!"

Her mother sat down on a stool by the kitchen window. The voices outside were clearly audible. Arnie was teasing his wife about the size of the piece of blueberry tarte she'd taken.

When Ursula spoke, Pix had trouble hearing—and believing—what her mother said.

"The Athertons didn't kill Adelaide, but the quilt was not a coincidence. I know she'll tell one of us soon. I've been waiting and waiting. Perhaps me, maybe Earl, or maybe you. She's a good woman, though very disturbed in mind, and is probably home thinking about it right this very minute."

"You can't mean Rebecca!"

"Addie was very difficult to live with, especially these last years," Ursula said slowly, "and Rebecca did long for a room with a view."

Myrtle Rowe Miller, better known as Pix, lay flat on her back in the cemetery. The bright blue sky seemed very close, almost brushing the tip of the long piece of grass she was chewing on. She'd slipped out from Arnie and Claire's going-away party at The Pines, ostensibly to see how the plot had fared in the heat and subsequent rains. She doubted she'd be missed.

The last two weeks had been filled with picnics and excursions of one sort or another. Arnie had, in fact, taken her to Vinalhaven, a lovely long, lazy sail.

Samantha had not remained jobless for long; the camp having obviously shut down, much to the loudly expressed sorrow of Susannah and Geoff, who had begged Samantha to take over. Now Arlene and Samantha were working for Louella, rising early to help bake, then tending the register while Louella kept cooking.

And Seth seemed to be accomplishing miracles of construction at the Fairchilds'. Pix went every day, watching the house rising from its foundation before her eyes.

Everything had turned out all right after all—except two people on the island were dead who should still be alive.

She rolled over and propped herself up on one elbow, looking at the stone that marked her father's grave. What was the line from Edna St. Vincent Millay? "I am not resigned to the shutting away/of loving hearts in the hard ground"? That was it. And Pix was not resigned. Not for her father, nor Mitch, nor Addie.

Rebecca had told Earl, the same day as the party Pix gave for her brother. Possibly while the Millers and Fairchilds were gazing at a magnificent pink-and-purple sunset from a spot on the Point where all hoped a deck would be by Labor Day.

Lilies of the valley—they grew in dense clusters on the edges of the cemetery. A British friend of Pix's had once told her it used to be considered very bad luck in her country to plant a bed of lilies of the valley, that the person who did would be the next to die.

But it was not the person who sowed who perished. Rebecca had given Addie the plant poison in every way imaginable. She'd brewed her sister-in-law's tea from the deadly roots and added the water in which she'd placed the cut leaves to Addie's juice. She'd even, she confessed to Earl, pushed Addie's tiny quilting needles into the berries, hoping she might mortally prick herself. One or all had worked.

And the quilt was no coincidence: End of Day. Rebecca had made it herself years ago, hiding it away when Addie had criticized the handiwork—hidden away, but not forgotten.

Had she wanted to be caught? If she hadn't wrapped Addie in the quilt to try to link her crime with the other, no autopsy would have been done on someone Addie's age. And the autopsy, like so many others, had not been able to pick up this natural poison. It mimicked heart failure. A failure of the heart—Addie's. Rebecca's.

Pix lay back down again. It felt good. Peaceful. The only noise was the raucous cries of the gulls and, if she listened very hard, the sound of her own blood pulsing. Slow, steady—reliable. She sighed. Another epitaph? But the reliable part wasn't so bad. They were reliable women: her mother, her daughter, and Pix herself. So different—and so alike. She was looking forward to spending the rest of the summer in their company.

Maybe she'd get to the attic.

Maybe not.

Have Faith in Your Kitchen

by Faith Sibley Fairchild and Friends

PIX ROWE MILLER'S FAMILY FISH CHOWDER

6-7 slices of bacon, 1/4"
thick
3 cups diced yellow onions
5-6 medium potatoes, peeled
1 lb. haddock
1 lb. cod

2 cans (3 cups) evaporated
milk
1 cup whole milk
salt
freshly ground pepper

Fry the bacon, remove from the pan, and place on a paper towel. Sauté the onions in the bacon fat and set the pan aside.

Cut the potatoes in half the long way, then into 1/4" slices. Put them in a nonreactive pot large enough for the chowder. Cover the potatoes with water and boil until tender. Be careful not to put in too much water or the chowder will be soupy. While the potatoes are cooking, cut the fish into generous bite-sized pieces. When the potatoes are ready, add the fish to the pot, cover and simmer until the fish flakes.

When the fish is done, crumble the bacon and add it to the pot along with the onions and any grease in the pan, the evaporated and whole milks. Bring the mixture to a boil, cover, and turn the heat down. Simmer for five minutes and add salt and pepper to taste.

Chowder invariably tastes better when made a day ahead.

The word "chowder" comes from the French, "la chaudière," a very large copper pot. Several centuries ago, French coastal villages would celebrate the safe return of their fishing fleets with a feast. The main course was a fish stew made in la chaudière into which each fisherman would toss part of his catch. "Chaudière" became "chowder" as the tradition made its way across the Atlantic to Canada and Down East. Chowders have continued to be just as idiosyncratic as these long ago concoctions. Pix does not even want to hear about the Manhattan version, but others of us are more open. The Rowe recipe may be happily modified in all sorts of ways.

The chowder is still quite delectable with olive oil instead of bacon fat. You may also use salt pork. Two kinds of fish make for a more interesting chowder, but these can be any combination of the following: haddock, cod, pollack, monkfish, and hake. Finally there is the question of garnishes: dill, chopped parsley, oyster crackers, butter are all good. And Faith and Pix's friend on Sanpere, Jane Weiss, swears by her chowder to which she adds curry spices!

LOUISE FRAZIER'S SOUTHERN CORN BREAD

1 1/2 cups stone ground corn meal	1/2 tsp. salt
3 tbsps. flour	1/2 tsp. baking soda
2 tbsps. sugar	1 cup buttermilk
3 tsps. baking powder	2 eggs, well beaten
	4 tbsps. dripping

Preheat the oven to 350°. Combine the dry ingredients and stir in the wet. Pour the mixture into a lightly buttered 8″

square pan and bake for 40 minutes, checking after 30. This is a dense, chewy cornbread and serves 6-8. Again, substitutions can be made: skim buttermilk, Egg Beaters, and butter substitutes for the dripping and to grease the pan. Do try to find stone ground cornmeal, though. It gives the cornbread a wonderful flavor and texture. The batter may also be fried in a large pan on top of the stove, flipping it over so both sides are crunchy.

FAITH'S EMERGENCY SEWING CIRCLE SPREADS: CHUTNEY CHEESE AND CHÈVRE WITH HERBS

Chutney Cheese:
8 ounces plain cream cheese, room temperature
1 cup chutney

Cream the chutney and cheese together by hand. Do not use a food processor or blender otherwise you end up with cheese sauce. Pix used her own green tomato chutney, which is a spicy combination of the tomatoes, onions, raisins, and walnuts. All and any varieties of chutney work well.

Chèvre with Herbs:
4 ounces plain cream cheese, room temperature
4-5 ounces chèvre (100% goat's milk cheese)
Herbs to taste

Herbed chèvre is readily available in most markets and cheese shops. Pix likes to keep things simple and buys the herbed variety. Combine the cheeses by hand. The cream cheese makes the combination easier to spread. If you are using your own herbs, rosemary, tarragon, and summer savory are good choices, alone or in combination.

Use both spreads to stuff snow or sugar snap peas, spread on cucumber or zucchini rounds, sweetmeal biscuits, water biscuits, or slightly toasted miniature bagels. The chutney spread makes a tasty sandwich when combined with smoked turkey or Virginia ham or by itself on date and nut or buckwheat walnut bread.

BAINBRIDGE BUTTERSCOTCH SHORTBREAD

1 cup unsalted butter
1/2 cup dark brown sugar
2 cups flour
1/2 tsp. baking powder

1/4 tsp. salt
1 cup finely chopped
    walnuts or pecans

Sift the flour, salt, and baking powder together and set aside. Cream the butter until soft and gradually add the sugar. Add the flour mixture a little at a time and mix well. Refrigerate for one hour.

Divide the dough in half and keep one portion in the refrigerator while rolling out the other to approximately 1/4″ thickness. (The dough gets soft quickly.) Sprinkle the dough with the nuts and gently press them in with the rolling pin. Cut into 1 1/2″ squares. Pix uses a paper pattern as she is hopeless at estimating things like this, unlike Faith. Prick with a fork and place the squares on an ungreased cookie sheet. Repeat with the rest of the dough.

Bake until golden brown, approximately 15 minutes in a preheated 350° oven. Makes 6 dozen squares. This is a devastatingly rich, crumbly cookie.

FAITH FAIRCHILD'S MAINE BLUEBERRY TARTE

Pastry:

1 1/2 cups flour
1 tbsp. sugar
a pinch of salt

12 tbsps. unsalted butter
3 tbsps. ice water

Filling:

3 cups blueberries
4 tbsps. sugar

2 tbsps. flour
1 tbsp. lemon juice

Put the flour, sugar, and salt in the bowl of a food processor. Pulse once. Cut the butter into pieces and add to the dry ingredients. Pulse again until the mixture resembles coarsely ground cornmeal. (You may also cut the butter into the flour mixture with two knives or a pastry cutter.)

Add the ice water through the feeder tube with the motor running and briefly process until a ball is formed. Wrap the dough in wax paper and refrigerate for 1/2 hour. Faith makes ice water by adding a few cubes to a glass of water before she starts making the dough.

Roll out the dough on a lightly floured surface and line a 10″ fluted tarte pan—the kind with the bottom that comes out. Prick the bottom of the dough-lined pan with a fork.

Combine 2 tbsps. of flour with 2 tbsps. of sugar and dust the bottom.

Add the lemon juice to the fruit and spread evenly over the dough. Sprinkle 2 tbsps. of sugar on the top and place on a baking sheet. Bake in the middle of a preheated 375° oven for 40 minutes, or until the edges turn slightly brown. Let cool for ten minutes and remove from the pan to a serving plate.

Tastes best warm or at room temperature. Serves 10. This recipe is also delicious with other summer fruits. Caution: do not use frozen blueberries or you will have a soggy mess. Pix knows.

Author's Note

There are cooks—and cooks. Pix represents one school; Faith another. I fall somewhere in between. As with the recipes in *The Body in the Cast*, these can be made successfully by cooks of all natures. Substitutions have been suggested in some cases and certainly feel free to experiment. I'm told I make great chili, but since I put different things in each time depending on what's to hand, I may never develop a recipe for it.

A relative once told me that anyone who could read could cook, a notion I heartily endorse. Cookbooks are always in the stack of books next to my bed (along with mysteries). Crime and food go together well. Occasionally a passion for one will lead to the other—as in Faith's and my case. There's nothing we enjoy more than sitting in the backyard with a plate of Bainbridge Shortbread and a cup of tea . . . or a glass of wine and a stack of crackers and Chutney Cheese or . . . being transported to whatever world a favorite mystery author has chosen this time. I hope you will join us.